Praise for Thom Racina's riveting novels

The Madman's Diary

"Fast-paced momentum . . . crisp dialogue and quirky characters."　　　　—*Publishers Weekly*

"Takes off at a rapid clip and never eases off the throttle. *The Madman's Diary* is an exciting thriller with an unexpected ending that begs for a sequel."
　　　　　　　　　　　　　　—BookBrowser

Secret Weekend

"Brimming with harrowing situations, romance, and mysterious characters, *Secret Weekend* is a suspense lover's dream. Thom Racina has packed many surprises into this page-turner, with a special shocker saved for the end."　　　　—*Romantic Times*

"*Secret Weekend* starts as a breezy read that quickly turns into a pulse-pounding suspense thriller. . . . Thom Racina has written an exciting winner."
　　　　　　　　　　　　　　—Harriet Klausner

continued . . .

Praise for *Hidden Agenda*

"A fast-paced thriller . . . a smart, up-to-date read."
—*San Francisco Examiner*

"Colorful . . . fiendish . . . good entertainment . . . could be a heck of a movie."   —*Publishers Weekly*

"A timely story . . . filled with recognizable people."
—*Library Journal*

"A wild romp through my news terrain. . . . I had a great time with it!"

—Kelly Lange, NBC news anchor, Los Angeles, author of *Trophy Wife*

"*Hidden Agenda* is a thrilling and savvy ride through the worlds of broadcasting, politics, and religion. Real names make it feel chillingly nonfictional, and the ending is a triumph of integrity over hypocrisy. It's unique, and I was spellbound."

—Sally Sussman, head writer, *Days of Our Lives*, NBC-TV

"The power of television news taken to its logical extreme. Thom Racina's ingenious story gives the reader a peek into the media's well-hidden backstage."

—Bill O'Reilly, anchorman, Fox News, author of *Those Who Trespass*

Snow Angel

"Chilling suspense."   —Judith Gould

"Breathtaking read, a devilish treat that will leave
you crying for more. You may think you have this
one figured out, but Racina pulls out all the stops
and gives the reader one of the most exciting tales
of the year. *Snow Angel* is topflight entertainment, a
sure treat for any season."   —*Romantic Times*

"Fast moving . . . Racina spins a highly cinematic
tale set against dramatic backdrops . . . a memorable
villain who generates considerable suspense."
                                      —*Publishers Weekly*

"A chilling cliff-hanger chase."   —*Booklist*

"A tale of obsessive love run nastily amok."
                                        —*Kirkus Reviews*

"Powerful, compelling. . . . A highly charged thriller
with a surprise ending."   —*Tulsa World*

Also by Thom Racina

Snow Angel
Hidden Agenda
Secret Weekend
The Madman's Diary

NEVER FORGET

Thom Racina

A SIGNET BOOK

SIGNET
Published by New American Library, a division of
Penguin Putnam Inc., 375 Hudson Street,
New York, New York 10014, U.S.A.
Penguin Books Ltd, 80 Strand,
London WC2R 0RL, England
Penguin Books Australia Ltd, Ringwood,
Victoria, Australia
Penguin Books Canada Ltd, 10 Alcorn Avenue,
Toronto, Ontario, Canada M4V 3B2
Penguin Books (N.Z.) Ltd, 182–190 Wairau Road,
Auckland 10, New Zealand

Penguin Books Ltd, Registered Offices:
Harmondsworth, Middlesex, England

First published by Signet, an imprint of New American Library,
a division of Penguin Putnam Inc.

First Printing, August 2002
10 9 8 7 6 5 4 3 2 1

Ⓟ REGISTERED TRADEMARK—MARCA REGISTRADA

Printed in the United States of America

PUBLISHER'S NOTE
This is a work of fiction. Names, characters, places, and incidents either
are the product of the author's imagination or are used fictitiously,
and any resemblance to actual persons, living or dead, business
establishments, events, or locales is entirely coincidental.

BOOKS ARE AVAILABLE AT QUANTITY DISCOUNTS WHEN USED TO PROMOTE
PRODUCTS OR SERVICES. FOR INFORMATION PLEASE WRITE TO PREMIUM
MARKETING DIVISION, PENGUIN PUTNAM INC., 375 HUDSON STREET, NEW YORK,
NEW YORK 10014.

For Sue Breeze,
who even loved it back in the old days,
and
for Joan Jordano,
who made it possible for it to be finished today

ACKNOWLEDGMENTS

Thanks to Genny Ostertag, my amazing editor; Kara Welsh, my terrific publisher; Leslie Gelbman; Claire Zion; and all the other wonderful and supporting people at NAL; Jane Dystel, my knock-out agent; Pat Golbitz, for the original idea so many years back; Carole Hennessy, for her loving friendship and generosity; Andrea Wendell, who taught me everything I know about Aspen; and all the great readers out there who lift my sales a little higher with each title. You are more appreciated than you know.

Prologue

Telluride, Colorado
Late March

He stood inches from the edge of the cliff. The sun had just risen, and a light breeze was blowing. He took in a deep breath, then slowly let it out. Invigorated, he walked back to the place where he would begin his run. He donned the rest of his gear, watching the bright yellow nylon skin shiver in the breeze.

This was going to be perfection. Not only were conditions right, he'd learned something a few minutes before that made his spirits soar. He could envision Kristen's happy face when, after the flight, he told her what he now knew. It would make everything right again, explain away all the pain and misunderstanding. With a thumbs-up to Maggie and the others who were watching him intently, he began his forward run. The brink came fast, quicker than he had thought, and when he leaped and was no longer touching the earth, he gratefully felt the wind catching the sail and knew he was safe in God's magnificent sky.

He felt like a soaring eagle. Though this was probably the hundredth time he'd done this, the experience was as filled with excitement as the first moment he had ever flown above the earth on nothing but cloth wings. Hang gliding, from that moment on, had been his passion. He'd started out on California beaches, easy and safe for a novice, then challenged himself with ridges, cliffs, eventually flying over forests, hills, and now these rugged snowcapped Rockies, warm in the cocoon of his pod harness. He loved the sound of the airstream over the taut glider skin, the feel of the wind on his face, the might and power of his weightless body careening over trees and lakes. Safe or risky terrain, it was all a matter of trust in himself, in the elements—the wind and air currents, the heat or cold—and in fate.

He clung to the control bar, knowing he was not aloft today simply for his own fun. Gripping the trapeze bars, he controlled the flight back around to where he'd taken off, over the Colorado countryside in all its glory. He saw Lizard Head, the giant monolith whose features resembled a reptile until a gigantic chunk of it fell off. It wasn't nearly as interesting from above, he realized. Then Yellow Mountain and Pilot Knob and finally Sheep Mountain, cradling Trout Lake, shimmering, blue, beautiful. He passed over several mountain cabins, a small river, and around again to the flat, jutting rock of the plateau he'd started from. He hoped they could see him grinning from the ground.

"Max," Maggie said to him on the little radio unit attached to his ear, "this is looking good."

"Hell, yes," he said into the mouthpiece.

"Come on, flyboy, buzz us up here," Maggie said.

"Yes, ma'am." He shifted his weight so the glider turned to fly over the group again. He saw everyone watching, pointing to him. Behind the extras, he could clearly pick out Nicole, her arms crossed, leaning against a station wagon. And that's when the revelation came to him. "Oh, my God," he shouted.

Maggie sounded alarmed. "What's wrong?"

"It was *her*. Nicole! She took the picture!"

"What?"

"She was on the boat that night." He smiled with delight. "I'm right, I'm positive. I *know* it."

The earphone crackled. "Max, have you lost your mind?"

"No," he responded, "but tell Kristen it ain't over yet, not by a long shot."

"Concentrate," she warned him. "This is hardly the time for personal problems."

He buzzed the crowd as instructed.

"Perfect, Max, just great. Now, swing around to your left, give us a sweeping movement over the edge of the lake." He obeyed her directions, seeing his reflection in the big blue mirror of Trout Lake. "Fabulous."

Then, abruptly, he felt a vibration. And for a moment fear shot through him. It was a feeling he'd never experienced before, not in all the contraptions he'd been up in, gliders both sophisticated and primitive. A glance at the variometer showed nothing unusual. After a quick look to the right, then the left, to the battens and the flying wires, he put it out of his mind. Nothing was amiss. It had been the wind. He didn't mention it to Maggie. This was going to be spectacular, an incredible sequence.

He moved his legs inside the pod, dancing a kind of aerial ballet over the edge of the lake, then continued at Maggie's urging to cross a nearby stream, where he saw a woman waving to him from the drawbridge of a magnificent old white stone château. "They don't build them like that anymore," he said into the mouthpiece.

"Especially in Colorado," Maggie said.

"Just like you," he said. Forgiveness was rushing through him. He'd taken a bold step by belting Borger, the first positive action toward winning Kristen back. He felt good about himself. Free, and not only because he was in the sky. Free of the blame that had been manufactured for him to bear. "Fuck Nicole," he shouted happily. "Fuck Borger!"

"Max," Maggie ordered, "stop it. Concentrate."

He dipped and turned right. "I'm sailing, Maggie. I'm soaring."

"Okay, baby," Maggie replied, "let's steal a little from *The Stuntman* here. Give me something wonderful."

"Want the flip?"

She gritted her teeth, he could tell. "Only if you think it's one hundred percent safe."

"Yeah," he said determinedly. "Let's go for it."

Turning right, the whole glider did a dance, a great yellow creature sailing on the power of its wings. He soared upward, high enough on the thrust of the thermal to glimpse another lake in the distance. He crossed the stream again, dipped lower, almost dusting the treetops where, over a meadow, he completed the dangerous maneuver, a show-off somersault that took everyone's breath away, including his own. But he didn't falter.

The second unit director's voice said, "We're ready up here."

"Fabulous," Maggie purred. "Up here" was one cliff over, clearly visible to all the people gathered, where a small dilapidated cabin had been constructed on another open bluff. "Max?"

"Ready."

He used his weight to turn west, back toward the starting point. The wind lifted him quickly again. He went so high that he could see Rioco, and even higher still. It was his job to make this scenario work. Curious about the seemingly abandoned cabin on the bluff near the one he'd taken off from, he would fly in very close to it, but a crazed young woman who would emerge from that cabin would scare the hell out of him and drive him away. He would then attempt to land back where he'd started, miss it because he was so shaken up, fly out into the wild blue yonder again, then eventually set down safely.

"Great, now go on in to Kristen," Maggie said.

Kristen. Who was going to realize everything had changed once he got his feet back on the earth.

They'd already filmed her sequence of looking fearfully out the ripped shade of the cabin's window and then emerging from the structure with shock on her face. All they needed to do here was get her carrying out the action on the next page of the script, which would be inserted into the sequence later. Max was to fly low, maybe fifteen feet above her, and then pull out of there in a hurry.

"Everyone ready?" Maggie inquired with a snap in her voice.

"Ready," the second unit director replied.

"Kristen in place?"

"All set."

"Props?" Maggie asked.

"Kathy Tam says we're set," the second unit director assured her.

Maggie reminded them, "We've only got one chance. Let's go!"

Max headed for the bluff. From his vantage point he could see the camera, the unit director, and the crew all standing on the sidelines as Kristen rushed out the cabin door, looking up into the sky with a terrified expression on her face, standing there frozen for a moment. She wore almost no makeup, was costumed in worn jeans and a dumpy sweatshirt. Max thought she never had looked more beautiful. He saw her rush back into the cabin just as he swept around for another glide over the weathered shack. The timing was perfect. He was closest to her when she hurried back outside, the rifle in her hands. She stopped in the middle of the yard, lifted it, aimed, planting her feet squarely on the earth, and fired at him, twice.

He let out a deep, muffled, agonized cry. Maggie started laughing. "Magnificent, Max," she congratulated him, "but you don't have to sound like she actually shot you."

Kristen was supposed to get off a third blast, but she set the butt down on the ground, chillingly captivated by a sight no one had expected. The underside of the bright yellow nylon pod that encased the lower half of Max's body was turning dark red, and his right arm was dangling in the sky.

On the main cliff, Maggie blinked, looked up at one of the cameramen, then over to a stage manager, who all had the same shocked look on their faces. She brought her binoculars back to her eyes. "Max? Max!"

There was only a low groan from the glider.

But he could hear Maggie shouting at the property manager. "Borger! What the hell is going on? You put a blood packet in the pod?"

"No. The script says—"

"I know what the fucking script says!" Max heard her scream at him. "Max? Max, talk to me, answer me!"

He was floating silently in the magnificent sky. Nothing seemed to be wrong, nothing seemed to be differing in the slightest way from the script. Except for the ever-enlarging round spot of blood on the underside of the pod's yellow nylon. And his limp arm.

"Max!" Maggie shouted again so loud that the speaker crackled in his ear.

"I'm . . . I think I'm bleeding," he said, in fierce pain.

"What?" Maggie gasped. "For real?"

"She shot me." He could barely talk.

He could hear everyone around her uttering the same two words: *Real bullets?*

"Max, talk to me. We know you're hurt—"

"My shoulder," he gasped.

"Honey, you need help, you gotta land."

"I'm supposed to do the abort first."

"Are you *crazy*? To hell with the film! Get down, Max, let us help you!"

"Okay," he whispered. There was a pause. Then he said, "Maggie, it hurts like hell . . . I can barely move my right arm." With great effort, he lifted it back to the control bar.

"You've still got control, Max. You're okay. Just come on in, we're waiting." He knew she must have covered the mouthpiece with her hand, but he still heard her shouting for a doctor, asking for paramedics to have an ambulance ready to roll.

Max was sure he could do it. He felt hot, wet liquid from his shoulder all down his front, and the pain was so intense that he could barely keep his fingers squeezed on the control bar, but he was positive he could land this thing. He had to. Yet as the open space where she and the others were standing came back into view, something else happened.

In a flash, he heard a ripping, tearing sound. The sun suddenly blinded him where it shouldn't have—where the right wing should have been. The nylon skin had ripped in a slit from the front of the wing all the way to the back. But it was okay, he told himself. The material was strong, it wasn't going to shred. He would get this baby down—not as Maggie wanted, not with an aborted attempt, but one final, lifesaving landing. He started to tell her what he was faced with. "Maggie, the nylon—"

He could not continue the thought, for he felt the craft stall. Panic seared his brain. He was losing airflow over the wings. The wind was perfect. Even though he was above dense snow, where the mountain air was thinner, he had no difficulty identifying the signs of lifting air. A quick look up told him that the wires were holding, but that same glance showed him that the straight rip in the aircraft's nylon skin was now starting to flap, to peel off the battens. And not only on the right side, where the rip had occurred, but on the left wing as well. It was shredding, disintegrating before his own eyes, like the sheet metal of an airplane's fuselage peeling off during flight.

He was certain that if he could make it to the top of the cliff, where Maggie and the crew were, he could land safely. Well, with maybe a broken ankle. But to do so meant he had to find a thermal, a rising current of warmer air than what he had here. He was unable to do that. The glider was fighting him.

"Max!" Maggie shouted. "What's happening? We see it!"

"I'm fucked," was all he could say. Explaining it wouldn't help. He needed his concentration to get himself down alive. "I gotta land this."

"My God, Max, the wings!" She sounded stricken.

"The bullet must have torn through the nylon," he

said. He turned right, felt a sudden lift, of both the wind and his heart, and then soared up—where he could see the crew standing with mouths open on the top of the ridge. Hope surged through him. "Yes! I'm gonna make it—"

"Max, don't panic. Of course you can make it, darling."

"Why did she do this to me?" he cried.

Then, just as suddenly, the craft dropped, diving to the right, where the adjacent mountain ridge came into focus only yards away, a forbidding solid granite wall. He was going to miss the bluff he'd stepped off from.

In the final seconds before the impact that he now knew was inevitable, he told himself he should have checked the battens more closely again this morning. He had gone over them last night but had given the aircraft only a cursory glance before he took off, trusting that that was enough. He should have tightened the flying wires, for the structural shape was giving away now as the material disappeared, exposing the bright sky above him. No, none of that would have done any good. It wasn't any kind of natural rip. This was a hole from a bullet that the wind had enlarged. What shocked him was that it was deliberate, that someone had purposely put real ammunition in the gun.

To kill him.

No! He wouldn't give them the satisfaction. He tried desperately, with all his expertise, to turn the aircraft away from the rock wall, but nothing

worked. The glider was uncontrollable, disintegrating above him. The bird no longer had wings that
worked. He saw the jagged, flat rock to his left and
knew—seemingly in slow motion—that in seconds
he would hit it, and that it would undoubtedly kill
him. And, just in case it unmercifully did not, he was
certain that the fall to the valley floor below would
be his last terrifying moments on earth.

He felt as though he could not breathe. He
coughed up blood. He thought it odd that he was
going to die so young, so unexpectedly, at the feet
of all three of them, the terrified girl he adored and
the conniving little French slut and the powerful
woman who had loved him so dearly.

As the glider soared shakily, with just the sound
of the ragged nylon flapping in the breeze, he
thought he could hear screams from the people on
the other cliff. Or was it in the background of Maggie's panicked voice on the earpiece? Or was it just
his imagination? The thing he was sure he did hear,
with all his heart, was the sound of Kristen's voice,
telling him she loved him still. He was sure she
hadn't fired real bullets on purpose. "I love you too,
Kris," he said.

"What?" Maggie cried in response.

But he was not listening. He cried out, "Kristen!
I didn't do it, no matter what the picture made it
look like . . ."

The radio communication went dead as his body
hit the rock wall so hard that any lingering impulse
was knocked out of his head. Blood sprayed every-

where, staining the gray slab of mountainside. He lost consciousness instantly and fell, entangled in the mess of fiberglass and nylon and stainless-steel wire and leather that had been a state-of-the-art hang glider, to a jagged resting place far below.

One

Two Years Earlier

At precisely ten-thirty in the morning on the Thursday before Christmas, Constance Heller left her Bel Air mansion. As she stepped out from behind the oversized carved walnut doors that in another time had secured a monastery near Florence, the gardener, who'd been planting red poinsettias near the monastic entrance, stopped and leaned on his shovel. He shook his head, glanced toward the chauffeur, who was adjusting the cap on his forehead as he moved from a military "at ease" stance to "attention" position at the side of the aging Bentley. "Can set my clock by the old bag," the gardener muttered.

"Morning, ma'am," Lawrence said as he opened the rear door of the gleaming automobile. The whiff of a mixture of tanned hides and years of too much perfume wafted into his nostrils.

The plump little woman brought her hand up to secure her holly-berry-bedecked sun hat as she slid into the dark recesses of the automobile. But she stopped suddenly, inhaling, and then sang, in her high, girlish voice, "Oh, poinsettias! What a scent! Christmas is in the air!" The chauffeur rolled his eyes and shut the door behind her.

The gardener snorted. "Poinsettias don't have a scent. She's smelling her goddamned hat." He went back to work as the big blue car wound its way down toward the gates.

From the backseat, Constance chatted about her Christmas list, which was the purpose of this morning's trip to Rodeo Drive. "My niece, so hard to buy for . . . impossible . . . got to remember David Geffen, I'll never live down forgetting him last year . . . Barbara Walters, remind me, Lawrence, a scarf maybe . . ."

As the gatekeeper saw them coming, he pushed a button to open the huge wrought-iron gate, on which hung a sun-bleached Santa Claus. He'd been dangling there so many years running that his outfit had turned a muted shade of pink.

Constance lowered her window. "Hank, darling, are the angels working yet?"

The gatekeeper proudly extended his hand to indicate that the angelic Styrofoam chorus was in place and ready to sing. Constance said to Lawrence, "Drive out a little farther. I want to get a look at them." The car rolled to the middle of the street and stopped. The gatekeeper pushed a switch. Twenty-two angelic cherubs lining the top of the stone wall surrounding the estate started chanting in unison,

"We wish you a Merry Christmas, we wish you a Merry Christmas, we wish you a Merry Christmas, and a Happy New Year!" Their little mouths moved just like at Disneyland.

The neighbors would die, but Constance was pleased, nodding approval to the gatekeeper as she raised the window. "Delightful, aren't they, Lawrence?"

"Miss Heller, you want my honest opinion?"

"I'm afraid I'm going to get it whether I want it or not."

"Garish."

She giggled. "Such a grinch. Put the tape on."

"Doctor Dre?"

"You know which one." She jotted yet another name on her list: Barbra. The other one.

Indeed, Streisand filled the speakers. "The sun is shining, the grass is green, the orange and palm trees sway. There's never been such a day, in Beverly Hills, L.A . . ."

They passed a fake Tudor mansion that had white plastic snow spread all over the grounds. "How lovely!"

"Looks like a Cuisinart full of Parmesan cheese exploded," Lawrence muttered. The sundowner winds of the previous evening had blown a good amount of the phony flakes into the street, and a horde of Mexican gardeners were sweeping the glittery piles into bushel baskets for the trek back to Winter Wonderland.

As they continued, she pulled the upcoming issue

of *Vanity Fair* out of her bag. Besides writing a daily column for the *Los Angeles Times*, she was employed by the magazine as its prime gossipmonger. She had just received the new copy this morning and was thrilled to find they'd only cut three lines. Not bad. Well, they didn't *dare*. She had become the Hedda Hopper of the new millennium, the hip Louella, the new Taki. No one was going to mess with her.

She glanced out the window as her mind jumped to another time. "Lawrence, stop!" she cried. They were taking a different route from the usual, Lawrence had said, because there was construction on Sunset. She had not been down this street in ages. There in front of her was a very grand house, an aging Mediterranean villa nestled among mature palms and overgrown ivy. The Nash house. She could picture Charles standing there in the driveway, dressed in blue jeans, clippers in hand, cursing that gardeners were a waste of time and money. She could see his crusty face before her, the face of one of the greatest film directors of all time, covered with little scratches from his fight with the bougainvillea. Her face suddenly flushed with emotion at the memory. "Charles and Louise Nash lived here. Oh, the memories."

"He still alive?"

"In Southern France. Remind me to have something sent. For Maggie too."

In traffic on Santa Monica Boulevard, Lawrence said, "Ask you something personal, Miss Heller?"

"Do."

"This Christmas stuff you get so excited about. Aren't you Jewish?"

"Only married Jews. I've been Korf, Ziederman, Gould—well, that was only for a month, a bad dream—and Hellerman, which I shortened when he had the good sense to die on me. I made them all celebrate Christmas. Maybe that's what killed them." She repositioned her hat on her head. "My love for the holidays began in the Nash house. They epitomized the true joy of a warm and loving spirit."

"The daughter's that famous director, right?"

"Yes, Maggie, my goddaughter. Louise died when she was only five, but Charles is still alive."

"Wasn't the mother Garbo's lover?"

"Don't believe everything you read, Lawrence."

He laughed. "You ought to know, Miss Heller, you ought to know."

At the corner of Rodeo and Dayton, Constance told Lawrence to meet her at Neiman Marcus in three hours. As he pulled to the curb, she noticed a tall, shapely woman standing with her back to Constance, next to a convertible, barking orders to a parking attendant who seemed to be staring at her in awe. Constance felt she knew this person. The hand gestures, the wild mane of chestnut hair, the tight skirt and long legs. Then it dawned on her—she looked like Maggie Nash. Impossible. Maggie seldom set foot in Los Angeles. And when she did, Constance was always the first to know.

Lawrence opened the rear door, and Constance emerged into the sunlight, adjusting her floppy bonnet in the late-morning heat, looking again just to be sure. Couldn't be. Probably some Saudi princess showing off her new Bimmer toy. The woman was now crossing the street, walking almost directly toward her.

What convinced her was the woman's *style*. She radiated class and elegance, had an aura about her that made everyone take a closer look. And the cheekbones, the high, strong bones of her mother, in a face that seemed to draw the sun. The slim but voluptuous frame, the high European heels, legs that stopped traffic even in Paris. Maggie Nash, all grown up. And in Beverly Hills!

"Maggie!" Constance cried. "Oh, my God, is it really Maggie Nash?"

The polished woman did not hear Constance, did not even see her. She avoided the curb, turning her back to Constance as she glided across Dayton. In the crosswalk, she extended her hand to her forehead to shield her glasses from the glare of the sun, then brushed her hair from her face, and that's when Constance was positive. That feline stroke of the paw over the brow, almost practiced, a signature gesture that even the drag queens couldn't get quite right.

Constance dashed into the middle of the street, dodging cars and risking her life against the light for the first time in her seventy-two years, calling, "Maggie! Margaret! Maggie Nash!"

The object of her bellowing heard her this time, stopped, and turned back, as a van overloaded with Japanese tourists braked just in time to avoid running into the fat lady with the funny hat. Maggie lifted her sunglasses when Constance reached the curb. "Lord Almighty," she gasped. "Connie?" A happy smile crossed her face, and she opened her arms wide to hug her very dear old friend.

Their ages differed by almost thirty years, but Connie and Maggie had once been close. Louise and Charles had helped Constance get her start in the business, and when Maggie was born, Connie flew to France to be her godmother. She had been especially close to Maggie after her mother had died, often visiting Europe when the girl was young. Connie had always loved her, and protected her.

"I was going to pop in on you later," Maggie said. "You just robbed me of that pleasure. I was going to ring the bell and surprise you."

"Just like old times! But why aren't you staying with me?"

"Your husband hates company, as I recall."

"Irving? He's dead."

"No. How did I miss *that*? Probably shooting a movie."

"He passed away just after I saw you last, in London."

"I'm so sorry."

"Me, too. Irving was the one I loved."

"You loved them all. And their bank accounts."

Connie waved off her "sorrow" for the sheer delight of this unexpected pleasure. "Maggie Nash back in California. Your father know?"

Maggie laughed at the implication. "Anger keeps

him alive." They moved out of the way of a girl dressed as a big holiday cookie, handing out flyers for a yogurt place. "We certainly are in California, there's no denying that."

"Some things are constant," Constance said. "Now, seriously, what are you *doing* here?"

"Shopping."

"Like hell. Gorgeous blouse, by the way." Constance fingered the silk.

"Thirty bucks, Hong Kong."

"Oh, just a layover on your way back from Asia?"

"Maybe."

Connie's eyebrows lifted. "Lost, dear?"

Maggie smiled. "You're sly."

"My job. So, coffee? Starbucks owns this country now."

"Europe, too, if you can believe it. Okay, an espresso."

Connie led the way. "So, there's been talk of Hollywood wooing you to do a picture."

"Still call them *pictures*?"

"Old habits die hard. Come on, honey, you didn't drop in just to buy a bag at Barneys. You *must* tell me."

"I'm on Rodeo to find something for Marty Stern."

"Marty Stern is as dead as Irving is."

"Marty Stern, *Junior*."

"Oy." She shook her head. "You know, these pathetic Juniors, all clerks or accountants or lawyers or former hippies or Coca-Cola bottlers. What has happened to the business? Where have all the creative people gone?"

"There are *some* good movies being made."

"Yes. Yours." And then it registered. "Marty Stern, the little *pischer!* He's going to bankroll your first Hollywood film."

Maggie put her fingers to her lips. "Shush. I'll tell you everything as soon as I know it, okay? An exclusive. But it's too early. I'm only here for the day, flying to Aspen later for the film festival tomorrow, then back to Paris."

They walked into Starbucks. Joining the line, Connie asked, "You still have the chalet in Aspen?"

Maggie nodded. "No one uses it, though. In fact, I'm staying in a hotel for the one night I'm there. No sense opening the place."

"Shame. We had good times there in the old days."

Maggie smiled. "That we did."

Connie ordered a caramel Frappuccino. Maggie asked for a double espresso and a piece of cheesecake. Constance shook her head. "Amazing. You Europeans. Not only do you keep your figure eating all that fat, you live forever."

"Forever?"

"Look at your father."

"You have a point."

"I bought something called a cross-trainer machine. It's sadistic. Haven't touched it in two years." Connie shrugged as they sat at a table. "All right, what are you and the little putz up to?"

"Junior? You guessed it. He's producing my first American movie."

Connie started jotting on a notepad. "Title?"

"None yet. Too early. Script's not even done. I haven't even found a guy to play the lead in *Fibs*, the film I start in January. Big dumb hunk with a heart."

"We have the market cornered on those here."

"So tell me where to shop."

Constance beamed. "Thank God I risked my life crossing that street to get to you. This is the kind of news this town needs. EUROPEAN DAZZLE HITS TINSEL TOWN. You're the major female filmmaker in the world today."

"Don't tell Liv Ullmann that."

Connie was hungry for details. "So, who are you considering? All the usual suspects?"

"No one I have ever heard of. I want someone fresh, young and intelligent and brooding and sensual and strong." She gave Connie an arch look. "The new Brad Pitt, next year's Ben Affleck. Know him?"

"Every waiter in Los Angeles. Oh, sorry—you said intelligent."

"Enough to remember his lines."

"At my age, I'd be happy to find someone who can remember his *name*."

"You haven't aged a day since I last saw you."

Connie giggled. "Writing sleaze keeps a person young." She sipped her coffee. "How is Charles? Really."

"Cantankerous as ever, but slowing down. Has a new partner, you know, a gold digger who drove up in a battered Peugeot one day and never left. They're quite happy."

"Charles Nash takes a mistress." She was writing again. "What's her name?"

"Nicole Richaud. I call her the sparrow."

"Can I print that?"

"*Paris Match* already has. Scrawny little thing. I'm quite sure she hates me, but she's young and silly, so I don't care much. Dad will dump her like all the others when he gets tired of her. By the way, he detested my last film, but warned the French film industry that if they didn't submit it for Oscar consideration, he'd bolt for Germany, with all his money."

"Never Germany!"

"They do know how to make a car, though." Maggie stood up, suddenly spirited. "Call me at the villa during the holidays. I mean it."

"Where are you going right now? Oh, right, Stern."

"Two o'clock meeting. And I'd best show up bearing gifts. A tie, do you think?"

"A pacifier would be more appropriate."

Two

Maggie figured she couldn't go wrong with Gucci. Anything sporting the double "G" would make Marty Junior happy. The elder Stern had been Maggie's godfather, and each year a lavish gift would arrive on her christening anniversary. Now it was her turn to lavish something on his son. Maggie entered the store and made a beeline for the neckties. She eyed several of them for a few moments. Then a salesman with a great voice said, "I'd be honored to help you."

Without looking up from the display case, Maggie said, "A baby rattle, please. No, just kidding. A tie. Silk, one of those, perhaps . . . the stripes . . ."

Young male hands opened the case, slid out a tray of expensive silk ties, and the deep voice said, "I think the diamonds are way more cool myself, but stripes always work if you are buying for someone conservative."

"He's pretty young—" As she glanced up and her eyes suddenly locked on the salesman who had just spoken, her voice stopped in midsentence. "—like you." But his youthfulness wasn't what shocked her. It was the immediate attraction of his eyes—dreamer's eyes. The shade of blue astounded her, a shade she'd seen only once in her life—on a marble egg that Ingrid Bergman had given her when she was little. He had a large frame, but not overly developed, striking blond hair, strong hands with prominent veins running up into his rolled-up linen shirtsleeves. The guy was a specimen.

"Too flashy," she said as he lifted a different tie for her. "I don't know how risky this kid is." The salesman turned around to find something else. She estimated him at six-three, and the shirt didn't hide the fact that he worked out, nor did the loose rayon pants covering the curve of his buttocks like a cashmere glove.

Did I sleep with him? Entirely possible, she realized. She liked boy toys, liked them a lot, especially since she had never, in all her forty years, had a real relationship. She was always too busy, too preoccupied, too strong and demanding, the men too soft for her. And here she was, standing in Gucci drooling over a mere salesclerk. Reality check. *Hollywood.* Goofy people, plastic Christmas paraphernalia, deranged coeds in cookie costumes. Her father had warned her. This was LaLaLand. The espresso and sun were getting to her, rendering her horny before lunch.

One of the ties he pulled out of a lower drawer was perfect. Muted red with little gold triangles, indeed cool-looking. Marty Senior would have hated it, but she trusted his son had not inherited his father's taste. This was a hipper Hollywood by far. "I'll take it. Can you gift wrap it, please?" Her inflection made it sound like she had just asked if she could go to bed with him.

"Sure, Miss Nash." That's when he started to lose his cool. And admitted it. "I recognized you the minute you walked in. I beat out two other guys to wait on you."

"I'm flattered," she purred. She never took her eyes off him as he started to wrap the box. She could see the effect she was having. His fingers trembled as he attempted to tie the bow around the package. He was so unnerved by her constant staring that he found it totally impossible to fasten the ribbon, making a mess of the whole thing.

"Having a hard day?" she asked.

"Understatement." He started again from scratch. But this time she stuck her thumb on the ribbon so he could tie the bow, and when her flesh lightly brushed against his, sparks flew.

"I'm . . . I'm not usually this nervous."

She smiled at his candidness. "Have we . . . have we met before?"

"No. But I admire you." He ran her credit card. "You make me laugh."

"Laugh? God, I've been waiting years for someone to say that. Everyone thinks my films are so damned serious."

"I find a lot of irony in them. Which is funny."

She blinked. "You're an actor?" She didn't let him

answer. "Wait, this is Bevery Hills. Hello! Of course you're an actor."

He manufactured the sexiest smile she'd ever had thrown at her. "Loved your new film." He handed her the package.

"Me, too."

"Merry Christmas." The blue eyes dazzled in a way Ingrid Bergman's egg never had.

She clutched the wrapped box to her chest as she looked at him. "Ciao," she said, and started out. At the doors, she stopped. She turned and walked back to him. "You had lunch?"

He looked startled. "Um. No."

"Hungry?"

He seemed unsure this was really happening. "I only get forty-five minutes, and I was planning—"

"Come on, I've got a meeting in an hour anyway. I'll buy."

"You're kidding."

"Your meter's running," she said. "Let's go."

"What's good and fast?" Maggie asked, out on the street.

"Follow me," he said. She did, around the corner, down past the Starbucks she and Connie had visited, to a nondescript 1950s coffee shop on Canon Drive, one of a dying breed in L.A. called the CharLite. As he held the door for her, he asked, "So, you always lunch with strangers?"

She smirked. "Hate eating alone."

"Oh."

"But I only invite strangers with cute butts."

His face reddened. And he grinned.

A waitress who looked like she had just stepped off Mars greeted them with coffee they didn't even ask for. She was petite, in a starched uniform, with a pile of reddish-blond hair that looked like cotton candy lacquered with Aqua Net. "X, babycakes," the woman said, "whatcha having? Francheezie?"

"Yeah, Nicky."

"Big weenie platter," she yelled over her shoulder. She put a hand on her hip. "How about you, Mom?"

Maggie glared at her defiantly. She at once promised herself to use this caricature in a film someday. A Revlon nightmare.

"Honey, you eating or just warming the seat?"

"Bacon cheeseburger and fries, please."

"Hey," the waitress said, pulling a pencil from her big hair and pointing it at Maggie's face. "I know you."

"Maggie Nash," Max said by way of introduction. "Maggie, meet Nicky Dee."

"Maggie Nash," the waitress replied, "and I sling hash. Big deal. That don't tell me nothing."

"She's the famous film director."

Nicky was unimpressed. "Don't go to movies no more. So what's a high-class broad like you doing with this bum?"

"I plan to have sex with him."

Nicky wasn't flustered. "I hearda child care, but this beats 'em all." She snorted and walked away.

"Do you?" Max asked.

"What?"

"Plan to have sex with me?"

"Haven't really decided." Maggie sipped the coffee Nicky had delivered. "Why'd she call you X?"

"Last name's Jaxon."

"Jackson?"

"Sounds right, but you're saying it with the *cee kay*."

"Huh?"

"J-A-X-O-N."

"First name?"

"Max."

She laughed. "X is right." She threw her head back and tousled her hair, flipping it from her forehead with a flick of her wrist. It was a calculated move she had perfected over the years since the day her father's great friend Audrey Hepburn had told her she needed a unique gesture, a "Holly Golightly" kind of personal stamp. They'd worked it out in the summer house her dad had rented on Lake Como, where Maggie actually practiced in front of a Baroque mirror. She could tell it was working on X here. "Unique name, actually. How old are you?"

"Twenty-eight," he answered. "You?"

"Still the easy side of forty," she said with a smile.

Nicky brought him a chocolate malt. "Growing boy, my little Maximilian," she muttered, then turned to Maggie. "But I guess you'll find that out yourself later."

"Nicky, come on," Max said, "give her a break."

"She gonna make you a star?"

Maggie blinked. And remained silent.

"Hell, he don't need no favors," the waitress said, rubbing his shoulder. "He's gonna get there on his own. And you know what? When he does, he's gonna remember the little people."

"Little people like you?" Maggie chimed in.

Nicky yanked Max's hair just behind the ear. "You ever get full of yourself, I'll kick your ass."

Max grimaced and Nicky laughed and sauntered off.

Maggie said, "So what brings you to Hollywood?"

"Figured it's the best place to do *Hamlet* and maybe some Strindberg."

She smiled. Nice sense of humor. And at least he was smarter than most of the dolts who wanted to become TV stars.

"After drama school, I first went to New York. But I couldn't afford to live there, so I came west."

"I loathe Manhattan. I have an apartment there, but I never use it." She eyed him sucking the thick malt up his straw. "Been to Europe?"

He shook his head.

"That's why you like New York. Tell me what you think after you see Rome, Istanbul, Stockholm. Older cities are more voluptuous."

"Like you?" he said with the straw still in his lips.

She grinned, glancing at the waitress. "Like older women?"

He qualified his answer. "*Some* older women." Then he mustered the courage to say, "I find you terribly attractive."

"That's simply because you know I want to suck your dick."

He spit air through his straw. The shake erupted like a lava pit. "You sure get to the point, don't you?"

"Listen, I'm thirty-nine, so I don't have all day. Let's be frank. You're sitting there with an erection in your Jockey shorts thinking the very same thing."

"Boxers," he corrected her with a smoldering look.

Maggie seriously considered changing her plans, taking a hotel here another night, flying to Aspen early in the morning, but at the very moment of decision, Nicky waltzed up with two plates balanced almost directly over her head. Maggie thought she should have simply delivered them on a tray on her helmet hair. "Patty for the Queen Mum, stuffed dog for little Maxie." She slammed the plates down in front of them. "Pickles on the house."

"Nicky," Max kidded, "you're a dream."

"More nightmare," Maggie muttered as the waitress walked away.

They stared at each other almost the entire meal, the attraction intense. Max was eager to continue it outside the restaurant, and was asking how they could meet up later, when Marty Stern Junior walked into the place. It was as if he'd been sent to rescue Maggie, for the moment he noticed her he took possession.

"Maggie, Maggie," he said, "lovely to see you. You're due in the office in half an hour, right?"

Maggie nodded. "Hi, Marty. This is Max. Max, Marty Stern."

"Hey," Max said.

"How are you?" Marty threw back, but it was clear

he didn't care what the answer was. His focus was Maggie. "Listen, I just popped in for takeout. You're almost done, why don't we walk back together?"

"Well, I guess—" She looked at Max.

"Hey, I'm gonna be late for work anyhow," Max offered smoothly.

"Listen, Maggie," Marty said, "you're going to Aspen today, aren't you?"

She glanced at Max. Then nodded. "Doing a seminar tomorrow."

"Me, too. Listen, fly with me on the Fox jet. That gives us the whole afternoon and we don't have to cram, we can talk on the plane."

Maggie relented.

As Marty approached the counter to order a veggie hero to go, Maggie put money down on the table. "I'm sorry," she said, apologizing for plans unsaid.

"Another time," he added.

She turned. Marty was ready. He motioned her to the entrance, and that was the last image of this knockout woman imprinted on Max's mind, disappearing through the revolving door, out of his life. Easy come, easy go.

When he got up to leave, Nicky was astounded. "No rice pudding? First time in two years. You sick?"

Max whispered into her ear, through the starched hair. "No, in love."

Three

He tossed and turned all night. About three in the morning, he went out on his balcony in his boxers, but the cool Los Angeles night air chilled him to the bone, so he crawled back into bed and pulled the duvet to his neck. An hour later, he swallowed an Ambien tablet, which Nicky had given him for emergency use only, but even that didn't work. All he could think about was the woman, and how he'd let her go. *I should have been more forceful. I should have offered to carry her bags. I should have gotten her cell phone number.* He beat himself up till the sun was rising and then collapsed into what seemed like a coma.

He awoke groggy at ten, made some coffee, then turned on his computer. The opening AOL screen promised great holiday travel discounts, even though Christmas was less than a week away. And a thought popped into his head. Nutty, risky, off the wall.

He typed in "www.priceline.com."

* * *

She noticed him halfway through her late-afternoon lecture on women in film. He had plopped himself in the center of the third row of folding chairs, and was draped over two seats in a casual and sexy way, dressed in baggy corduroys and a turtleneck sweater. His blue eyes seemed to reflect the lights of the stage. Maggie was dazzled. She faltered for a moment, then, being a pro, picked right up on her speech. He gave the impression of being interested, and maybe he was. She was, after all, an international film figure, and most audience members were young, starstuck film buffs or actors. Like himself.

She found she couldn't take her eyes off him. X. In Aspen. He must have followed her here. That took guts. She liked that. She could barely keep her mind on what she was saying. Her focus was only on him. And the sexual heat he was generating.

After her talk, she welcomed questions from the audience, mainly from brave young feminists who wanted to become her one day. There wasn't a peep out of the stallion in the third row. Her distraction only intensified at the post-lecture coffee-and-cookies gathering. She was feeling what she'd felt in the restaurant: a desire not so much to know him as to simply touch him. To feel the texture of his curly, bright hair. To find out whether it was on his chest as well. To run her hands over that muscular ass. To peer deep into those eyes and close them with her lips. To feel him naked against her flesh.

As a female refugee from the 1970s with granny glasses and ironed hair cornered her in the lobby, Max sauntered past, chomping nonchalantly on a brownie. When the girl asked if she disliked American actors, Maggie answered, "On-screen, usually. In bed, however, it's another story." She said it looking right at him. The girl paled. He did not.

But by the time she extricated herself from the group, the object of her lust had disappeared. Shit, where did he go?

She hurriedly retrieved her mink coat from the checkroom, put on the fur hat she had bought the last time she was in Moscow, and ventured outside. Walking Red Square in the winter was only a rehearsal for the snowbound streets of Aspen Village. The place seemed deserted. There was no one in the Hyman Street mall, or on Cooper Street. Even the teens who normally hung out around the Paradise Bakery were missing. And Max was nowhere to be seen.

She suddenly felt lonely and unfulfilled. It was snowing, it was dark, and she was freezing. She headed in the direction of the hotel. And that's when he came up from behind and put his arms around her. "Thought you'd never get out of there," he said matter-of-factly, as if they had made a date.

"What are you *doing* here? I almost lost it when I saw you."

"I was going to Telluride to do some hang gliding and thought I'd detour to Aspen."

"Bullshit."

He smiled. "Truth is, I figured this deserved one more shot."

"Bold little bastard, eh?"

"I like risks."

"How'd you get here?"

"The Fox jet wasn't available, so I went to Priceline dot com."

She blinked against an icy gust. "To hear my lecture."

"And for the blow job you promised."

She laughed, but the air she sucked in seemed to freeze her lungs. "This is worse than goddamned Russia. Close your jacket."

He did.

They hailed a four-wheel-drive taxi to her hotel, the legendary Jerome. In the backseat, he put his arm around her, brought his lips to her frozen chin, and warmed it with his breath until she could stand it no longer. She pulled away—their eyes met in the semidarkness of the SUV—and came back to him with her lips parted, her tongue meeting his, kissing in a frenzy of passionate anticipation.

In the suite, she watched him undress. He was not the least bit self-conscious; in fact, he did a kind of striptease for her. She recognized the performer in him, unafraid to take chances. He lifted his sweater and slowly pushed it up over his head, then let it fall softly to the floor. His chest was smooth, not hairy as she'd imagined, but well developed and firm. He faced her and opened his belt. She lay on the bed in her slip, urging him on with her eyes.

He kicked off his boots and pulled his socks off his feet. Then he stood there, planting his legs wide apart, and carefully, slowly, unzipped his worn corduroys. They spread apart at the waist, revealing pubic hair darker than his head. It curled around his fingertips as he held his hand on the waistband of his undershorts. As he moved slowly toward the bed, her hand reached out and replaced his, feeling the wiry dark-golden-brown curls. She hooked her fingertips in the elastic of the boxers and yanked them down. He stepped out of his clothes and knelt on the bed.

She took him first in her hands. This was what she liked best, feeling the young stallion's cock, hard thighs, the muscles in his legs, the weight of his balls, touching the warm spot just under them as if she were blind and learning him with only her fingertips. And then she sucked in the sweetness of the damp hair, kissing up and down the length of him, licking him, teasing him, inhaling the musky odor of cologne and sweat and the natural scent of his body. She pulled him down to her and wrapped her arms around his thighs and held him tight.

He undressed her. He was good at it, expert. The slip glided to the carpeting, her panties melted from her middle and her French bra found its way into his teeth. He chewed on it for a moment before unfastening it that way and dropping it to the side of the bed.

He took her nipples, the color of raspberry sherbert, between his lips. His index finger ran down the length of her body. She was firm everywhere. There wasn't a spot on her that felt soft or cushy, not even her buttocks; they were tight, like his. He kissed her feet, her hair, her eyelids, her underarms. He licked her from head to toe as she wrapped a hand around the base of his penis and closed her eyes to float with the madness of passion. He positioned himself atop her body, then rolled over so she was atop him, and she straddled him.

Their eyes communicated something both were thinking but not saying. She reached over to her bag and fished in it for the foil packet. She opened it and unrolled the condom, and he helped her, moistening his fingertips with its lubrication, which he then rubbed over the head of his cock. She fitted it to him with both hands, sliding it down, feeling him filling and strengthening even more as she covered his erection with the silk skin.

And then, finally, when he entered her, she knew this was something special. She got laid often, and it was always just physical. There was something more here. She wondered if he was as good an actor as he was a lover. They rolled over again, putting him atop her once more, where his thrusts seemed to move right through her and penetrate the mattress.

The climax was endless. It was as if an avalanche had struck and they were tumbling headfirst into the pure white, the freezing beauty of the blizzard, drowning in the excitement and incredible sensations of a joy that had never been experienced and could never be repeated.

He rolled over her, she over him, he over her again, and they fell noisily to the floor. She pulled his hair and screamed and then all at once began to whimper and cry, digging her teeth into his shoulder, begging him not to stop, forbidding him to stop, hating him because she knew she would never see him again.

When it was over, he sat for a long time holding her in his arms. She played with his hair, running her hand through the loose curls, remembering how she'd longed to do it from the stage, twisting her fingertips through the thatch above his penis, even pulling the hair on his legs and arms. She felt herself becoming defenseless and susceptible, which had happened rarely in her life. She'd learned, the hard way, through tears and sleepless nights in a short marriage and an even faster divorce: get laid but don't get involved.

Yet she knew her heart was pounding for Max, sitting there naked on the floor of a hotel room, his potent body making her forget it was winter outside. Just as she knew she could not give in to the temptation to generate anything more. She had her work, her life, she had to go on. It had been special, but that was that. Another notch on the belt. Anything more wasn't in the script. She got up and put on one of the white hotel robes and sat in a chair.

He seemed self-conscious suddenly, probably be-

cause he was now the only one naked, so he slid his
shorts, cords, and sweater back on and picked up his
heavy jacket, which had landed near the door. The
look on his face was as plainly vulnerable as the one
she was masking, and she read the forlorn expression
in his eyes. She sensed that he wanted to talk, but
that would get her heart in trouble. Better he go back
to L.A. for his francheezies and tell that bizarre waitress all about the heat.

She knew that if she allowed him to stay, they
would make love again, have breakfast. She'd never
make her plane to Denver, then she would miss the
connection to Paris, screw up all her plans. Hell, this
was probably just starfucking for him. He probably
only wanted a job. But . . . but she knew that she
didn't want him to be just another piece of meat.
"Ciao, Max," she said.

He opened the door, gave her a forced smile. "By
the way," he said.

"Yes?"

"Good lecture." He winked, nodded, and was
gone.

She went to the window and waited till he
emerged from the front doors, watching him as he
walked along frigid Main Street, crossed it, slid between cars on the ice. He leaped a snowbank, continued up the sidewalk till he disappeared behind some
big candy canes and Christmas trees that an estab-
lishment had erected.

She went to the sink, splashed cold water on her
face, opened a Diet Pepsi, sat down and picked up

the script. In a few minutes, all thoughts of him had been banished, and she was pondering the wisdom of building a set for the interior mill scenes or shooting on location somewhere.

But somewhere in her consciousness he remained.

Aspen, Colorado
Police Investigator's Office

In his tight office in the basement of the Aspen City Building, Christopher Daniel rubbed his chin. He'd forgotten to buy more Edge, so he hadn't shaved today. He'd inherited his father's dark eyes, his strong, squarish jaw, and French Canadian heavy beard. Women found the combination irresistible, but Christopher himself had no such romantic illusions; it was simply a pain in the ass. With his longish hair he knew he must really look like a mountain hippie today, and the chief would no doubt make some kind of a redneck comment. He looked at the clock on his desk to see if he had time to shave before his meeting—a bar of soap would be primitive, but the lather would work. Before he knew it, however, he could hear the bulky frame of Chief of Police Hans Schierling marching down the hall. There was no escape.

Christopher Daniel, whom almost no one ever called by his first name, at thirty-two was Aspen's hot new detective, the rising star on the force. The reason was the notoriety he'd gained in the previous year when he solved a well-publicized missing-persons case, proving his hunch that it was a homicide. A twenty-four-year-old attractive, status-obsessed ski instructor had disappeared from her hillside condo one summer afternoon without a trace. In the ensuing search for her, a scandal erupted. She'd been the secret lover of a very powerful—and very married—Colorado Springs businessman, a vocal proponent of Christian Right family values. His wife alibied him. But Daniel didn't buy it.

The fact that the girl had left without taking her purse bothered no one else—jogging, hiking, swimming were mountain activities that didn't require identification—but it disturbed Daniel. He thought it odd that her bag was left on her kitchen counter. Her friends agreed. She was a native New Yorker and never went anywhere without her wallet.

It haunted Daniel, even after the papers stopped writing about it. He spent weekends in Colorado Springs, getting to know the businessman's household staff. He learned an interesting, and seemingly unconnected, fact: the husband liked motorcycles. The man had, in fact, secretly gone on weekend bike runs with the missing girl when he was supposedly on business trips. Daniel already had the long hair, so he stopped shaving and rented a Harley. He met other bikers, rode his hog alongside them, gained their confidence. When bikers' girls joined them, he was struck by the fact that most of them wore fanny packs. "Sugar," one of them told him, "you don't take a purse when you're gonna ride a motorcycle."

It took him three months, but he finally arrested the businessman's biker buddy who had driven off with her that day, killed her, and buried her in a remote area, paid for by the businessman. Motive? Tests proved the girl was pregnant, and when he finally confessed, the businessman admitted that he was enraged because she refused to abort it. It threatened his public image, so he'd done away with her. He and the biker got life in prison. And Christopher Daniel, sans Harley and beard, became a hero.

"Chief Schierling," he said, pointing to the stack of newspapers on his desk, "this case is getting higher-profile by the day."

"We're in Aspen, Daniel."

"But we got laws too. The rich and famous aren't exempt."

The chief folded his arms over his ample belly. "My wife's a big Max Jaxon fan. In fact, she belongs to a fan club called the Max Jax Faxers. They fax each other gossip about him. Christ, it's embarrassing. I mean, Toni is way too mature for this kind of nonsense."

The tragic hang-gliding incident near Telluride just a few days before had made headlines all over the world. Max Jaxon was one of the biggest stars Hollywood had seen in many years, and it seemed that someone had tried to kill him and make it look like an accident.

The chief grumbled, "We don't want another Jon Benet here."

"With Hollywood, turning an investigation into a circus is a surefire way to circumvent the law. I won't let this become another O.J. Galls me how entitled these people think they are." He lowered his voice. "I just watched the sequence again."

"The film they were making?"

"Yes, sir. And I listened to the tape of the radio communication between Jaxon and Maggie Nash, the director. He seemed to have had a revelation of some sort when he noticed a woman named Nicole on the ground. Went on to talk excitedly about a 'picture,' saying 'she was on the boat that night,' and got angry about someone named Borger—who turns out to be the prop guy on the movie. He asked, 'Why did *she* do this to me?' after he was shot."

"Well, he meant Caulfield. She pulled the trigger."

"Maybe. Maybe not. I talked to her, and she's pretty upset. I doubt she did it on purpose."

"I don't know. Women."

"I reread the initial statements that the eyewitnesses and members of the cast and crew gave the Telluride police. Everyone agreed that the emotional climate of that movie shoot was filled with jealousy and anger."

"Sounds like just another Hollywood day to me." The chief shifted his weight.

Daniel leaned back in his chair and clasped his hands behind his dark, shaggy hair. "Nothing they have said—nothing anyone has said—has convinced me that this was sabotage, that someone purposely set out to murder Jaxon. But then again, nothing reassures me otherwise."

"Start," Hans directed, "like with our Colorado Springs Bible spouter, with your gut feeling."

"Real bullets accidentally replaced blanks? Come on. What were real bullets doing anywhere near there in the first place?"

"Right. One tore through his chest and the other shot a hole through the wing?"

"That's what it looks like, Chief. I've got an expert—he runs the annual Telluride hang-gliding festival—rigorously testing the remains just to be sure."

"What else?"

Daniel brought his hands down and sat erect. "I'm fascinated with the relationships here. I mean the major players—Nicole Richaud, Kristen Caulfield, and Maggie Nash herself."

"Richaud was her old man's mistress, right?"

"Recently became his wife. Tabloids say she had a thing for Max."

Hans smirked. "Like my wife." He loosened his belt a notch. "Too much chili on the fries at lunch. Listen, how about the prop people? Who was in charge of putting the blanks in the rifle?"

Daniel nodded. "That's Bruce Borger. In his initial statement he professed shock. He was distraught."

"I'd be too," the chief said, " 'cause I'd know I'm the first suspect." He stood up. "I'm curious about that French broad, Richaud. Find out why Jaxon reacted to her the way he did." The chief stopped near the door, remembering something. "Hey, you were born in Montreal, you're a Frog yourself. Talk a little *oui oui, mademoiselle*, with her and get her to spill. And all the rest of them too. I want this wrapped up fast." He turned the doorknob. "And listen, son, do me a favor."

"Yes, sir?"

"Shave your goddamned face."

Four

Max was in a rotten mood the next day, which was less than conducive to Christmas sales. His boss commented three times that he had to "shape up, get into the spirit." But his humiliating return from Aspen made him glum. The point of the jaunt had been to see her again, well, have sex with her, which he'd accomplished. He'd gotten laid, but he hadn't put out money for a plane ticket just for that. He could have gotten sex free right here in Los Angeles, with any number of women. No, he had hoped for something more. He'd gone to Colorado hoping she could do something for his career.

Fool. "Hello, ma'am, may I show you some neckties?" *Dumb risk, especially when you don't have any money.* "I can start gift wrapping those if you'd like to look around some more." *You were just another lay for her.* "We have some very cool socks to go with that." *Stupid. Just a stupid move.* "Can I help . . . you?" The words caught in his throat when, at three-thirty in the afternoon, he found himself looking into her eyes again.

"Bonjour."

"What are you doing here? You were going back to France."

"Changed my mind."

He was dumbfounded. "Why?"

"You."

"Me?"

"I'm at the Beverly Hills Hotel. Pick me up when you get off work."

"I'm here till nine. Christmas hours."

"Fine. I'll be waiting."

"Where will we go? I mean, what's the plan?"

"Mmmm. It's your town, you decide. Someplace where we can just be alone and talk."

He picked her up outside the Beverly Hills Hotel twenty minutes after he'd punched out. He had changed from his Gucci outfit into the jeans, sweatshirt, and sandals he kept in the trunk of his beat-up cream-colored Mercedes. It was so aged and rusted that the valet looked embarrassed. She got in apprehensively. "This thing run?"

"It's a classic."

"Prewar, but I think that's a plus only with apartments."

"All I could afford."

"At least it's European." She touched his thigh. "Where to?"

"How about the beach?"

He gunned the motor, and the car careened down Sunset Boulevard, winding the curves toward the Pacific. "I want to know more about you, Jaxon," Maggie yelled above the roar of the wind and the engine. "I didn't give you a chance last night."

"We were pretty occupied last night."

She smiled, drawing her knees to her chin, heels on the ripped leather seat. "Yeah, but I shouldn't have let you go."

"You came all the way here to talk to me?"

"Don't let it go to your head. Spill."

"Not much to tell. Single mom, dumped me with relatives in Tulsa. I hated it there, bummed around doing odd work, construction stuff. Never wanted a real job—"

"Like you have now?"

"My future isn't in silk ties. Pays the rent, I meet people." He boasted, "I'm shooting a national commercial next week, then a guest spot on a series in January."

"Why acting?"

"Always lost myself at the movies, the big escape. It really hit me when I walked into my first legit theater, the feeling that I could have gone up to the stage and *into* it. That's when I knew I had to go to drama school."

"Watch out!"

They were almost up the ass of a lumbering Cadillac. He downshifted—the gears ground something awful—and swung into the passing lane. "I succeeded in whatever I took on, like I was the best cement pourer, the best bartender, the best fuck—if I may be so modest—but I knew the script was never going to get better. Theater was passion. I felt alive for the first time ever."

"Where did you study?"

"The Theatre School at DePaul University."

"Ah, the old Goodman School of Drama. Why not New York?"

"Figured there were less distractions in Chicago. But I did later go to New York. I rented a room from Nicky Dee down in the East Village."

"Nicky? That waitress?"

He nodded. "She'd just divorced, needed money, had an extra room. I joined an improvisational theater group, but man, we were broke. When Nicky decided to come out to California to live with her sister, I followed her. It's the place to get discovered."

"The mystique of Lana Turner at the tie counter. I mean soda."

He downshifted into third, and the car rattled and shook. "There's a beach I know . . ."

She closed her eyes. "I swear, Hitler himself might have motored in this thing."

He turned left onto Webb Way and barreled up the smaller road, paralleling the water. "Nicolina DeAngelo is my best bud and biggest fan."

"She certainly is . . . colorful."

"Protective too. She's always said I have the charisma and determination to make it. I have good feelings about my future."

"You said you got a gig coming up?"

"I aced a great role on an episode of *The Practice*." He turned into a parking space and shut off the engine. "It goes up, it goes down, but no matter how tough it gets, I don't give up."

"I wish you'd give this *car* up," she joked.

They got out and started walking toward the cold, dark beach, hearing the roar of the waves. "When do you shoot it?"

"January. I had a few lines on *ER* last year. But this is a real part. Come through here." He swung a gate open between two high-tech town houses. "Shortcut to the sand. I went to a party in this house once." He took her hand and led her down the narrow redwood-and-glass alley, where they found themselves facing the black ocean.

Maggie said, "You ever been to Hong Kong?"

"Chinatown count?" Max spread the blanket he was carrying on the cool sand.

She sat close to him, drawing her legs up as she had in the car, arms around her knees, head resting there. "How good are you? Really."

"Damn good."

"You sure of that?"

"Yup. I'm gonna make it."

"Determined to work hard for that?"

"Hell, yes."

"Was New York too tough for you?"

He blinked. "What is this, an interview, an inquisition? Foreplay? I don't mind any of those things, but I gotta know what you want from me."

"I want—" She hesitated, needing to get it right. "I want to know what's inside. I've already been with the handsome man I see in front of me. I see the exterior, but how's it furnished inside?"

He took a breath. "I don't know if you can comprehend any of this, but I'm really on the other side of the fence from your life. Your father is a Hollywood legend; I don't even know who mine was. Mom deserted me, handed me off to strange relatives when I was four. I've slept in viaducts I worked installing. I went to drama school on my own money. I tended bar nights and had a paper route in the morning—don't laugh, you don't have to be eight to deliver newspapers."

"What was so compelling about acting?"

"I didn't have to be me. Whenever I went to the movies and saw Dustin Hoffman, I envied the fact that he didn't have to be Dustin Hoffman every moment of his life."

"Don't like yourself?"

"Like myself just fine. It's my life I have problems with." He shifted his body, moving to his stomach on the blanket. His hair flopped over his suntanned forehead, and when he lifted his feet into the air, sand poured from his sandals down his legs and into his jeans. She was looking at him as if she were seeing him through the lens of a camera.

"I wanted to be a classical actor. But my acting coach, this great woman named Bella Itkin at DePaul, said why in the world would you want to play Hamlet when you're made for Stanley Kowalski?"

She curled up next to him, running her index finger over the seam of his jeans, right along his hipbone. "I think I like this gal."

"She's the greatest. She told me to use my assets: my age, my face, my body, and the driving force I had to become a—" He stopped, embarrassed.

She finished it for him. "A star. What's wrong with that?"

He shrugged. "Dunno. People make you feel weird about wanting it."

"Crap. Happiness is what's important, and if being a star makes you happy, then be one. I mean, it's a lousy job, but somebody's gotta do it."

He brightened. "That's what was wrong with New York. Everybody there *wanted* to do Hamlet. There's no stardom even on Broadway. It's only in the movies and music."

"I suppose you sing too?"

He grinned.

"What do you really want?" she teased, hooking and tugging at the belt loop of his jeans. "Besides validation?"

"Nothing much," he said, shrugging. "Just the simple things: fabulous wealth, fame, a gleaming new SL in the garage, the AFI Lifetime Achievement Award, and maybe a good francheezie now and then."

A wave crashed behind them, and the night suddenly felt damper, colder. He reached out and lightly touched her hair with his hand. She shivered as his little finger brushed her ear. He saw how prominent her nose was when her hair was pulled tight, how petite and delicate her ears were, her classic chin in the moonlight. He whispered, "You are so beautiful. I didn't want to leave last night."

"I know. I had to kick you out."

He pulled his hand away, looking hurt.

"I'm blunt, you'll learn that about me. And I can be very closed off. But I'll open up with this: you have done something to me." She put her hand to his chin. He hadn't shaved since morning. "I think I may have found what I've been looking for."

He brought his hand around the back of her neck, pulling her down to kiss him. As her face met his, he took her in his arms, one hand on the firm flesh of her buttocks, the other buried in tangled, wind-tossed hair. "I've been hard since I left you last night," he growled. "You're gonna remember this night when you're back in France." He found the clasp on her trousers and undid it, yanked them down, hooking her panties with his thumb. He quickly unzipped his jeans, freeing himself with one hand.

"Max, not here!" She was startled. People had been strolling along the beach as they'd talked, and figures could be seen in windows in the houses above them. "Not like this."

His answer was complete defiance. Nothing she could do at this moment would change his mind. He kissed her hard and moved his body to hers, as close as possible. She held her breath as his hands prepared the way, then in one strong move, he entered her. He would not move his lips from hers, letting her cry out into his mouth, two clothed figures on a blanket on the beach, making love as the waves crashed.

Finally he was on top of her. He looked down. She had thrown him out into the freezing street last night. Tonight was his turn to be the aggressor. He breathed hard into her ear as he lunged one more time, and her nails dug through his shirt into his back. Her face contorted with the delicious agony of desire as her hair matted into the damp sand. He looked into her eyes, his almost brimming with tears in his fury.

"My God," she gasped.

He held her hands down with his own. And unleashed the longing, the pent-up frustration from the previous night. As he'd walked from the Hotel Jerome to a cheap motel, he hated her, resented her. He felt like a toy she'd used and discarded. Now he took it out on her body, making love to her with all the anger he could resurrect. He made her hurt, and beg, and love him back. If she wasn't going to give him a job in one of her films, he sure as hell would give her something to remember him by. He brought himself to the point of climax, held back, whispering, "Should I stop now? Should I throw you out into the street?"

"Max," she groaned, her mind awash in sexual passion, "come . . . make me come too. Please."

"You used me." He thrust into her so hard she felt she had been lanced.

Her eyes were closed. "Darling, yes, yes, fuck me."

"Fuck you? Fuck you?" he said, sweat forming on his forehead now. "Wind me up so I can fuck you and you'll be gone in the morning?"

The scream that came from her mouth as he finally came was silenced by his hungry lips on hers. She gripped his shoulders as his body arched and fell, arched and fell, convulsively. He was pressing her so hard into the sand that she ached all over, but once his orgasm tapered off, he began to moan like a little boy. Then the brutal passion subsided. He freed himself from her body and lay next to her on the sand.

She reached out and touched him, stroked his back, ran her fingers over his buttocks, up around his ears, kissing him on the back of the head. His hair smelled of the ocean. It was colder, and she curled up against him for warmth. She thought about what he said before he had come so fiercely. *No, I won't be gone in the morning, Max. I'm not going to throw you into the street.*

And though it seemed corny, and had it been spoken in one of her films, she'd have cut the line because it was just too romantic to be real, she actually said to herself, *Tomorrow morning might be just the beginning.*

Five

When he pulled himself out of bed the next day, having managed only about two hours of fitful sleep, Max was sure he would never see her again. She had been strangely silent all the way back to Beverly Hills, as if her mind were in another place. She'd seemed so preoccupied that his insecurities started to tell him that he had indeed been just another lay—twice. At least it was on his terms this time.

At the hotel she'd given him a big hug, a passionate kiss, even a smile under the portico. What did it mean? A reward for being a good screw? All the questions about his life, would she have asked them had she only been interested in sex? What was it about her that had gotten so deeply under his skin? Christ, Aspen was alive inside him. Memories of Malibu made him shudder with desire. The scent of their passion still lingered. He could taste her, feel her, touch her in his fantasies today. That was why he had tossed and turned, his head filling up with possibilities—all that they could have together—and why he had to protect himself. She wasn't going to change his life, enhance his career. He needed to return to the tie counter. With armor on.

He stepped out on his little balcony and filled his lungs with smoggy air, glancing up at the former Cecil B. DeMille mansion just a hill away, where a maid in a white uniform was shaking out a rug. When the coffee was ready, he showered, shaved, dressed, feeling antsy. He swiped the *Los Angeles Times* from his neighbor's door, opened Calendar to see what movies were playing, only to find Maggie staring at him in a color photo. "Internationally renowned filmmaker and jet set personality Maggie Nash flirting with the American paparazzi in Aspen yesterday." Jet set? Who the hell still used that expression?

He read Constance Heller's column telling the world that Maggie would be returning to Hollywood sometime next year to do a movie with Marty Stern Jr., whose father had produced so many pictures with Charles Nash, her famous father, blacklisted in the McCarthy era. But first she was searching for a young leading man for her upcoming film—will the new Tom Cruise please stand up? So while she was making love to him, some other goddamned actor was already watching the ink dry on his contract with her. Terrific.

Feeling like shit, he had trouble starting the aging car. The floorboard was full of sand, which brought the night back, and like it or not, it made him hard. She was the most intense and exciting woman he'd ever met. He slammed his fist on the steering wheel. He had to erase her, block her out. Yet every time he tried that, when he pictured her . . . man, what she did to him.

Work sucked. He took out his anger on his customers, which was not cool in the new hip Gucci; in the haughty old days it would have been expected. He felt the hours would never move fast enough. He felt like a kid with the mumps passing the time with comic books and TV. He was aching, he was mad, he was jealous. If only she could have seen him act, seen his audition tape, she might have asked him to read for her. He shouldn't have opened up to her. It totally pissed him off.

Then, at noon, Maggie walked in.

She marched to the counter. Her hair was pulled back and tied with a scarf, a large leather bag that looked heavy was draped over her shoulder, and the jeans she had been poured into reminded him of what she looked like naked. She wore very sexy, very serious boots. She slammed the bag down and caught his eye with a curious, mischievous grin. "Do you have a passport?"

"What?"

"You heard me. We don't have much time. Do you have a passport?"

His heart leaped. He had always had one, ever since he learned what they were; it kept the dreams alive. "Yes."

"Valid?"

"No, fake."

"Funny." She grabbed his arm. "Let's go." She tried to pull him around to the front of the counter, grabbing her bag with her other hand.

"Go where?" he sputtered, flustered.

She just grinned.

The manager was right there. "May I ask what is going on?"

"Sure," Maggie answered. "Mr. Jaxon no longer works for you. He got an acting job that's going to keep him busy for some time."

The manager glared at Max. "What?"

Max stared at Maggie. "What?"

"I screened that *ER* you did today," Maggie almost yelled, "and I liked it."

"This for real?" Max asked.

"You don't trust me?" She pulled him toward the door.

The manager shouted, "But it's the Christmas rush!"

"You'll do better without him," Maggie assured the man, " 'cause he can't wrap a present for shit." With that, she dragged Max out of the store.

As the blast of warm air hit them, Max stopped moving and stood his ground. "Okay, listen, if this isn't on the level, don't fuck with my head, okay?"

"Come on," she said, waving to the valet attendant for her car, "we have a plane to catch."

"A plane? To where?"

"Paris."

"You're kidding," Max said as they got into the car. "She's kidding," he said to the valet holding the door. Maggie pulled out with a squeal of the tires. Max looked at the store he would no longer enter as an employee. Perhaps as a customer, he thought, and that made him grin. But he was reeling. "Paris? You're not talking about Perris, California, by any chance, are you?"

Maggie put her sunglasses on and turned up the air-conditioning, even though the top was down. "Where do you live?"

"You're *not* kidding, are you?"

"We have reservations on the four o'clock Air France, the nonstop."

"What?"

"You heard me."

"I can't." He suddenly remembered. *"The Practice."*

"Huh?"

"I'm shooting in January."

She seemed impatient, dismissing it. "Twenty lines on an episodic TV show or a substantial part in a major motion picture, take your pick."

Was there a choice?

She continued on about a costume fitting tomorrow, something about contracts being sent to Paris from New York, going down to see Daddy for Christmas, a villa, but Max couldn't take it all in. He was lost in wonder. And shock. He did manage to tell her he lived in the Los Feliz area, and she turned east. "The film is called *Fibs*. It's about you and an older woman, and spare me the cute remarks, okay?"

He smirked.

"Last night, on the beach, I knew you were right for this. And I knew I was right in what I was planning. We start shooting in Stockholm just about the time they'll have replaced you on *The Practice*."

Stockholm.

"Verna Zimmermann plays your mother. And lover."

Verna Zimmermann. He couldn't believe it. She was the best actress Europe had produced since Catherine Deneuve. "What's it about?"

"Incest."

He swallowed hard. "You're kidding."

"Not in the least. It's filled with longing, fantasy, intrigue, and intimacy all rolled up in a ball of lies, the little fibs we tell to protect people, and save our own butts." She swerved to avoid a van, nearly snapping his neck.

"You drive like a maniac!"

"I drive like I'm in Rome." She laughed. "And you should talk."

On Los Feliz Boulevard, he said, "This isn't a game, is it? You're not fucking with my head?"

"Who's your agent?"

"William Barber at United Talent."

"Ah, Billy. I can deal with him." She put in a call to the man from her cell phone, advising his secretary that this was urgent, return it as soon as he could.

He pointed to a driveway, and she turned in. "You live *here*?" It was a typical Hollywood apartment complex, a stucco box surrounding a swimming pool.

"Yes." He got out when she parked behind his car.

"Grab what you need, what you can't live without, a carry-on. I'll wait here."

"What? Paris isn't Pasadena. How long will I be gone?"

"How the hell should I know? Six months for certain."

He shook his head, like a dog shaking water out of his fur. "I have stuff."

"Stuff?"

"Stuff!" he said defiantly.

"You said you liked taking risks," she reminded him. She unfastened her seat belt and turned to him. "Listen to me. Take what you absolutely can't live without and leave the rest behind."

He blinked. "You really want me to do your movie?"

"I'm a hell of a director, so trust my instincts. I liked what you did on *ER*, and even if you're not as good as you claim, remember I'm the only person alive who ever got a good performance out of Ali MacGraw. And if you make me miss that plane, keep in mind that Keanu is always available."

"I'll be right back."

She went with him, on second thought, to see if she could help. It took him nearly an hour deciding what mementos and treasures to take, plus enough clothes for a few days. She told him she'd buy him what he needed in France.

He looked around. He knew she thought he should set fire to this place. But everything had meaning for him. A birdcage with Barbie and Ken dolls in a 69 position inside. A garish poster promoting hang gliding. His DePaul University Certificate in Acting, cheaply framed. Photos of skylines, buildings, architectural renderings that he'd drawn. Plants in Lean Cuisine trays, books on hang gliding, film, biographies, thousands of matchbooks from restaurants he couldn't afford. His free weights, a worn teddy bear. He saw Maggie pick up a framed photograph of Nicky Dee, his best friend. He shot her a look. Maggie blew the dust off it and slipped it into the bag he was packing. "No waitress-from-hell jokes," she promised.

"What about my car?" he asked.

"Donate it. To the enemy."

"People will wonder where I've gone."

"Ever heard of French postcards?"

His spine tingled. "Do I need a heavy coat? Does it snow in Paris? I don't even know."

She wrapped him in her arms. "Yes, it sometimes snows in Paris, and it's enchanting. We'll go ice skating together. Take your leather jacket and the bulky sweater you wore in Aspen." She tossed in the unwrapped copy of GQ she spied on the coffee table. "Take this too."

"Why?"

"Article on me. Good one, actually. Save me a couple of hours explaining my life."

He went to the bathroom, sweeping everything from the counter into a Ziploc bag—toothbrush, toothpaste, Chlor-Trimeton, floss, rubbers, tweezers, nail clippers. "What do I do about my landlady?"

"Wish her well."

"I have a lease."

"You're not breaking it, just vacationing." Maggie pulled out her checkbook and started writing. "How much does she overcharge you for this rathole?"

"Eleven hundred a month."

She wrote it to cover his rent for six months. "Who do I make it out to?"

"Beverly Mattioli."

"Maybe Beverly will do a little refurbishing while you're gone." She set the check on the coffee table. "Ready?"

He pulled the *GQ* out of the bag, then zipped it up, slipping the magazine into his backpack so he could read it on the plane, and took one last look at what had been his home for almost two years. "Scary," he said.

"I'll say."

"I mean what's happening."

"Thrilling," she corrected him. "An adventure." She took his bag. He picked up the backpack. And they went out the door.

The sunlight nearly blinded him. It was an odd sensation, no brighter than it had been before they went inside, but it seemed as though the sun were pulling him, guiding him, giving him permission to risk everything for accomplishments he'd only dreamed of. "You okay?" she asked as he stopped hesitantly.

"Nicky always talks about spiritual blessings. Maybe this is what she means."

Maggie pinched his butt and forced him on ahead of her. But after putting his things in her car, instead of getting in himself, he went to the carport, where he unlocked a storage locker at the rear. "What the hell is in there?" Maggie asked. Time was not on their side anymore. He struggled with what looked to her like a folded tent wrapped in a travel case. "What the hell is that contraption?"

"My glider."

"Your what?"

"Hang gliding is my hobby."

"We can get you one in France."

He was determined. "Some people go to church, I go gliding. With *this* glider. You want me, you take the glider too." He tucked the bulky contraption under his arm. "Now I'm ready," he announced. Indeed, his heart was already on the airplane.

Six

Kristen Caulfield walked into the prop room and un-fastened her necklace. Bruce Borger, the property manager on her debut film, *Snow Angel*, turned around and lit up with a smile. "Hi."

"Hi," she said. "God, I hate giving this back. It looks like Harry Winston."

"More Wal-Mart. Paste and rhinestones."

"Sure looks real in the rushes."

"*You* make it glimmer."

She blushed. "Thank you. You've been so kind to me while we've been shooting . . . putting up with my stupidity."

"Stupidity?"

"I didn't know what I was doing half the time. We're finished tomorrow, and it's like you have to pinch me to make me realize this is real. You've been great."

Bruce smiled. He'd been enamored of her since the day she appeared on the set, mesmerized by her physical beauty and talent. Now that they'd shot scenes all the way from Yosemite to Honolulu, he was certain that she was going to be the next big thing. He'd known it from that first day, and now word was spreading. "You're being written up in all the columns. You're the one to watch, Constance Heller says. So, what comes next?"

She shrugged. "I don't know. I miss my parents, so I think I'll go back home for a few months." He knew she was very close to her family. She had lived with them in Wisconsin until she started the movie.

"I enjoyed meeting them when they were here. Did they like being extras in the Christmas sequence?"

She smiled and nodded. "But then we drove down to Mexico for a few days. Dad was the only one who ate strawberries. He got hepatitis. That's another reason I want to be there. He's had a hard time."

"Sorry. But I'm glad it wasn't you."

"That would have been the end of my film career."

He looked at her with awe. "It's just beginning."

She giggled. "I've been getting amazing offers. Bill says there's a stack of scripts for me to read. I'm honored."

"Bill?"

"Bill Barber, my agent."

He looked relieved. "Thought maybe you meant a boyfriend."

"No boyfriend."

"That's impossible. I mean, someone as attractive and talented as you are?"

"I don't want a romantic involvement. Not now."

"Been burned before?"

"No, never really been in love. I'm focusing on my work. I want to be really good."

Bruce put the necklace in a coffee can. "You are really good, and you know it. And since the movie will be wrapped tomorrow, you don't need to focus on anything but your dad and that pile of scripts. So, how about being my date for the wrap party?"

She gave him a warm and genuine smile. Her cornflower-blue eyes looked at him with a kind of wonder that he would ask her out, as if she didn't deserve it. "I don't know."

"What don't you know?"

"I don't know if I should."

"Why not?"

"Well, I promised myself I'd put all my energy into my career. No emotional involvements beyond that."

Bruce laughed. "Hey, I'm not asking you to marry me. I only want you to go to a party with me." Plus, he thought, she could do worse.

He was older than her, in his mid-thirties, with a good physique, hair graying slightly at the temples, and a winning smile to go with his dark brown eyes. He was successful in Hollywood precisely because he was the opposite of all the actors; he was not a dreamer. He was a realist. He would work forever.

She looked embarrassed, bit her upper lip. "God, I must sound so silly. Sure, I'll be happy to go with you, Bruce."

He grinned. "So there's hope?"

She looked at him, sizing him up. She couldn't help but laugh at his flirting. "I just want friends right now. I told myself that I wouldn't get involved with anyone here in Hollywood."

"I'm no actor."

She blinked. "You say that like it's bad."

He laughed. "It's what you have to avoid. You deserve better."

She abruptly changed the subject, to get things more on a business level. "Now, the last scene we're shooting is where I drop the champagne bottle to the floor on New Year's Eve. Can I have a bottle to practice with so I get it right?"

"I can do better than that. I could buy us some Dom Perignon at dinner tonight and you could use that one."

She had to giggle. "You don't give up, do you?"

"Never." He handed her an empty Cold Duck bottle.

She grinned. "I'll see you tomorrow, Bruce."

He winked and she left. Then he opened the coffee can again, lifted the thick necklace to his face, and drew in what was left of the scent of her.

Seven

A Parisian newspaper made the announcement: AMERICAN NEWCOMER TO APPEAR WITH ZIMMERMANN IN NASH FILM. Max discovered it on a stand on the boulevard St. Germain. Maggie told him she'd thought about holding a press conference, but it was best to wait until Verna Zimmermann joined them in Stockholm. They'd get better coverage.

He stared at his name in the article. "Max Jaxon, American newcomer." "Nicky won't fucking believe this." He bought a copy to mail to Los Angeles.

Paris was a wonder, the little he saw of it. He caught a glimpse of Pei's pyramid at the Louvre, toured the Eiffel Tower and Notre Dame, but most of his time there was taken up with business managers who confused him with a mix of French and English as they talked about his contract. He was fitted and refitted for costumes while a seamstress with her hair in a tight bun stuck pins in him, lamenting that he was too tall, too big, too many muscles. Maggie watched it with amusement. The making of a star. It was proof to her that she could take a struggling nobody and turn him into something big.

They dined at the Bristol Hotel, where Maggie introduced Max to Yves St. Laurent, who was with a prominent member of the French government, an old friend of her father's. Yet the real shock came when they ran into Julie Christie on the way out. Max was numb, so impressed he could not find words. He loved old black-and-white films, and *Darling* was one of the first movies he had ever purchased. Now he was kissing her hand.

They made love in Maggie's apartment on the rue Monge, and walked hand in hand on the cold cobblestones at night. Thousands of twinkling lights danced on Christmas trees behind the iced panes of French doors. They stopped once on the Pont-Royal. "I think this is the loveliest spot in all Paris," Maggie exclaimed. "It was built under Louis XIV, and I don't think a stone has been changed. Look at the water, how the images reflected are so precise."

He was amazed. "You see things that everyone else misses."

"That's what I try to do with a camera."

He put his arm around her shoulder. "This reminds me of walking together in Aspen that night."

"Colorado was colder. Now I've got my love to keep me warm."

He wondered if she meant that. Love? Did that have anything to do with this? He doubted it. But there certainly was passion. "I always wanted to see

Paris. The buildings, the cafes, the museums. Why do I feel at home here?"

"Maybe you were Parisian in another life."

"It's a stupid feeling, like this city has always been inside me."

"It didn't feel so stupid to Hemingway." She kissed him lovingly and then turned and gestured to the thousands of windows lining the Left Bank. "If you are lucky to have lived in Paris as a young man, then wherever you go for the rest of your life, it stays with you, for—"

He knew the line. "—for Paris is a moveable feast."

They walked alongside the Quai Conti and watched a fisherman toss a line into the icy Seine. "Paris was once called Lutetia," she said, "and these fishermen knew her when. Guys like him have been throwing their lines for hundreds of years."

Max watched a couple of other old-timers toss their lines in. "They always fish this late at night? In the dead of winter?"

"Paris never sleeps." She pulled his arm. "Come, buy me a Cinzano."

"Nicky?"

"X, baby!"

"How are you? I miss you."

"Oui, monsieur, fine, miss you too," the waitress bellowed. "How's the bitch treating you?"

"She's being wonderful."

"Gush attack. Don't trust this."

He could envision her pantomiming putting her finger down her throat. "It's overwhelming, Nicky. Honestly, I mean it's all a blur."

"Whoa. You sound like you did in New York when you thought you had that role at Lincoln Center."

"I'm not getting carried away. I signed contracts."

"Honest, babe, it's on the level?"

"Honest, honey."

She cautioned him. "Don't get too swept up. That broad's got a lot of power, but you might just be her current boy toy. *Capisce?* Keep your options open for the future."

"Nicky," he said, "if anyone's using someone here it's me. I mean, this movie could make me famous, you know? She's already got a career, I don't. She could do that for me."

"Now you're talking. God, X, I love your enthusiasm. That's the gift you bring to the world, you know that? It's contagious."

"Honey, I'm gonna make it. This film is going to turn my life around. You'll move in with me in palatial splendor in Malibu and sling hash no more."

"But I'll still make you rice pudding."

Two days later, Maggie and Max boarded the train for Avignon, the steam rising from the tracks sizzling in their ears. Max read her revised script of the film on the way, and marveled. It was wonderful. Maggie had toned down the suspicion that he, the mysterious American stranger, and Zimmermann were related, making it more subtle. But he still did not like the ending.

"Good," she said, " 'cause I'm not crazy about it either. I've got a few more ideas."

"Like?"

She bristled. "Hell, I don't know." She looked out the window at the rolling countryside, covered with a low fog. She seemed in a funk.

"You're preoccupied."

"Daddy, in a word."

"I thought you were excited about seeing him," Max said.

"I always am—until I board the train." She continued to stare out the window glumly. "We have a conflicted relationship. Not aided by the presence of the sparrow."

"Sparrow?"

"Nicole Richaud, the frail little thing who passes herself off as being his devoted mistress."

"She's not?"

"Frail or devoted? Truth is, she's a scheming piece of steel masquerading as a lover and nurse."

"So, tell me, how do you *really* feel about her?"

She turned to him. "Your sarcasm isn't welcome."

He took her hand. "Does your father love her?"

She nodded reluctantly. "I think she makes him happy in his golden years."

"Then that's all that counts."

"Old fool," she muttered.

"How old?" Max asked.

"Eighty-eight. I think."

"Then he has every right to be a fool." Max squeezed her hand.

"I'm always so apprehensive. It's so uncomfortable sometimes."

"Hey," he said brightly, "this time I'll be there."

She just shook her head. "You'll see."

An hour later, she led him up the steps of an enormous weathered pink stone house which was surrounded by cascading beds of brightly colored winter flowers. The man who met them in the open vestibule held a glass of Vichy in his hand. His white linen pants and wrinkled shirt complemented his suntanned, leathery skin. His face was old, craggy, but pleasing and welcoming.

"Papa," Maggie said, giving him a peck on each cheek, "I want you to meet Max Jaxon. Max, this is my father, the legend."

Charles stuck his tongue out at her and smiled at the young man.

Max extended his hand. "It's an honor, sir."

Charles Nash said, "Welcome to Avignon," as he shook Max's hand, then clapped his other arm over Max's shoulders and led him inside. Two big dogs lounged in front of a fire roaring in a huge stone fireplace. Charles sank into an easy chair at one side of the hearth, indicating for Max to join him in a matching one. He virtually ignored Maggie as she instructed the servants with the luggage.

Nicole Richaud fluttered down the staircase, as if a gentle breeze had propelled her from a cloud. She was slight, pretty in an almost ethereal way, enchanting. She moved directly to Nash's chair, hugged him from behind, then lovingly kissed him on the cheek, smiling.

"Ah, *ma cherie*," he said, "we have a guest tonight."

Nicole turned to Max, who had gotten to his feet. She seemed almost overwhelmed by the gorgeous young man she was facing. Her delicate hazel eyes moved from his face, down to his feet, and back up again, almost in slow motion. With a sensual smile that was thoroughly French and reeked of desire, she approached him with an outstretched hand. He took it in his, bent forward, and lightly kissed it. He felt her fingers curl into his palm and lightly rub him there. It was an exotic, secret, enticing move. "How nice to meet you," he managed to say.

"The pleasure," she purred, dramatically emphasizing the word *pleasure*, "monsieur, is all mine."

When Maggie stepped into the room, the dogs rose languidly to welcome her. She sat on the floor, petting them. Charles did the same to Nicole, who curled up at his feet. But her gaze remained on Max, and didn't waver.

"You have to understand," the old man bellowed at dinner, "there was a kind of virus infecting everyone back then. People were obsessed with the Reds. Pinkos, they called us. Anyone too liberal or who made the slightest criticism of America, they got the shaft—from their peers, no less. I stuck it out till I couldn't take it anymore. Democracy, my ass. It's a wonder they didn't put AIDS victims in concentration camps in the Reagan era. Pass the mutton."

"Though it seems Daddy has a certain prejudice against the American way of life," Maggie said to Max, handing her father the platter of rosemary-and-garlic-encrusted lamb, "he continues to increase his fortune through Wall Street."

"Charles," Nicole cautioned softly, "your cholesterol."

"Who gives a good goddamn at my age?" He heaped the fattiest slice he could find onto his plate.

Maggie could see that Max was mesmerized by the old man. "You ever meet the Kennedys, Mr. Nash?" Max asked.

"Oh, my God," Maggie moaned, setting her fork down, "here comes Camelot."

"I knew Joe when he was banging Gloria Swanson, but that's another story. Jack told me he liked a movie of mine, can't recall which one." When Charles laughed, his bushy eyebrows seemed to stand up. They were scraggly, with the same white hair that protruded from his open shirt collar. He was balding slightly on top, but he seemed, at his age, ruggedly virile. They were the perfect match, for Charles Nash was, in his own gruff way, paternal, and Max was a boy in need of a father. Charles seemed to be so taken with Max that he was oblivious of Nicole's constantly staring at him.

Maggie wasn't. "Nicole," Maggie said, "you seem preoccupied."

"I love the old stories."

"Francine never did. She used to grow bored."
Francine had been Charles's previous mistress. Her
very name rankled Nicole so deeply it almost made
her spit.

"Maggie, don't start trouble," Charles warned.

"I'm merely saying how good Nicole is for you,
Papa."

"Dinner is delicious," Max said, attempting to
change the subject.

Maggie went with it, in her own way. "Nicole, you
haven't touched anything on your plate."

"I had a big lunch."

"I swear, Daddy, you'd better make this girl eat,
or she's just going to blow away one day."

"There is no mistral strong enough to take me
from Charles," Nicole stated emphatically, matching
swords with Maggie. She leaned on Charles. "Darling, tell Max about the time Jackie O came to the
villa. That's one of my favorites."

Before Charles could begin, Maggie offered another suggestion. "Max, dessert and coffee on the
terrace?"

Max said, "I'd love to hear about Jackie."

Wrong answer. As Charles started in, Maggie
tossed her napkin on her plate, got up and went to
the grand piano in the corner of the living room,
framed by French doors and lush red-silk drapes. She
noticed a crucifix on the wall, wondered where in
the hell that had come from. Religion had arrived in
the house along with Nicole, but this was a bit much.

She tinkled a few keys, keeping an eye on Max.

And on Nicole watching Max as Charles told a story Maggie had heard too many times before. Before long, Maggie moved her fingers expertly over the Bosendorfer keys. She had studied classical piano as a girl, and played a little Brahms. But she soon tired of it, and switched to Sondheim, to "Send in the Clowns," a subtle jab at the two men talking animatedly at the table. Bored with that, she got up, took a cup of coffee from the maid, and stepped outside. Here, not so very far from the Mediterranean, the night was warm, and the prospect of soon shooting in frozen Stockholm made a balmy evening outdoors all the more enticing. But she had no desire to stand there alone. She put her head back in the open door. "Max, enough politics?"

Nash rapped his knuckles on the table. "If you could find a little room in that mushy romantic brain of yours for political sensibility, the social commentary in your films might carry a little sting."

"Since when do I make social commentary?" she snapped right back.

"It's inherent in contemporary cinema."

She nearly spat. "Bullshit."

"That's a cop-out, Margaret," he growled.

She disappeared, slamming the door.

"Women," Charles said to Max as he got up. "Except for you, my darling." Nicole smiled as the maid took her untouched plate. Charles reached for a humidor. "Cigar? I only do it when Maggie's not looking. Nicole doesn't care."

Max looked at Nicole. She nodded her approval.

"Men should have what makes them happy," she said, more to Max than to Charles.

Max appeared on the patio an hour later. Maggie was nestled in a chaise behind a potted palm and a pile of books, so he didn't notice her at first. She watched him stop at the stone wall and put one foot up, looking out over the hillside into the night. He leaned forward on his right knee, seeming to drink in the place, the stars, the smells.

From her angle, in the glow from the burning lantern candles, Maggie thought Max had never looked so attractive. She wished she were behind the camera now. She drank in his strong, pouty lips, his chiseled nose, the slightly dimpled chin, and how—she noticed for the first time—his earlobes were quite large. Big lobes, but normal ears, actually perfect ears that sat close to his head and that his hair just dusted. She wanted to suck on them. Hmmm. Perhaps she'd write that in for Zimmermann to do. The meat displayed in the front of the case, her father had taught her, is there for a reason.

Max seemed to be growing restless looking around the garden for her. She figured she'd tortured him enough. When it looked like he was about to walk away to hunt her down, she whistled. He turned and discovered her hiding in the corner, ensconced in the wicker chair with a beautiful throw covering her legs. He smiled and went to her. "Don't be mad."

"Me?" she said with soft sarcasm. She moved her legs to one side as he sat down, and when he saw her shoes on the tiles, he began to rub her feet. "Miss me?" she asked. He nodded. "Liar. You couldn't tear yourself away from Nicole."

"Nicole? I like her, but—"

"And I'm more than sure she likes you, too."

"Well, she did come on a little strong." He nestled in next to her and nibbled her ear. "But I stayed inside because of your father."

"I'm warning you: beware of her." She glanced toward the house. "Did they go to bed?"

He nodded. "Think so." He went on dreamily, "He told this remarkable story about Dash Hammett and your mother."

Maggie groaned. "The time Hammett almost burned the house down? I think he actually just lit a cigarette. Papa embellishes."

"Maggie, what was she like? Your mom."

She flinched. "I hear she was warm, generous, temperamental, and very troubled." She seemed lost for a moment in the cobwebs of memory, then laughed, as if tenderness was too hard to talk about. "I don't really remember her well. Made good bread dumplings. That's what I remember best, sitting around the kitchen while she was baking, listening to her tell stories about her life in the movies before Daddy rescued her."

"Rescued her?"

"She hated it. Just wanted to be a housewife. She died too young. We would have become good friends." Maggie stood up, as if to force away the memories. "Did he tell you how we actually ended up here?"

"Nope."

"Everybody else put money into steel and cars and gas and oil in those days, but Daddy always fancied himself something of a farmer. He used to clip hedges around the Beverly Hills house like a mad barber. He shopped the Riviera for a farmhouse and vineyard, good old Dick Diver–style digs, and found this place, so most of my growing up was done on the Rhone River, and I thank God for that."

"It really is *Tender Is the Night*, isn't it?"

Maggie blinked. "You know, I just realized, he carried the Fitzgerald thing to the hilt. Not only did he get his villa, but he got his own bona fide Nicole to go with it."

He shook his head. "The grace before the meal was pretty intense."

"Nicole is a religious fanatic. She's converting Daddy. Which is a joke."

Max finished the cold espresso in her cup. "She seems devoted to him."

"She's a money-hungry slut, if you ask me."

"She's pretty."

She gave him an expression as cold as Colorado.

"I only said she was pretty," he said with a laugh, "not gorgeous, hot, fantastic like you." He pulled her down to him and kissed her full on the lips.

"Let's go for a walk."

"Christ, don't you ever sit? We've been moving ever since we met—the plane to Aspen, the car to Malibu, a jet to Paris, train here. Relax a little."

"I try."

"Not enough. But okay, let's walk." He took her

hand. "And let's make it a vow: no matter where we are, every night we'll walk somewhere together. Just us."

She smiled. "Just us."

She showed him a weathered old shrine to the Virgin behind the olive trees. They passed a barn and a small guest cottage, which looked like it had been shuttered for years. "Who built this place?" Max asked.

"A cardinal who was very tight with the pope when they ran the church from here."

"The Catholic Church?"

"No, the Holy Rollers." She gave him an arch look before she continued. "Avignon was the Vatican for a time—1309 to 1377, if I remember my history."

"Why?"

"A sleepy little French village was the perfect hideaway for the horny Princes of the Church to keep a stable of mistresses. I'll have to take you to the Palace of the Popes."

He was scandalized. "You're kidding."

"Nuns never taught you that, huh?"

"I'm not Catholic."

She chuckled. "Good. Then Nicole won't be dragging you to church." She sat down under the spreading whitish-green leaves of an olive tree. It was starting to feel damp, with a mist creeping up the hillside. She pulled up some of the grass and brought it to his nose.

"Smells like a park in Tulsa I remember. I played

in the clippings when I was a kid." He took a deep breath. "Maggie, is that what you see me as? A kind of kid?"

She waved away the idea. "Hey, you already have a mother in that waitress. I see you as a man, strong-willed and intelligent, but with the ability to be as delighted with wonder as a child. Never lose that mix; it's your key to fame. I'm going to capitalize on it."

"I think I love you, you know."

She smiled patiently, knowing that he did not.

"How much of us is in that script? How much of you? How much of it is your fantasy?"

"You mean, how much of *you* is my fantasy? Max, the subject of *Fibs* has nothing to do with our lives, yours and mine. If I wanted a young stud for the sake of lost youth, I'd pick up one of the muscle boys hanging out on the beach at Tropez. They're ten years younger than you—no offense—and their private parts weigh more than their brains, though you do give them a run for the money in that department."

"I don't want to feel like a toy."

"Right now," she said lightly, "you probably feel as though you're on a carnival ride. Give it time. Be easy on yourself. Let me take care of you for a while. Look up to the sky and reach for it." She lay back and peered up through the crinkled leaves of the tree. "Lose yourself in those stars and make love to me and you will discover the man you really are."

"I love you."

"No, you don't. Not yet." She pulled him down to her, already moving her fingers inside the waistband of his pants. "But you will."

"Well, well, well," Nicole said, standing in the master bedroom window, watching Max and Maggie return to the villa, hand in hand. "The loving couple is back. How long do you give it?"

There was no answer. Just a snort.

She turned to Charles, who was fast asleep under the thick duvet. She gave him a look of utter contempt. "I'm talking to you and you fall asleep on me." In response, he began to snore, and she bristled. "Old man," she hissed, turning to the window again.

The young man beneath her was kissing Maggie. Her heart leaped. He was so attractive, so utterly masculine, but with a little boy's wide-eyed wonder about him. She had felt drawn to him instantly, and not only because of the powerful physical desire. She understood him, she got him. She turned back to look at Charles. Who would accomplish the task first? Max or her? Would Maggie marry him before Charles said yes to her? Would he have to put in less work than she had? Maggie certainly seemed taken with him, but with Maggie it was hard to tell. She had a veneer that Nicole had never penetrated, and for that she detested her. Nicole prided herself on her ability to read people. Maggie confounded her.

She closed the curtains and knelt at her side of the bed to pray. Her fervent wish was silent. Then she crossed herself and slipped into bed. "A double wedding, my love?" she said to the comatose Charles. "Father and daughter. The press will go mad." She pulled the covers to her chin. "A double honeymoon." She giggled. "Adjoining suites." She turned to face Charles. "One for you and Maggie, one for me and Max." Satisfied with her fantasy, she reached up and clicked out the bed lamp. *"Bonne nuit."*

Charles continued to snore.

Telluride, Colorado

"Hey, Chris, sorry I'm late," Christopher Daniel said as he jumped from his vehicle.

A very tall, blond-haired man shook Detective Daniel's hand warmly. "Hey, Chris," he mimicked him, "no problem."

"You're the only person who ever calls me Chris," the detective said.

"That's 'cause I know you from the old days."

"I think it's more the curse of having two first names." Daniel laughed. "Good to see you again."

"Yeah, buddy, ditto for me." The two Christophers had been friends since childhood, and even though their interests had taken them in different directions, they had never lost their affection for one another.

Daniel shivered. "Colder than I thought it would be." He pulled the collar of his parka up around his neck. He'd dressed for the excursion, putting on corduroys and a wool sweater instead of his usual indoor

office attire, but the wind whipped through them on
top of the barren bluff. "I was warmer up here the
other day when they were shooting the movie."

"People think Colorado is icy," Chris joked. "This
is nothing compared to Vermont last week. That was
real long johns weather."

"What were you doing there?"

"Gliding competition."

"Middle of winter, you crazy ass?"

Chris Larsen smiled knowingly. "Hard-core fanatic,
what can I say?"

"Did you win?"

"I was a judge."

"Ah, of course." It made perfect sense. Chris
Larsen was one of the world's foremost authorities on
hang gliding. And that's why he was here today. Daniel needed him.

Larsen looked around. "This the spot where she
shot him, right?"

"That mark there," Daniel explained, pointing to
the right, where the Telluride cops had painted a yellow X. "He hit the mountain just down there, to the
left."

"I found it with the binoculars. Blood's still there."
Larsen looked sick for a moment. "I still can't believe
it. I competed with Jaxon once."

"I didn't know you knew him."

"He was a very good flier."

"Could anyone have landed that thing?" Daniel was
very curious to know that answer. "Could you have
done it?"

"I doubt it. 'Cause you were right, Mr. Detective."

Daniel's eyes brightened. "My hunch?"

Chris Larsen nodded. "Murder."

Daniel said, "Well, well."

"Let's go look at the glider," Chris suggested. "I didn't bring my long johns."

"Meet you there," Daniel said, already heading back to his Blazer.

Ten minutes later, they were standing in the Telluride police evidence room, peering at the wreckage of Max Jaxon's hang glider. Daniel took off his parka. "You have a chance to go over this thoroughly?"

Chris nodded. "Sure did. Studied the film footage too, in slow motion. You were correct that this didn't come down because of the bullet, like everyone thought."

"Even Max himself," Daniel said

"Bullets don't do what was done to this glider."

"I knew it. I knew there had to be something more. Some kind of sabotage."

Chris nodded. "The second bullet missed."

Daniel looked at the crumpled mess that had been a world-class aircraft, twisted metal and shredded yellow nylon with bloodstains everywhere. "Okay, if the bullet missed, why did the wings rip apart?"

Larsen crouched down. "See this?" He indicated a piece of the nylon material of the right-hand sail.

Daniel nodded. "The rip? The tear?"

"No, rips and tears are imprecise, jagged. This is

too clean a cut. Too precise to be caused by a rifle shot or the force of the wind."

Daniel's eyes widened. "This a slice from a razor?"

Chris nodded. "Old fabric sometimes gives with force, but this nylon is brand-new. It's a deliberate slit from a blade or some kind of very sharp scissors or knife."

"You sure of this?" Daniel asked.

Larsen stood up. "Bet my reputation on it. Listen, watch the film in slo-mo. You'll see a moment—unnoticeable to anyone not searching for it—just before he flies out over the lake."

"What kind of moment?"

"A shudder. A vibration. Max felt it, I'm sure. He didn't know it then, but it was one of the initial cuts on the wing—the right wing—starting to rip back."

"Cuts, plural?"

"Slashes. There were two of them."

"Two?"

"Look over here." Larsen reached out for another piece of the mangled wreckage and turned it over. "On the left side here as well, where the wing rounds the batten frame, is another deliberate slit, about two inches in length. See how just beyond that the nylon is jagged? That's because the force of wind took over and pulled it apart."

Daniel peered at the rip closely. "Both wings were sabotaged?"

"It was a kind of insurance policy. If one didn't give, the other would."

"So," Daniel theorized, "if the bullet didn't kill him, the glider would."

Larsen nodded. "Just a question of which went first."

"Which *wing* went first?"

"The right. You can see the damage is more severe on that side. The right caused the loss of control, and when the fabric started ripping, the force on the other wing, trying to balance it, pulled the other slit open as well."

"So that's what caused the accident."

"That and the wires. On a glider, the stainless-steel wires provide great durability for flight. The flying wires, the webbing, cables, they all add up to creating a safe experience, even if you have been shot in the shoulder. But one of the cables was loosened." He crouched down again. "Here, where it joined the battens."

"I see."

"It was just a matter of time before it would give way under the extreme pressure of the wind."

"More insurance?" Daniel asked.

"Assurance, really. This baby *had* to crash, there was no hope." Larsen stood up, looking puzzled. "Damn, Max was good. You can see it on the tape. He was amazing, he tried so hard. Somebody wanted to kill him real badly. They knew exactly what they were doing to him."

"Would it have to be someone who knew gliders well?"

Larsen shook his head. "No, you could learn how to screw it up from any number of books on the subject. I mean, the simplest book on gliding can tell you how the thing is held together."

"From which you can figure out how to make it come apart."

Larsen nodded. Then he looked down at the smashed wreckage of what once had been a beautiful flying machine and shoved his hands in his jeans. "Poor Max," he said. "He never had a chance."

Eight

They stayed in a lavish suite at the aptly named Grand Hotel, in the heart of Stockholm. Max met the great film star Verna Zimmermann that evening, and after some initial hesitation—he was too eager, she a bit distant—they hit it off pretty well. They talked mainly about the movie they were to make, and Verna remarked, "Thank God someone still writes good parts for old broads." Dazzled by her class and bearing, he thought, *Yeah, right, this is some old broad.*

The three of them read through a scene that quickly became problematic, in that Max and Verna just didn't seem to connect. Maggie wanted her stars to be comfortable, so rather than work problems out on location, she ordered up refreshments and snacks, and kept at it. Zimmermann kicked off her shoes and curled up in the chaise, cozy under a cashmere throw Maggie had brought with her. Max, in sweatpants and tee, was less relaxed. In the scene he had to declare his love for Verna, despite their age difference. Verna—and Maggie as well—did not believe him. He wasn't authentic. Maggie thought he was letting the outcome of the story—that they were related—influence his feelings. She told him, "You're jumping the gun. You must see her only as your lover here, a passionate older woman to whom you are irresistibly drawn."

"Forget what the outcome is," Verna suggested. "When you do the lines, do them to some girl you have loved, do them to Maggie, do them to a fantasy figure you desire with all your heart."

"Yes, Max," Maggie added. "You have no clue about the mother thing yet. You must act out of passion here."

Max agreed, but objected to several lines that seemed to him to foreshadow the ending. Maggie gave it some thought. Verna said that now that Max had pointed them out, she agreed, and Maggie edited them. Max got the right feeling finally. Maggie, who had secretly harbored skepticism that he would, sipped her coffee and said nothing.

She never knew how the chemistry between actors would work. Many a lousy script had become a memorable movie because of the spark between the stars. Conversely, many a fine love story had been rendered laughable because there was no magic. Maggie's reputation would be on the line if they did not heat up the screen. She was putting an unknown actor in a film with one of the legendary stars of the cinema. Was it insanity? Or genius? As she watched them talk, she soon began to feel it was the latter. This seemed a match made in heaven.

And it came through that way on film. They were simply magnificent together. Max had many weaknesses before the camera, Maggie quickly discovered, but she could fix that. She was a master at hiding an actor's flaws. Plus, those very weaknesses were inherent in the personality of the character Max was playing, so Maggie tailored the daily rewrites to enhance the character rather than diminish him. Max's shortcomings would look like expert acting on-screen.

Verna took Max under her wing, supporting him when he needed it, smoothing his feathers when the pressures ruffled them. She was the consummate professional, taking direction easily yet retaining her independence. Maggie guessed she was feeling more toward Max than just a pro to a novice. Max was a stud who could raise any woman's blood pressure.

Much of the movie was shot on location in the Gamla Stan, Old Town, on the cobblestone streets winding around ancient corners of crumbling red brick and cracked plaster, under colorful signs indicating shops, bakeries, eye doctors, handicrafts. A shot of Verna and Max running hand in hand down the Drottninggatan was wonderfully romantic, almost fantastical; Maggie knew instantly she'd use it on the poster. It rained right on schedule for a passionate argument on the balustrade of the Parliament Building, and when Verna embraced Max after the fight, the rain mixed with his tears.

Yet at the entrance to the Grand Hotel on the water in the harbor, hundreds of people gathered to watch them make an entrance from a Volvo, only to have Max split the seat of his pants, Verna get her skirt caught in the door of the car, and the doorman forget—in three takes—that he was there to do just that, open the door for them. Nothing went right except the rain. Maggie finally tossed in the towel. "It's hopeless," she said, laughing along with all the rest of them, sending everyone home to rest.

She and Max had a romantic dinner in their suite, celebrating Maggie's very understated fortieth birthday, then went for their customary walk, ducked into a theater to see the new Spielberg film, and ended up eating a slice of what they deemed "birthday cake" at midnight in a sweet shop on the Kungsgatan. They made love that night, for the first time since shooting began almost two weeks ago, bringing each other a comfort that helped their working relationship; it created a balance.

The next morning, they went to a studio that had been rented, just outside the city. It contained the sets for Verna's apartment and the hotel room in which the lovers spend so much of their time. Under grueling pressure, the actors occupied the soundstage for three weeks, coming up for air only when shooting was finished each day.

Max grew ornery, sitting off alone during the breaks, having a rough time sleeping nights. Maggie did not try to change his mood; it was what she wanted. He was becoming the brooding young man she'd envisioned. She was demanding, hard on him. She was "too tired" to sleep with him, she "had a meeting" when he wanted to share dinner, she often didn't answer his questions in the car on the way back to the hotel. His anxiety and anger pained her as a woman, but as his director she loved it.

The camera recorded his growing turmoil, and when the big scene came where Peter is told by the sensual older woman that they cannot be together again because she really doesn't love him, a fib to protect him from her suspicion that they may be related, it all burst out of him in an explosion. Maggie knew she had to get this take the first time, for he would never be that good—that *real*—again. She stopped the cameras, called *finis*, and gave everyone several days off so she could rewrite the ending now that the actors had "inspired" her.

She wrote all that night and the next day. It wasn't until that second evening, when he slipped naked into the bed beside her, that she even spoke to him. "You look marvelous in the rushes," she whispered, and drifted back to sleep. He ran his hand through her hair, lifting the soft strands from her face, and let the rise and fall of her breathing lull him to sleep.

She was long gone when he awoke at noon.

He grabbed a Whopper at the Burger King on the Kungsgatan—you can take the boy out of America, but you can't take America out of the boy—where he wrote another postcard to Nicky Dee:

Nicky!
On the front is the sailing ship Wasa. *See me*
argue with Verna Zimmermann (yes!) on its very

deck in the Maggie Nash film Fibs *opening at a
theater near you in about seven months. I'm
on my way, baby! Thanks for believing in me . . .
Constantly, X*

That night, Verna invited him to join her and some
old friends for dinner. He came in as the group was
raving about someone.

"She's incredible," a man said.

"Fabulous," a woman agreed.

Verna said, "I was mesmerized. I have never seen
anything like it."

"What are you talking about?" Max asked.

Verna introduced everyone to her costar, then told
him they were talking about Kristen Caulfield.

"Who's she?"

"You'll know soon," one of Verna's friends said.
"She will be a household name."

Verna explained, "They're saying she's the most
astonishing new talent to come along in years."

A costume designer who had been silent said, "I
saw an early cut last month. Every actress on earth
is going to faint away with envy. She is gorgeous,
absolutely stunning. But the talent! *Mon dieu*, the
talent!"

"Did you see what the *New York Times* wrote about
her last Sunday?"

"No," Verna answered, "but I heard about it. Sam
found her playing Shaw in some regional theater,
right?"

"The Guthrie," a man affirmed. "This is her first

time in front of a camera. No training, nothing. And you'd think she had the career of Meryl Streep behind her, the way she controls the screen. Are we all going on Friday?"

Everyone enthusiastically said yes.

Everyone but Max. "Going where?"

"Her film is being screened," Verna said, "and you and Maggie must come."

"Can't answer for Maggie, but I'll be there."

"Drag her along," the costumer urged him. "Maggie Nash simply has to see this girl. She's going to want to get her hands on her, mark my words."

Max's eyes danced with excitement. "Then we'll both come," he promised.

"Maggie, her name is Kristen Caulfield. Seems everyone is talking about her." Max followed her around the room as she dressed after her shower. "They say she's the new Gwyneth Paltrow."

"Really. Do you know where my jade earrings are?"

He jumped on the bed, crossing his legs. "You have to come to the screening with me. Promise me."

Maggie found her earrings behind the cosmetic case. She put them on in front of the big mirror. "Darling, I'd love to see this Christine Whatever, but—"

"Kristen. Kristen Caulfield."

"Kristen. But I can't let these people down, they're investors." She retouched her red lipstick and then stepped into her shoes and gave herself a pat on the ass. "Plus, I'm going to the studio after dinner. Ellie Storey, my editor, has previewed some new footage, and I want to see it before we resume shooting."

"How's the ending?"

She cocked her head, and her hair danced the way Audrey Hepburn had taught her. "Still lousy." She sat on the bed. "Listen, go see the film, enjoy the new Gwyneth, and I'll meet you in the sack at midnight, fair?"

He winked. "Fair."

She picked up her bag, grabbed her mink, stood for a moment. "Well?"

"Hot." The dress clung to her in all the right places, making her appear taller, slimmer, and even more striking. "You're a knockout."

"You can eat this off me when I get back," she said, and was off.

After the film, Max declined Verna's invitation to join her and her entourage for coffee and pastries at a café. Instead, he walked in the drizzle, completely stunned. His life had become one astonishing wonder after another since he'd met Maggie, so this night shouldn't have surprised him. But it had. The movie was a good one. It was a thriller about a cunning, likable man who murders a young woman's parents to be there for her—a victim of breast cancer, no less—in her grief. In making her feel like a woman again, he has her indebted to him forever, and in terrible danger. Yet what knocked Max out—and made the movie unforgettable—was Kristen Caulfield.

He had no words to describe her performance. Her fresh beauty, combined with her expressive and vibrant eyes, communicated a strangely appealing mixture of corn-fed sweetness and sophisticated charm. Not since *Darling* had a performer so completely drawn Max into the character she was creating. It was as if his own life had ceased for two hours and four minutes.

Then he came to his senses. It was only a movie. And he, better than anyone, was learning just what that was about. Manipulation was key. Trying to be pragmatic and less the little-boy fan, he suddenly knew what he really wanted: to make a movie with Kristen one day. He would urge Maggie to consider it. But he knew he'd have to be careful not to push too far. If he were really clever, he'd make her think it had been her own idea.

When Maggie showed up at the hotel at two-thirty in the morning, she found Max not in bed but propped astride a dining chair, his chin resting on his hands on the back, looking out the windows at the pouring rain. The room was dark and she could just see his silhouette from the streetlight outside the spattered glass panes. She set her bag down, hung her drowned mink on the door hook, and went to him. He hadn't moved a muscle when she walked in. "Max," she said softly, touching his shoulder, "are you okay?"

"Fine," he said, peering out the window.

"I think it may snow." She stood next to him. He looked up at her, they kissed, and then she took his hand and led him to the bedroom.

As she removed her jewelry and he flopped on the bed, she asked, "How was the movie?"

"Great."

"What's it called?"

"*Snow Angel.*"

"Oh, yes, sure." She had read the novel. The buzz on the girl playing the lead in the movie was good. "What's the name of the actress?"

"Kristen Caulfield."

She let him strip the clothes off her body as she had promised, and they spent nearly an hour teasing with exquisite foreplay. But she surprised him. They did not make love. Something else was on her mind. She curled up next to him and said, "Okay, tell me."

"Tell you what?"

"Tell me about this actress."

Nine

Kristen couldn't believe her eyes. When she and Bruce emerged from the restaurant, they were greeted by photographers and reporters eager to get a piece of her. Bruce pulled her close to him as they waited for the car to be brought around. Kristen, though a little frightened, loved the attention. Obviously, popular enthusiasm matched the reviews. *Snow Angel* was a hit. Overnight, she had become a star.

She answered as many questions as she could. Yes, she was proud of the film. Yes, she was going to make another. No, she didn't know what it would be yet. Yes, she was taking a little time off to be with her parents. No, this man next to her was not her boyfriend. Oh, God, no, she had no idea about the Oscars, she couldn't even think about that yet.

In the car, she felt a rush of adrenaline. "That was just too incredible."

"Scare you?" Bruce asked, piloting his Jaguar through the waving throng of people.

"No. It gives me energy."

"Your life has changed. This is what it's going to be like from now on. Think you can handle it?"

She took a deep breath. "I'm going to have to."

At her apartment, they had a nightcap together on the terrace. She'd rented a place near the beach in Santa Monica when she'd gotten the job, and it was beginning to feel like home. Rather than give it up and move back to Wisconsin, as she'd planned to do, she had decided to keep it in case she found another movie that was compelling enough. She was now besieged with offers, from every famous director and major studio in the world. But she was going to be careful and pick the right one.

She had enjoyed Bruce's company at the wrap party. She had really started to feel comfortable with him. He was a good man, a sexy man, older than she was, with a secure job in a very insecure business. She laughed thinking about that, for he was the kind of guy her parents would want her to marry. What was there not to like? Plus, he was in the same business, yet removed from the pressures of stardom, the crazy world of actors. He seemed to have none of the insecurities associated with show business.

Only she did not love him. She did not feel anything for him but a caring kind of affection. There was no sizzle, no passion. They'd gone out together a few times after the wrap party, never calling it dating, but it was. He drove her to the airport when she went back to see her parents, called her every few days, picked her up on her return. She told him she'd do the same for him, that they were very much alike. But his feelings went deeper than hers, and tonight he admitted it.

"Kristen, listen," he said as he finished his vodka. "I have to confess something."

She waited. "Yes?"

He took her hand. "I'm feeling . . . well, feeling something for you that keeps getting stronger."

"Bruce, I feel very close to you, too. I'm very fond of you."

"*Fond* isn't exactly the word I'm thinking."

She pulled her hand away. "I told you, I like you very much, but I'm not ready to date anyone."

"What are you waiting for?"

She stood up and went to the railing, looking up at the stars. "I was brought up very straitlaced. I've never had a boyfriend, and my only date before college was on prom night. I went out with a couple of guys at school, but they only wanted sex."

"Did you do that?"

She was taken aback. "No! Not then. My God."

"Well, sorry, but people do these days, you know."

She laughed out loud. "I did. Once. I'm a dinosaur, I think. I just . . . just have to feel something deeper. I don't know. I guess I'm scared."

"Protestant?"

She shook her head. "Catholic."

"I got the Jewish guilt. Much the same thing. You have to unlearn a lot of the stuff you were taught."

"That's probably true."

"Let me help." He walked over to her and put his hands on her shoulders, turning her to face him.

"Kristen, I adore you. I'm falling in love with you, and you know that. And yet you're not running away from me. I know that somewhere, down deep inside, you're considering it."

She regarded him a long while. Finally she said, "I can't say what you want me to say, Bruce. I just don't know my heart yet. This is a time of big changes in my life." She walked over to a gardenia bush in a pot. She crouched down and smelled the blossoms. "I grew up thinking a white knight was going to sweep me off my feet."

"Only in the movies," Bruce assured her.

"I guess I have to set my sights on something more realistic."

"I could dress up in white and rent a horse."

She giggled. Then she went back to him and threw her arms around him. "Give me time, okay? Too much is happening. It's a roller coaster and I can't think straight. Can you wait a little bit?"

He took a deep breath, looking like he was going to explode, and then he did explode, with laughter. "Sure, for you, anything."

They kissed. It wasn't passionate, yet it wasn't casual. It made her feel she had someone who truly understood her.

But it made Bruce crazy. He had trouble getting into his Jaguar down in the basement parking garage. When he turned the key, something erupted inside him, his desire shifting to fury. He slammed the transmission into reverse and gunned the engine, backing right into a washing machine that had been set in the garage awaiting the trash pickup. When he hit it, he whirled around, angrier than ever, saw what it was, moved the gears to drive, jerked forward slightly, and then put it in reverse again. This time his bumper almost cut the machine in half, destroying it. When he pulled out of the building, his dented rear flank still had chips of white paint clinging to it.

Once he reached his little house in Studio City, his rage only intensified. He had wanted her for a very long time, with a passion he'd never before felt for anyone. He would do anything to have her. She was only asking him to wait. Could he? He wasn't sure. He walked into the kitchen and turned on a light. His cats rubbed against his trouser legs. He grabbed a bag of Iams and dumped it haphazardly into their bowl. Then he picked up the mail where it had fallen from the front door slot. On the cover of *Premiere* was Kristen's picture.

He poured himself some straight Grey Goose as he read it. "Talented, charming, sensitive, intelligent." Yes, he thought. " '*Snow Angel* is my first film, so it's all new to me. What's really important is to know who I am. That's what I want to hold on to.' " *She doesn't have a goddamned clue.* " 'I don't worry about survival or stardom. I suspect that's why it's happening. I'm free and easy about my work. I'm twenty-four, not a child, and probably a lot naive. Frankly, I look at Hollywood and wonder: What am I doing here?' "

Bruce felt the unmistakable pang of sexual desire.

It had been increasing daily as they did the film. There were scenes on location in the snow near Yosemite when he was glad he was wearing a heavy coat, for she never looked so alluring as when lying there in the white powder making an angel with her arms.

He read on. "Only a small blemish on her left cheek keeps her from being a deity." *A goddess*, he thought. He closed his eyes, finishing the vodka. He rubbed between his legs. He leaned his head back, feeling the deep frustration that had been building all these months, and hurled the glass across the room. It sailed through the sliding glass door that led to the pool, shattering the huge pane into a hundred jagged pieces.

Ten

When *Fibs* wrapped, Maggie told Max they were going to London for a few days on business. When they arrived at Charles De Gaulle Airport, Max found seven groupies and three publicists waiting for him. He loved the young girls' adoration, but was surprised that the media were interested not only in Maggie or Verna Zimmermann, but in *him* as well.

"*People* wants to do a piece on you."

"*Entertainment Weekly*, too."

"Do you sing? Cook? Any special talent? Something for the morning shows."

"I hang glide."

"If we could get Oprah to do a segment on incest," one of them said, "we might have a chance to tie in the film."

"We have to get a fan Web site set up for you, Max."

"Jeez," Max said with a shrug, "you guys are treating me like a star."

"You are a star." The man turned to Maggie. "Doesn't he know that?"

She giggled. "Convince him."

The reporter ticked off his fingers. "Your picture has already appeared in twenty major newspapers. All the teen rags have run a photo of you. Next week, you and Verna Zimmermann will be in *Time*."

"Jesus Christ," Max muttered, not knowing how to react.

"Overwhelmed?" Maggie asked.

He looked like a child discovering his first snowfall. "I'm speechless," he said, heading to the Air France gate.

Maggie called to the bathroom door in their suite in the Savoy. "Hurry, darling. We're having an early dinner."

From behind the paneled door came, "Why?"

"We're joining Joanne and Paul."

Max stuck his head out. "Joanne and Paul who?"

"Woodward. Newman."

Standing in his shorts, Max looked into the steamy bathroom mirror. "Joanne and Paul? Jesus Christ." Would he ever get used to this?

She walked in and pinched his butt. He jumped. Then she bent forward and pretended to take a bite of it. "I like you in those tight white things better than boxers," she said.

"Easier to eat, huh?"

She started fluffing her hair. "Oh, there's an interview set up for you tomorrow."

"With whom?" He tucked his crisp new white shirt into his trousers and found himself a black belt.

"My old friend Connie Heller."

He paled. "They say her cunt has teeth."

"She's a pussycat."

"Cats scratch and draw blood."

She finished her lipstick and looked at him again. "Fat ladies like studs like you." She held up the Hedi Slimane jacket she'd bought him in Paris, and he slipped into it. "Just tell Connie she's got the most beautiful eyes you've ever seen, some such horseshit, and she'll be yours for life."

"You know something, Miss Heller," Max gushed, his own eyes ablaze, "you've got the most beautiful eyes I've ever seen. And I mean that."

Constance blushed. "She pay you to say that? Oh, hell, don't tell me, let me continue to live my delusional life."

"Maggie warned me I'd fall in love with you."

"Hush!" She composed herself. "So, truth now: was it frightening to work with The Diva on your first film?"

"Verna Zimmermann was hot."

"I meant Maggie!" She giggled.

Maggie entered the suite at that moment with what looked like a hundred shopping bags. "Constance, darling," she said, with air kisses, and then set down the Sloane Street spoils and kissed Max quickly on the lips. "Get all the dirt out of him?"

"Just starting," Connie said.

"I didn't mean to interrupt," Maggie apologized.

Connie said, "So tell me, are you two a couple? Is this serious?"

Maggie slumped in the chair. "Our sex life is nobody's business."

Connie pulled her glasses down to the tip of her nose and bent forward, looking into Maggie's eyes. "Your sex life has been my readers' business for twenty years."

"I kinda like it," Max said, his legs crossed under him.

"This a relationship, then?"

Maggie looked at Max and then nodded. "Just say that we're dating."

"Bull. You're in love. Admit it."

Max looked at Maggie again. Maggie looked at Max. Then at Connie. She said, "Mmmmmmm."

Max did the same. "Mmmmmmm."

Connie said cattily, "That's intriguing. What is that supposed mean, exactly?"

Together, laughing, they said, "Mmmmmmm."

"Well, all right, at least tell me how many *M*'s there are in that word so I can spell the goddamned thing."

There was nothing more to be said.

On the flight back to Paris, Maggie warned Max what was coming. "The next few weeks are going to be a test. Of our devotion to one another."

"Huh?"

"I'm going to hole up in the cutting room. Editing is the most crucial part of the process. I immerse myself in it with Ellie. I don't even remember to pee."

"I understand."

"No, you don't. Not until you live through it with me. It's what really ruined that early marriage."

"I knew there was more to it."

She shrugged. "Every man I have ever cared for has been threatened by my work."

"I can handle it. It's my film too."

"Remember that night in Tropez after Christmas in Avignon, when you felt so abandoned 'cause I was hours late meeting you at that restaurant? That was nothing."

"I'll be fine. I love Paris. I'll learn more French. I'll go gliding. I like being alone sometimes." That was untrue; he hated being alone, and she knew it. He could feel her fingernails pressing into his arm. "I'll be okay, honest."

She withdrew her hand and let the flight attendant put down her tray for dinner. "It's going to be hell. I promise you."

The first week wasn't so bad. He was a tourist, plain and simple, doing the Louvre, a night at the Bastille Opera, an afternoon in Versailles. Three days in the Impressionist Museum. Hanging out at the Beauborg. Discovering new and funky restaurants in the Marais. The Picasso Museum. But the boredom soon set in, for he had no one to share it with. They hardly saw one another, barely found the time to talk even when they did, and their love-making all but ceased, as Maggie slept on a cot in the edit room many a night. He felt like a child surrounded by wonderful toys, but there were no other playmates.

He remembered a night when he was small. He wasn't sure how old he was, but he did recall his hair was still dark—it didn't turn blond until he was eight. He had been sitting on his bed in his room at his aunt's house, looking out at the setting sun. Sunset on the plains seemed to go on for hours, spreading over the landscape from one side of the window to the other. As the darkness came, he saw less and less. The field he'd been looking at had one sticklike tree on the horizon, and even that had been obliterated in the blackness. He felt choked, fearing the night was going to take him too. The darkness was going to come through the window and swallow him whole. Filled with fear, he ran to the parlor, where his aunt and uncle looked up, seeing the desperation in his frightened eyes.

Even after his aunt held him in her arms and assured him he was simply having a "bad feeling," he knew it was more than that. His panic wasn't about the night at all, though throughout his life this feeling returned almost always at night. He was simply afraid of being alone with himself.

It was silly, he knew that. He had told himself so many times, and yet here he was, in the wonderful City of Light, feeling the "bad feeling" yet again, and nothing—not booze, sex, late-night television, cold pizza, or the finest Croques-Monsieur—could take it away. Three in the morning, and Maggie had not come home. He walked to the Seine and bummed a

Gitano off a cute whore, even though she said she didn't smoke, kept them for johns. He assured her he wasn't one. Four-thirty and still Maggie did not come home. He read an interview with Kristen Caulfield like a starstruck teenager. Five forty-five and still no Maggie. She was not returning tonight. He was sure of that now. He took a sleeping pill and sat waiting for first light, hoping it would chase away the fears and give him some peace. At seven, he was mercifully asleep.

She called late in the afternoon. "Ellie and I are like two madwomen," she told him. "Go down to the villa and see Daddy or fly to L.A. and have what's-her-name make you a hot dog cheese thing."

"Nicky. And it's a francheezie."

"I probably block her name out because it reminds me of Nicole."

He laughed. "You know, actually Avignon sounds good. I'll go tomorrow. I want to hear more of those great stories."

"Give Papa a kiss for me. And stay out of the sparrow's clutches."

Max went to Avignon feeling frustrated, but when the dogs started licking him at the door, his mood began to soften. Nicole was delighted to see him arrive there alone, and unannounced, but it was Charles Nash who really cheered him. Because Max mentioned at dinner that he'd always been interested in boats, Charles took him to Monaco to show him the Nash yacht, which he seldom used anymore. Max's eyes widened in wonder at the number of floating palaces moored before him. "Let's take the tub for a spin, shall we?" Charles said.

Out on the Mediterranean, Charles taught him to tie a line and hook bait. Though the one fish Max caught would have fit in an anchovy can, he was proud of it. Nicole remained in the background, lapping up the late-winter sun in her bikini, not nearly as overt as she had been at Christmas, but her smoldering interest in Max was clear.

The three of them dolled up and went clubbing that night, dancing at the disco at the Hotel Byblos, where Nash, something of a legend in these parts, put the young folk to shame with a dance routine that was right out of the 1970s—with an old France Joie record blaring to match. In the heat of the dancing, Max took his shirt off, and Nicole, having abandoned Charles to a group of adoring sycophants, rubbed her head against Max's sweaty chest in the middle of the floor. The music heated up, driving, pounding, and soon they found themselves in a sexual heat, dancing a kind of erotic dare that left both of them trembling. At the end of the music, Max grabbed Nicole and kissed her on the lips.

The moment he pulled away, he apologized. "I'm drunk. I'm hot. I'm . . . lonely."

"You're hot for me," she said.

"I don't think so."

She clung to his chest as they talked. "I think we are both the poor partners to a Nash."

"What?"

"There is fire there, with them, the Nashes, intellectual and spiritual fire, and God knows they have power, but we live in the background, in the shadows."

"Maggie's making me a star."

"But you are still just one of her boys."

The music started again. Max began dancing, wanting to end the conversation. Yet Nicole bent forward and licked his right nipple, then closed her lips around it. He felt himself stirring. Then he saw Charles making his way over to them, and he was glad. He was rescued.

They slept on the boat, where, over morning coffee on the main deck, Max confided his fear that Maggie was too much in love with her work to love him. Charles told him just what she would have said: trust her. "My daughter is driven. Because of that drive, a lot of good men have run the other way. Can't say I blame them. She's tough. So be as tough as she is. Hang in there. I know she loves you."

Talking with Charles about it only made him miss Maggie more, and as the hours went on he grew more restless and anxious. "Go back to her," Charles said firmly, "because she misses you, too. This I know. You can't curl up at night with celluloid."

Nicole had other ideas. Late that night, back at the villa, long after Charles had gone to sleep, she surprised Max by showing up at the olive tree under which he was sitting. "Want company?" she purred.

"As long as you behave."

She sat next to him, close enough that their shoulders were touching. "Charles tells me you are leaving us tomorrow."

"Yes. I miss Maggie."

"Do you think she misses you?"

"Of course." But her doubtful tone gave him pause. "Don't you believe that?"

"Are you in love with her?"

He shrugged. "I don't know. I think so. It's hard to separate the wonder of all that's happened from my feelings."

"Be careful. Don't be too vulnerable."

He nodded. "Do you think Maggie loves me?"

"Do you?" It was clear her answer was no.

Her distrust left him uneasy. "Nicole, will you be honest with me?"

"*Oui.*"

"Have there been others like me? I mean, is this a pattern of Maggie's?"

Nicole paused a moment. "Maggie is a powerful woman. She is very strong, very much in control. She gets what she wants. Right now she is focused on you."

"I want things too, and she's giving them to me."

She laughed. "Oh, yes, stardom."

"More than that."

"Like what?" she asked with bite. "New clothes?"

"Self-esteem, self-assurance. She makes me feel wanted, desired. She makes me feel bigger than life. Granted, sometimes she makes me feel inconsequential, but that's my problem with not feeling good enough. Maggie really makes me feel better about myself than anyone in my life ever has. With the exception of Nicky Dee, my best friend."

"Your own Nicole?"

"Her name is Nicolina DeAngelo."

Nicole asked, *"Italiano?"*

He nodded. "As she proudly says, 'A dago from way back.'"

Without warning, Nicole put her arms around his neck and kissed him passionately.

He gasped, tried to pull away, but she kept her hold on him. Soon he returned the raw desire with a thrust of his tongue. He kissed her hungrily, but then, finally, stopped, as if coming to his senses. He stood up shakily.

"Does Maggie make you feel like that?" Nicole whispered.

Max fought the intense attraction. "I can't do this. I mean, this is great. But my God, Charles is sleeping just above us."

"Oui, so? What's your point?"

"I'm in love with his daughter. This is just too weird for words."

She leaned back in the moonlight and looked up at him with a smile. "Maggie is too old for you."

"I could say the same about you and Charles."

"Yes, he is," she responded simply.

"Nicole, please."

"And she is too manipulative. With Maggie there is always a condition. *Fuck me and I'll make you a star.* With me it is just sex."

"With you it's just danger." He thrust his hands into his pockets and shook his head. "Nicole, you're gorgeous, but I think you had better take your gorgeous body upstairs right now before this gets us both in trouble."

She said nothing, stretched out on her back, lifted

her legs slightly. The hem of her dress slid down to her waist, and Max could plainly see that she wasn't wearing panties. He was mesmerized for a moment at the sight. Then he turned and hurried back to the house. He locked the door of the guest room, perhaps more to keep himself in than to lock her out. He couldn't do this to Charles. Nor to Maggie.

But he was enthralled. So much so that he slipped out of the house and left for Paris that same night, sleeping to the gentle rocking of the rails. In the morning, as the train pulled into the Gare de Sud, he felt like a heel. He promised himself that he would never sneak around behind Maggie's back again, even though he hadn't been trying to.

Maggie was leaving the apartment for the editing studio as he entered. He was thrilled to see her, but she merely said hello—as if not very surprised to see him, or was it she hadn't even noticed he was gone?—then good-bye, gave him a kiss, and left. She didn't ask how he was, about her father, if he had had a good time, hell, if he had even been there. He could have seen the Egyptian pyramids and she would never have known. Or cared.

It sent him into a deep funk.

Aspen, Colorado
Police Investigator's Office

Maggie Nash seemed bigger than life as she swept into the room. She held out her hand, and Christopher Daniel rose to shake it. "Thank you for coming, Miss Nash."

"Maggie."

"Maggie."

She seated herself facing his desk. "What I really want to know is, how can you work like this?"

His eyes flickered. "What do you mean?"

She looked around. "No windows. Subterranean. My God, I'd go buggy."

He grinned. It wasn't the first time people had asked him about this. "We have been begging to be moved upstairs for years. Guess it's not a priority."

"A police station in the basement. That's a first for me."

"I'm sure you're used to significantly upscale digs."

"Touché." She softened her tone. "So what do they call you, Inspector? Detective? Or just Chris?"

He shrugged. "Daniel is what I get called. No one ever uses my first name."

"*Christophe*—Christopher—is a lovely name. Tell them to start."

"I'll do that," he said, not interested in her opinion of his name. "Now, ma'am, tell me something. Do you know anyone who might have wanted to harm Max?"

She gave him an assessing look. "You don't believe this 'accidental' bullshit either."

"Nope."

"That's what Max thought."

"Would Kristen have wanted to hurt him?"

"No." Then she stopped to qualify that. "Well, yes, but no. Nothing like that."

He asked if she wanted some coffee, and she said yes. He got up and went to the oak credenza and a Mr. Coffee machine. "It's fresh, made it about half an hour ago. How do you take it?"

"Black."

He poured a cup and handed it to her. "Let's talk about the glider. The ripping of the wings was not caused by the bullet."

She stopped in mid-sip. "What?"

"The frame-by-frame record of your movie shows a vibration, a slight loss of control, when Max initially flew over Trout Lake. The wing material was already ripping open."

"Max didn't say anything," she said slowly. "I mean, wouldn't he have felt it?"

"He probably didn't realize the cause of what he felt. He must have thought it a little wind shear."

She looked unsure. "What did cause the wing to rip if it was already happening before the gunshots?"

"Both wings were sliced with a razor."

She appeared stunned. "My God."

"How could Max have missed that?"

She set her coffee mug down, shaken by this revelation. She tried to think back. "I was busy setting up the sequence, so I'm not positive. I do know Max didn't take his flying lightly. The night before, he told me he had gone over every inch of the aircraft. But there was a lot going on, a lot of pressure on the set."

"Was anyone near it the morning of the flight?"

"Of course." She looked at him as if he were some kind of idiot. "We were filming a movie."

"I mean touching it, in a position to do something to it."

She shrugged. "Probably not."

"How about the previous night?"

"No. It was locked in a prop trailer."

"But you just said he had told you that he had gone over the aircraft the night before."

She nodded. "Yes."

"When did he tell you this?"

Her answer did not come right away. "I don't recall. The morning of the shoot, probably. Or perhaps late that night, the night before. We slept together, you know."

"All the world knows. But you weren't sleeping together anymore by then, is that right?"

She sipped some more coffee, turning away. "That's right."

Daniel was getting what he wanted—inconsistencies in her testimony. "Ma'am—and correct me if I am wrong—someone said during initial questioning that you were in the prop trailer with Mr. Jaxon the evening before the accident."

"Yes," she said, "but so what? I don't see your point."

"Why would he have to tell you about going over the aircraft inch by inch if you were there when he did it?"

She bristled. "Listen, I did not see Max inspecting the aircraft when we were in the prop room together."

"Then what were you both doing there?"

"I assume he was there to check the glider. He may have even assembled it that night. I don't know when he did that, perhaps that afternoon, I'm not sure."

Daniel kept pushing. "Who got there first?"

"Pardon me?"

"Was Mr. Jaxon in the property trailer when you arrived?"

She had to think for a second. "Yes."

"Are you sure?"

"Detective, what is this?"

He instantly backed off. If she knew anything, he didn't want her to clam up. "I suppose you'd call it an investigation."

She glared at him. "More like interrogation."

"I apologize for sounding so gruff," he said, nice and easy. "I know this is hard for you in your grief. I lost both my parents in a car crash, so I have some idea what this is like for you."

"I'm so sorry. Recently?"

He shook his head. "When I was younger."

"It really makes us mortal, doesn't it? I mean, what we really believe in comes into focus when we lose someone we love."

He didn't want to talk about that. "So, what do you think?" Daniel said. "Who had the strongest motive to do this?"

She grinned slightly. "You mean, who hated Max the most?"

He was pleased by her candor. Now he was getting somewhere. "Precisely."

She thought about it. "Listen, I have wanted to blame someone because that would be easier. Then it might not have been so tragic. There are lots of reasons that certain people would want to harm Max, but are these people killers? I think not."

"About the gun," he said, abruptly changing the direction of the conversation. "Who chose a 30.06 automatic rifle?"

"I did. I wrote the script."

"Why that particular gauge?"

She shrugged. "I don't know guns, but my father was an avid hunter in his earlier days. I suspect he had one in the gun cabinet in Provence, and I just used that gauge in the script."

He nodded. "Everyone, even Kathy Tam, the prop girl whose responsibility it was to have the gun in the cabin for Kristen to use, claims astonishment at the fact that real bullets were substituted for the blanks."

Disturbed, she got up and began pacing. "It was shocking."

"Where had the bullets, real and fake, been stored?"

"The fake ones were stored with the other props. There *were* no real bullets. None that I knew of, anyhow."

Daniel leaned forward. "Maggie, did Bruce Borger, your property manager, hate Max?"

She smiled. "Detective, everyone is going to tell you that they loved Max. That's true. Except for Bruce."

He scratched his head. "You know, I'm not looking just at those who hated the victim, but those who loved him, too."

She didn't understand. "Why is that?"

"Well," he explained, "love turned to hate is the most dangerous kind of passion there is."

"Then there are two other suspects," she offered. "There are two people who loved him passionately."

"Kristen Caulfield, for one," he said, "who shot him, after all."

"Yes, and Nicole Richaud. The night before the accident, she told me she would rather see Max dead than end up with me."

His eyes widened.

"She was crazy jealous."

"Because she loved him?"

"I don't know about love, but she was obsessed with him. I think it was more sexual than of the heart. But I guess, yes, you could say she loved him too."

There was no mistaking her hatred, and Daniel focused in. "But isn't there a third?"

"A third what?"

"Person who loved him."

She blinked in confusion. "Who would that be?"

"You," he said. "You loved him most of all."

Eleven

More endless days passed after Max returned to Paris. He saw Kristen's movie again on the Champs Elysees, standing in line like everyone else. He walked around for hours. He gazed up at the well-lit Arc de Triomphe, paused to look at flowers that people still placed at the site of Princess Diana's fatal car crash, then found a little cobblestone alleyway where a bistro was just opening—he was shocked to see that it was five in the morning—and had a café au lait.

Needing some reassurance, he went to see Maggie in the screening room. He did not let her know he'd entered, just slipped silently into a leather seat in the rear. She and Ellie Storey were viewing the scene they were preparing to cut. The dubbing was off. The color not yet corrected. But Max sat there turning to putty in his chair as he watched himself on a big screen for the first time. It wasn't Kristen Caulfield by any means, but it was a damn good start. His spirits lifted. Verna Zimmermann had never looked more sensual, and with her help, *he* radiated an erotic magnetism that astounded him. He thought this must be what Maggie saw that night on the beach in Malibu. He seemed sure of himself—what a joke!—utterly masculine yet sensitive. Scared but confident. There was no anger to see as yet, but *some*thing smoldered under the surface, so when it exploded in the final moments, it would not come as a surprise. And his smile—his smile, he was pleased to assess, was pretty damned winning.

Lights! The room burst into brightness, and Maggie let out a gasp upon discovering him. "I had to peek," he said. "Forgive me."

She kissed him. "And?"

"Wow. If I say so myself."

She kissed him again. "Now I have to get on with work." And she tossed him out into the street.

But the bad feeling was gone. In its place was a sense of being high, riding on a cloud through the sky. Excitement bubbled in his blood, flashbulbs went off in his brain. He boarded the Metro and rode all over the city for hours. He rested on the steps of Sacre Coeur and let himself feel dwarfed by its white opulence.

He was sipping strong espresso in Café Lipp an hour later when he had the sensation that someone was watching him. He glanced over his shoulder to make sure he was not being paranoid. A girl was staring at him, and it unnerved him. But when he gave her a second look, he realized the girl was Nicole.

He quickly picked up his cup, saucer, jacket, and scarf, and joined her near the window. "*Bonsoir!* What are you doing in Paris?"

"A gallery opening, some shopping, seeing friends," she said, eyes looking mischievous. "I am staying nearby, at the Hotel Lenox-Saint-Germain."

"Is Charles here?"

"In Avignon. Working on his memoirs. I think he wanted to get rid of me for a few days." Her face lit with a sly smile. "I really came to Paris to see you. I was going to ring you up tomorrow."

"Yes?"

"*Oui,* because I felt ashamed of what happened. When I found you had left in the middle of the night, I felt terrible." She said she understood how he could be so filled with love that he would feel sexually stimulated and in need of satisfaction, especially at a time when he was feeling shut out by Maggie. She had taken advantage of him, and for that she was very sorry. "I think we must remain just friends."

He nodded enthusiastically. "*Oui,* Nicole. Oh, there is an attraction. I wouldn't be a man if there wasn't one. But we have to keep things in perspective."

She smiled. "Well, that's that, then, yes?"

"Yes." He warmly took her hand.

"Now, if Maggie is editing, and you are lonely, I will be in Paris almost a week. Would you like a companion?"

He smiled. "I would."

He walked her to her hotel when they had finished their coffee and sweets. They strolled together down the winding Left Bank streets, stopping to view some ceramic tiles hand-painted with cats in an antiques store. She showed him the massive chestnut tree in the courtyard of the Hotel Marronniers on the rue Jacob, from which it derived its name. She and Charles had first met there and stayed in an attic garret overlooking the tree. It had felt like a fairy tale. She had wanted never to come down.

"Can I ask you something very personal? Do you really love Charles?" Max asked.

"*Mon dieu*, how can one *not* love Charles? Being with him makes me feel . . . blessed."

"I feel that way with Maggie."

She winked. "Then we both have very good taste."

"Well, in Nashes, anyway," he joked. "But you indicated that you were frustrated."

She shrugged and looked away. "Charles is getting on in years. I know what they say about Frenchmen, they screw till they drop, but prostrate problems hit all kinds of men."

"He has trouble in bed?"

"*Oui*. But we make do. He pleases me in other ways. Yet—"

Max nodded. "You don't feel completely fulfilled."

She squeezed his hand. "But that is *my* problem."

When they reached the Lenox on the rue de l'Universite, Max gave her a friendly hug. "You saved my life tonight."

She made him promise to meet her in the morning at Galleries Lafayette. "But," she suggested, "perhaps it would be best not to tell Maggie I'm here."

He nodded. "Maybe we had not better tell either

of the Nashes we saw each other. Perhaps Charles wouldn't like it either."

"He can be jealous. Very Français."

Max smiled. "Very male."

"*Bonsoir*. I'll say a prayer for you."

"Ciao." He pecked her on the cheek and watched her disappear into the lobby of the elegant little hotel, and then he headed for the apartment.

Nicole, he thought, was—what? Charming, almost pixieish. Her eyes were huge and sad, her body bird-like (didn't Maggie say the sparrow never ate?), almost frail. And she was his friend. In another situation she easily could have been his lover.

As he stood on a corner of the boulevard St. Germain waiting for the light to change, his attention was drawn to a little dive from which an incredible voice beckoned. He peeked in the window and saw a girl singing her heart out, Edith Piaf style, tears rolling down her cheeks as she leaned against a fake lamppost. All she was missing was the beret.

The feeling of being high on life returned. He could smell the scent of yeast from the bread baking all over the city, and in the distance he could hear the sound of an accordion welcoming the clouds of early-morning light.

His mood changed the moment he walked through the door of the apartment.

Maggie was sitting there drinking coffee. "Where the hell have you been?"

Max was shocked to see her. "I had no idea you were coming home."

She was sitting in a kitchen chair, her feet propped up on the table next to the Melior coffee brewer, full of cold grounds. The film's script lay open on her lap, and on her face was an expression he'd never seen before. One he didn't want to tangle with.

"Son of a bitch," she muttered, running her hand through her hair, which he could see had not been washed. "That scene's for shit. Doesn't work at all. I've got to cut it completely. I've been looking at earlier versions to see what I can do with it."

"Was it my fault?" he asked.

"Was *what* your fault?"

"The fact that it's for shit. Did I fuck it up?"

She didn't answer. She threw the script to the floor, started digging through one with a different-colored cover. "Make some fresh coffee."

He nodded, started to get the beans from the freezer.

"Where have you been all night? It's four o'clock."

What was he going to say? Walking hand in hand with Nicole? Not with Maggie's current mood. It was the first time he was on the spot with her, and he knew he had a choice between truth and lies. He'd done nothing wrong. Admiring a pretty girl was not a betrayal, and certainly Nicole had been a lifesaver. But could he bring himself to tell her about it? Could he be a man here?

A man would simply tell the truth. But he knew she would never believe it. Her anger was already boiling; the jealousy would push her over the edge.

So he chose the easy way out. "I went to see *Snow Angel* again. But I fell asleep in the theater. They woke me when they were closing."

She looked above the rim of her reading glasses. "Come on."

"Honest. Slept through the last showing of the night." He ground the beans so he could not hear what she was asking. When he was done—he kept his finger on the button so long that they were pulverized to the consistency of face powder—he said, "It was a crazy night. I had too much to drink, must have passed out, 'cause this usher woke me when they were sweeping the place already. I went to a bistro and tried to wake up."

"Sleep a lot these days?"

"I was very tired," he said, matching her challenging eyes.

As he boiled the water, Maggie dumped that script to the floor as well, then told him she'd have to invent something with what she already had on film. Verna Zimmermann wasn't available, and it would cost a fortune to reshoot. She told him what scene it was, and he remembered that he'd felt unsure of it. Verna had too. He thought the problem was in the writing, but he didn't dare tell Maggie that. She was too ornery to accept criticism today. He fled to the bathroom and closed the door.

He was in the tub, soaking under a sea of bubbles, when she wandered in, mug in hand, and sat on the toilet seat. "Max," she said softly, "please tell me that you're not lying to me about tonight. I know I've been ignoring you, and I fear you might have done something to hurt me."

He pretended astonishment and hurt. "Why would you think that?"

"I'm a director. I'm a pretty damn good judge of people. The way they react to things."

He stared at the bubbles. He thought about the humiliation he'd feel if he 'fessed up now. How this whole dream could go to shit if she blew up. "Max?" she said, waiting for an answer.

He looked guilty as hell, but he said, "I don't know how you can think I'd lie to you."

She said nothing more, just got up and left.

Max and Nicole spent a great week together. They did the Musee d'Orsay, shopped Galleries Layfayette, ate hot dogs in the place des Vosges, rented a Renault and drove to the country on Sunday afternoon, where they watched a big family picnicking, and the family watched them, probably thinking them young lovers. In Las Closerie des Lilas, Nicole showed Max tables in the bar where tiny plaques were etched with the names of former patrons: Lenin, Sartre, Hemingway, Apollinaire. At the Montparnasse Cemetery, she pointed out the graves of Maupassant, Baudelaire, and Saint-Saëns.

Max felt very comfortable with Nicole. The common denominator in their relationship was that they both loved a Nash, and that was turning them into *compadres*. Perhaps this was the sister he never had. She assured him that they were friends, and that was more rare, in Paris, than lovers.

"Does Maggie frighten you?" he asked one night.

"Sometimes. I sometimes see things she does not

want me to see, and she is stronger than I, so I am the one who runs up the stairs."

"I'm not sure I understand what you are saying."

"You don't? Hasn't she ever made you feel like running up the stairs?"

Out of the blue, Maggie called Max to invite him to the studio, grandly announcing the first finished cut of the entire film. It was supposed to be Nicole's last day in Paris, but she was in no hurry to leave. She told him she would take an early-afternoon train tomorrow instead.

Max appeared at the screening room, seeing Maggie for the first time in four days. She looked like hell. He was suddenly aware how hard she must have been working. "It's really ready?"

"I hope so." She pushed him into a leather chair, sat next to him, took his hand, and called out for the film to begin.

The lights dimmed. Music swelled. *Verna Zimmermann. Max Jaxon.* Max's flesh erupted in goose bumps as he saw his name on the screen for the first time. *FIBS. A Film by Maggie Nash.*

The movie that followed was terrific. He was remarkably strong for a newcomer, especially up against a seasoned veteran. There were nuances in the character he had tried to capture that eluded him, but all in all, his star did shine. Maggie embraced him when the lights came up.

They dined alone that night, celebrating, and in the booth she put her head on his shoulder and told him how much she'd missed him. He said the same about her. She began kissing him, and just about the time it started to heat up—Christ, he'd not made love to her in more than nine days!—she dropped the bomb. She had to return to the studio tonight. She had just a few more days to tweak the final print. She had to change this and fiddle with that. Some of the music bothered her. The titles needed her personal touch—

Max went into a funk.

She saw she was losing him. "Darling, don't brood. We'll leave for Avignon a week from Thursday, perhaps even Wednesday, how's that? After seeing Papa, we'll take a vacation, anywhere in the world you want to go."

He managed a smile. "Hong Kong?"

She moaned. "Already? I feel as though I just left. Well, hell, why not? I'll book the Mandarin Oriental, whatever your heart desires."

"It desires to make love to you tonight."

"No, your penis does."

"That too."

She laughed. "Oh, Max, I adore you! It's going to be glorious."

"What is?"

"Our life together. Look at your performance, you're wonderful. We'll travel and see the world and finally settle down one day, in our wheelchairs— well, you can push mine for a few years—and not lament one moment of the entire thing. No regrets, ever."

"Maggie?"

"Yes?"

"Before you go to the studio, could we maybe stop home for a fast fuck?"

They didn't. She kept her word and returned to her obsession with the film. Max faced another night alone. And it was unbearable. He could not sleep, could not read, could not watch TV. He was so horny that he thought he was going to come in his shorts just thinking about Maggie, but he didn't want to masturbate because he knew he'd feel worse when he finished. Yet the loneliness was getting to him. He had to get out. Finally he called Nicole. "Do you have plans tonight?"

"No," she said, pleased to hear from him.

"Let's do something, go somewhere. Let's celebrate."

"Celebrate what?"

"My movie. I saw it, Nicole." He almost burst with enthusiasm. "I saw it and I'm *good!*"

They went to La Poule au Pot, where Max had the best onion soup he'd ever tasted, an intense broth bolstered with white wine, with a blistered dome of melted Emmentaler on country bread floating on top. Contrary to Maggie's assertion, Nicole downed a salad, and they shared a pistachio soufflé for dessert. Afterward, they went to a blues club down the street. Nicole ordered champagne, which Max was not used to drinking. In fact, he'd never much liked it before, but the sum of his experience had been a whole lot of bottles of Cooks and one taste of Dom Perignon at a friend's engagement party.

The bubbly went to his head. And to his crotch. Though he kept things light, being friendly, he could feel his penis stirring as if it had a life of its own.

When they danced, a slow, sultry number, they drifted to the corner of the tight, smoke-filled room. Max pulled her closer to him, for there was hardly any room to move. She took advantage of it, clinging to him. He felt her small, hard breasts pressing against his chest, and knew she could feel that part of him down a little lower. The movement of their bodies to the rhythm almost brought him to climax. He drank in the scent of her, his head popping like the bubbles of the champagne, and he tried to pull away, to stop.

"Max," she whispered, "don't. Just enjoy." She laid her head on his chest. She was smaller than Maggie, shorter, softer, lighter. She moved her left hand down his back to touch his ass. He could feel her breathing hard. Then he nervously did the same, sliding his right hand down. He could hold almost her entire bottom. His left hand moved behind her head. She looked up and kissed him gently on his chin. And then licked down his neck to the line of his shirt.

And the music stopped.

As the lights rose slightly, Nicole extricated herself from his grasp, turned and hurried to their table. Max went to the washroom, threw cold water on his face, and peed when his erection finally subsided. He left the room with the resolve that there would be no more dancing.

At the table he said, "We promised each other that we would just be friends."

She looked into his eyes. "In Paris, there are many kinds of friends."

"Not this kind of friends. This is a dangerous kind of friends."

"I think," she said with a hint of arrogance, "Americans could learn a great deal about passion from the French. Certainly, they could take lessons in overcoming shame." She lifted her glass. "But, no matter—friends. Here is to our friendship conquering our desire."

"It isn't right," he protested. "That desire."

"Oh, *oui, oui,* you are with Maggie." She crossed her legs and looked at the singer, who was starting a new number. "And Maggie is with her movie."

Nicole gave him an impish look. She knew how much he resented Maggie for deserting him yet again, for leaving him wanting her, telling him the film was more important. She didn't love him as much as her work. He told himself he would not be unfaithful to Maggie, even while he moved to hold Nicole's outstretched hand. But she pressed it down between her legs, and in a few moments his fingers were crawling under her short skirt. Another glass of champagne and he was powerless.

They took a room in a small hotel just down the street. It was old, shabby, pungent with the smell of Indian cooking. They had to walk up four flights because the tiny elevator was out of order. Two bright-eyed dark kids in underpants were chasing each other up and down the hall, squealing as they played a game like tag.

Once inside the room, they didn't turn on the light. The glow from the neon outside the window lit up the bed. Max fell backward onto it, partially to lure her down with him, but mainly because he didn't think he could stand up any longer. The room was spinning.

She opened his zipper, withdrew him, and did all the work. He had no idea how long it went on, for he was tumbling in somersaults of pleasure. She massaged his organ with her hands and then slid it between her lips. He grasped the two musty feather pillows and pulled them to his face, covering his eyes, muffling his moans until he felt her knees suddenly planted on either side of his chest. She grabbed the pillows and flung them to the floor.

He ripped her panties off, and she pressed her body down onto his mouth. She cried out in passion, feeling the intensity of his hungry tongue, screaming so loud when she came that he feared she'd be heard over the squeals of the brats in the corridor. Then the world started to spin some more. Max realized he was entering her, though lying there flat on the bed, his feet still touching the floor, his pants still on. She was riding him, thrusting up and down, the bed creaking in rhythm, his hands gripping hers at either side of his hips, until he could take it no more and he came. And passed out.

When he awoke, the sun was peeking through faded curtains. He slid out of the bed, no easy feat, for he had to lift Nicole's legs off him. His pants were still undone, his penis still protruding from the fly. He pulled it inside, zipped up, then stepped into the hall, found the toilet a few doors down, and vomited the minute he stepped inside.

The retching brought a reality check. The thought of Maggie terrified him, making him feel like a heel. Not only was he a liar, now he had betrayed her. With Nicole! With someone who was virtually her stepdaughter.

Looking blearily into the cracked mirror above the rusted sink, he said, "What kind of asshole are you, man?" He hurried back to the room, to wake Nicole and get her to tell him that nothing had really happened, he was just drunk, but when he saw his wallet lying there next to her, he remembered it had fallen out of his pants as she had been riding him. It had indeed happened. All of it. He could not bear to speak to her. He grabbed his billfold, turned, and fled.

At the apartment, he showered, soaping himself again and again, until he finally felt clean. Self-righteous denial kicked in. He told himself Maggie deserved it. Hell, had she seen to his needs in the slightest way, this wouldn't have happened. Why should he feel guilty? Could he deal with it? Come on, hadn't he just made a movie called *Fibs*?

It was only nine, but he was feeling sick. His head pounded and his heart ached. He felt sick to his stomach again, took some Pepto-Bismol, and stretched out on the bed. He awoke a few hours later feeling someone's arm around his waist. Half-dreaming, he first thought it was Nicole, and he grabbed the hand that held his penis, wanting to stop her, wanting not to do it again, not allowing it to move. Then he realized it was Maggie's hand, that she was home in bed with him, naked too, whispering, "I missed you so much I couldn't stand it anymore . . ."

Nicole wheeled her Vuitton case to the bench, sat down, and waited for her train. A smug smile had filled her face since she left the grungy hotel room. She had finally had him. It had taken some planning, some deception—she smirked at the "best friends" scenario—and some fancy dancing, but she had succeeded. It was why she had come to Paris. To get him. And to get Maggie.

Oh, wouldn't the powerful Margaret Nash just die if she knew? She was well on her way to marrying Maggie's father, and now she had fucked her boyfriend. It could only be sweeter if Maggie knew, but that would risk everything. No, there was time. She needed time to marry Charles before he croaked. Her charms had infected Max like a kind of magic potion, an elixir she knew he would need again. And again. If it worked according to her desires, she'd become Mrs. Charles Nash, and then the Widow Nash, all the time feeling fulfilled by the stud Maggie had dragged in. When she owned the villa, the yacht, the vineyard, the bank accounts, when she had what she deserved, then she could inform Maggie of Max's betrayal. Or, perhaps Maggie would drive him away by then, as she'd driven away every man in her life. By then Max would be a big movie star and wouldn't need Mother Maggie anymore. By then he would be in love with Nicole.

The train chugged into the station. Nicole boarded a first-class coach and tipped the steward for stowing her case. She settled into her compartment with a blanket and pillow. A few moments later, as the train began its way south to Avignon, she bade farewell to Paris. And to Max, to whom she blew a kiss.

Twelve

To Max, it seemed like months had passed before Maggie finally entered the apartment with a glow. "The movie is fucking magnificent, if I say so myself!" She hurried to Max, kissed him, and then pulled a bottle of champagne from the refrigerator.

"No!" he cried.

"Oh, you don't like it. I forgot."

He couldn't bring himself to tell her the real reason. The night with Nicole was something he was trying to bury. He'd felt awful ever since.

"Wine, then?"

He mustered up some enthusiasm. "What are we toasting?"

"Our next film." She uncorked a bottle of chilled white wine.

"Huh?"

"Us. You and I. I want to sign you for another movie."

He was speechless.

"I'll call Bill Barber and do it through the proper

channels, but I swear, I don't know why you're paying an agent a commission."

"Why?" he asked. "I mean, what made you decide this?"

She grabbed him and threw her arms around him. "Because you're good! And because I love you!"

He could barely face her.

"I warned you, I'm no walk in the park. I told you how difficult it would be. But the movie's done, it's great and you're great in it. You understand?"

He just nodded. And sat down.

She was dumbfounded. "What the hell kind of reaction is this? I thought you would be jumping for joy."

"I'm . . . just . . ." The words would not flow.

"Max? What is it? I've never seen you like this."

He had a choice here. He could make up something. Or tell the truth. And throw away his career.

"Max?" she said again, not demanding, but concerned.

Self-preservation won out. "I'm overwhelmed, Maggie. I guess it just hit me. The reality of it all." At least he was telling the truth about that. "I mean, my life will never be the same. I felt so insecure, like this would be my one and only film and I'd be back selling ties or something. I am stunned."

"Oh, honey," she said, hugging him.

"I didn't know if I was . . . I don't know how to say this."

"Just get it out," she urged patiently.

"I thought maybe I was using you. I mean, yes, the passion was real and all that. I mean, when you get kidnapped to Paris and put in a movie with one of the great stars of the cinema by one of the greatest filmmakers on earth—"

"*The* greatest," she joked.

"Maggie," he said seriously, "this isn't funny. You told me I would come to love you, and I didn't really believe it when I first said I did. And I think that's happening. I mean, this week, the past days, I'm coming to understand my feelings." But he stopped there, when he could have admitted the whole truth.

She believed him. "Darling, I told you to trust me. I wanted to be sure I could get a performance out of you. That's why I said let's just do one picture and see where it takes us. Now I know the future. It's together." She slugged the wine down. "Let's go out to dinner."

At an outdoor table at La Fontaine de Mars, he was uncharacteristically silent all through the meal. She took it as his being quietly romantic, for he held her hand and whispered how much he had come to love her. Afterward, when they strolled along the Seine, taking almost the same path as the first time, she suggested that they go down to see her father for a few days. "I've been cooped up in editing way too long. Time for a little fun. Why don't we go back down to the villa?"

"I don't know," he said reluctantly. He could not see Nicole again, not this soon, perhaps never. The guilt was eating him up.

She seemed surprised. "Really? Oh, sure, you've just been to Avignon. But hey, don't be so selfish. Do it with me this time. We could take Daddy's yacht to one of the Greek islands, would you like that?"

"Well . . ."

"How about Turkey, then?"

He didn't want to go anywhere near that yacht. "I'd rather stay here."

They watched a sight-seeing boat go by on the river. "All right, if you promise to make love to me every night after our walk."

He took her hand, getting an idea. "Maggie, could we maybe go see *Snow Angel* tonight? Please? It's going to be a classic by the time you see it."

"I already did."

He froze. "Huh?"

"I saw it, weeks ago."

He stopped walking, turned to her and blinked as if he were not hearing right. "You saw Kristen Caulfield's film?"

"Actually, it's Sam Mendes' film, but have it your way."

He was stunned. He couldn't believe it. "But you didn't mention it? You didn't say anything?" Then he figured out why. "You didn't like it."

"I loved it. And her."

He smiled broadly. "I told you. What made you finally go?"

"An interview Kristen gave that announced to the world that her all-time favorite film director is Maggie Nash. That she'd give anything to work with me."

His heart started pounding. "My God! You kept all this secret?" Before the words passed his lips, he realized he had no right to be surprised that anyone would keep secrets.

"She gets your dick pumping, huh?"

"You know that's not what I meant," he said. "So, were you blown away?"

Maggie pulled him in the direction of the apartment. "Yes, but I was more impressed in person."

He stopped walking again. "In *person*?"

"Remember the morning Connie interviewed you in London? I was having tea with your Betty Bacall. That's why we went there."

Betty Bacall? Then that made him Bogart. In a flash it all came together for him. He'd be her partner. "I don't fucking believe this," he shouted. He gave her a huge smile. "And you didn't tell me?"

"Darling, then it wouldn't have been a surprise."

He blinked. "What wouldn't have been a surprise?"

She walked to a nearby bench, set her trusty weathered-leather bag down, then withdrew a script and tossed it to him. "This."

He caught it before it hit his chest, righted it, and read the cover:

SCANDALS

A Film by Maggie Nash
Marty Stern, Jr., Producer

STARRING

Kristen Caulfield
&
Max Jaxon

He gasped. No words would come.

"Happy birthday a week early."

"Jesus." He was glowing.

Maggie explained, "For the past six weeks I've been putting this together. The fact that you two share an agent made it easier."

"Bill is her agent too?"

She nodded. "Plus, we had Marty Stern on our side, so I believe we can count on starting to shoot in Hollywood next spring." She gave him a grin. "I'm signing her to a two-picture deal."

"What are we going to do in the meantime?"

"We're going to promote *Fibs*, promote you, travel a bit, spend Christmas down at the villa, and spend a lot of time in bed together."

"You're the most incredible woman in the world, you know that?"

She winked. "Bet your ass."

Thirteen

Three Months Later

The lobby of the Peninsula Beverly Hills had returned to elegant sobriety now that all the Christmas decorations had been removed. It was January, and Tinsel Town was getting on with business. The foreign press was now in the spotlight, seeing that the Golden Globe nominees had been announced. Maggie, Verna Zimmermann, and Max were all nominated for *Fibs*, which had opened to great reviews and even better business before the end of the year. Kristen Caulfield, who'd already won the New York Film Critics Award for Best Actress and the National Society of Film Critics Award as well, was up against Verna Zimmermann. The nominations generated a winter's heat, but tonight in this lobby that should have been bustling, just one lone Hollywood ranger was making a deal on a cellular phone. And, sitting in a chair across from him, Kristen Caulfield was as calm as could be.

The first time she'd met Maggie, in London, she'd been terrified. Maggie Nash was a legend, a woman she grew up regarding as an icon. She remembered how nervous her devout Catholic mother was some years back when she traveled from Wisconsin to St. Louis to see the pope. Meeting Maggie was like that for her. But the icon had put her at ease. Now Kristen was simply eager to see her again, to get to know the woman, and to work with her.

She wasn't sure how she was going to like Maggie's lover, however. She'd seen Max Jaxon's first film, and while she liked the movie, she didn't think he was all that good. She agreed with the notices: *Fibs* probably made him seem more gifted than he actually was. Oh, he was gorgeous, and he had the most winning smile and a gaze that penetrated like a bullet, but Kristen's real respect was for actors, not movie stars, which he had become in one easy move.

A shrill "There she is!" from Constance Heller brought Kristen back to reality. Yes, the gossipmonger was with them, wearing her signature Hedda Hopper hat, gushing already, though she was not even halfway across the lobby. "Darling, you look simply divine!" She rushed to Kristen and greeted her energetically.

"We picked up this *shrew* on the way in," Maggie said with fake scorn, gesturing toward Constance, "and just can't shake her."

Kristen laughed. She'd done several interviews with the famed and feared Heller already and knew what to say. "We'll give her ten minutes, but we draw the line at letting her dine with us."

"Oh, shucks," Constance muttered good-naturedly. "I'll have to hurry."

"Wonderful to see you again." Maggie gave Kristen a little hug and air kisses over both cheeks. "And this is Max."

He beamed and extended a sweaty palm. "Hi."

She flashed the screen smile he'd fallen in love with. "Hi."

"He's your biggest fan," Connie gushed.

Kristen nodded toward Maggie and said, "So I've heard. Oh, thanks for the flowers when I got the awards. It was very sweet of you."

Maggie teased, "The florist is ready for another delivery in about three days," referring to Golden Globe night.

"Your lips to God's ears," Kristen replied, crossing her fingers. "For all of us."

With no time to waste, Constance took over, pulling out her pad. "So, Max, you've wanted to act with this young lady ever since you laid eyes on her in the first moments of *Snow Angel*. How does it feel to finally meet her? Both Golden Globe nominees, my goodness."

And on it went, a comfortable interview in the overstuffed chairs in the lobby. But after fifteen minutes, Maggie sent Constance packing. "This is one film I'm going to really want to see," the columnist said as she grabbed her bag. "You two have a chemistry going already."

Indeed they did. Maggie saw it too, and she was relieved, for her greatest fear was that Max and Kristen would light up the screen individually, but together would fizzle. Nothing of the sort was going to happen. During their first interview together, Max and Kristen already had a natural rhythm.

"Tell me about your life together," Kristen said as their appetizers arrived in the hotel dining room. "I only know what I read, and when I see what they print about me, I know I shouldn't believe any of it."

"In our case, it's all true," Maggie boasted jokingly, "every salacious word."

Max almost blushed. "They portray our relationship like it's some kind of porn film."

Maggie smiled devilishly. "Now, *there's* a way for us to make some money!" She ate a bite of her salad, then turned serious. "It's the difference in our ages. It gives them more spin. But I'm not complaining. Publicity works, any kind."

Kristen nodded in understanding. "It really stunned me, the things they started printing about me, digging up old boyfriends like I was Monica Lewinsky. I mean, who cares that I had a crush on Franz LaMacchia in Middleton High School?"

Maggie said, "They care about *everything*." And lifted her wineglass to that.

"Actually," Max explained, "they can't dig up old dirt on me. This is my first real relationship."

Kristen admitted that she had never been in love. "Boyfriends, yes, but I knew it never was love. Something wasn't happening."

Maggie said, "The stuff you see in movies?"

Kristen agreed. "The violins didn't play."

Max laughed out loud. "In drama school, we used

to break up in the middle of really gushy romantic scenes and call out, 'Cue the violins.' "

"They have their place," Maggie said. She speared another forkful of salad. "But then I'm a hopeless romantic."

"Oh, me too," Kristen added, "old Bette Davis movies, *The Way We Were*, even those Lana Turner tearjerkers of the 1960s."

"Nineteen fifties. Ross Hunter epics," Maggie offered. "And Troy Donahue and Connie Stevens down on the tobacco farm."

Kristen knew it well. "*Parrish*. My mother's favorite film. I think I had to sit through it twenty times growing up."

"You're a stage actress," Max said, remembering what he'd read about her, "but did you always have a secret passion for movies?"

"I never saw myself working in film. This is all still very startling to me."

"I'll have to write you a play," Maggie offered. "My secret ambition, but I never had the guts. Or the time. But if you promise to star, Kris, I'll do it."

"Deal," Kristen said, buttering a roll.

Maggie elbowed her. "How do you eat all those carbs and stay so slim?" The girl was digging into her third sourdough biscuit.

"Three letters: G-Y-M."

"Ugh," Maggie groaned.

Max, feeling a little left out, said to Maggie, "You do a play, you'd better write me in opposite her. We'd knock Broadway dead."

Maggie smiled, as if humoring him. "Let's conquer Hollywood first, shall we? We'll start at the Golden Globe banquet. I'll arrange for us to sit together. It will help generate interest in *Scandals*."

After dinner, Kristen joined them—driving her own car—at the Beverly Hills Hotel, where, because Maggie refused to ever again set foot in the apartment that Max still kept in Los Feliz, they had taken a bungalow. They sat outside, on comfy lounge chairs just beyond the French doors to the living room, sipping decaf coffee with Kahlua. Maggie asked Kristen what she did for fun. Any hobbies?

"Swimming, running, went bungee jumping once, want to hang glide."

Maggie looked over at Max. "He'll teach you."

Kristen was enthused. "You glide?"

Max nodded. "I'm pretty good. Been doing it for years. Nothing makes me feel more—what's the word?—powerful? Omnipotent?"

"Oh, come on, say it," Maggie prodded. "You feel like God flying around up there."

"Do you glide as well, Maggie?"

Maggie choked. "Are you kidding? Put me in Seat 2A, encased in steel. Gliding positively sends shudders through me. I won't let him do it once the film starts."

"Oh, come on," Max moaned.

"Tell that to the insurance company when you crash into a lake before we've completed principal photography."

He turned to Kristen. "She's like a mother some-times," he whispered, "but I love her for that too."

Kristen had surmised there was a mother/son dynamic in their relationship, for she herself felt a maternal pull toward Maggie. It wasn't a mother thing like with her own. This was earth mother sensual. Maggie had a magic that Kristen had never before seen in a woman. No wonder she was so revered.

When Maggie went inside to take a phone call from Paris, Max admitted to Kristen that he'd been scared to death to meet her. "I think I built you up in my mind for so long that I was afraid I'd created an image that no one could live up to."

Her eyes twinkled in the light of the candle burning on the patio table. "You saying I'm less than you had thought I'd be?"

"No, not at all," he corrected, hastily. "I'm saying you're real, not at all unapproachable."

"Listen," she said, "I'm just a girl from Wisconsin. All this is like some kind of dream. I pinch myself sometimes just to make sure. I won't take any of it seriously because I feel it's some kind of wonderful vacation I'm on, but that I'll have to pack up and go home someday."

"Oh, no," Max said, "not you. Never."

She was pleased by his earnestness. "Fame is fleeting."

"Not yours. You've got the stuff to back it up. I'd give anything to have your talent."

"You've got your own," she said pleasantly.

He squirmed a bit. "I'm okay. But I'm the kind of

guy that people see on-screen and fall in love with. You're the kind of actor people are in awe of."

"Aw, shucks," she said.

He laughed. "You know, I really *like* you. As a person."

Her return smile was warm and genuine. "I like you too. Very much."

"I'm glad we're going to work together."

"Likewise." She brought a finger to her chin. "You know, I was wondering before. Anyone ever call you X?"

He smiled. "Yes. A waitress from New York. My best friend."

"Can I?"

"Only if I can call you Krissy."

Max did not take his eyes from hers, and she didn't avert her gaze. The connection was genuine. Max brought his hand to hers on the table and clasped his fingers over her palm. He held it firmly, smiling, but careful not to reveal the tingling sensation running through him. He was glad they were sitting down in the dark because his pants would have given away the truth about how she was affecting him.

What they didn't know was that Maggie was watching it all from inside the darkened room, talking on the phone just past the little panes of glass, seeing the chemistry—the magic—she had hoped to see on the screen begin its life away from the camera. It thrilled her.

And worried her.

*   *   *

"Well, what did you think?" Maggie had just crawled into bed, where Max had been curled up for half an hour.

"About what?"

"*Krissy.*"

"You heard that?"

"Big ears."

Max wasn't embarrassed, though. He hadn't done anything wrong. "She's everything I had hoped she'd be. Warm, loving, sincere, sexy, honest."

"And hot."

"And hot," he admitted. "I still can't believe we're going to work together. I mean, I really was a fan, like one of those guys who come up to me sometimes, somebody working construction, who says, Man, I really liked you in that flick, man. I'm just boggled."

"Want to fuck her?"

He flinched. He knew he should not have been startled by her bluntness, certainly not at this point, but it still took him by surprise sometimes. He answered with a bluntness of his own. "Sure. Who wouldn't? What man doesn't?"

She giggled, covering any hint of jealousy. "If I were inclined toward women, I daresay I think *I'd* want to fuck her."

"But we won't."

She played with him. "We won't?"

He kissed her. "No, we won't. First of all, you're not gay, and second, I'm committed to you."

"But you have to make love to her in the film. A lot."

"*That*," he said, "I can do."

"Can you also, now, do me?"

With a sexy wink, he lifted the covers and started to move down her body, whispering, "I can try . . ."

Aspen, Colorado
Little Annie's Restaurant

Little Annie's was Christopher Daniel's favorite chow palace. It was funky and fun, with red-and-white plastic tablecloths and weekly fried chicken and all-you-can-eat spaghetti specials. The minute he walked in, the bartender slid a basket of popcorn his way and said, "What will you have, Detective?"

Daniel made a face. "I'm working, Kip."

Kip rolled his eyes. "Me, too, but that doesn't stop me."

Beverly, Daniel's favorite waitress, was passing by. "Don't you believe a word he says," she told Daniel. "You here for lunch?"

Daniel said, "Looking for someone I've never met."

Beverly was sharp. "The movie guy?"

He smiled. "That was easy."

"Honey, he was telling me a story about Mel Gibson you wouldn't believe." She pointed to the man. "He knows *every*body."

"He doesn't know me."

A minute later, Daniel slid into the booth. "Mr. Borger. Glad you're still around."

Bruce stared at him. "Do I know you?"

Daniel extended his hand over a half-eaten burger, which Bruce limply shook after he licked some mustard from his fingers. "Aspen Police Department."

"So you're the guy who has prevented me from leaving town."

Daniel ignored his challenging tone. "Most people would love being trapped in Aspen."

"I'll admit it's better than Dubuque." Then he turned serious. "But I want out. I've got a movie starting in Albuquerque."

"I'll let you know." Daniel indicated Bruce's food. "Hey, eat, don't let me stop you."

"Want some fries?"

"That's all right." The cop fixed him with a stare. "Mr. Borger, did you work with Maggie Nash before *Never Forget?*"

"Several times, yes."

"With Mr. Jaxon before this film?"

"Yes. On *Scandals.*"

"Then you worked with Miss Caulfield as well."

"Yes, and I knew her from her first movie."

"Are you friends?"

"Yes. I adore Kristen."

"I've heard that," Daniel said. He tried to summon a waitress, but the place was buzzing and no one saw him. He looked back at Borger. "Tell me about the accident."

Bruce dipped his fries into a puddle of ketchup.

Then he met the detective's eyes. "I don't know how real bullets made it into that gun. It was my responsibility."

"When was it out of your control?"

Bruce thought about it. "From the moment I set the rifle into the van that went over to the next ridge."

"I spoke to Kathleen Tam, your assistant," Daniel added. "She said she took over from there."

"Right. But that means it was pretty much up for grabs. I mean, no one can account for the gun minute by minute from the time the van left for the cabin."

"Why not? Kathy did. Said it was never out of her sight until she put it in the cabin for Kristen, and that no one else entered the cabin."

Borger shrugged. "She didn't tell me that."

"Who loaded it?"

"I did. Before I put it in the van."

"Wasn't that dangerous?"

Bruce gave the detective a disbelieving look. "They were blanks, remember?"

"Kristen could have substituted real ammo for the blanks when she went into the cabin," Daniel offered.

Bruce let out a long sigh. "Look, the idea that somebody wanted Max to die and make it look like it was Kristen's fault is really out there."

Daniel was not to be deterred. "Tell me about the hang glider."

Bruce hesitated, thrown off by the quick change of subject. "Okay. Ah, Max and I put the contraption together late the afternoon before the shoot. We waited till then because he was worried about the weather, it being Colorado, you know? But the forecast said the next day was going to be great, and since we were filming early in the morning, he needed to have the glider ready. I helped where he needed help, and then he checked it over, and that was that."

A waitress who looked as though she was competing for the title of Miss Winter Chill stood suddenly next to Daniel with pad in hand. Beverly told her to get lost, he was her customer. She smiled. "Sorry it took this long. Whatcha having?"

"Turkey sandwich, light mayo, chocolate shake, and fries," he said.

As she walked away, Daniel went right back at Borger. "How did Max 'check it over' to make sure everything was okay with the glider?"

Bruce seemed less sure about this subject. "Kinda like a pilot going over the checklist before the plane leaves the gate, I guess. He was very thorough, Max was. Well, hell, he was an expert hang glider."

"Thus he would have found ripped nylon or a loose cable in his preflight check?"

Bruce nodded. "X would have found anything like that."

"X?"

"That's what Kristen called Max. We all kinda got to doing that on the set."

"Anybody else have access to that trailer?"

"Only two people had keys, myself and the director."

"Max did not?"

"Nope." Bruce added irritably, "You don't trust actors with anything."

"Did you know that Max checked the glider again that night?"

Bruce looked mystified. "How? That can't be."

"Maggie Nash said that she found him in the property trailer looking over the aircraft." Daniel nodded as Beverly set down a chocolate shake.

Bruce shook his head. "You must be mistaken. If Max was in there, then she let him in."

"Maggie said she found him in the trailer when she was looking for him."

Borger stuck to his guns. "You have it backwards, man. Max didn't have a key."

Daniel filed that thought away. That was an inconsistency. Then he went back to his questions. "Someone cut the nylon on the wings and loosened one of the stainless-steel wires that controlled it sometime after you and Max set it up but before the flight. Who would have been able to do that? Besides yourself?"

Bruce frowned at the implied accusation. "Maggie would have been the only one."

Beverly set down Daniel's food, but he didn't miss a beat. "Think she wanted to kill him?"

Borger didn't understand. "Think who wanted to kill him?"

"Maggie."

Bruce almost spit out his food. "Maggie? She certainly didn't want him any more dead than I did."

"How dead was that?" Daniel asked.

Bruce laughed at the sick joke. "My God, Max and

Maggie were in love. I mean, what an incredible story! A little crazy, that love, but you know, I live in Hollywood, I've seen it all."

"Aspen might outdo Tinsel Town," Daniel offered, "if you lift the rocks." Then he sounded a sharper note. "What *was* the state of the relationship between Maggie and Max at that time?"

"How do you mean?"

Daniel looked at him as if he were stupid. "Happy, rocky, blissful, miserable? All partnerships have their ups and downs. What was this one like at the end?"

Bruce stopped eating and seemed to think hard. Finally he said, "I'd call it difficult. Professionally, it was fine; they were pros, the best. But they were having real troubles."

"Was there animosity?"

"Hell, I don't know. Maggie is a ballbuster on the best days, and for most of that shoot she was hell on wheels. There was a lot of tension between her and X. And between Kristen and X. Poor kid, I think he got shafted."

Daniel stopped sucking his thick shake into the straw. He wasn't buying this now-I-care-about-Max scenario. "How?"

"Well, man, look, their relationship is falling apart, and he tries to do his best, does the movie, does a good job despite the anxiety and pressure he is under, and then what happens? Someone inserts real ammo in the gun Kristen is supposed to 'shoot' at him with, and then, like if that wasn't enough, he slams into a mountain. Anyone deserved better."

Daniel felt he was finally getting someplace. "Was the animosity that Maggie directed toward Max intense enough for her to want to harm him?"

Bruce oddly didn't seem surprised to be asked that. "Maggie didn't hate him. They were fighting because they loved each other. And I mean, it wasn't like they were married and Maggie wouldn't let him get a divorce. If Max really wanted out, he would have just walked out. No, she's no suspect. She's about as much a killer as I am."

"So you think Kristen tried to bump him off?" Daniel asked it to see the reaction.

Bruce shoved his plate away. "Jesus."

"Why do you look so horrified?" Daniel knew the question rankled. He wanted to see how deep.

Bruce's face grew tight and red. "Kristen's no murderer either."

"She shot him through the shoulder, collapsed a lung. Looked like she was aiming for his heart."

Bruce said staunchly, "She didn't do it on purpose. I rehearsed her, taught her how. She was a terrible shot. And she was *supposed* to miss. No, she's no killer."

Daniel shrugged. "Hey, in my line of work, everyone's a killer until I'm proven wrong." He finished his sandwich. "So, who *did* you know that might have wanted Max dead?"

Bruce Borger stirred on his side of the booth. He seemed reluctant to answer, but then let it out. "Nicole Richaud. Everyone knew she was in love with Max from the day she set eyes on him. Everyone knew she was jealous of Kristen. Jealous of Maggie. Maggie may not be a walk in the park, but I think, from what I've seen and heard, that Nicole Richaud is truly evil."

"Why would she want Max dead if she loved him?"

"Jealousy."

"Sounds like a motive to me." Daniel felt he was finally learning something useful. He wanted to tap deeper into Bruce's feelings for Kristen, so he went there again. "Try another possibility on for size: Kristen figured she'd never be blamed for putting real bullets into the rifle, and she was a lousy shot. She was alone with the gun in the cabin while she was waiting for her cue. She could have loaded it then. If she missed, having sliced the glider wings would be insurance that he wouldn't come back alive."

Bruce started to smolder with anger. "Why would she *do* this?"

"Because she wanted revenge for the harm he'd done to her."

"Kristen's no killer," he insisted. "Everyone loves her. For good reason."

"Do *you* love Kristen?"

Bruce Borger looked very uncomfortable. "Everyone does, I just said."

"I mean, do you *love* her?" Daniel probed, staring at him. "There are people who believe you were jealous of Max."

"Come on."

"There is a rumor that you were obsessed with her and hated him."

Bruce said defensively, "I had a thing for her. No denying that."

"And were you jealous of Max Jaxon?"

Borger shifted in his seat. "I see where this is going, and I don't like it at all."

"No one is accusing you of anything, Mr. Borger."

"Damn right they're not," he answered heatedly. "You want to know something? I was very jealous of Max. Extremely." His nostrils flared and then he took a deep breath. "Wouldn't you be?"

The detective nodded. "I suppose."

"But I don't try to kill people I'm jealous of. I took it like a man. Kristen chose Max, and there was nothing I could do about it. I gave up on her. Ask anyone who worked on *Never Forget,* I was as professional as they come. Unlike Nicole Richaud."

He wanted to deflect Bruce's anger before the guy got up and stormed out. Borger had been so hard at first, but now he was talking. "Tell me what you know about her."

"She wouldn't give up," Bruce said intensely. "Kristen told me that she'd been trying to get into Max's pants since the day they met. Nicole coveted everything Maggie had, and was violently jealous of her relationship with Max. She was jealous of every woman who even looked at Max. Her rage was directed at Max for not choosing her."

"Did she ever speak to you about it?"

Bruce waved his hand. "She talked to anyone who'd listen. She was all over the set. She lives in Aspen as well as someplace in Southern France, so she was always in our faces. Maggie even tried to have her barred from the set, but she just kept showing up."

"Was she around the night before the accident?" Daniel asked mildly.

Bruce nodded. "In fact, she told me that night that she was going to take Max off on a cruise on the Nash yacht, that she'd win him over. Then she had a fight with Maggie. That was near the prop trailer. Jesus, maybe she could have found a way inside, I don't know—maybe she took Maggie's key."

"Did she ever say she wanted to hurt Max?"

"She said, she would rather see him dead than with Maggie."

Fourteen

The next Saturday night, Kristen Caulfield did not win the Golden Globe for Best Actress in a Drama. She lost to Verna Zimmermann. Three weeks later the Oscar nominations were announced. Max was not one of the nominees, but Kristen was. Her competition was her contemporaries Charlize Theron and Jennifer Aniston, and two seasoned stars: Jane Fonda, who had made a spectacular comeback with an aging version of the hooker she'd played in *Klute*, and Zimmermann for *Fibs*. Neither the movie nor the director was nominated, probably because of the story. Incest, despite the good reviews, was still touchy subject matter in Hollywood.

In the meantime, the three of them read through the *Scandals* script together on a weekend trip to Aspen. Maggie rented an SUV there and opened the house, which she hadn't visited in ages. It was more a mountain cabin than anything—the family had always called it the chalet. Built by Charles and Louise Nash in the 1940s, when Aspen was nothing more than a mountain village some skiers had discovered, the lodge was made to accommodate guests from Hollywood. Off a foyer was an enormous living room, the scale of which was kept warm and comfortable by small groupings of rustic furniture, wood-paned windows hung with drapes that puddled on the hardwood floor, a huge rock fireplace, and two walls of books piled on oak shelves. The dining area was part of that room, holding a table that could—and often did, back in the old days—seat eighteen comfortably. There was a sunporch filled with antique wicker and a patio made from natural stone, surrounded by towering aspens. Upstairs were five bedrooms, each with its own bath, unheard of at the time it was built, and the master bedroom boasted another fireplace. Now the canyons were surrounded by mansions and châteaus, but the Nash house had never lost its allure. Indeed, real estate people constantly called Charles to see if he was ready to sell. He said he'd die first. He probably would.

As Maggie reopened it, she thought her father had been right in holding on to it. She liked being there, especially with her two young stars. Kristen said it reminded her of cabins in northern Wisconsin where her parents had vacationed when she was young, although not on such a grand scale. The only thing it was missing—the treasure that most Wisconsin cabins had—was a lake outside the back door.

So they found one. As a girl Maggie had gone swimming at the nearby Reudi Resevoir, but Turquoise Lake had later become her favorite when she started vacationing in Aspen—as she first discovered America—in her twenties. She booked a nearby A-frame cabin for a night and planned a day at the lake to do the first read-through of the script together. They packed a picnic lunch, lots of canned soda and bottled water, and set off.

The clear blue water of Turquoise Lake shimmered just that color in the sunlight. It was almost as beautiful, Max said, as Fallen Leaf Lake near Tahoe. He had worked there one year in summer stock after moving to California. It was also a place he loved to glide. Kristen loved the mountains, lake or no lake, and wanted to hike. She was the most athletic woman Maggie had ever met, and Max offered to try to keep up with her, but when Kristen returned after doing three miles in what Maggie was sure was Olympic record time, Max was nowhere to be seen. "I lost him after the first ten minutes," Kristen revealed. *Well*, Maggie thought, *at least they weren't off screwing in the woods.*

The beach where they had rented the cabin was fairly secluded, nestled into a cove and surrounded by trees. They read through the lines sitting on the deck, eating their lunch, then repeated it later on the sand, acting out portions that were easy, pages that required nothing more than a gesture, touching, imagined props. Maggie gave a little direction here and there, when she had an inspiration, and even took notes on her master script when Max or Kristen did something that seemed right on the money. Even in the bright sunlight, hardly trying for the emotion of the story, the sexual compatibility between Max and Kristen was undeniable. Maggie was sure she wasn't imagining it when she thought Max's skimpy Speedo trunks were bulging.

One key scene would be filmed in Mexico, where Maggie feared the Pacific Ocean would be even colder than it was here. She suggested that they wade in, thinking it would be good practice. Just touching her fingers in the water, though, made her shiver. She could already imagine Max's voice rising a few octaves as his balls shrank into his body.

In the movie, Claire, Kristen's character, is a tour guide, chased by Tom, played by Max, everywhere she goes. Tom worms his way into a party that Claire is attending with her new boyfriend. She is angry to find he's followed her yet again. He seems to be stalking her, obsessed with her since she told him the affair was over. But he doesn't understand the word *no*. She sees him duck out after humiliating her date, so she follows him to the beach just beyond the terrace, attempting to get him to talk it out. He ignores her, shedding articles of clothing as he nears the water, planning to take a drunken midnight swim. The fact that he is butt naked doesn't stop her. She walks right into the surf in her evening gown, screaming at him. Tom **rips** the dress off her, drags her into the water, makes love to her right there in the ocean.

Max did his lines and ran into the water—and howled. It startled Kristen for a moment. She had not brought a suit, so she followed him up to the bottom of her shorts, but stopped there. Even in the sunlight, she shivered as well. Turquoise Lake was frigid. He did what the lines suggested, grabbing her, pulling her to him, holding her as she protested, kicked, fought. "After he kisses Claire and she slaps his face, Tom starts to lose his footing in the water, grasps for her, and rips open her front, revealing her naked torso."

"Oh, Jesus!" he said, realizing he'd just done that very thing with her blouse. She was naked underneath, and the sight of her breasts shocked him. He hadn't realized he'd gotten so deeply into the character. "I'm sorry!" From the rocky beach Maggie watched with interest. She almost wished she had a camera now.

"It's okay." Kristen didn't try to hide herself, but giggled. "I guess this is how we're going to have to do it, huh?"

He blushed, unable to take his eyes from her beautiful breasts. "I guess."

She cried, "This feels great!" She dunked herself under the water and came up again, splashing, shedding inhibitions. Then she reached under the surface with both hands and pulled her shorts off. She felt as rebellious as a teenager disobeying her parents. And this boldness protected her shyness. "If we are going to be naked in the water in the film, we had better start now."

"Right." He didn't sound convinced. He glanced at Maggie, but she looked like she was enjoying this immensely. Then he threw caution to the wind. With a fast jerk of his thumb, the bright blue Speedos slipped down over his butt, off his legs, and flew into the sky toward the sand. Maggie caught them in midair before they slapped her in the face. Max whooped and hollered and splashed Kristen with water. "This is wild!" he shouted.

They played like children. There was no salaciousness about it. Rather, they enjoyed a freedom that broke all inhibitions between them and would certainly make for an easier time once the cameras were rolling and they had to do the nude scene for real—in front of some thirty crew people.

Max dunked Kristen and managed to pull her panties off. They floated away on the water as she responded, slapping him on the bottom. Then he ran out of the water, his penis swinging in the wind. Grabbing Maggie's hand, he pulled her up from the towel and toward the lake. "Come on, we need a director!"

Maggie protested, cried out that it was too cold, laughed, warned him, and then she was all wet. Four hands were pummeling her, ripping her clothes off, her shorts, shirt, bra, panties. Suddenly she—the European, who had been used to nude beaches her entire life—felt like the prude who was being tested. "The hell with it," she cried before they dunked her.

Showing her true colors, she rose to the surface of the water like a porpoise, laughed out loud, then dove under and grabbed Max's penis in her hand. With the other, she took hold of Kristen's firm buttocks and they both squealed. The childlike game of

touch and feel went on like that for about ten minutes, the three of them groping, joking, playing,
teasing.

Maggie, an expert swimmer, did the breaststroke
out to a diving raft, and came up winded, beaching
herself there on her belly in the hot sun. Goose
bumps covered her from head to foot. Kristen, almost
as fast, joined her, breathing hard, catching her
breath, as they watched Max doing the backstroke
toward them. Both were amused that his male ego—
showing that big dick—made him choose this particular swimming stroke. When he sat on the platform
and gasped for breath, Maggie said, "I think we're
all in the finals."

Later, as they ate fresh mountain trout at a local
German restaurant, Kristen said, "I'm glad we're
staying the night. I'd hate to have to drive back in
the dark."

Maggie nodded. "Especially after all this beer."

"Anyone wanna play Upwords when we get back
to the cabin?" Maggie asked.

"What's that?" Kristen had never heard of it.

"Like Scrabble, only you put letters on top of
letters."

Max shrugged, though she'd beat him a dozen
times before. "You just can't use French."

They sat in the sparsely furnished cabin and
played the word game, drinking dark beer and
chomping popcorn. At moments Maggie saw Max's
eyes gleam with desire for Kristen, but Maggie had
known the dangers of this minefield all along. She

would do everything she could to encourage his feelings for the girl—the ultimate director's quest—but she would not allow him to step over the line. If he did, she might be finished. As long as she remained in control, everything would be just fine. And she would. That's what her life had been about.

Kristen slept in the loft, on a lumpy mattress lying on the floor. Max and Maggie wished her a good night, each giving her a kiss on the cheek, but when Max had trouble falling asleep, Maggie knew it was because of the proximity to the flame—Kristen was just above them, lying virtually on the ceiling of their bedroom. Maggie rather enjoyed his torture. In the morning, she encouraged him to make love to her as they heard the shower running, knowing that he was thinking about Kristen standing naked under the rushing water.

The three of them returned to Los Angeles for the Oscars. It was a momentous year, not only because *Fibs* had been nominated in several categories, and Kristen was an odds-on favorite to win, but because the Irving Thalberg Award, for "his lifetime contribution to the art of filmmaking," was being presented to Charles Nash. Maggie at first was sure her father would refuse to come. He had not set foot in America, after all, since the blacklist scandal of the 1950s. But Charles was older now, and even though he spouted off to anyone who would listen, he had a soft spot for the industry where he'd been such a trailblazer. Max helped convince him with a phone call. "It's your chance to forgive," he said.

"Forgive," Charles echoed, "but never forget."

"I'm gonna use that as a title," Maggie said when Max reported her father's reaction. She was working on the script of another movie. "But I'll never believe he's coming till he shows up at my door."

He did, at their hotel suite, only a few days later. Max found himself again having to face Nicole. He'd seen her in Avignon at Christmastime, the first time he'd seen her since their tryst in Paris. Neither of them had talked about it, but Max was painfully aware that Nicole still wanted him. By the time Nicole and Charles showed up in Aspen, Max had buried his memories of the affair, but Nicole had not. He could see that the moment they set eyes on one another.

What Maggie saw was the diamond ring on Nicole's hand, a chunk the size of a walnut, surrounded by emeralds. It was almost bigger than the pencil-thin finger that supported it. "What does this mean?" she asked, fearing the answer she knew was coming.

"Made it legal," Charles said, hugging Nicole to his side, "just like that picture of mine." *Making It Legal* had been one of his earliest hits, a classic.

Maggie held her tongue while Nicole gave them the details. They'd been married only a week before, by the priest in the little church where they had taken Maggie and Max to midnight mass on Christmas Eve. "Since Charles found Catholicism, he has felt badly about living in sin."

"Crap," Maggie said. She knew the old buzzard had been forced into it by Nicole's prodding. She probably threatened to leave him if he didn't finally say yes. Religion had nothing to do with it, even though it seemed his newfound passion for everything Catholic was real.

"I hope you'll be very happy," Max said.

"I hope you signed a prenuptial agreement," Maggie said.

Nicole glared at her. "Why do you find it impossible to believe that we love one another?"

"Love comes easy, doesn't it, when there's a fortune at stake?"

"Margaret, enough," her father warned. Instead he turned his attention to Kristen, who had just walked in the door. "You're miraculous, my dear, just what the American cinema has needed for years, a kick in the ass. Those idiots had better give you the Oscar or I'm not accepting the Thalberg."

Kristen took his hand gently, smiling. "It's wonderful to meet you, Mr. Nash, but I think they present the Thalberg before they give Best Actress."

"Then I'll give it back," Charles muttered. "Have you met my wife, Nicole?"

Kristen blinked when Nicole showed her the ring. "My goodness!"

"That's what I said," Nicole added, and they shared air kisses. Then Nicole went to Max and threw her arms around him. "I'm so sorry you weren't nominated," she said. "It must make you feel awful." She giggled. "Well, stick with me. We're the only non-nominees in the room. We'll support each other and get through this."

"I never expected to be nominated," Max said, pulling away from her. "I'm thrilled for all of you," he said to Maggie, Charles, and Kristen.

"You'll be there someday, darling, we all know that," Maggie offered.

But the damage had been done. Nicole's dig had

gotten to him. Once again, he was reminded that he was second-rate.

Later, alone on a lounge chair, looking up at the swaying palms surrounding the pool, Max tried to dismiss the feeling of inferiority, but it gnawed inside him. Here he sat, bronzed, buff, sexy, women glancing at him from the pool area, desiring him, admiring him—and he felt like shit. Was his success only reflected glory from Maggie? Without her, he'd still be nothing, selling ties only a few miles south. Maggie had raised him light-years from his former life, but his success felt tenuous. He didn't trust it because he didn't trust himself. He wasn't brilliant like Kristen. He was a hunk who got lucky.

He dressed and walked down past Santa Monica Boulevard to talk to Nicky Dee. He'd spent hours with her the night they'd arrived, but he hadn't been able to open up the way he did at lunch now. Or was he coming apart? "Nicky, Jesus," he said over rice pudding, "I feel pulled in two directions. I'm in love with Maggie, and at the same time I'm afraid she's going to throw me away."

"Never liked the broad."

"Am I me or am I just some creation of hers?"

"Jesus, X. I thought you were getting some confidence. Maybe you shoulda stayed in town and done that TV show you had lined up. This movie star stuff's made a mess out of you."

"Nicky, come on, that's not it. I'm just . . ." He didn't know the word.

"Scared."

He nodded.

"Listen, Maximus. You're good, you know that. I seen you from the start, back in those ratholes in the Village where you used to do Chekhov and Ibsen. I think this bitch keeps a hold on you by keeping you insecure."

He objected. "What? She's given me everything! Christ, we've only done one movie and are starting another in a few weeks." He licked his spoon and set it down. "It's Nicole who got me feeling glum."

"Ah, the new Mrs. Nash?" Nicky lifted a folded newspaper and showed him Connie Heller's column with a photo of Charles and Nicole arriving at LAX. "She's the one you fucked in Paris, right?"

Involuntarily, Max glanced around. "You're the only one who knows."

"Besides her. X, listen, don't play with fire. I think you gotta tell Madame about it before Nicole does."

"Huh?"

"You'll look like a cheater if you tell her, but if Nicole does, then you look like a liar as well."

"You have a point." He shook his head wearily. "Man, how'd I get myself into this mess? I was going to tell Maggie, but then she offered me another film and I was afraid she'd tell me to take a hike."

Nicky pulled a compact out of her apron and dabbed on more lipstick. "You're a star, baby, you don't need her anymore. Why can't you believe that?"

"I love her."

She clicked the compact shut. "Do you really?"

*   *   *

If Kristen and Max had any doubts that they were movie stars, the week leading up to Oscar night convinced them. They did television shows, newspaper articles, Internet interviews, and that night, outside Hollywood's Kodak Theater, they were besieged by fans who couldn't get enough of them. Joan Rivers, of course, dissed Kristen's dress, and made a few off-color comments about Max and Maggie living the story of *Fibs*. But the older woman–younger man concept seemed to work for everyone else. People ate it up.

Charles Nash caused a sensation, and Nicole loved the limelight she was experiencing for the first time—it had never been like this in Europe. "Guilt works for Americans," Charles muttered to her as they swept into the auditorium to a standing ovation. The only disappointment was that Kristen's father had had a recurrence of hepatitis and was too ill to fly out, so her mother had decided to stay with him and watch in his hospital room. When her name was announced, Max took her hand and said, "This is for your parents."

But Kristen lost to Jane Fonda, who later, when she was back in her seat just behind them, whispered into Kristen's ear, "This is my last one. You've got many coming."

And Charles did not give back his Irving Thalberg Award.

At the Governor's Ball, Nicole grabbed Max's hand and pulled him to the dance floor. They began to move to a slow, languid a "Moon River." "So, you got what you were working for," Max said to her, feeling her huge ring touching his ear.

"Did you?"

"How do you mean?"

"Is Maggie going to marry you?"

He drew back a little. "That's not what I'm after."

"Oh, that's right, *pardon moi.* You are with her for fame."

He stiffened. "You're not going to make me feel insecure, not again."

"One cannot make a person feel that if they are not."

"Can we just not talk and dance?"

She pulled herself closer to him, reaching up on her toes to touch his cheek with hers. "You smell the same," she said softly.

He said nothing.

"You look wonderful. Better than on-screen."

He remained silent.

"Did you ever tell her?"

He bristled, starting to pull away.

"Have you?" she demanded.

"Yes."

She smiled and melted in his arms. "Oh, good. I have felt so guilty all this time. Maggie is my stepmother now. I should talk to her about it, tell her I'm sorry as well—"

"No!" He stopped moving in the middle of the floor as the orchestra began to segue to another movie song. Max tried to leave, but Nicole held tight to his arm.

"So you didn't tell her. She doesn't know, does she?"

Max glanced over to where Maggie and her father were talking with Emma Thompson and a group of European friends. Guilt raged through his blood. And fear, the fear that Nicole had a secret she could hold over his head. He looked into her eyes and gave her a warning. "Don't you dare."

In response, she put her arms around him in a dancing position again, pulling him back to the floor. "But, Max, what do you take me for?"

He was afraid to tell her.

They moved in rhythm for a few minutes, then she said, "It haunts you, doesn't it?"

"No."

"Liar."

He tried not to show her any fear. "I don't even think about it."

"Arrete de nier."

"I'm not denying it." The song was coming to an end. Nicole dipped backward, and he held her. When she came up and faced him again, as applause began, his anguish was clear. He bit his upper lip. "Yes. It haunts me."

"Good," she purred, and walked away.

Late that night, with Charles snoring next to her in their hotel bedroom, Nicole, to take her mind off Max, opened *Anthem*, the novel she'd been reading for the past two months. The author, Jerry K. Loeb, had been a budding screenwriter and pilot when Charles was still making movies. He sold Charles a script, but it never got made, and Jerry went off to a career in the navy. Now retired, he'd written a novel and sent a copy to Charles and Nicole. It wasn't Nicole's usual cup of tea, but she was determined to read it for a friend. And by now she was thoroughly engrossed.

Tonight she was reading a section set in South America. Half concentrating on the story and half listening to her old husband's annoying snoring, she found certain words jumping out at her. *Murder. Poison. Rosary beads.*

She closed the thick book and stared at Charles. Murder. Poison. Rosary beads. And another word she'd just read filled her mind: *undetectable.*

Fifteen

The next morning, Kristen attended mass with Charles and Nicole at the Church of the Good Shepherd in Beverly Hills. Maggie joined them for breakfast back at the hotel, where Charles announced that he and Nicole were going to the airport at noon, but not to return to France as planned. Nicole had suddenly decided she wanted to see Argentina, Brazil, Peru. Charles seldom left the continent, she explained, so this was her big chance. Maggie said good riddance when Nicole finally departed with her father, but Max breathed a heavy sigh of relief. Nicole had kept the secret.

Maggie went back to Aspen that afternoon to speak at a film seminar, leaving Max and Kristen in Los Angeles to prepare for the movie shoot. They both had to take some crash courses, to learn how to skateboard, drive a bus, and shape a pizza by hand.

The pizza lesson was provided by Giancarlo, an ancient Italian who owned a small restaurant in Westwood that was, people said, the best pizza joint in California. Kristen had eaten there several times while making *Snow Angel*, for it was Bruce's favorite place. Indeed, when she walked in for instructions, Bruce and an attractive Chinese girl were just paying their bill. When Bruce first heard that *Scandals* would be Kristen's next film, he jumped at Maggie's offer to work on it. They hadn't seen each other in ages—he was pissed that she hadn't let him accompany her to the Oscars—and hadn't talked, except for a few phone calls in which he would ask her out and she would tell him she was busy.

"Kristen!" Bruce's eyes lit up. He took her hand warmly.

Kristen greeted him and said hello to Kathleen Tam, his assistant. "This work or pleasure?"

Kathy said, "Both."

"What are you doing here?" Bruce asked.

Kristen explained about the pizza lesson. Bruce laughed, because he had come here not only for lunch but to talk Giancarlo into letting him borrow one of his pizza peels for the movie. "Maggie loves authenticity."

"She does."

"So, when are we going to see each other?"

Kristen saw that Bruce wasn't going to give up. He had feelings for her, but she could not return them. No, that wasn't really true. She liked him immensely, found him attractive, enjoyed his company. But she didn't feel anything stirring deep inside the way he did for her. She told him she would call him and they'd go out for dinner as soon as she had a moment. She was busy memorizing the script, she said, and Maggie was on a roll.

Kathy said, "Typhoon Nash has blown into town."

Bruce nodded, trying not to show that her turning him down had stung. "We're a little overwhelmed. But the hoopla is great, her first American movie and all."

"I'll call you," Kristen promised, and then let him hug her.

Bruce whispered, "I miss you, honey."

At that moment Max walked in. He was surprised to find Kristen in the embrace of a stranger who was whispering in her ear. Max approached them as they parted, and Kathy told Max she thought he was wonderful in *Fibs*. Bruce said little, sizing him up, very aware that he had taken Kristen's hand the moment he'd come near, telling her they were running late and had better get to the kitchen. "Hey," Max said to both of them, "see you on location, soon."

As they left, Bruce glanced over his shoulder a second time, and watched Max leading Kristen into the back of the restaurant, still holding her hand. He did not hear, though, what they said:

"Who was that guy?" Max asked.

"Just a friend."

The pizza lesson was a disaster at first, but after an hour Max was tossing rounds of pizza dough like he had been born in Naples. In fact, they made their own dinner. "Well," Kristen said, finishing a glass of red wine, "we can always get a job here if our careers fall apart."

Max laughed. "I think Domino's is more our speed."

"You going to join Maggie in Aspen tomorrow?"

He shook his head. "Not for a few more days."

She nodded. "Me too. I want to relax a little. And I promised Bruce we'd have dinner."

"You dating him?"

"No. But he thinks he's dating me. At least that's what he tells himself."

Max got it. "Ah."

"What are you doing tomorrow?"

"Going to heaven."

"Huh?"

He answered with a teasing wink. "And if you're good, I'll take you with me."

The next morning Max drove up in the bright red 330i convertible that Marty Stern had provided for Maggie when they arrived in Hollywood. It was a good thing too, for Max's old Mercedes had been sitting idle so long that it wouldn't turn over. Nicky had promised to start it for him now and then, but it had been more then than now. "Where are we going?" Kristen asked when she got in.

"San Diego."

"That's heaven? What for?"

"Torrey Pines."

"Where?"

"Ever heard of Blacks Beach?"

She blinked. "I didn't bring a suit."

"You won't need one."

It dawned on her. "My God, that's the nude beach north of San Diego!"

"No," he laughed, "we're not going to do *that* scene again. We only swim naked on-camera."

"Then why to the beach?"

"That's where the Gliderport is."

"Huh?" She was clueless.

He motioned behind them. "That's my glider wrapped up back there. Torrey Pines is a launch site for gliders. A three-hundred-and-sixty-foot sandstone bluff overlooking the ocean. I won a competition there, actually."

"Best naked male?"

He laughed out loud. "On a glider? I don't think so."

"We're going gliding?"

"*I'm* going gliding. You're going to watch."

"I want to do it too."

He shook his head as he merged onto the 405 Freeway. "You've been in Wisconsin way too long. It takes learning, practice, lessons."

"Oh," she said, feeling dumb.

"It's my passion," he admitted. "There is nothing that feels as powerful, as weightless, as magical, almost like you're not human anymore, you're suddenly like a bird."

"Is it dangerous?"

"Yup," he said with a smile, "and that makes it even more compelling."

"I know nothing about hang gliding. Just that I think it's cool."

Obviously. But he didn't say it.

As they drove down the coast, he told her a little about the sport. He led off with some history. "Otto Lilienthal was the father of hang gliding, even though he crashed and died in 1896."

"Wonderful."

"Francis Rogollo designed felixible wings during the Second World War. Then an Aussie added a control bar and somebody put a seat on the big kite and presto, modern hang gliding had been born."

"How'd you begin?"

Max told her he started when he first changed coasts, with a simple glider on beaches and low hills, and how it took root in his soul to the point where he'd won three competitions and had even flown for two hours once. He had considered becoming an instructor, but took the job at Gucci instead, where he was more likely to be noticed by the film industry. "But there is nothing I love more."

At the vast Gliderport parking lot, she helped him get his gear out of the backseat of the car, and watched with growing interest as he unrolled the contraption—it looked to her like golf clubs wrapped in a travel bag—and fastened the pieces together on the grass. "This is the sail, anywhere from thirteen to twenty-eight feet across," he explained, pointing at the bright red Dacron cloth. "It's stretched across aluminum tubing called the A-frame. It'll look different in the sky because it flexes and changes shape with the weight and movement."

"How do you attach to it?" she asked.

"This harness." He showed her. "Hangs here, from the top of the control frame. The ones for long flights have swing seats."

She eyed it doubtfully. "Like Maggie, I think I still prefer a 747."

He smiled. "I steer it with this, the control bar. It's rounded, triangular, for best control in the air."

"Why's it padded?"

"Comfort."

"No chapped hands?"

He smiled. "This is the most popular kind, a Rogollo type, simple and beautiful." He raised his hand to feel the wind. Others had already taken off, and the horizon was filled with the bright colors of the man-made birds. "My weight has to be right for the glider. Too small, I'll fly too fast and sink faster. Too big, I can't control it. Watch that guy."

She saw a man start running toward the stunning drop-off into the ocean, then he became airborne. "Jeez! It scares me."

"It's great!" Max said with enthusiasm.

"Now I'm turning chicken. I don't think I could hack it."

He looked into her eyes. "Never say never."

She blinked. "Well, maybe I'd go with you, but since they only hold one—"

"There are some made for two people," he interjected.

"My big mouth."

He pinched her cheek. "I'm holding you to it."

"I think I'd pass out from fright."

"I won't let you. Trust me, okay?"

A few minutes later, watching him effortlessly gliding through the sky over the beach and water below, she started to understand why he'd said he was going to heaven. After getting over the shock that he had not fallen off the cliff to his death and seeing that he was flying with ease, she stood on the wooden observation deck growing curious. What was it like? What did he feel? What did he see from that height? In the midst of her questions, she found herself pondering something entirely different, what he'd said about her going with him. She did already, in this short time, trust him, and she wanted to experience it with him.

She trusted him, in everything. She knew this was the start. She was coming to feel something for her costar, no matter how much she wanted to deny it.

Kristen and Max flew back to Aspen two days later. They got Kristen a room in the sumptuous, hundred-year-old Hotel Jerome, where he and Maggie had made love that first time, then walked down Main Street to have veggie sandwiches at Explore, a comfy bookstore/café. On a front table were flyers about Maggie Nash's lecture, so they made their way to the Aspen Club Lodge, where she was speaking at the conference center. They entered the ballroom, to find her holding a question-and-answer period. They stayed at the back until she noticed them, interrupting a question to introduce Max Jaxon and Kristen Caulfield. They received excited applause from the attendees, mostly college kids mad about film.

Maggie walked down the aisle of folding chairs to hug and kiss Max passionately, which surprised Kristen enough to make her gasp slightly. The audience roared their approval. Maggie held Max's hand, forcing him and Kristen to take a few questions from the audience, and then told them they were off the hook, they could go. The students were not happy she was dismissing two big stars they hadn't counted on meeting, but when she reminded them this was an *educational* experience, they relented. She told Max and Kristen she would meet them for dinner. A boy in the audience asked, "So, like, what restaurant?" and Maggie smiled. She could picture it: an intimate evening with a hundred of their newest best friends.

After they left, Max and Kristen strolled down Main Street. "She really loves you," Kristen remarked.

"Yes. Well." Max blinked, a little unsettled. "I actually thought Maggie was being a bit possessive."

She flashed her most photogenic smile. "You mean, you don't always carry on like that?"

He laughed. "Well, sometimes. But I think she was showing off."

"I'd show you off too."

"No," he said, "I mean to you."

"Oh."

She looked away, uncomfortably, and he hastened to add, "It's new to me. All of this. The career, the lifestyle, love."

She took a moment to reply. "No relationships before this? Honestly?"

He shook his head. "Not that I didn't try. Just

never happened." They crossed the street at the corner, and resumed the conversation on the other side. "How about you?"

"Well, you met Bruce." At his frown, she laughed. "That's about the closest thing I've had to a relationship, and I mean, we didn't even come close."

"Before that?"

"Well, for years I was madly in love with Bill Ogden, but that was in grade school. He grew up to be a fireman and married my best friend, Lori. Plus, I had a crush on my dramatics coach in high school, but he was gay. Fell passionately in lust with Frank Tousignant on my college graduation trip to Paris—"

"You've been to Paris?"

"Hated it."

He stopped dead in his tracks. "How could anyone hate Paris?"

"Simple. Frank swept me off my feet, first man I ever slept with, but then dropped the bomb, on the Eiffel Tower no less, that he was married with two kids." The bitter memory still rankled her. "Asshole."

Max chuckled, but he knew she had felt real pain. "You can find jerks everywhere. Don't blame Paris."

Kristen noticed an ice cream store and shot Max a look that told him she would love one. "What's X's favorite flavor?" she asked as they headed inside.

"Guess."

She hit it right. They licked their butter pecan cones as they sat on a bench outside the shop.

Max said, "How are you handling the success?"

She intercepted a drop coming down the side of the cone. "It's pretty overwhelming. But then, you'd know."

To her surprise, he didn't agree. "Mine's different."

"How so?"

"You're a brilliant actress. I'm a personality. Here today, gone tomorrow."

"Come on," she said, turning to him with genuine concern, "don't put yourself down. You were wonderful in *Fibs*."

"Not like you. You have talent that comes along once in a lifetime," he told her, certain of what he was saying. "I've have seen your film about five times."

She laughed, not taking him seriously. "You sound like some crazed fan."

"Oh, I am." He bit into his cone and closed his eyes.

When he didn't reopen them for a few seconds, she asked, "What are you thinking?"

With his eyes still closed, he said, "Youth. Butter pecan reminds me of being a kid."

"I'm thinking how fattening it is." Then she laughed.

Three women, tourists, came up to them and asked them for their autographs. They ate it up. Then they walked some more while they finished their ice cream. "You excited about the movie?" he inquired.

"*Scandals*? Oh, very. I just wish I could get my

personal life in some kind of shape before we start shooting."

"Huh?"

"Don't know what to do. I'm new to Hollywood, never planned on going to California, so everyone, all these advisors say I should buy this and that for tax reasons and such. I'm overwhelmed."

"Maggie knows about that stuff. She'll help."

She laughed. "Just what I need, another opinion. Though I do admit she seems to have a maternal side that's very appealing. Probably why she's a good director."

"Sexy earth mother, I call her."

Kristin nodded. "She is. Very." Then she giggled. "Listen to me, the little protected girl from Dairyland."

"Strict upbringing?"

"Catholic farm family. Heavy-duty guilt."

"Aha. We'll change that."

She flashed a daring look. "Promise?"

"My challenge," he said with a nod.

"She didn't get laid till she graduated from college?" Maggie asked in disbelief that night at the Nash chalet. "You must be kidding."

Max said, "I think the innocence is part of her screen magic."

Maggie sipped her tea. "Innocence, my ass. Waste of time."

"She's from the Midwest. I think she has a pent-up sexuality just waiting to explode."

She gave him a shrewd look. "And you'd love to ignite the rockets."

He held his hands palms up in innocence. "I didn't say that."

"Oh, come on," she said, calling him on what they both knew to be true. "You've been lusting for her since the day you first laid eyes on her."

He swallowed. "I'm just entranced by her talent."

"And she's beautiful!" Maggie purred. "Honesty, baby. Come on."

He leaned toward her, until they were forehead to forehead. "She's attractive, but I'm in love with *you*."

She pulled back. "My father would put it this way: you want to pork her." She laughed out loud. "You Americans and your sexual guilt. Admit it, you'd love to fuck her."

Seeing her light mood, Max nodded. "It's a fantasy, I guess."

"Oh, Jesus, can't we be genuine here? Your desire to sleep with her doesn't diminish me or our love any. In fact, it shows me you're a full-blooded male and that you have exceptionally good taste." She sipped more of her tea. "The fact that she's young makes me a lot less jealous than if she were my age."

He thought back over the past few days, how wonderful they'd been, and asked, "If I actually carried it out, how would you feel?"

She stopped the cup near her lips, pressed it to her cheek before she answered, mulling over the question. "I think I'd be very hurt," she admitted finally. "I want to feel you're mine."

He winced, thinking of Nicole. "I am. So it will stay a fantasy."

"Promise?" She closed her eyes for a moment. "Allow this big strong worldly mature director a moment of insecurity, okay?"

He took her hand. "I promise."

Aspen, Colorado
Paradise Bakery

Christopher Daniel walked into the Paradise Bakery and recognized the tall, balding man just paying for his order. "Corky Propsom," Daniel said. "Haven't seen you in ages."

"Detective, how's things?" Corky swatted him on the back. "Hear you got your hands full with the movie folk."

"Meeting one of them here, as a matter of fact."

"I was an extra up there that day. Boy, that was a shame, what happened."

"See you around." Daniel turned to the counter girl. "Debbie, give me a couple of éclairs and coffee. And tell me something. I hear Mrs. Charles Nash bought hundreds of Bismarcks the morning of the accident."

"Who?"

He tried her maiden name. "Nicole Richaud."

That tripped her memory. "Yeah, Frenchy. Sweet thing she is, but too skinny. She wanted to treat the whole cast and crew. Yeah, I remember, five o'clock in the morning she made me have them ready," Debbie said. "I bake that early, but I sure never opened the shop at that hour." She handed him his coffee and two luscious éclairs.

Then Nicole herself walked in. *"Bonjour, mademoiselle, comment ca va ce matin?"*

"Oui, monsieur, parlez-vous Français?" She offered her hand.

But his were full. "I grew up in Montreal."

"Oui. I have visited there. Have you been to Paris?"

He smiled. "Paris is Mecca for people who live in Montreal."

"So you have."

Daniel indicated his hands. "Coffee, tea? Bismarck?"

She declined. "I'm so glad you suggested we meet somewhere other than the police station. Where can we talk?" She saw that there were no tables.

"Outside, on the bench."

She smiled and nodded, then noticed Debbie and gave her a little wave.

Debbie recognized her. "Hey, honey, how are you doing?"

"Well, thank you," Nicole said with a nod. "Nice to see you again."

Daniel thought she certainly was as attractive as everyone had told him. Whether that should set off alarm bells, he wasn't sure. He let her open the door for him, and they sat together on the bench outside. "How well did you know Max Jaxon?"

"We were dear friends."

"Might you have been more than that?"

"I do not understand."

"You know what I mean."

She looked stunned. "Inspector!"

She was trying to jerk him around. "He was a sex symbol, a movie star, bigger than life. Women fell for him. Even the chief's wife is nuts about him."

"Women who don't know him. Fans, people from afar. I knew Max, and I adored him, but it was never romantic."

"Sexual?"

She blinked. "Inspector, I am offended."

"I have reason to believe, from what others have said, that you had sex with him."

She leaped to her feet. "I did not come here to be insulted. How dare you accuse me of having an affair with Max?"

If he didn't know better, he'd guess *she* was the actress. "I accused you of no such thing. Please, sit down and be less dramatic."

"I do not like your tone."

"I'm not wild about yours," he muttered. He took a sip of his coffee and bit into one of the éclairs.

"I'm going to get tea," Nicole said, going back inside.

"I'll be right here." He would give her time to understand he wasn't going to be played for a fool. He watched a cowboy get out of his pickup truck and go into Kemo Sabe, the upscale Western store across the street. A girl with a pierced lower lip walked by holding her boyfriend's hand. His pants were worn so low that the hems were chewed up from dragging behind him. Just another day in Aspen.

He was wondering about the photo Max had referred to in his last moments. When Nicole returned, he asked her about it. "What was he talking about? What kind of picture? Of what or whom?"

She shrugged, warming her hands on the cup of tea. "I have no idea."

"Mrs. Nash, this is an investigation. You need to be straight with me."

"I am, sir."

"Were you in love with Max?"

"I am still in love with Charles Nash."

"Did you not have an affair with Max Jaxon?"

"No. How dare you infer such nonsense?"

"Because there are people who believe you did."

"I was devoted to Charles. There has never been a man in my life but him. I will love him forever, till the day I die. I doubt that any other person on earth could come close to pleasing me, on every level, as Charles did."

"That's wonderful," Daniel curtly said, "but we don't have time for games. All you say about Charles Nash may be true, but it has been common knowledge around the movie set that you had had a sexual affair with Max and wanted a relationship with him."

She glared at him.

His coffee was gone, so he got up and disposed of his cup. "Care to take a walk?"

She didn't seem happy about the idea, but she followed him as he started up Cooper Street. "People heard you declare your desire for Max in public, and also witnessed you stating that you would do almost anything to get him."

"That must be Maggie talking. She has always hated me, so it makes perfect sense that she would try to throw suspicion on me."

"Why did she hate you?"

"For the reason you just stated. Because I once slept with Max. See? It was not *l'affair*, as you so pompously assume." She stopped walking. "It was simply—if you pardon the American expression—a good fuck."

He blushed, then continued on. They entered the Cooper Street Mall, a brick street closed to cars. Benches lined either side of a landscaped center with a small ditch built to resemble a brook. Daniel put his foot up on one of the benches. "Mrs. Nash, did you not plan to whisk Max off on a cruise once the film was completed?"

"Yes. It was going to be his birthday present."

"Did you say something to the effect of 'he will be with me or he will be with no one'?"

"Perhaps. Inspector, I am French. We have passion."

"Passion is often motive in a murder investigation."

"Maggie did it."

He blinked. "Excuse me?"

"Because she didn't want to lose Max. She was desperate. The Nashes always get what they want. She would rather have seen Max dead than lose him to another woman."

These two women really did hate each other. "Do you have evidence to support this theory?"

"In fact, I do." She set her purse down on the bench and reached into it. "Here," she said, thrusting bound pages at him.

He saw it was a screenplay for a movie, titled *Never Forget.* "But I've seen this. I read it right after I got assigned to the case. I wanted to see what they'd been filming."

"*Non, c'est different!* This is the proof you need."

He had no idea what she was talking about. "Proof? Of what?"

"Turn to the folded page. In the original screenplay, the one they were filming, Kristen's character is on the run, holed up in the cabin. When the unsuspecting dolt, Max, flies over her, she mistakes him for the FBI or some such thing."

He nodded. "And she shoots at him."

"*Oui,* and misses, which scares him, and then when they later meet up, he hates her for almost killing him, but despite the obstacles, they fall in love. It's a stupid story, if you ask me. I don't know where the title comes from. She has been living with some criminal who abducted her two years ago and has fallen into the Stockholm syndrome of growing to love him."

"Until Max comes along."

Nicole said, "Read this version."

He humored her and did so. It was like reading an adaptation that had incorporated the accident into it. The scene they had shot that morning was moved to the end of the film, after the girl had gone back to her criminal lover. "So what?" Daniel said, closing the script.

"Look at the date on the cover. It was written *before* the accident."

Indeed, he saw that it was dated several months before shooting of the film even began. "Where did you get this?"

"In her things at the chalet. There is a copy in her computer as well. I was working on Charles's memoirs at the desk when I came across it. See the date?"

"You're saying that—"

"I'm saying, Inspector, that this proves that she tried to kill him! This was her plan all along. This was what she wanted, to have him dead, out of the way."

"This script certainly raises an eyebrow, but it proves nothing."

"She wanted him dead!"

He wasn't convinced in the slightest. "A screenplay is not motive. This is only one version of who knows how many versions she wrote. While it might help prove to a court that there was intent, it does not even suggest a reason as to why she would do such a thing."

"You can't arrest her?"

"Arrest her?" He had to laugh. "I can't even detain her. I can't detain anyone at this point. I need more than circumstantial evidence to proceed. I need motive and hard proof of it."

"You sound very frustrated."

He wasn't interested in what she thought. "Tell me about the morning of the incident. You arrived at the set before anyone else, with pastries for all, did you not?"

"*Oui, oui.* Usually they only have dry bagels."

"When you got there before sunup, was the prop trailer open by any chance?"

She blinked. "How would I know?"

"When did Bruce Borger arrive?"

She shrugged. "I'm not sure."

"After Bruce got there and unlocked it, was the trailer ever left unattended before they brought the glider out?"

"I was busy with the food. I have no idea."

"But didn't you tell Bruce that you took some coffee and sweets into the prop trailer for him, but he wasn't there?"

She tried to recall. "Yes, I think I found him in his own trailer, his office."

"So the prop trailer was empty when you were there looking for him?"

"I think so. Yes, probably."

"And anyone could have walked in there, loaded the rifle with bullets, slit the sails, and been out in less than a minute, never detected."

She looked uncomfortable. "Probably. That's when she could have done it, Inspector."

"That's when anyone could have done it," he said, "from the director of the film to the prop man to the girl who was starring in it . . . to the person who brought rolls and coffee."

Sixteen

The press had a field day once *Scandals* started production. Pairing the two hottest young stars in the business was an incredible coup for Maggie Nash, who was having a torrid affair herself with the male stud half of the partnership. Already the tabloids had printed scandalous headlines like MAX SNEAKS OFF WITH KRISTEN and WHAT MAGGIE DOESN'T KNOW! Though photographers weren't allowed on the set, the three were photographed everywhere they went, alone or together.

One titillating picture made it to the covers of nearly all the supermarket gossip rags. It showed Maggie holding a weeping Kristen to her breast, with Max looking on with an abandoned expression on his face. The truth was, Kristen had broken down in tears talking to Maggie about a scene she couldn't make work, and when Maggie had gotten Kristen to admit that the reason was it was too close to home—to Kristen's own relationship with her mother—she let Maggie hold her and comfort her. It was a woman thing, a moment that had no room for Max, or for any man. But the accompanying text made it seem as if Maggie and Kristen were having an affair under Max's nose. The threesome ignored it, knowing that all publicity was ultimately going to help them.

Max and Kristen were so comfortable with one another that several scenes were done in one take, which blew Maggie away. "I'll never hire anyone else for the rest of my career," she crowed.

It also blew Bruce Borger away. On set for every moment, the property master often found himself overcome with jealousy as he watched Max and Kristen create magic. Their sexual chemistry was palpable. He felt as if he were about to burst, for the more he watched Kristen do her scenes, especially the sensual, half-dressed ones, the more he wanted her.

The movie required a number of locations. They moved outdoors for a car race, filming in Long Beach, where a Grand Prix racetrack had been recreated just for the film, then up to San Francisco, where the rain and fog interrupted their plans for several days, and then to the wine country, where the weather cooperated and the last scene of the film was shot—long before others that came before it. In that scene, Tom, not able to give up on Claire, tracks her down to a little cottage her family owns but never uses. Claire, thinking him dead, is startled and shocked, and then thrilled at his appearance, with the happily-ever-after last moment a real tearjerker. The script called for dialogue, but Kristen was so overcome that she could not speak. Maggie left it as it was shot; there was no need for words when such powerful emotion burst from the screen.

Then they went to Seattle. They took the ferry to Bainbridge Island, one of the alluring San Juan Islands off the coast of Washington, and set up the cameras. In the scene it is night and there are few passengers. Claire is crying because she is so uncertain of what she wants in her life, especially now that she's engaged to Carl, whom she doesn't love. She really loves Tom, and finally, in this improbable place, Tom walks up to her on the deserted deck, presses her against the steel wall, her head against a porthole, and kisses her with fiery passion. Tom says, "You're never going back. We're here for a reason. We're here because we are supposed to be. You. Me. The two of us. I love you."

The passion of their kiss leads them to make love right there while standing on the deck under the quiet stars. It was a chillingly romantic scene, yet one that was startling, compelling. Anger and frustration fed the passion, leading to a power Maggie had not thought possible. She'd known it would be good, but not *this* good. The crew was absolutely mesmerized. Bruce Borger seethed as he watched. He actually thought Max was going to fuck Kristen right there in front of them with the cameras rolling. They did give a good impression of doing it, despite the fact that they did not go that far, but everyone believed that Kristen's screams of pain and delight and Max's orgasm were the real thing. And it was for Max, though he admitted this to no one.

The love scene they shot the next day in a grassy meadow on Bainbridge Island, feeding each other raspberries after they'd picked them in the wild, was nearly as hot, and the subsequent scenes in an old sleigh bed in a farmhouse location were as beautifully romantic as the others had been intense. This was an incredible screen couple, everyone thought.

Were they destined to be the same offscreen? The crew talked, as they always did, and provocative questions surfaced in the press. Constance Heller asked if Kristen was going to step in as the "other woman" in the great love affair between Maggie and Max. Other articles made comments about Maggie's age, and the fact that Max and Kristen were younger. Some portrayed Max as a stud puppy who had nailed the older woman as a career move.

Whatever the slant, the gossip rags had a field day, with leaked pictures of some of the scenes. One of them, which a wardrobe person had secretly snapped, showed Maggie looking at a near-naked Kristen and a very sweaty Max curled around one another in the sleigh bed. Maggie's expression was not that of a calm director. It was of a jealous woman scared to death.

Maggie's true feelings came out the morning after that scene was shot. Max had made love to her the night before, only hours after the filming was completed, like a wild man. Maggie was sore when she woke up. When Max dragged himself out of bed in the Seattle hotel, a silent and brooding Maggie was sitting in the window, smoking a cigarette, looking out over the Pike Street Market at the mist hugging Puget Sound.

He helped himself to coffee and joined her. "I love it here."

"America gives me the willies," she said acidly.

"Huh?"

"I never feel comfortable with everything in English."

This side of her he still didn't understand. "Are you trying to be cute?"

She turned to face him. "I'm being honest."

He sipped his coffee nervously, suddenly feeling much younger. To dispel her dark mood, he said, "Last night was great, huh?"

"Last night as in the movie? Or last night as in here?"

His eyes flickered. "Both."

"Mmmm. The scene was incredibly sensual. It'll play. Here was a little rough, if I do say so myself."

He grinned. "You like it exciting."

"You hurt me. What was that all about?"

"Passion. Feelings. You know."

"Guilt?"

He blinked. "Guilt? How so?"

"Oh, come on, Max."

He thought out his response before he gave it. "That scene with Kristen was acting, Maggie. It's in the script. I saved the real passion for you."

"Was that what it really was?"

"I don't get what you're after."

"The truth."

"The truth," he said, folding his arms on his naked chest, "is that Kristen turns me on, like you told me to admit, because I'm a guy and a guy can't help that. But you're my lover, and I respect that boundary. If you're thinking that the scene heated me up for you, you're wrong."

"I don't believe you," she snapped, hating herself for it, for she knew she was losing control.

He picked up on it instantly. "Stop being insecure. It's not like you."

"I'm a woman too, Max, not just a director and someone to screw."

He stood up and walked back to the bed. Sitting down hard on it, he said, "I don't think we should be having this talk now. You're too jealous."

She looked at him angrily. "What were you thinking about when we made love last night?"

"What?" he asked, perplexed. "What does anyone think of when they're making love?"

"Were you thinking of *her* as you fucked me?"

He got up and left the room without deigning to answer her.

On the set that afternoon, things were tense. Maggie took out her aggression on Kristen, who managed under the duress, but she wasn't being fair to the girl and she knew it, hating herself even more. Her apology was accepted, but Maggie knew that Kristen had figured out the real reason and was hurting because of it. For Kristen, it might be acting—Maggie knew she could pull it off. But she knew Max even better, and understood his limitations.

During a break, Maggie went up to him at a water cooler and said, "I'm sorry. You were right. I'm feeling insecure."

Max looked at Maggie with frustration. "That's your problem. I haven't given you any reason to feel that way. I love *you*. I'm in a relationship with *you*. I sleep with *you* in real life, with her only in the movies, and movies, as you know, are make-believe."

She kissed him on the cheek and walked away.

But the tension remained.

The scene where Max rips Kristen's evening clothes off in the water brought the issue to a crisis point. Maggie had decided to shoot in Mexico, near Rosarito Beach, so the crew relocated there. In the studio scene that preceded it, Max and Kristen were brilliant—Max was snide, drunk, awful, while Kristen teased him, egged him on, put him off, drove him crazy. The subsequent argument pulled out all the stops.

When they shot the outdoors scene, the sequence they had "rehearsed" at Turquoise Lake, the steaminess between Max and Kristen had never been hotter. Even the crew was astounded at how freely sexual they were with one another. The consensus was that this wasn't acting. Max had no shame showing his erection, and Kristen pranced around like a porn star. When he pulled her under the water and simulated making love to her, everyone—including Maggie—was sure, just like on the boat the week before, that was exactly what he was doing. The director in her wanted another take for technical reasons, but the woman in her couldn't go through it again.

She was moody back at their hotel that night, and Max knew why. "I didn't fuck her."

"It looked like it on camera."

"It was supposed to, wasn't it?"

"You're a fine actor."

He blew up. "Are we always going to have this problem? Are you always going to be jealous?"

"I'm not jealous."

He was scathing as he went on. "I was told Europeans aren't. I thought they had different values, weren't all screwed up by hypocritical morality the way we are. Man, you could sure fool me."

Maggie marched out, slamming the door behind her.

She had a glass of wine in the hotel bar and walked around the hotel grounds, then sat for a long time with her legs dangling in the pool. When she returned, she heard Max's voice softly talking on the telephone. The door to the suite's bedroom was slightly ajar, and she was sure he hadn't heard her enter because she had wanted to be careful not to wake him. Through the crack she could see that he was holding the phone in his left hand. She could hear him saying, "I think it's time I was honest with you. And maybe myself." Who the hell was he talking to at three in the morning? She moved closer to the door. "I can't do this in person, Krissy, because I'm a real coward." Maggie blinked. *Kristen.* "Listen, no—let me say this before I lose my nerve. I feel something for you, Kris. I know it's no secret I'm powerfully attracted to you sexually, but I think . . . I think I might be falling in love with you."

Maggie's breath was frozen in her throat. She wanted to walk in and slam the receiver in his face. Or pick up the extension and tell them their little talk was finished. But she knew that being so dramatic would only make them want one another more. Or was she jumping the gun? Did Kris feel the same way? "I'm confused," she heard him say, "because I do love Maggie, very much. That's my dilemma. That's the problem here."

Maggie couldn't stand it. She left as silently as she'd arrived.

In a fit of anguish, she shed her clothes and jumped into the hotel pool. A security guard came running, followed by a guy in a suit, wanting to see if she was all right. She told them in perfect Spanish that she was fine, wanted to be alone, just needed a fucking swim. Get lost, in other words. Since this was one of the best hotels on the Mexican coast, where odd requests were common, they accommodated her, though the security guard kept close watch from behind a palm tree, knowing that Hollywood people were even more litigious than others.

Swimming laps, Maggie thought about it. Hard. By the time she was exhausted enough to sleep, she knew how she would hold on to Max and not let Kristen steal him away from her.

From what she had discerned about Kristen, her sense was that she was the small-town Catholic girl suddenly awash in a glamorous world that she longed to taste. Maggie was sure her plan was going to work.

Seventeen

Kristen could not bear to look Maggie in the eye the next morning. She flubbed her lines, spilled coffee all over her dress in a key scene, and seemed agitated and annoyed whenever anyone spoke to her. The chemistry with Max, at the heart of the film, was suddenly nonexistent. She kept to herself, ate lunch alone, and locked her dressing room trailer each time she entered it, which was completely unlike her. No one knew what was wrong. Maggie did. She'd gotten the Catholic thing right; Kristen's guilt was overwhelming her.

Max showed no such signs of remorse. He acted as if nothing had happened. Maggie felt that he should at least feel some kind of shame after declaring his "confused" love for both of them. It only increased Maggie's feeling that inside his great strong man's body was a little boy. And, like all men she'd known, Max was unable to keep his dick in his pants.

Maggie didn't let on what she understood. She remained completely professional, trying to help Kristen get through the scenes, demanding her complete concentration, but when Kristen continued to stumble, she dismissed them both and continued with other scenes—upsetting the schedule—with the other actors.

In time, over the next few days, their rhythm returned. Kristen seemed to be back to her old self. Maggie figured she'd said a few Hail Marys and begged God's forgiveness. The fact that Max seemed to perk up the more Kristen did was even more worrisome to Maggie. His entire creative state now seemed to depend on his attraction to this girl.

After they did several scenes in Rosarito, in the studio originally built there for *Titanic*, they took a few well-deserved days off. They shopped the endless stands featuring everything from smelly dried starfish to intricate ironwork to charming handcrafted Mexican curios among a lot of kitschy crap. They gorged on lobster at Puerto Nuevo, a little town that was nothing more than a string of lobster restaurants, just down the coast. They took suites at Las Rocas, a whitewashed Moorish-looking place with turrets and vaulted ceilings made from brick and rough beams.

On the third night, they dined down the coast at La Fonda, a tattered, funky expatriate palace clinging to the side of a steep bluff overlooking the ocean, feasting on rare steaks and the best fresh tortillas they'd ever tasted. The margaritas were oversized, frosty, and tangy. Kristen was buzzed on her first one, and by the third she could barely remember her name. She sucked on the limes left in the bottom of the glass till Maggie pulled the goblet away from her face.

For dessert they ordered a delicious vanilla flan. It was time for the experiment to begin. Maggie dipped her index finger into the flan and let Max lick it. Kristen watched, giggled, then did the same, sticking her finger into the soft custard and letting him sensuously lick it from the tip. Then Maggie repeated the invitation, this time offering her finger to Kristen. The girl sucked the sweet off Maggie's finger.

When they left the restaurant, they walked along the road in search of a taxi. It was late, and the highway at this hour was deserted, even though the restaurant was one of the most popular places along the coastal route. "I'm scared," Kristen said as they walked in the darkness. Crashing somewhere beneath them could be heard the roar of the waves.

"You're drunk," Max said with a laugh. "And I think I am too."

Maggie put her arm around Kristen. "I'll protect you."

Kristen giggled. "Promise?"

"Promise."

Max said, "Great, 'cause I don't think I could protect myself right now. They got bandits on this highway?"

Maggie saw a set of car lights far away. "Yes. They rob drunken gringos." She felt Kristen's body tense, and she whispered into her ear, "Just kidding."

As the lights came closer, Max walked in the middle of the road and waved his arms. "Hey, help, three gringos *tres* sheets to the wind need a ride, *por favor*."

"Watch out," Maggie warned sharply. "You'll get mowed down."

Sure enough, the pickup truck roared by them without even slowing. Max would have been thrown a hundred feet had he stayed there. "Jesus," he muttered.

"Hey, behind us," Maggie said. More headlights approached, and they could clearly see it was a cab. Max waved, and the car stopped.

Safely deposited back at Las Rocas, they ventured out behind the building, settling in on lounge chairs near the spa. A couple was just leaving, and so they had the place to themselves. A wind was blowing from the ocean, almost making them feel cold. Max reached his hand down into the spa. "Nice and hot. Anybody up for it?"

Kristen barked, "Sí!"

"You'll pass out," Maggie warned. "Your blood alcohol surpassed the legal limit hours ago."

"Nobody's gonna arrest me," Kristen said petutantly.

"Nobody's gonna *revive* you after cardiac arrest in that pressure cooker, either."

Max kicked off his sandals and put his feet in. The jets were still running from the previous inhabitants' dip, and he loved the swirling sensation. He took his shirt off, shivering for a moment in the wind, and then quickly pulled off his cargo shorts. Naked, he slid into the churning water. Kristen kicked off her shoes, sat on the rim and dropped her feet in as well, but Maggie held her back from toppling into the water. "Just sit here," Maggie ordered. Kristen nodded.

"Man," Max said, stretching his arms out along the rim, "this is excellent."

"I'm thirsty," Kristen said.

"No more booze for you," Maggie warned.

"Water?"

Maggie thought that was a good idea. "You're probably getting dehydrated."

"They have bottled at the desk," Max offered.

Maggie stood up. "Be right back. And don't let her go into that water." She took off toward the building.

When she returned, she saw Max had risen halfway out of the water, his butt on the coping, leaning back, eyes closed. Kristen was leaning forward, kissing him. Maggie stood in shadows, not surprised, but gearing up for her move. It was now or never. After tonight they'd be fucking. If she didn't stop this—alter this—now, it would never again be in her power. She emerged from into the ghostly light of the pool area and said, "Water, children."

Instantly Kristen pulled away as Max slid back into the bubbling water. Maggie handed Kristen a bottle, Max grabbed one, and then Maggie, without a word, took off her shoes, slowly pulled the light shift she was wearing over her head, took off her bra, slipped her panties down and off, and joined Max in the spa, facing him. She saw Kristen watching her intently. Max, surprised and enthused, put his arms around her and felt her reach between his legs for his erection. "Mmmmm, knew I was coming?"

Max smiled. "Hoping."

Kristen was downing the cool water as if she had just crossed the Sahara. "Krissy," Maggie said when she was finished, "X's got a woody." She was making it clear this was *her* territory and she welcomed invaders.

"I know," Kristen giggled.

"Show her," Maggie said to Max.

"Huh?" he said, jarred.

"I said, *show* her. Modesty has never been a virtue you hold dear."

Max looked at her curiously. "All right." He lifted his pelvis above the water level for a moment, then leaned back down.

"Just like in the movies, huh?" Maggie asked Kristen, but didn't give her time to answer. Suddenly Maggie reached her arms around him. Grasping his buttocks with her hands, she lifted him above the water again. In front of Kristen, her eyes looking up to her, she took him in her mouth. Max closed his eyes and moaned, even more excited because Kristen was watching. He kept his pelvis arched upward while Maggie sucked him under Kristen's watchful eyes. Then Maggie took her lips away from Max and said to Kristen, "Your turn."

Kristen looked shocked, but the margaritas had turned her inhibitions into lustful eagerness. She brought her head down to Maggie's level. "Oh," she whispered, looking at Max's organ up close.

"Oh, yes," Maggie assured her. "It's okay, go ahead, he won't mind."

"No," Max gasped, agreeing. "He won't." He watched, propped on his elbows.

"But—"

Maggie said, "*I* won't mind either."

Kristen went down on him. Slowly, trembling a little, moving lightly up and down as Maggie held the base of his organ firmly. Max closed his eyes, flopped back on the cement, and gasped, not believing this was happening. Maggie whispered, "Good girl, he likes that. Yes, very good . . . take more, a little more . . . it's big and thick, isn't it?"

Kristen crossed from timidity to exuberance as Maggie urged her on, putting her other hand on the back of Kristin's head, guiding her, forcing her face down farther, until she had taken almost all of Max in her mouth. When she started to choke, she pulled her head away, and Maggie stroked her hair, kissed her gently on the cheek, purring, "It's okay, you did very well."

Then, only inches from the head of Max's throbbing organ, Maggie kissed Kristen lightly on the lips and said, "Give me some, honey. There's enough to share."

"*Grande chorizo*," Kristen giggled as Maggie licked it. Then Kristen did. They both laughed a little. Then Kristen took him between her lips again as Maggie moved down and gently touched his balls with her cheek. They switched places, and met as their lips crept up to the tip of the engorged shaft. Their tongues touched, and they found themselves kissing, kissing each other passionately, almost as if the point had been the kiss and Max's penis had somehow gotten in the way. They licked and sucked hungrily, kissing one another with their tongues searching until Kristen rolled over into the spa and joined them.

Max slipped down into the water and kissed Kristen hungrily as Maggie pulled the girl's water-logged blouse from her breasts. As Max sucked on Kristen's pert nipples, Maggie unzipped Kristen's shorts and pulled them down. She brought her hand up between the girl's legs and rubbed the soft silk of the panties, massaging her mound with her fingers, and then eased them inside the underwear to gently caress her. A moment later, she pulled the panties down, and off, and brought both hands to Kristen's buttocks and kneaded them, as Kristen moaned, biting Max's shoulder. Maggie reached down again and guided Max's hard cock between Kristen's legs, rubbing it as she did, kissing the girl's shoulders from behind. Max did not enter Kristen, but rather kept his penis there, hard between her legs, moving just slightly, driving her wild. Kristen and Max kissed madly. Maggie and Max kissed madly. Kristen's hands started to explore Maggie's body, first her hips, then her back, then her breasts, and finally they made their way down to her pelvis, around the spot, between her thighs, but never quite touching her lips—until Maggie grabbed her hand and forced it against her. Kristen shuddered. Maggie did too. Then Max put one finger inside Maggie, one finger inside Kristen, and told the women to grasp him as well. In only a second Kristen felt a wild orgasm, letting out a scream and biting her lip. Maggie groaned with pleasure as she dug her fingers both into Kristen's firm butt and Max's penis. Then Max cried out and felt himself exploding. He gasped and groaned and closed his eyes.

No one spoke another word.

They dressed after a while, went back to Maggie and Max's room, and fell into bed together, all three of them in a queen-size bed, and into a hazy, drunken, sensual sleep.

All but Maggie. As she lay next to the two younger lovers, her eyes were wide open, her mind sharp. She had done it. And it had worked. She'd counted on Kristen's inexperience, her desire to break free of convention, to experiment, her infatuation with Max, her vulnerability. The tequila had helped, certainly, but Maggie was quite certain they would not hear a "Christ, was I drunk last night!" defense from her in the morning. No, Maggie thought, the girl had enjoyed it.

As for Max, what could she say? He was a man. What man wouldn't get off on that scene? Wasn't that every man's fantasy, to have two women at once? She had them both where she wanted them.

Max would remain hers. Kristen was no longer a threat. There were three of them now. And, something Maggie hadn't counted on, she had liked it as well. The future just might be more interesting than she had anticipated.

Aspen, Colorado
Atop Ski Lift Number Four

"Bruce," Christopher Daniel said, walking over to Bruce Borger, who was just unbuckling his skis.

"Fancy meeting you here," Bruce said unhappily.

"The slopes are in my blood. How'd you do?"

"You don't care how I did," Bruce shot back at him. "So why don't you just ask me what you want to ask me and get it over with?"

Daniel set his skis against the wall of the building. He indicated for Bruce to follow him and moved to where there were fewer people, behind the chair lift station. "I failed to go over something with you when I saw you in Little Annie's. Can you give me some details about the morning of the incident?"

"Detail is what I do. I'm a prop man. My mind is a series of endless lists."

"The morning of the accident, can you recall what the director was doing?"

Bruce didn't understand. "You want a moment-by-moment account?"

"Whatever is necessary."

Bruce pulled his ski cap off and tousled his sweaty hair. "I opened the property trailer while Maggie and Max got coffee. They showed up together. Nicole had brought sweet rolls and stuff."

"What about the aircraft?"

"After coffee, we—Max and I—dragged the glider out. We set it in position. Max started to look it over, as I recall, when hair and makeup grabbed him."

"So he didn't have a chance to do his preflight checklist?"

"Don't think so."

"You didn't see him do that?"

Bruce said, "I wasn't studying Max. I was setting up."

"The glider?"

"The whole shoot." Bruce leaned against the building as if he were bored. "Movie making takes time."

Daniel smiled. "I wouldn't know."

"Like investigations."

"You in a hurry?"

Bruce shrugged, pulled a candy bar from his pocket, and bit into it. "So what are you getting at?"

"What were you doing prior to Max going to your trailer to get gloves?"

Bruce shot him a cold look. "Opening boxes."

"What kind of boxes?"

Bruce shoved the candy wrapper back into his ski jacket. "Costumes for the extras were shipped to us at the last minute. Maggie and I opened them."

"Directors usually do things like that?"

"Maggie does. Participates in everything."

"What were you opening the boxes with?"

"What?"

"Knives? Scissors? Fingernails? Teeth?"

Bruce didn't appreciate his attempt at humor. "Maggie used a box cutter and I had my Swiss Army knife."

Daniel raised his eyebrows. "You cut anything other than tape on a box?"

"My little finger." Bruce held up his left hand. "See, there's still a scab."

Daniel realized he wasn't going to get farther in that line of questioning. "Why did Max slug you?"

Bruce didn't answer. It had come out of left field and he wasn't ready. He bent down and made a snowball.

Daniel crouched down as well. "He hit you so hard he almost knocked your teeth out. Why?"

"He hated me," Bruce said, tossing the snowball at the wall. "Jealous that Kristen liked me, I guess. Hell, I don't really know."

"What happened in your trailer?"

"How would I know? He was alone in there."

"Come on, Bruce, speculate."

Bruce shrugged. "He goes in for gloves, emerges with a right hook. Little crazy, if you ask me."

"You think Max was paying you back for the punch you threw at him?"

Bruce blinked. "What punch?"

"At the Club Lodge. At the wrap party. I hear you called him a 'fucking asshole' and slammed your fist into his face."

"And he hit me back. Hard."

Daniel shot back, "Max said you were sick and dangerous."

"Had you been there, Detective," Bruce assured Daniel, "you would have seen that Max started it."

"Officer Stonecipher seems to think you did."

"That little brat with a badge?" Bruce laughed. "The kid isn't old enough to wipe his ass, much less know what came down that night."

"Tell me about the photograph."

Bruce sobered suddenly. "What photograph?"

"The one Max mentioned when he was flying."

Nervously, Bruce said, "Why do you think I know something about it?"

"Could Max have been referring to a photograph he'd found in your trailer when he went to get the gloves? Could the picture he talked about have been yours?"

Bruce glared at Daniel.

"You're sweating, Borger."

"The sun."

"What happened in your trailer that enraged Max enough to come out and slug you?"

Bruce took a deep breath. "I wasn't there, I told you."

"Come on, Borger."

"I already said, hell if I know."

"I think you do," Daniel said. "I think you know a lot more than you're telling me. But if you refuse to cooperate, there are others who will."

"What's that supposed to mean?" Bruce said angrily.

"Think about it," Daniel said, and walked away.

Eighteen

Maggie was right: there was no guilt at sunup. In fact, the morning began pretty much the way the night had ended—when Kristen woke up, she saw that Maggie's eyes were open as well. They glanced at each other over Max's sleeping form. He was lying between them, wearing only the boxer shorts he'd put on when they had gotten back to the room last night. Maggie looked down at his erection tenting the fabric, and Kristen giggled slightly. Maggie mischievously brought her fingertip down to the tip of the outline of his organ and tickled it. Max moaned a little in his sleep, and Kristen giggled again.

Now it was her turn, as Maggie urged with a nod. Kristen reached over Max's heaving chest and took a little lick of the nearest nipple. He didn't move. Then she bit it slightly. He jerked, feeling the pain, then tried to turn to his side, but Maggie's body prevented that. One arm flung itself across Maggie's stomach, and he covered her legs with one of his, giving Kristen the chance to pull the boxers down and pinch his ass. This time he jumped and moved onto his back again. "Don't tell me it's time to get up," he muttered, keeping his eyes closed as he brought his hands up to block the light coming through the window shutters. Maggie pulled open the fly on the boxers and freed him. Then she bent forward and licked.

"What the hell?" Max sat up, obviously wondering where he was and what was happening.

Maggie, her head still in his crotch, said, "*Buenos dias*, Mr. Jaxon."

Kristen moved her head to where Maggie's had been and kissed him there. "Time to get up. But I guess you're already up."

Max sighed. "Why can't I wake up like this every day?"

Maggie winked at him. "You can if you play your cards right."

Max kissed Kristen lovingly on the lips, then said, "Morning." He pulled Maggie's face up from his lower half and kissed her too. "Wow," he said, eyes riveted to hers, communicating to her he still didn't believe what was happening.

Maggie winked again. "I don't think I've had this much fun in years."

Kristen said, "I've *never* had fun like this. Not this naughty." With that, she wrapped her hand around Max's penis.

"I think it grew in the night," Maggie assured them. "Two women together really turns you on, huh? Typical male."

Max flopped back into the pillows. "Go ahead," he said with sappy resignation, "use me, do to me what you like, I'm just your love slave." He closed his eyes and waited. He could feel them moving on the bed, but nothing seemed to be happening. When he opened his eyes he saw why: they were exploring one another's bodies again. He watched.

And watched.

And the wonder never stopped.

The hours turned into days and the days turned into weeks and Constance Heller reported, "Not since the Liz-Richard-Eddie-Debbie (for those of you old enough to remember) scandal has there been such an interest in the sex lives of movie stars. And for good reason. This one—this threesome—tops them all."

At first they denied it in a demure, ingenuous way. "We are just great friends," was the official line, until photos started proving that a lie. When a reporter asked Kristen if she feared she was going to come between Max and Maggie, she replied provocatively, "I usually do!" When Maggie was asked what she thought of the photo some paparazzi shot of Max and Kristen lying nude together on Capri, she replied, "I think it's darling, don't you?" When someone wrote of "Maggie's intense embrace with Kristen" at a party at the Cannes Film Festival, Max said, "I'm the luckiest guy on earth. I get them both." Indeed, two days later, the threesome posed for photographs as erotically charged as they could muster keeping their clothes on. They couldn't keep their hands off one another. Finally, a brash reporter said, "Stop teasing. What's really going on? What's this thing all about, you guys?"

"We love each other," Max said.

"Equally," Kristen added.

"Deeply," Maggie said.

But even then the media didn't quite believe it. Some reported that Maggie had "put up with this from the kids" and pretended to be part of it for publicity or until the infatuation blew over. Others said that Max was having an affair with Kristen at the same time as he was having an affair with Maggie, and that jealousy was simmering between the women and it was only a matter of time before it exploded. One reporter wrote that Kristen and Maggie were doing the lesbian thing because it was chic and attracted attention. A man in England was paid by one of the British tabloids to tell "the shocking true story" of how he had had secret sex with Max endless times and this nonsense was all a cover for his staying in the closet. Michael Musto said it was *all* nonsense, all faked for shock value. Liz Smith was the only one who got it right: "This is a ménage à trois, pure and simple. It's real, folks. The only thing we don't know is who does what to whom on any given night. And, frankly, it ain't our business. Not that that will stop us any."

She was right. The threesome became the toast of the gossip rags, and as the stories got hotter and wilder, the publicity only snowballed. They rode a tidal wave of titillation and sexual openness that was unprecedented. Kristen told a reporter, "This relationship is genuine. We did not manufacture it to get us on this program, or in the papers. This is no stunt. This is real. There is a deep affection here, that we share in a way we will never be able to explain."

Max offered, "I'm the lucky guy, the man in the middle, and yeah, I'm worn out a lot. But Krissy is right. Jealousy doesn't exist. For instance, Maggie and Kristen have run off for a few days without me, and I was happy knowing they were each with someone to love."

Max's cell phone rang. Before he could even say hello, he heard a voice screaming at him. "I just saw that interview! Are you nuts? Who you trying to kid?"

"Hi, Nicky."

"Hi, Nicky, my ass. You made me start smoking again, you little prick. What are you doing?"

Max smiled, for she always made him feel better with her candor. "I'm not sure I know what I'm doing, Nicky."

"I know you're having fun."

"Yeah, well, sure."

"Hold the line." He heard her take a drag on the cigarette. "Now, you listen to me. I think this is all Mom's publicity stunt."

"I'm not sure. At times I think that, then it seems so real."

"My aching feet are real," Nicky snapped, "not your roll in the hay with two broads."

A doubt that had been nagging him for a while came to the surface, and he voiced it to Nicky. "The thing that worries me is, if Maggie needs someone else in the act, does that mean she's tired of me?"

Nicky snorted. "I've been around the block a few times, and I can tell you one thing. This ain't gonna end well."

"Nicky, I think most guys would really get off on this. I mean, hell, what a fantasy. And I love them both, in different ways. I really do. But rather than make me feel secure, it does just the opposite. With two of them, I can't sort out what I think about either one."

"Okay, you listen to Nicolina. First, did ya finish that film?"

"Yes. It's going to be released soon."

"Great. Don't do another with her."

"Who?"

"Maggie Nash."

"She's writing another that—"

"I don't care. She's already made you a star. Tell her thanks, and run for the hills. X, I'm telling you this 'cause I love you. You're a goddamned actor. So you're vulnerable, you don't want to hurt nobody. But, hey, Mom can take it. I just don't want to see you hurt."

"Nicky, to tell you the truth, part of me wants to break away, to see what Kristen and I could have. But I don't know. She's very into this too, and it's great fun and—"

"Hey, I'd knock on your head if I was there right

now. Maybe I'm just an old-fashioned broad, but the minute you got into this kinky stuff you dug your own grave. You wanna know what I think?"

"Yes."

"I think you're in love with Kristen but can't bear to leave Mom 'cause she's too powerful and you're too afraid to go it alone."

He ran his hand through his hair. The thought had occurred to him as well. "We're on such a roll right now, Nick, with the movie about to open and all the press we're getting. I just don't know when—"

"Don't sling hash to a waitress. And, more important, don't bullshit yourself."

In Avignon, Nicole and Charles attended a christening at their little church. Afterward, Nicole asked the priest to bless a rosary she had bought in a jungle market in Peru. "I find them very special," she said as she handed the rosary over, encased in a felt bag.

"I've never seen anything like this," the priest remarked as he slid it out of the bag into the palm of his hand. "The beads, they are so very different."

"Ah, exquisite," Nicole agreed.

"You don't want to know what we went through to find them," Charles commented with a shrug.

"I read about them in a novel," Nicole explained. "How they are made from beans harvested by Peruvian natives. They apparently feel the beans possess mystical qualities, which seems to me a blending of pagan superstitions and missionary Catholicism."

"Indeed," the priest said. "Well, we need all the help we can get with our prayers, don't we?"

Charles laughed. "We crawled up a goddamned hill—forgive the language here in church, Father—in the heat and rain to find the market."

"Only place they sell them," Nicole assured him. Then she hugged Charles. "It was worth it, wasn't it, darling?"

"You love them," Charles said, "and that's what matters to me."

The priest lifted his right hand, pressed his fingers together, and began the Latin blessing over the beads. When he was finished, Nicole took them and handed them to Charles. "I want you to have them."

"Me? But, my dear, you love them so much!"

"*Oui*, that is why I want you to have them. I love them as I love you."

Charles kissed her on the cheek. "You are the great blessing of my life."

That night, as Charles said his prayers kneeling at the side of their bed, Nicole handed him the beads, which he'd forgotten were in his pocket. He wrapped his fingers around them as Nicole knelt next to him, holding a rosary of her own. When they finished saying the rosary, she kissed her beads. He did the same with his. Then she kissed him on the cheek and helped him into bed.

An hour later, when she was sure that he was in a deep sleep, she picked up the Peruvian rosary and again pressed the beads to his moist lips. The stall owner where she had bought them had assured her—when she had sent Charles to rest in the shade of a palm tree—they were not dangerous unless you touched them to your wet lips. So she held them to

Charles's lips for several minutes as he wheezed deep in sleep, breathing in and out.

At one point, he coughed. When his tongue protruded from his lips, she pressed the blessed beads against it, making sure the beans got wet with saliva but careful not to touch the damp part herself. After replacing them in the felt bag on the dresser, she hurried into the bathroom to wash her hands thoroughly.

Snuggled in bed next to her husband, she remembered the stall owner telling her that they would take some time to have the desired effect, but that they were foolproof. The beans were lethal. But what was so good about them—she remembered the man's toothless grin, filled with childish glee and the sadism of a killer— was that the poison was impossible to detect.

Maggie holed up to do the final edit on *Scandals* with her trusted Ellie Storey, and Max knew she would not come up for air till she was finished. He welcomed his first real break from the camera in more than a year. And a break from the threesome, especially after speaking with Nicky Dee.

He had none of that nervous, aimless feeling of ennui that he'd experienced back in Paris when Maggie had edited *Fibs*. The difference was that this time he had Kristen. He suggested that they leave Maggie in Hollywood with her obsession and get away from it all in Aspen. Kristen had loved the Nash chalet, and she was delighted when he suggested they return there to unwind.

They flew to Denver, where Max rented a Subaru Outback. It took them a while to get out of the parking lot because they had to sign autographs for the thrilled tourists who recognized them. Once inside the car, Kristen popped open a bottle of water. "Is it true Maggie is setting the next film in Aspen?"

"She's rewritten an old script for us to do. It's the one she's now calling *Never Forget*."

"What's it about?"

"Revenge," he said with raised eyebrows. "She's changed the setting from a little lake in France—Le Lac Leman, it's called, near the Swiss border, I glided there—to Aspen. Pretty easy fix, actually."

"The Alps become the Rockies. Hey, how far is Telluride?"

"Farther than Aspen. Why?"

"I want to see where you won that glider competition."

He smiled. "You will. Maggie's writing it into the movie."

They drove through Colorado Springs, marveling at Pikes Peak and the Garden of the Gods, then through Cripple Creek and west to Aspen.

Everyone was predicting winter to be early and harsh this year. Snow already dusted the mountaintops. A light rain started to fall as they turned onto Snow Canyon Road, and it was pouring as they made their way up the steep incline to the cottage. They lit dozens of candles that they found in one of the pantry closets, and when the fire was roaring in the stone fireplace, they nestled in front of it and held each other, relaxing and enjoying the romantic atmosphere. With rain beating against the windows, they made love that was different from ever before.

"Let's sleep right here," Kristen whispered as Max curled up next to her on quilts they'd dragged to the floor in front of the hearth.

Holding her in his arms as she dozed off, Max realized something: he wasn't thinking about Maggie. In the past months, there hadn't been a time that he and Kristen had made love that Maggie was not a part of it. The force hovered over them constantly, which seemed inherent in a three-way relationship. But Maggie was more than just the third party. She was the foundation, the rock, the glue. Tonight, for the first time, their lovemaking had nothing to do with Maggie. Even in Maggie's house, he had thought only about Kristen.

The rain washed over the windows, and she said, "It sounded like this when I was a kid, up in my room, hearing it pounding on the roof."

He kissed her cheek. "I love you."

"And I you."

"No," he said, trying to explain. "I talked to my best friend, Nicky Dee, the other day. She said she believed I really loved *you*. And I do."

She looked deep into his eyes. She too knew this time was different. She let herself be swallowed by his arms and closed her eyes against his chest.

The rain-soaked terrain was iced over in the morning. Even the towering trees were covered with a frozen coating. After the sun poked through the clouds, though, the landscape became soggy, then had pretty much dried by two o'clock.

Max took Kristen to a nearby pass he loved. It was a brisk autumn day, and only a few crusty leaves still clung to the trees. The evergreens were unbowed, defiant with their brilliant green canopies. Max started bellowing, "The hills are alive, with the sound of music . . ."

"You know what?" Kristen interrupted. "You've got a great voice."

His lips twitched with humor. "Hmmm. Maybe we should turn *Never Forget* into a musical."

"I don't think so. I did *The Unsinkable Molly Brown* in high school," Kristen warned, "and one Colorado musical is enough."

They drove on to Telluride. Max showed her where he'd glided, a plateau that ended with a sheer drop from the mountainside, first discovered by gliding aficionados as one of the "perfect" ports. The valley was surrounded by mountain peaks, the winds were perfect, not too strong, especially at this time of year, and the view was astonishing. They could see all of Trout Lake from there, protectively surrounded by Sheep Mountain. "I love flying here," Max said. "This is where we're going to do it in the film." Max indicated the other hang gliders, aloft in the blue sky. "So let's do it. You and I."

"Huh? Now?"

"Why wait?"

In an hour, they were back, with a rented glider made for two.

Kristen looked down at the heart-stopping drop

from the edge of the plateau. "Are you sure it's smart to start *here*?"

"You only live once."

"X! Jesus, can't we try a beach first?"

"Don't trust me?"

"I don't trust jagged rocks, that's what I don't trust."

"That's what makes it exhilarating."

Finally, Kristen put her reluctance aside. He explained everything, showed her how to check the frame, the wires, the skin, the harness, again and again. Safety was the first and foremost consideration. And her fears melted into sheer wonder once they were airborne. She could not believe the feeling—weightless almost, her heart soaring with her body. She could feel the thermals—the rushes of hot air—that lifted them even higher. But the stillness was the most amazing part. Her ears could discern the wind through the trees. She actually heard birds' wings flapping as they got out of their way.

She held his hand as he guided them left, then right, up, down, in circles. She thought of the scene in *Superman* where Clark Kent takes Lois Lane flying. Her spirits had leaped when she watched that for the first time, and now she knew how Lois had felt. This was bigger than life, one of the most magnificent experiences she'd ever had.

"How long can we stay up here?" she asked after half an hour.

"Forever!"

Max kept them airborne for nearly an hour. When

they did land, it was a little hairy. Kristen put her feet down too fast, Max wasn't ready to touch down, and when her toes met the ground, she shouted in fright. He nearly fell himself, worrying about her at the time he was supposed to be in control of the craft. They tumbled to earth, ripped a little of the skin of the glider, but neither of them was hurt. Instead, they started laughing. When they unhitched themselves from their harnesses, they rolled around on the ground like kids. Kristen had brought a picnic lunch, which they ate there, watching other gliders taking off and dotting the sky. They broke open a bottle of wine, and by the time they returned to the chalet, they were both almost as high as when they'd been in the air.

The evening turned freezing. They cuddled in front of a roaring fire Max made, filled with logs and pinecones, read, relaxed, even dozed off. Around eight, Max made popcorn in a hand-held antique popper directly over the burning logs. Kristen melted salty butter and poured it over the kernels. They shared more wine. Then they made love.

The passion was intense, but this time it did not manifest itself in the usual acrobatics. They were like new lovers discovering one another's bodies. They took their time, savoring the pleasure, giving themselves time to feel everything the other was doing, losing themselves in a sea of passion. And that was the difference. This was not just sex, not just sensual pleasure, this was love. Max held himself inside her body for as long as he could without moving a muscle, looking deep into her eyes, kissing her, licking her lips and chin. His eyes seemed to say, *I want to stay inside you forever. Joined with you. Deep within you.* Kristen ran her hands over his buttocks and his strong back and his muscular shoulders as if she were pulling him further into her heart.

In the morning they had to fight to open the front door, for the snow that had fallen had already accumulated to eight inches. They shoveled a path to the car and dug it out. Then they built a lopsided snowman that they tried to fashion after the Oscar statuette, followed by snow angels they made in the blanket of untouched white behind the cabin.

When they left for the Aspen airport the next afternoon, it was with heavy hearts. Maggie had called. "The editing is done, and we're going right into the next one. Come back here." It was time to return to reality. The storybook vacation had come to an end.

In the car, Max seemed anxious. Kristen sensed it and asked him if it was because they were returning to Maggie.

"Yes. And no." He glanced over from the driver's seat. "See, I don't know what you think. I'm not sure how you feel."

She looked out the window at the white hills. "I love you, Max. I'm not really thinking far into the future. I've never been in love, you know that, so I'm not sure how it plays out or what you're supposed to do next. This has all been an education for me."

"Kris, the time's going to come when we have to decide. I mean, this can't go on, this three-way thing."

"Do you want it to stop?"

He swallowed hard. "Yes. I mean, the pleasure is great, but it's nothing anymore compared with what I feel for you. Something's changed. I only want you now."

She closed her eyes for a moment. "But we're going back to the opening of our film, and we're tied to Maggie for another. That's pretty impossible."

"Hey," he joked, "I thought I was the insecure one."

She put her hand on his on the center console. "I want to be with you, Max. Like today, like the other day in the sky, like last night in front of the fire. I want us to be a couple."

He could feel his heart soaring. Happiness flooded through him. "We have to tell Maggie. I mean, *I* have to tell Maggie. This is my responsibility. I just don't want to hurt her. She's been good to me."

"You know her much better than I do," she said softly. "I'll leave it to you to find when the time is right. But I'll warn you of something, X."

"What?"

"It's not going to be easy."

Nineteen

The first thing Max did when he and Kristen returned to Los Angeles was arrange dinner with Maggie. She truly had finished editing, and the final print was being rushed to open in theaters on Thanksgiving Day. Max was glad to hear it, for he knew this way she'd be more receptive to what he and Kristen had to tell her. Besides that, she was excited about the film, pleased with the outcome, sure it was going to be a smash. Max dropped Kristen at her apartment, then went to the hotel to shower and change, planning to meet Maggie, who was coming direct from the studio, at a restaurant. A quiet, intimate place in Santa Monica where they could have the discussion they needed to have.

But Maggie surprised Max in the shower. After he'd soaped up and covered his hair with shampoo, she suddenly appeared next to him. He gasped, caught water in his mouth, and started to choke. "Well," she said, "I know you're excited to see me, but please don't expire before the movie breaks."

"What are you doing here?"

"I was a mess. Needed to freshen up. You'll help me." She kissed him on the lips and took his hand, which still held the soapy loofah, and pressed it down between her legs. "Oh, Max, you're going to love your performance. It's incredible."

He didn't know what to do. He felt his dick rising, but that was an automatic response he had little control over, especially now that she was fondling it. What he knew was that his emotions weren't there. His heart was with Kristen. He could not do this. He felt he was betraying the girl he loved. He backed away slightly.

She pressed him to the cold marble wall, her breasts pinning him. "Max," she said, "I'm so horny, I'm so psyched, I've got so much to tell you both . . . wish Kris were here." She tried to kiss him again, but he turned his head. "What's wrong?"

He knew he could tell her. But this wasn't the right time. Maybe he would be stronger in Kristen's presence. He had to get out of this situation. "I have to pee," he said weakly.

She blinked, looked down at his hard penis, and said, "How?"

It was the perfect excuse. "That's why I gotta get out of here." With that, feeling stupid, he opened the glass door and jumped out, still covered with soapsuds. He toweled himself slightly, then walked into the adjoining toilet room just for effect, and stood there wondering how he was going to get the shampoo out of his hair.

"You are going to be nominated this time," Maggie called from the shower. "Mark my words. Everyone who's seen it, even Marty, is struck by your performance. You and Kristen have a chemistry on-screen that you don't even come close to off. Max, this film is going to make you."

"Wow," he said, believing her. And with that, he felt he owed her even more. And that was just the problem.

"The buzz is, Elvis Mitchell is giving you a rave in Friday's *New York Times*. Max, when you're done whizzing, bring one of the robes over here, okay, darling?"

Max flushed the toilet. He found one of the robes in the closet and hooked its hanger on the towel bar near the shower, where steam and Maggie's singing voice were rising. He turned on the water in the sink and stuck his head under the faucet to rinse his hair. And felt himself sinking. Was this how he was going to repay everything she had done for him?

"Great dinner," Kristen said, finally pushing her chair away. They were at Ivy at the Shore in Santa Monica. The food had been exquisite, but Max had barely eaten a thing. Maggie had talked of nothing but the film and the heat its impending release was generating. She told them there was a good chance that if the opening was as big as they had predicted, they might be on the cover of *Newsweek*. Under the table, Kris had felt for Max's hand, and squeezed it, knowing how difficult this was going to be for him.

Then, over coffee, Kristen took the lead. "Maggie, there's something I have to tell you, something *we* want to talk to you about."

Maggie's demeanor changed at Kristen's grim tone. She knew the news was not going to be good. "Yes?"

Kristen continued, "I know this is hardly the time, but timing is something we can't always control. Being together has been wonderful, all of what we have, what we've done, the fun and the intimacy, the—"

"Get to the point."

Max grasped Kristen's hand again under the table. Kristen said, "Maggie, I just can't go on with it. I've been uncomfortable for some time now, and I think it's best to be open about it."

Max was amazed that she put it that way. And he was glad. It sounded less like a conspiracy. It would be easier on Maggie if they individually stated their points of view. Kris was going first, and then it would be his turn.

"I have loved this, every minute of it, but it's run its course."

Maggie's eyes flashed to his. He bowed his head, avoiding her glare.

"It snuck up on me," Kristen explained.

"In Aspen, I suppose?" Maggie snapped.

"It's been coming to the surface for a while."

"You're in love with Max, right?"

Kristen nodded. "Very much so. Very deeply. So this threesome has to end."

Maggie fingered her coffee cup. "I see. So. You two

are planning on going off and setting up housekeeping?" There was no answer. "Max?"

Max knew what he was supposed to say. He was supposed to say yes, that he and Kristen were going to move in together and be a couple. But he had heard this tone from Maggie before, and he was fearful of it. She could create, but she could also destroy. Plus, she had a right to be angry, after all she'd done for him. At that moment he realized he wasn't willing to hurt her. Maybe he would take a small step rather than a big one, and let things happen more naturally.

"I think," he said unsteadily, "maybe all three of us should live apart for a while. Give us all time to think things over."

Kristen's mouth dropped open in astonishment.

Max could see she was shocked and disappointed. He had promised to tell Maggie they were going to be a couple, and now he was backpedaling. He started babbling on about how "it had gotten too intense" and "we all need to clear our minds." As he talked, Kristen stood up. Without another word, she picked up her bag, gave him a hurt look, and walked out of the restaurant.

Maggie watched her go. Then she shrugged. "Oh, well, all good things must come to an end."

Her attempt at humor only made him feel worse. "I'm sorry."

She wasn't. "We were fine pre-Kristen, and we'll be fine post-Kristen." She reached across the table and took his hand. "Perhaps she's right. Perhaps it has run its course."

He withdrew his hand. "I meant what I said," he reiterated.

"What?"

"It's over. We all need time alone."

She began to tremble. "I have no such need."

"Maggie, it's never going to be the same, ever again."

She looked into his eyes for a long moment and then slumped against the banquette, looking like someone had just shot her.

"Kris, open the door, please!" Max begged just outside her apartment.

Through the wood, she said, "There's nothing more to say. Go home to Mother."

"Kris, please, give me a break here."

He heard the chain move, the click of the lock. She yanked the door open, standing in her nightgown. He could see she had been crying.

"I went back to the hotel and moved out."

She blinked, then brightened slightly. "Are you moving in here?"

"Can I get out of the goddamned hallway?"

She let him in, and he took a seat on the sofa. She chose a chair as far away from him as possible, as if to protect herself. "Okay, talk," she said.

"I'm not the heel you think I am. Maggie has feelings too. She can get hurt just like anybody, and I just don't want to destroy her."

"U.S. Special Forces couldn't destroy Maggie Nash."

He brought a hand up to his forehead, rubbing it

fiercely. "Listen, nothing's changed. I meant what I said in Aspen. We are going to have a life together. It's just that we have to take it slow. We have another movie to do with Maggie. She'll sue our asses if we try to walk out on that commitment."

"Who said anything about not working with her professionally?"

Max was exasperated. "It'll be hell, you know that! She brought us together. We can't just say thanks and shove her aside and then expect to work with her like nothing's happened. All I'm asking for is some time, Kris. Time for Maggie to get used to the idea. We'll make it look like we're living alone, but we'll be together. It's just that Maggie won't have to know. Until she recovers."

His speech took her breath away. "How dare you suggest that? Until Maggie *recovers*." She stood up, raising her voice. "Why don't you pick up your balls from wherever Maggie tossed them after she cut them off? Tell her you love me and you're going to be with me, and if she doesn't like it, too bad. Max, I'm not sneaking around for anyone." She walked to the door. "You go live alone, or go live with her, I don't care. Just don't expect me to be waiting for you when you decide you can jump off the Nash yacht and swim for yourself." Without giving him a chance to say another word, she opened the door and ordered, "Get out."

Max sat in the borrowed car for nearly an hour, feeling damp and cold from the ocean fog. He had two choices tonight: return to Maggie or go back to his own apartment. It was still vacant, rent paid up, used only by Nicky Dee's relatives when they visited town. To return to Maggie would mean he would lose Kristen forever, he knew that. But going to his own apartment might cause the same result. So the question was, Whom could he ultimately not live without? The answer was Kristen. So he would go to Los Feliz.

As he started the car and headed through town toward his old neighborhood, he told himself that Kristen would calm down. She would hate him less tomorrow, and even less as they went on their publicity tour for *Scandals*. In time, she would see that he was committed to her and that pulling away from Maggie gradually was the best thing for them all.

At two in the morning, he slid into a bed he had not slept in for almost two years, feeling lonelier than he had ever been.

At the same hour, Maggie Nash sat on the balcony of her Beverly Hills Hotel suite, drinking straight gin. She had been alone most of her life, she wryly thought, so what was so difficult about tonight? She figured things would be bumpy for a few days, but then they'd get back to what they had had before Kristen came into their lives. But was that going to work? Or had things changed too much? Maggie had instigated bringing Kristen into their relationship to hold on to Max anyway, so losing her really wasn't that much of a loss, or a surprise. Or was it? Maggie was mature enough to know that no three-way love affair could sustain itself over time.

But what she hadn't counted on was the terrible

emptiness she was trying to ignore. And Max sticking to his guns. She thought his little speech after Kristen had left the restaurant was just a bluff. When he packed and told her again that he had to do this, she was dumbfounded. She ordered the bottle of Tanqueray from room service and waited for him to return. After an hour, she started to give up hope. Now she was certain he was not coming back. Perhaps ever.

And she was terrified. A feeling she'd never felt before. She'd always been the survivor, the strong one. No one had ever gotten under her skin. No one had ever stolen her heart. Until now. Now she felt adrift and exposed. Even the liquor wasn't helping to anesthetize her fears. And the growing awareness of what she'd lost.

Twenty

Scandals opened on Thanksgiving, and if the threesome had thought their lives were an open book already, now they were dissected in public. Newspapers and magazines gushed glowingly about the film and ran long articles on them. The media couldn't get enough because the public couldn't get enough. Though the film did not break the record for the biggest single opening in history—nothing would ever come close to *Harry Potter*—it did come in at number twelve. Maggie was thrilled.

Publicly. Behind the scenes, Maggie, Max, and Kristen were miserable. They did what they needed to do to promote the film, then retreated to their own individual corners. They hardly spoke to one another when cameras were not on them. Maggie made it clear that principal photography would begin almost immediately on *Never Forget* and that this Christmas would be a working one. The actors would have no choice.

Kristen had to tell her parents that she would not

be coming home to Wisconsin for the holidays. They worried that she would be alone, but she assured them she would not. She had someone who cared about her. Bruce Borger was not only waiting in the wings, he had been hired as the property master on *Never Forget*, so they saw each other daily as they prepared to go into production. He started picking her up each morning to take her with him to the studio, and in the evening they had dinner together, unwinding, enjoying one another's company.

That's why he became concerned one day when she didn't come down after he blew the horn. He dialed her cell phone, but there was no answer. At the door, he called her name, very worried. She opened it, looking pale. "What's wrong?"

"I threw up." She looked more startled than sick.

He made her some tea, made her rest a little, and tried to figure out what it might be. Flu bug? Anxiety? She'd shared with him all her feelings about Maggie and Max. He felt the tension she was under when she worked with Max in rehearsal, and especially when she was with Maggie. The director treated her like dirt, obviously blaming her for the loss of Max. Everyone knew he had left Maggie. Everyone knew the threesome had fallen apart.

Kristen got sick again, at the studio this time, two days later. Driving her home, Bruce said, "You're going to see a doctor."

"Maggie had the guy at the studio look at me yesterday when I almost fainted."

"What'd he say?"

"Stress."

"Could you be pregnant?"

She stiffened in her seat. "Don't be silly."

He shrugged. "It's not really such an outrageous possibility. You never know."

"I do know. I'm fine, really."

But she was not. She was moody, standoffish, ornery throughout the two weeks they filmed on the set. The day they were to fly to Aspen—most of the film was being shot on location there—Kristen suddenly felt dizzy while waiting in the airport. Max noticed it and steadied her. "You okay?"

She closed her eyes for a moment, then nodded. "I think so."

"Kris, what's wrong with you?"

She suddenly let down her guard, perhaps because he was the only person she could really tell about this fear. "Max, I'm scared."

"Scared of what?"

"What if I'm—"

Just then, Bruce walked up, and she never finished the sentence.

But Max wasn't going to let it go. In Aspen, he was determined to find out what she had held back in the airport. He found her, with Bruce, in the Hotel Jerome restaurant, Jacob's Corner, where they had just had lunch. "Okay," Max said, sitting astride a chair at their table, "what the hell is going on?"

Surprised to find him confronting them, Bruce said, "I don't think Kris is your business anymore."

"Krissy will always be my business," Max replied forcefully. He looked at her. "I want to talk to you. Alone."

Kristen touched Bruce's hand. "I do need to tell him."

"Tell me what?" Jesus, he thought, was she serious about this asshole? So quickly? He was giving Maggie time to adjust to life without them both, but his love for Kristen had not changed. Had hers for him? He couldn't believe it. He told himself he had to be jumping to conclusions.

Bruce started to say something, but Max cut him off. "Listen, we want to be alone, okay, buddy?"

She nodded to Bruce. "I'd like to do this alone."

"You'll be okay?" Bruce asked, touching her shoulder.

Max wanted to spit. "Yes, she'll be okay, for Christ's sake." Why was he treating her like she was in some kind of danger?

Bruce finally got up and left, but not without kissing Kristen on the cheek. When he was gone, Kristen said, "You have to understand, he's very protective of me."

He had to ask. "Do you love him? Are you having an affair with him?"

She was so surprised by the assumption that she laughed out loud. But in another second, her outburst turned to tears, and then she reached across the table and clasped Max's hands in hers. "I'm going to have a baby."

He felt like someone punched him in the gut. It jolted him. He stared at her, but she could not bear to look him in the eye. "That can't be."

"Why not?" she said quietly.

There was no answer to that, least of all from him. It was certainly possible, even probable. He touched her arm. "How long have you known?"

She pulled it away abruptly. "I suspected for several weeks. I missed my period at Thanksgiving. Bruce took me to a doctor this morning. He confirmed it."

"I used condoms."

"They don't always work." She shook her head in misery. "I didn't want this."

"I didn't either."

She sat bolt upright. "I didn't want this *this way*."

"Huh?"

She was holding back tears, and he realized what she meant. She did want a baby—if the right man wanted her.

"Bruce knew before I did?"

She nodded. "He was the only person I could talk to. He suspected it too."

"What about me?" he said, devastated.

She felt uncomfortable talking in the restaurant. "Let's get out of here, all right?"

They left and walked up Main Street without talking for a few minutes.

"I remember the first time we did this," Max said.

"Yes," she replied warmly. She took a deep breath. "Max, Bruce has been a good friend. He told me I had to tell you."

"Of course," he said, putting his arm around her in comfort. "But, Krissy, what are you going to do?"

"I have no idea. I've never been so confused in my life."

"I understand. Me, too. Man." He kissed her frozen cheek. "I love you. You know that. We'll deal with this."

"I know *I* will."

He faced her. "What does that mean?"

"It means that I don't think you will."

"Gimme a break here, Kris," he said weakly.

"That's why I've held it in, X! I was afraid to tell you because I know you don't want this."

"Don't put words in my mouth."

She pulled her hand from his grasp. "Well, do you?"

"Christ, how do I know? Talk about too much too soon. I can't process this fast enough to give you answers now."

Kristen was wound up tight. "Will you leave Maggie?"

"Hello? I did leave Maggie!"

The dogged look in her eyes didn't change. "I mean, face her and tell her that you are going to marry me. All you did was cover your butt, leading Maggie on, making her think there might still be hope for you two."

"I did not!"

"Oh, come on," Kristen said accusingly. "I see the way she looks at you still. I know you're too afraid to commit to me."

He felt his knees giving out. "Kris," he tried to say in a calm tone, "I'm not. I will commit to you. Hey, give me a little time here, I just got hit with this."

She stopped walking and suddenly seemed filled with despair. "I know what's going to happen."

He moved to comfort her, take her in his arms. "Krissy, you're very upset, you're almost hysterical. This can't be good for the baby."

"You *care* about the baby?"

He was startled. "Why are you so angry?"

She brought her fist to her lips and bit down.

He'd had enough. "If you won't tell me, I'll give you a chance to chill." With that, he pulled away and started across the snow-laden street toward his car.

"X!" she cried out, running after him. He turned to face her in the middle of the street. She grabbed his hand and tugged for emphasis. "I'm mad because you had a chance to tell Maggie already and commit to me, but you reneged. I don't trust you. I don't believe you're going to do it."

Max put his hand firmly on hers. "I'll tell Maggie it's over forever, if that's what you want, and I'll also tell her that I'm going to marry you, because that's what *I* really want."

A car skidded to avoid them. They hurried to the curb. "If we live that long," Kristen said, and started chuckling. He did too, pulling her to him. They held each other close, their laughter overriding their tears.

Before he got into the car, Kristen said, "This makes it easier for you."

"What does?"

"The baby. Telling Maggie. It's the perfect excuse."

He shook his head. "Don't ever call our child an excuse."

But after he kissed her and slipped into the cold car, the old fears kicked in. He put the key into the ignition and started the engine. As he waited for it to warm up, he felt his resolve hardening, and finally thought, yes, I can do it. He headed toward Snow Canyon Road. Determined that this time he would not let Kristen down.

All the way to the Nash chalet, Max marveled at something he never had given thought to in his life: that he would be a father. The idea both scared him and gave him confidence. He'd done a production of *Carousel* once, and started singing, "My boy Bill will be rough and as tough as can be . . ." Then he thought about what it would be like to have a beautiful little girl, a miniature version of Kristen, maybe an actress herself one day. How do you change diapers? he wondered. He had to save for a college fund, had to start now. Where would they live? He wanted to meet Kristen's parents now because they were going to be his child's grandparents. Yet when he turned up Snow Canyon Road, he almost headed the other way—to drive off, to the other side of the world and hide. All this frightened him to death.

It was his day for shocks. When he rang the bell at the chalet, he expected Maggie or the maid to answer. He steeled himself for what he had to say. But Nicole opened the door. He stood there in the falling snow with his jaw slack, gaping. "What are *you* doing here?"

"*Joyeux noel!*"

Charles appeared behind her, looking tanned and robust. "Happy holidays and all that crap," Charles said, swatting him on the back. "Come on in, get your ass outta that cold air."

"I can't believe you're here," Max said as he walked inside and unwrapped his scarf from his neck. "This a surprise visit?"

"Sure as hell is," Maggie said, coming down the stairs in sweatpants and sweater. "Just about floored me."

"Family should be together during the holidays," Nicole said, taking Max's hand. "And we are all family."

Max glanced at Maggie. "What are you doing here?" she asked.

"I wanted to . . . I was going to . . ." He just couldn't do it, not in front of other people. He shoved his hands into his pockets and made up something. "I was going to ask if you wanted to go caroling."

They all laughed. "Come on in by the fire," Charles invited him with a slap on the back. "We'll open a great bottle of Cotes du Rhone that I brought with me."

"Where's Kristen?" Nicole asked Maggie, but she did not answer.

Several hours later, the Nash family, along with Max, dined at the Century Room in the Jerome. Max had never found a moment to talk alone with Maggie back at the chalet, and he realized that now he would not be able to do it tonight. He'd had too much of the delicious Cotes du Rhone, and was still drinking, a fine Merlot that Maggie had ordered at dinner. In fact, he was feeling so good that when Kristen walked through the lobby and happened to notice all of them in the restaurant, he had his arm slung around Maggie's shoulder at the table.

Later that night, unable to sleep and wanting to do for Max what Max obviously was too much of a coward to do, Kristen jumped into the Subaru and drove out to the Nash chalet. Maggie was shocked to find her standing at the front door. "Kristen, what are you doing here?"

"I need to talk to you. Before we break the couple of days for Christmas."

Maggie was still mystified, but she stepped aside. "Sure. Tea?"

Kristen nodded. "I see that Charles and Nicole are here," she said, following Maggie into the kitchen.

"Asleep. Tired from the journey, plus we drank too much wine."

"Is Max here?" Kris really wanted to know if Max had come back with Maggie.

Maggie gave her a shrewd look. "No, he's not."

Kristen breathed easier, glad to hear it.

Maggie made her some herbal tea, poured herself a gin and tonic, and suggested they go to the living room. It was snowing again, and the fire would keep them warm. Kristen brought her legs up on the chaise there, pulling a knitted throw over her feet. Maggie set the cup and saucer down on a nearby ottoman.

"Thank you," Kristen said.

Maggie sat facing her. Had Kristen decided she missed the relationship? "It must be something big to bring you here alone. And this late."

Kristen got straight to the point. If Max couldn't do it, she would have to. "I'm pregnant."

Maggie's gin and tonic burned her throat. The enormity of the words was not lost on her. It fell into place for Maggie—Kristen's moodiness in the past weeks, how withdrawn she had become. Not knowing what to say, Maggie made an attempt at humor. Holding her glass in the air, she said, "Good thing I didn't bring you one of these."

Kristen managed a slight grin.

"Of course, my mom said she smoked and drank like a fish when she was carrying me." She laughed. "Oh, hell, maybe that's why I'm like I am." Maggie moved closer to her. "Does Max know?"

Kristen nodded. "He was going to tell you this afternoon."

"So that's why he came out here." Maggie understood now. "I guess with Nicole and my father showing up, he didn't get to tell me."

"Good excuse for him," she said dully.

Maggie asked, "Max going to marry you?"

"I hope so."

"You're his true love. I'm smart enough to know that. I've always known that. That's why I made it happen." She raised her glass, took down a good slug of gin.

"Made what happen?"

The rim of the glass lowered, and Maggie looked

over it. "I was the aggressor, if you've forgotten. I brought you into our relationship so I could hold on to him."

Kristen looked surprised. "It was planned?"

Maggie's face hardened. She laid it out for her. "I'm never not in control." Then she looked wistful. "Do you think he loves me?"

Kristen didn't need to think about the answer. "Yes. He does. But it's a different kind of love from what he feels for me." Kristen nodded and drank more of the soothing tea. "All my life I've wanted to have a child. I want what my parents had, what they have, that kind of security and those kinds of values. This has all been crazy, but it's been my—what? Rebellion, maybe? *Isadora goes wild!* I had a pretty strict upbringing and lived that way till you two came along. I'll remember this time fondly, no regrets. It was something I needed and wanted and did with open eyes."

Maggie tried to joke again. "Actually, your eyes were closed most of the time."

Kristen grinned. Then she softly said, "But it's over now."

Maggie took a gulp of her drink as the reality hit her. "I've known that for a while. Honestly." Her voice was genuine, almost spiritual, as if she were cutting through the layers to find the true emotion. "I have come to feel very close to you. It hurts thinking we three will never be together again."

This confession made Kristen uncomfortable. "You'll survive. You have the power."

"You sound like you blame me for that."

Kristen squirmed. "I love him, Maggie. I want to marry him. He says that's what he wants as well."

Maggie said sharply, "You really believe that?"

"I'm not sure of anything."

Maggie finished her drink. "Don't get your hopes up. Max is a child, we both know that. That's what makes him so appealing."

Kristen had to agree. "He'll never really grow up."

"Isn't that partly why we love him?" Maggie asked.

"You seem okay with this," Kristen said.

Maggie's voice took on an edge that Kristen had never heard before except when she was directing. "Yeah, well, who really knows or cares how I feel? We have a movie to finish together, the three of us. And that's just what we are going to do." She stood up. "We're on location at six o'clock sharp."

As Kris stood in the snow, shivering, waiting for them to set up the next shot, Bruce brought her some cocoa. "Listen," he said, "I know it's not the best time, but there's something I have to tell you. Max is a coward, we both know that. I'm not. I'm offering to marry you, Kris. It don't care that it's his baby. I'll raise it as mine, and I'll be the best father ever."

She closed her eyes. She didn't want to hear this, especially not now.

But Bruce continued. "I know you don't trust him. You keep pushing him away, even in this time of real need. He's never going to live up to what you expect of him, Kristen. Give me a chance, and I will. I'll make you very happy."

The assistant director called her to the cameras, thankfully giving her the opportunity not to answer.

But when she walked away, Bruce muttered angrily, "What the fuck does Max Jaxon have that I don't?"

After the shot was wrapped, Max, who had a terrible hangover, tried to explain to Kristen what had happened when he'd gone out to tell Maggie the previous afternoon. Kristen wouldn't listen. When he begged her to hear him out, she said, "Listen to me for a change. I told Maggie myself. I went out there last night and did what you should have done." With that, she walked away from him, disgusted.

For the next two days, shooting went on, and, being professionals, they did their best to mask their personal feelings and get the work done. But it wasn't easy. Off the set, they barely spoke to one another. They took their meals separately. They put on happy faces for the rest of the cast and crew, but Bruce saw the sadness and turmoil behind the facade. He seemed particularly anxious and overzealous in his caring for Kristen. In a piece of business on a ski slope, he so overreacted when Kristen took a small fall in the snow that Maggie, furious, ordered him off the set for a few hours to get his priorities in line. "You care for the props," she said harshly, "and leave the actors to me."

The next day, the takes went so badly that Maggie

decided they would not break for Christmas at all, that they would work straight through. After her speech, though, Kristen was unable to complete any of her scenes satisfactorily, and Maggie shouted at her. When she went to her dressing room later to apologize, Maggie found her packing. "What are you doing?"

"I'm going home to my parents."

"You're *what*?"

"I have to get away."

Maggie said sternly, "Let me remind you that you have a movie to finish."

Kristen slammed her suitcase shut. "I can't stand it, Maggie. I'm too angry, too disappointed. I can't do scenes with him like everything is all right!"

Seeing her distress, Maggie pulled Kristen into her arms. "I know, I know," she said softly. "You're under incredible pressure."

"I don't know what to *do*! I've got to get away."

"Maybe you do, maybe I would too," Maggie generously responded. "Listen, if I can arrange a week off for you, would you stay tomorrow to complete the ski run sequence?"

Kristen nodded, grateful for the offer. "I just feel I can't be here anymore." She slumped onto the bed.

Maggie sat next to her. "You've not spoken to Max in two days except reading lines in the script. He's had a chance to process the news by now. Why don't you talk to him?"

Kristen shook her head. "No point."

"No?" Maggie said. "Well, I have another, contrarian idea. We all seem to be miserable alone. We were happy together. We all three could raise the baby—"

Kristen snapped, "The three of us? What are you, demented?"

"I know it may be unconventional, but—"

"Unconventional? Your whole *life* has been unconventional, Maggie!" She burst to her feet. "You're from a different world, sophisticated and cosmopolitan and ironic. Hollywood, Europe, the Orient. Values are different on your planet. They're not the kind I was taught in Wisconsin. And don't smirk, please. I honor the way I was brought up. It's the way I want to live my life."

"I'm not laughing at you," Maggie said, subdued. "I envy you."

Kristen stopped dead. "What?"

"You have no idea what it's like never knowing what a simple, real life is like, never feeling the security of parents loving one another, being fearful of having children because you're afraid you'll do to them what your parents did to you, never giving up control for happiness. Oh, you have no idea, little girl."

"I can only be true to myself. I'm sorry if I've hurt you."

Maggie softened. "I know I haven't hurt you. My conscience is clear there."

Kristen set a hand on her shoulder. "I don't blame you for anything. You've been wonderful, my best friend, a partner, a lover. You've guided me and given me so much. I could blame you for your influence over Max, but he gives you the control because that's what he needs. But I'm me, and this is over for me. There is simply no alternative."

Maggie took a deep breath, knowing she would not win this battle. But there was one issue they had not yet cleared up. "We still have to finish the film."

"I wish I could just say get Gwyneth," Kristen laughed. "But I won't let you down. Give me that week with my parents. I'll think things through and I'll be back to finish it. I promise you."

Maggie was on the verge of tears. Emotion flooded her face. "I'm sorry. I'm so sorry."

Kristen leaned down to embrace her. "I am too, Maggie. I am too."

They finished the ski slope sequence without problems the next day, and Maggie announced the change in schedule to accommodate Kristen's sudden trip to see her family, saying that her father was very ill. It was a lie. And Max knew it.

Early that evening he knocked on her door. Kristen was almost packed. She was catching the last commuter flight to Denver, and then on to Madison.

"I know you don't have much time—"

"There's nothing more to say, X."

"A little while ago I finally found a moment alone with Maggie. I tried to tell her."

"You're a little late," she snapped, closing a suitcase.

He nodded. "I just wanted her to hear it from me

as well." He went to her window and stared out at the dark sky. "You know, if we were shooting at Turquoise Lake, I think I'd just swim out and never come back."

"Very *Star Is Born*. And a little too dramatic." She put some cosmetics into her purse.

He smirked. "Hell, I couldn't do it."

"Good. I'm not worth it."

He caught her eye from across the room. "I think you are, but it would be hell on the kid growing up knowing his father committed suicide 'cause he couldn't decide what to do with his life when he learned he was going to be a dad."

Her demeanor brightened. Was he coming around? Was he growing up? Her heart leaped. Then she felt caution grip her. She'd given him every chance. He was never going to commit. "It's too late."

He looked down at her stomach, as if seeing the baby inside her. "I'm trying to face the facts finally. What can I do to convince you that things will be different now?"

"Nothing." She grabbed her coat. He started forwards, but she held up a hand to stop him. "My heart hasn't changed, X. I love you more than you know. I want your child. I wanted *us*. But it's too late."

He bit his lower lip. "It's not!"

There was a knock at the door. "I've got to go now." She knew she had to get out of there fast or she wasn't ever going to be able to leave. She unlocked the hotel room door.

"I'm coming with you—" His voice stopped in midsentence when he saw Bruce in the doorway.

"Ready?" Bruce asked. Then he saw Max. "What's he doing here?"

"Saying good-bye," Kristen answered.

Ignoring Bruce, Max grabbed her, twisted her around, kissed her passionately on the lips, holding her so tight that she felt he would squeeze the life out of her and the baby. Yet she liked being held by him. She could smell the cold cream he'd used to remove his stage makeup earlier. She pressed herself to his flesh, clinging to him, tears suddenly flowing down over his neck and shoulder, loving him more than she ever had—and more sure than ever that what she was doing was the right thing.

When she broke the embrace, she saw Bruce looking at Max with fury in his eyes. She quickly wiped her tears and said to him, "I'm going to be late for the plane. Can you take the big suitcase?" Bruce picked it up. She took her purse, and without looking back at Max, left for the Aspen airport, from where she planned, unknown to any of them, never to return.

Maggie, who was again dining at the Jerome with her father, Nicole, and some friends, saw Kristen and Bruce walk through the lobby. Then she saw Max hurry past. She went to the window of the restaurant in time to see Bruce driving Kristen away in a van. Max stood in the street, crying. And as the van disappeared from sight, Maggie felt a gut-wrenching sensation, a feeling of desolation that she'd not felt since she'd learned her mother was dead.

She turned away from the window and dissolved into tears herself.

Aspen, Colorado
Police Investigator's Office

"Miss Caulfield," Christopher Daniel said brusquely, "I'm sorry to keep you waiting."

"That's okay, Detective."

"Please, sit down."

"Thank you." She took the wooden chair in front of his desk.

He saw the sadness in her eyes and wondered if it was real. "I wish we were meeting under happier circumstances."

"I've been a mess," she admitted. "Max is the only man I ever loved. What happened was unthinkable. The last few days, I've been paralyzed. I mean, I did it. I'm the one who shot him. Living with that—"

"You understand it wasn't a bullet that brought the craft down."

"Yes, I know. They told me. But still, look what I did."

"I understand."

She was trying to hold her emotions in check. "It's a sense of doom, a feeling that God is punishing us."

A warning light went on in his head. "For what?"

She shook her head. "Maybe for all the unconventional fun and games we had, I don't know."

"You're being too hard on yourself." He then shifted gears quickly. He'd find out soon enough how upset she really was. "Listen, what's the picture that Max was referring to? You know, while he was airborne."

She understood right away. "A photograph of him and Maggie naked in bed. Well, X is naked."

"When Max was flying and he saw Nicole, he was sure she had taken it."

Kristen nodded. "But Bruce was the one who showed it to me."

Bruce Borger again. "How did he get it?"

She shrugged. "I don't know."

"Why did Bruce show it to you?"

"He wanted to prove that Max was lying to me, making a fool out of me."

"And you believed that was true?"

"Of course. But now I think I may have jumped to conclusions." She looked exasperated. "*Fibs* was the title of Max's first film. It's what this is all about. Liars."

He couldn't agree more. These Hollywood types were champion liars. "Let me give you a few theories," he said, resting his hands on his desk.

She nodded.

"Motive one. Bruce wanted you, and to feel he really had a chance of that, he would have to get Max out of the way."

She seemed doubtful. "I can't believe Bruce

would . . ." Her words trailed off. She considered the idea. "God knows he had access to the gun and to the glider."

Daniel offered another point of view to see what she'd say. "Motive two. Nicole wanted Max, and would rather see him dead than have him end up with you or Maggie."

"Possibly," she said with more conviction. "And she was everywhere. She could have gotten to the gun before I fired it. And the glider too."

"Number three is Maggie, for the same motive. Rather than lose him to you or Nicole, she'd rather have him dead."

Kristen didn't agree. "That's pretty far-fetched. That's just not Maggie."

"And there's one more."

"Yes?" She seemed eager.

"You hated him so much, after all the pain he caused you, that you put real bullets into the gun and for good measure slashed the wings to try to hurt him."

She looked startled. "That's preposterous. I mean, for starters, when could I have done that?"

He answered her question with a question. "Where were you the night before the accident?"

"In my room at the Jerome. Max came there. We talked."

"What was the nature of that discussion?"

She closed her eyes. It was clear she was fighting her emotions. "He told me he loved me. That I was wrong in what I had believed."

"What the photo suggested?"

She nodded. "But he didn't know about it yet. He only knew I thought he was still sleeping with Maggie. He said he was sad that it had ended this way, that I didn't believe him, but that he held his head high because he had never betrayed my trust." Her lower lip trembled. "He had integrity. All through it. But I was too blind in my anger and my hurt to see that. I believed others. Others who had their own agendas."

"Bruce?"

"And, even more so, Nicole. If you really want to know what I think, Detective—"

"I certainly do."

She scowled. "I distrust Nicole completely. I think she took advantage of Bruce's passion for me to cover up her own plan."

"I'll take that under consideration."

She seemed nervous suddenly, as if she wanted to say something else but was hesitating.

"Is there something more?"

"I know I'm wrong about this." She reached into her bag and grabbed hold of something. She closed her eyes for a moment. "I feel like I'm making it worse for someone who might be totally innocent."

"What is it?" he probed.

She pulled out a book and handed it to him. *Hang Gliding and Parasailing*. It was a primer, a starter's book on hang gliding. "It's the underlined paragraphs and notes that worried me."

He opened the cover, found page 15 dog-eared. He started reading. "The sail is attached to the frame with bolts or screws. . . . The hang glider is kept in shape by flying wires. . . . The sail is the most important part of the glider. It must be perfectly balanced. If it is out of alignment just a little bit . . . the craft will not fly properly." He turned more pages, randomly. "Safety tips." "Flying in the mountains." There were notations everywhere, like *Check out Telluride terrain* and circles around various passages about flying mistakes.

"Where did you get this?"

This was the hard part for her. "Bruce's room."

"I see. Is this his handwriting?"

"Yes. But of course," she added, trying to explain, "he would have to know all this, being the property manager."

"You sound like you're trying to convince yourself."

She looked defeated. "Maybe I am." She swallowed hard. "Bruce told me not to tell you that he had the photograph, that he gave it to me."

Daniel nodded. "The one he told me he knew nothing about, even though I guess that was what Max discovered when he went to Bruce's trailer to get gloves. But it only points to what you said."

"What's that?" she asked.

"That this is all about liars."

Twenty-one

Life without Kristen was sheer misery. Max felt as though he had—by his own hesitation—turned out the lights on his life, and now he was groping in the dark to find the switch that would turn them back on. If the parting was awful, Christmas without her was even worse. He had never felt so alone.

Charles invited him to join them at St. Mary's for midnight mass on Christmas Eve, but Max declined, preferring to remain alone in his rented condo. He wondered what Kristen was doing in Wisconsin. Was she at mass with her parents, thinking about him the way he was about her? Had she really meant that it was too late? Or did she just need time to get over the hurt? He wanted to call her, but he put the phone down each time he picked it up. He didn't want to contribute more to her emotional distress. Thinking about her, missing her, made him melancholy, but then he thought about the wonderful memories—hang gliding together, making snow angels in Colorado—and they made him smile. He felt the sensual pull again, longing for her body to envelop him. He prayed for just the sight of her beautiful body, a slight touch of her lips on his.

He thought about becoming a father, having the chance to do it right, to give his son or daughter the kind of support that he had never gotten in his early life. He figured because he had gone through hell, he would never make the same mistakes with his kid. His kid would be *loved*. He would be there Christmas morning when his son awoke, and he would help him discover the toys and show him how they worked.

On Christmas morning Max couldn't stand it any longer. He dialed Kristen at her parents' house in Middleton. Her mother informed him that Kris didn't want to speak to him. He asked how she was doing. "Fine," Mrs. Caulfield responded. "Merry Christmas." And she hung up. He didn't blame the woman for hating him.

Nicole held an open house for Charles on Christmas Day, which Max dragged himself to because he liked Charles so much. Max hated that Borger was there, but at least he wasn't in Wisconsin. Maggie seemed the perfect hostess, but under her veneer Max could sense her loneliness as well. And an anger directed toward him that she could barely hide.

Nicole found him alone on the sunporch. "Isn't it cold out here?" she asked him.

"When you're numb, you're numb."

"So, you lost them both?"

He shrugged. "I guess."

"But you have your precious career."

Her arch tone made him look up. "Listen, I don't need more grief from you."

"I don't want to make you more miserable. I want to help you smile."

"You can't."

She looked at him as if he were being a fool. "I could make you very happy."

He was outraged at the innuendo. "Your husband is standing in the next room."

"You Americans," she laughed. "So moral, so righteous."

"Don't you have any decency?"

"Charles is ninety. He's almost dead."

Max didn't respond. In truth, the old man didn't look good. He was very pale, a sickly color. "Are you looking forward to being the bereaved widow?"

"Can't you be nice to me?" she asked. "Is your guilt still so deep that you have to hate me for one indiscretion? I mean, since you and Maggie are no longer together, my little secret couldn't hurt you now, could it?"

"That's right. You have no power over me now."

"Only the power of love. If you allow it." And with that she got up and walked away.

They went back to filming the next day, and Maggie did what she always did in a personal crisis: work. She was a pistol on the set, demanding and thoroughly unforgiving. The object of most of her derision was Max, who suddenly could do nothing right. She called Kristen that evening to check on her, to make sure that she would indeed return. Kristen's mother, as with Max, ran interference. Maggie sent flowers the next morning, along with Fauchon chocolates. But there was no call to say thanks. Maggie had to trust that the girl, whatever her emotional state, would return on New Year's Day, as promised, to see her contract through. This film had to be wrapped before Kristen started showing; Maggie could not write in a pregnant character.

On New Year's Eve, Max poured out his heart in a call to Nicky Dee. "What the hell should I do?"

"It's more like what you shoulda done, jerk," Nicky told him. "Kris gave you two chances to tell the old broad it was over forever and move in with her, show them *both* you meant it, but you blew it."

"I know what I should have done," Max said in his defense. "I'm trying to figure out what to do now."

"Go to Kris before it's too late."

"She's coming back tomorrow."

"You really think so?"

Nicky's thought sobered him. What if Kris didn't return?

"She doesn't need time, she needs you. She probably said screw the damned movie, and you should too. You're full of excuses, which is like being full of shit."

"I can't just walk out on the film. I can't do that to Maggie," he protested.

"Why?"

"She loves me."

"So do I. But I'm surviving without you. So will Mom."

"I just want to make it all right again."

"Kristen is carrying your baby, asshole!" Nicky suddenly shouted. "Go to her and make this right before it's too damned late."

But she was coming back in the morning. Max trusted that. He trusted that with all his might as he heard revelers outside his condo window welcoming in the new year. He put a pillow over his head and prayed that Nicky was wrong.

She wasn't. Maggie showed up at his door late the next afternoon. "I just got back from seeing Papa off at the airport," she said, storming in, flinging a dozen roses onto the sofa. "Kristen's flight landed. I stood there with those, like an idiot. She wasn't on it."

He felt himself sag inside. "I feared that."

"You heard anything?"

"No."

"We have a movie to shoot tomorrow!" she shouted.

"Fuck the movie," he yelled back. "We're talking about a human being, and my baby." He almost broke down, turning away from her before she could see the tears in his eyes.

Seeing him so upset, Maggie considered her options. She had to be clever, had to get them reunited to get them to finish her film. She hadn't come this far to let it go because he'd knocked up some actress. She touched his shoulder gently. "Max," she said softly, "I miss you the way you must miss her. I *hate* the loss of the actress. I *accept* the loss of the person. But what happened to my Max? Can't we still be close?"

He looked out the window and saw snow falling again. "I don't want to lose her."

"Then don't." Maggie planted her hands on her hips. "Longing for her won't accomplish shit. You want her back, do something about it. And remind her she's got a commitment to finishing this film." She grabbed the phone next to the bed and held it out to him. "Make it happen. Call, talk to her, beg her, promise you'll marry her, anything."

He thought for a moment, staring at the receiver. Then he said decisively, "I'm going to go one better." He opened the closet and pulled out a carry-on bag.

"What are you doing?"

"I'm going to see her."

She was stunned. "You can't go to Wisconsin! Not you too. Not in the middle of shooting."

"Listen," he said sharply as he pulled some underwear out of a drawer and tossed it into the leather bag, "would you rather shut down for a few more days in order to get your stars back or have your picture close down completely?"

Her stunned silence was the answer.

"Kristen?" Her mother knocked at her door. "Honey, open up."

"Mom, please, I'm reading. I want to be alone."

Her mother's voice was filled with distaste as she said, "Honey, there's someone here."

Kristen groaned. "Another reporter? Tell him to go away."

"No. Not a reporter."

"I don't want to see anyone, Mom."

"You'll want to see this person."

Kristen slammed her novel down on the bed, got up and unlocked the door. "Okay," she said, set for a confrontation, "why will I want to see this person?"

"Honey, please calm down."

"I am calm!" she almost screamed.

Her mother shook her head. "Come downstairs with me."

"Tell me who's here first."

"It's me."

Kristen almost lost her balance. Incredulity at the distinct, unforgettable voice took her breath away. Over her mother's shoulder, she saw him standing on the landing, just four steps down.

"I'm sorry, Mrs. Caulfield," Max said. "I couldn't help but hear." Then his eyes met Kristen's.

"Oh, my God." Her mouth fell open in a gasp.

He climbed the last stairs. "Kris, I need to talk to you. I came a long way."

Sarah Caulfield was standing between them, but she graciously got out of the way. "I don't like this," she muttered. "I don't like this at all." She brushed past Max in the narrow corridor as she descended the stairs.

Kristen swallowed hard. Then, suddenly embarrassed, she grabbed her hair, pulling it into a ponytail behind her head, holding it for a moment with her fingers, then let it cascade down her back. She knew she looked terrible. She was wearing old ripped shorts she used to help her mom in the garden, and a ratty T-shirt. For a fleeting second she wished her mother had simply told her so she would at least have looked halfway—

He came forward in a rush and threw his arms around her. Breathing hard, as if to keep back the anguish he was carrying inside him, he guided her back into the bedroom, kicked the door shut with his foot, then kissed her so hard that the force of it pushed her down to the bed. He tried to say something, and so did she, but words never made it past their hunger. In a few moments—she didn't even know how—she was naked, the shorts flung somewhere on the floor, the T-shirt ripped in their mad frenzy to join together. Without removing her lips from his, her hands removed his clothing as well, tugging, tearing, unbuttoning, unzipping, until his shirt was rolled down over his shoulders and his shorts were at his ankles. His several-days-old beard felt like sandpaper on her flesh. He smelled musty, manly. When he entered her, it was like she had just drunk the magic cure, as if life was beginning again for her.

She clawed his back with her fingernails, knowing she was hurting him, but she wanted to hurt him, for the anger was still boiling inside her. Without words, his violent, wild thrusts told her he knew he had been wrong. He had been a coward. He had come to realize it. But he was here now. He was back. He would be here forever. He was hers.

Her head reverberated with this chant as she felt

her body burning with a pleasure she had never felt
before. It was physical, but it was so much more. She
grabbed his buttocks so hard, guiding his thrusts,
that she left imprints on his flesh. She slapped his
ass and screamed, and tears flowed as she reached
climax. Then, as the ebbing subsided, as he let out a
long, guttural groan and nearly collapsed atop her,
she had the strangest thought. Somehow this beautiful, inflamed act had brought three people together
again—her, Max, and their child.

After a while, silent on the bed next to one another,
they heard the sound of the teakettle squealing
downstairs. "Just Mom," she said.

"I love you." His gaze was soft, his eyes almost
glazed. "I have never stopped loving you." He gently
put his hand on her stomach.

She started to cry.

Twenty-two

They sat on the sun porch watching the sun go down. The tea had mango in it, and it was delicious. Max dipped one of the scones her mother had put out into his tea, dribbling spots all over his shirt. "Doesn't matter," he said when Kristen handed him a napkin, "you ripped a couple of buttons off already."

She was still in shock. "I didn't expect you to come."

He nodded. "Christmas was hell."

"Does Maggie know you're here?" Then it dawned on her. "Or did she send you?"

"We haven't been getting along."

"I know I was supposed to be back already. I want to finish the film. But I just couldn't get on that plane."

"You're going to have to make that decision. Maggie is giving us both a little time."

"So she did send you?" she said more pointedly.

"No. I had to come. I've been a wreck."

"That's two of us." Kristen put her legs up on the wicker ottoman and just let him talk.

"I have never been so miserable. I've been so scared that you meant it. I didn't sleep at all, all week."

"Listen, I'm scared too. But I had to make a decision and stand by it." She touched her stomach. "We are going to have a child together. That changes things. No one can remain a kid forever."

The implied accusation hit home. "Maybe that's why I like acting so much. You get to pretend you're someone else, and if you work a lot, you almost never have to go home and be yourself."

"Grow up, X." She said it softly, without anger, almost lovingly. "This is no movie."

He looked sobered by the words. He finished his tea and looked out at her farm. "Coulda fooled me. So, this is Wisconsin, huh?"

She laughed. "Cows, cheese, boring. Right now, though, it's comforting."

"Gonna show me around tomorrow?"

She brightened. "Sure. Actually, I haven't been out of the house much since I got back, but I'll give you the grand tour."

"Your mom and I talked a little before she went upstairs to tell you."

"I'm surprised she even let you in the door."

"I flashed my movie star smile," he said ingenuously. "She is very worried about you."

"Oh, the baby, yeah. The doctor said I really have to be careful."

"Not only that," he explained. "Your depression, your sadness."

"I loved you," she explained, "more than I thought possible to love another person. Then I felt shattered. I have a piece of you inside me, but I wanted it all, wanted us to come first."

He took her hand. "I understand." He gripped her fingers tightly. "Are you coming back?"

She nodded. "Now that you're here."

"And if I hadn't come?"

"I think I might have died."

The words shocked him. "Kris."

"I almost wanted to. Not commit suicide or anything like that. Just go to sleep and not wake up. The pain was that deep."

"But you were so angry that last day. You seemed fine, over me."

"I'm a good actress, X."

Kristen woke Max with the sun—"Just like farmers do," she told him—and they descended to find a hearty breakfast waiting—buttermilk flapjacks, thick bacon, hash browns, steaming coffee. He thought it a wonder her parents were not obese. They seemed to be gentle, simple people, who were, obviously, not happy with the pain he'd caused their daughter. The tension was palpable. He and Kristen had gone out to a restaurant the night before, mainly to avoid the glares of her mother and father. Before bed, Kristen had assured them that it was "going to be all right." But Max felt their displeasure at having him in their house.

He noticed her mother had pasted the front and side of the refrigerator with clippings about her—

about *them*. None of the articles pointed up the salaciousness of the threesome, but Max knew they resented him for having dragged their daughter into sin. It surfaced only once at the breakfast table. "I think everyone has to explore the various paths life offers," Sarah Caulfield said, rather generously, considering. "I think when you're young and confused by all that is out there, all that's available now, you want to try everything."

Her father was more direct. "Just because you kids are part of that Hollywood scene doesn't mean you have to turn into dogs in heat."

Max swallowed hard, but felt better when Kristen gave him a knowing wink.

"Have you discussed a wedding?" Sarah asked.

Kristen knew it was too soon to get into anything like that. They hadn't even really sorted out where they were. "Give us time, Mom. We need to talk about a lot of things."

"Your mother was right," Max told Kristen late that afternoon as a beautiful brunette named Jody handed him a dark beer. She'd shown him Madison, taken him to the university, drove around frozen Lake Mendota, and now they were sitting at a picnic table inside a beer hall called the Capital City Brewery. Kristen told him it was a place she liked to hang out, where since she'd returned pregnant, Jody always greeted her with lemonade or root beer.

"Mom and Dad hated you at first, seeing me in such pain. They wanted to protect me. And they did. But they seem to be warming up to you."

He rubbed his index finger up and down the wet beer mug. "I think it's more 'Oh, thank God, he's going to marry her after all!' "

"Are you?"

He hesitated a split second. "Yes."

She didn't believe him. "Listen, lots of couples don't marry. They raise a family without ever having to do that."

"What do *you* want?" he asked her.

She answered without even thinking. "What I said I wanted when we parted. You, me, our child. Our work. A life together forever."

"Like your parents have."

She nodded. "They're my heroes, my role models."

"I didn't have that."

"It's what everyone really wants."

"Not so sure of that," he cautioned.

"Your first movie was called *Fibs*. I think that's the problem. It's so easy to lie to ourselves."

"I'm trying not to, Kris."

She said, "Overcoming fear is the big problem."

He shrugged. She was right about that. Just what Nicky had said. "Listen, come back with me. Let's finish the film. And then get married."

"You mean it, don't you?"

He downed a draught of beer and turned to her, propping his feet up on the wooden bench. "Kris, nothing has changed. I mean that in a good sense, my love for you, my desire to be with you, spend the rest of my life with you. Marriage scares me, of course, but I know one thing. I'm going to be a better father to our child than my parents were to me."

"Oh, X," she said, with gladness filling her heart. "Come here, kiss me."

He got up and slid around to her side of the table. And kissed her lovingly. Just then his cell phone rang.

Kristen sensed immediately, from the troubled, guilty look on his face, that the caller was Maggie. It was a short, stammering conversation. Max was obviously shocked by the news. "I'll be there as soon as I can," he said. "Chicago to Nice nonstop?" Then he hung up.

Kristen could not believe what she'd just heard him say. "Nice, France?"

"Yes."

She could barely breathe. "What's she doing in France?"

"That was Nicole on the phone," he said heavily. "Maggie is on her way to Paris right now. Charles Nash died this morning. I have to go."

Kristen closed her eyes, instantly depressed again. She fought the feeling that if he did get on a plane to France, she would never see him again as long as she lived.

Twenty-three

Though never once before he met Nicole did anyone ever hear Charles Nash say he believed in God, he died a rabid Catholic. Nicole arranged a high mass funeral the likes of which had never been seen in Avignon. Conducted by the same priest who had performed their small wedding ceremony, it was the exact opposite: big, sprawling, and public. But only Nicole, Maggie, Max, and a few close friends from Avignon, Cavaillon, Le Barroux, and Paris attended the burial, on the slope outside his villa, under his favorite olive tree, as he had requested. Maggie wept as they lowered him into the ground. Nicole, Max noticed, retained her composure. When he asked her why she didn't cry, she replied, "I feel only joy for the blessing of the time we had together. Maggie never made peace with him. That is why it was so hard for her."

Maggie had been thrilled to find Max on the villa's doorstep after thinking she had lost him to Kristen forever, happy to have his strong arms there to hold her, to comfort her. To Max she seemed oddly vulnerable through the first days of mourning. This was a different woman from the Maggie anyone had ever seen. She didn't seem upset that she'd had to shut down the film even longer to come here. She didn't even power up her cellular phone for three days. She read, walked in the garden, sat at the mound of naked earth under which her father now lay forever, in a trance, coming to grips, she told him, with what had been a difficult and trying relationship.

Max talked to her about forgiving her father, urged her to use the grief and pain to go on, reminding her how brilliant her work was. He made her feel protected in much the same way he had when they'd first started their love affair. When he assured her that both he and Kristen were returning to the set as soon as she was ready to resume shooting, a rekindling happened, making the old fire in her eyes dance once again.

But he did not tell her he had promised to marry Kristen. Not yet.

In the meantime, Maggie was trying to figure out what had killed Charles. He might have been old, and weakened, as Nicole said, by the holiday trip to America, but she too had noticed his unnatural color in Colorado. He had always been in very good health, up until the time of his marriage. Besides, Maggie thought, he was too ornery to die. Especially of "natural causes," as the death certificate read. She didn't buy it. She didn't trust it. Something about his sudden death bothered her. And she wouldn't let it go without doing some investigating.

She made arrangements to get the film back on schedule, which was no easy feat. Everyone had decamped, and the various conflicting schedules wouldn't allow them to reconvene on the set for nearly two weeks. Kristen told Max on the phone that she would be there on the newly set date. She asked what Max was going to do until then, and he explained that he felt he should stay in Avignon for both Nicole and Maggie. Indeed, he accompanied them to the reading of Charles Nash's will the next morning in Cannes. It left Maggie seething and Nicole buoyant. Mrs. Charles Nash got almost everything. "It's not so much a rebuke to me," Maggie told Max, "because what the hell, I have everything I'll ever want. No, it's more about rewarding the little slut who deceived him all this time."

To Maggie and Max over dinner that evening, Nicole said, "It is proof that family meant so much to Charles, for we are still family, Maggie, and we should spend more time together. We should not let distance come between us."

In a dead voice Maggie surmised, "That means you're coming back to Colorado, doesn't it?"

Nicole took Maggie's hand and reached out for Max's, bowed her head, and said, "God bless Charles."

Maggie looked like she was going to vomit. When Nicole left the room, Maggie said, "I think the little bitch killed him."

"Oh, come on," Max said, dismissing it as nonsense.

* * *

Maggie and Max flew to Paris the next day to attend the banquet for Les Cesars, the French equivalent of the Oscars. *Scandals* won nothing. Maggie, who already had nabbed four of the awards during her career, felt the Americanization of the film resulted in snobbery in France. Screw them, was her attitude. She'd show them at the Academy Awards, for which she was sure they'd be nominated for everything. After the Cesars ceremony, they accepted the Agnellis' invitation to spend a few days in the Greek islands aboard their fabulous yacht.

They were shocked, an hour out into the Mediterranean, to find Nicole onboard as well. "The little bitch got herself invited so she could flaunt herself in front of you again," Maggie snarled to Max.

"It won't work," he promised. "But I hope you're wrong. The Agnellis love her. That's what it's about."

He seemed to be correct, for Nicole kept to her widow's weeds, and on the whole the trip turned out to be a healing experience. Diving off a swim platform the size of Connecticut into a cool, crisp sea, Max and Maggie played like children in the water, feeling the months-old tension disappear. They visited an ancient whitewashed church on Mykonos, where they prayed for Charles. Maggie held Max's hand as they stood on the Acropolis, regarding the history at their feet.

Yet on Cyprus, their last night before flying back, Max sat alone, under the stars, thinking of Kristen, trying to find the right time to tell Maggie he was planning to marry Kristen soon.

Maggie joined him. "A drachma for your thoughts."

"A euro for yours," Max said.

In response, she gripped his shoulder tightly. "When I said I think she killed Papa, I meant it."

He winced at her tight hold. "You're not kidding, are you?"

She shook her head. "I talked to Agnes. That's the maid who came with the villa. She's been with us for years, and hates Nicole as much as I do. She told me she watched Daddy having these bouts, then recovering, then getting sick again."

"When?"

"All after they got married."

Max was very suspicious of her accusations. "What kind of bouts?"

"Dizziness, fainting, no appetite. When did my father ever lack an appetite?"

"He was old, Maggie," Max reminded her. "I think you don't want to face that."

"But he had the resolve—and the body, mind you—of a fifty-five-year-old. The maid thinks the sparrow may have been poisoning him."

"Nicole? She was devoted to him." But then he remembered the one-night stand he had buried for so long. Had Nicole's desire for Max been the actions of a woman who truly loved her husband? Max felt a shiver.

"What is it?" Maggie said, seeing the change on his face. "What do you know?"

"Nothing. I just think it's absurd."

"I called her a money-hungry slut, from the start,"

she said, darkly. "I knew she would stop at nothing to get what she wanted, and once he wrote the will her way, she hastened his death. She's got it all now. Everything she came for."

No, Max thought, *perhaps not*. He remembered the moment she found him on the sunporch on Christmas Day. *No*, he thought, *she might still want me*.

"It's late. We should get back to the boat."

As they walked, she took his hand. "One thing I am sure of. I have loved being with you again, Max."

He smiled.

She stopped and faced him on the dirt road in the moonlight. She ran her hands through his hair. "You look as wonderful as you did that night when we first saw the fishermen on the Seine. Kiss me, darling," she urged. "Kiss me like you used to."

He turned his head.

"Max?"

"I can't do that, Maggie. We aren't ever going to make love again. Ever." Max finally mustered up his courage, getting out what he'd meant to say for the entire trip. "I'm going to marry Kristen soon after we return tomorrow."

She shrank away from him. "What?"

"Kristen is coming back to complete the film only because we are a couple now. But we'll finish it. We won't let you down."

She took it in and sneered. "Gee, thanks, honey." Her syrupy voice dripped with anger.

"Maggie, I don't blame you for hating me."

"Hate you?" she cried. "I don't hate you. I despise

the whole situation. But I knew this was how it was going to play out." She started to walk off.

"So, is it all right?"

She turned back to face him. "Do I have a choice?"

He shrugged. "I guess not."

"Then it's all right. Now, I have to get back to *Never Forget*. And maybe try to forget myself." She grinned at the thought. She started away, but then turned again and called back, "Max, just make sure your fiancée is there, okay?" And with that she disappeared down the hillside.

Later that night, on the boat, Max fell asleep looking out at the stars in the sky through the lavish stateroom's window. Suddenly he felt warm, smothered. His naked body was heating up as someone squeezed him tight. He opened his eyes to find Maggie had crawled into bed with him.

"Darling, hold me, hold me," she begged. She sounded distraught.

He realized this was no dream. He didn't know what to do. She had silently come through the connecting door of their adjoining staterooms. His arms automatically moved around her, but at the same time he wanted to jump of the bed. He thought she was trying to seduce him.

That was far from her mind. "Max, please, forgive me for being so nasty. I hate loss, don't know how to deal with it. Probably 'cause I'm always in control and you can't control that." She let out a little laugh and then cradled her head on his shoulder and neck, a place she had spent many nights before. "I admire you for your decision to do the right thing with Kristen, I really do, despite my own jealousy and fears. Fears, they rule us all, don't they?"

"That's for sure."

She placed her hand on his chest, resisting the natural urge to move it south. "I was walking the deck and ran into that little cunt three times . . ."

"Nicole?"

She nodded against his chest. "It made me think of Papa, and then I had this panic attack. I wanted to drown myself."

He was astonished hearing this from her.

"I can't stand the idea of Kristen hating me. It paralyzes me."

It sounded so genuine that he believed every word of it.

Until she said, "And maybe someday, who knows? Maybe someday the three of us will be together again, baby and all."

That's when he froze. Maggie had not truly given up on him or on Kristen, on them. She was simply going to ride out the crisis out and hope that it brought the threesome back together. No, he was wrong, he realized. Maggie was never that passive. She was going to direct them, manipulate them, back together. He promised himself, even as he held her in his arms, this woman in her nightie and him lying there stark naked, that he would never be so weak again as to betray Kristen the way he'd betrayed Maggie with Nicole.

*   *   *

What Max didn't know was that Nicole was present in more than his memory. At that very moment she was outside the stateroom window, peering in. The bed's headboard was to the wall beneath the window, and she was looking right down on them.

She ran back to her stateroom and fetched her digital camera. It was so sophisticated that low light, as the small night-light on Max's wall provided, was no problem. She didn't know how she was going to use these photos, but she knew they would come in handy with her other rival for Max.

As Max held Maggie in his arms, Nicole clicked the shutter.

Twenty-four

Kristen was elated when Max returned to Aspen. He found her waiting for him in an even more sumptuous suite at the Jerome than the last time. Bouquets of flowers sat everywhere. "I think they really want to hang on to me this time," she said with a laugh, enfolded in his arms.

"Krissy, honey, I've never felt so good." He took off his leather jacket, glad for the warmth. The weather was a far cry from the Mediterranean, worse than when he'd left: icy cold, snow everywhere, a frigid winter wonderland. "I told Maggie. I told her everything."

She was thrilled, but cautious. "Everything?"

"Everything."

"Thank you." She kissed him. "I'm proud of you."

"And I'm staying here, with you. I'm not going back to that condo."

"God knows, there's room. How did she take it?"

"Better than I'd expected." He sat down, pulled her into his arms on the down-filled sofa. "I think Maggie is a survivor before a sentimentalist. She may harbor some fantasy of having me back—maybe of having us both back—but it's not going to happen if we stay strong."

Kristen put her head in his lap as he stroked her hair. "All I want is for us to be happy. All of us, Maggie included."

"We're going to be fine." He kicked his shoes off in front of the fireplace. "So, what are we going to name the little devil?"

"How about Xavier? Xavier Caulfield Jaxon."

"Another X. Cool. I love you, Kris." He bent forward and pressed his lips to her forehead. "And I've missed you."

On location, Maggie treated Kristen with kindness and affection from the day they started shooting again. If she harbored any lingering animosity, it remained hidden. The casual onlooker would not have known anything had happened among the three of them. Only after the cameras stopped rolling did the different dynamics become apparent. Max and Kristen went to the Hotel Jerome. Maggie went home, alone.

Until one night when Maggie arrived at the chalet to find a woman sitting in the living room, nursing a Campari and soda. "What the hell are *you* doing here?" she snapped at Nicole.

"I live here."

"Pardon me?"

"*Cette maison m'appartient, au cas ou tu aurais oublie.*"

"My God, you're something." Maggie looked as

though she was going to spit. "No, I haven't forgotten that you own this house."

The sparrow smiled. "I was bored with France and thought I would do a little skiing."

"Switzerland would have closer."

"But less fun. Here I can watch a movie being filmed. Besides, we are family still."

"Jesus," Maggie muttered, "you're a rich widow, a free agent, and you want to be here? Level with me. It's Max, isn't it?"

"Max is in love with Kristen. He's made his choice."

"But you still want him. I see it in your eyes. You can't fool me. You have some deluded notion you're going to get him one day, don't you?"

"Whatever fantasies I have are no more delusion than your thinking *you* will have him back."

"What makes you think I believe that?"

"All this crap, this 'Oh, I'm so happy for Max and Kris' bullshit, it doesn't fool me. You'll never convince me you're ready to be a bridesmaid at their wedding."

Maggie was seething. "I'll tell you one thing. Even though it is painful to lose him to Kris, it is a hell of a lot more pleasing than the idea of losing him to you."

"You already lost him to me once."

Maggie recoiled. "What?"

"He fucked me back in Paris."

"Liar."

"When you were editing *Fibs*. I seduced him. Max's passion for me is not my imagination, you see."

Maggie held in her anger, ready to burst. She picked up her bag and headed toward the staircase. "This discussion is over."

"Don't like it when you're not in control, do you, Maggie?"

"You monstrous little piece of shit." Maggie glared at her from the bottom of the staircase. "Now I know that my loathing of you has never been misplaced. And, if you'll excuse me, I'm going up to bed—or did you corral the master bedroom as well?"

As Maggie ascended the stairs, Nicole called after her mockingly, "I know you, like your father knew you. The leader/destroyer, they call the personality type. Always in charge, always with a plan." She put her short, slim legs up on the ottoman, making herself comfortable. Then she sipped her drink. "I'm just going to sit and watch. I'll bet what unfolds will rival any movie you've ever made."

Maggie slammed the upstairs bedroom door.

In the morning, she figured she should move out, but where would she go? She couldn't go to the Jerome. Max and Kristen were there. Nicole was right on the money. Maggie knew it wasn't over for them, not by a long shot. She would be involved with them again, but she had to take her time, give them what they thought they wanted right now, that space to enjoy planning to play house. She needed to keep her distance. All in good time. And in that good time she could go to the Aspen Club Lodge, where some of the others were staying. Hell, she could move into the condo that Max had vacated to be with Kristen.

But that would only be more painful, more reminder of his betrayal. The gall of him. He had lied to her. She had suspected something had happened with Nicole. She questioned him about it, and he had denied it. He'd made a fool of her. How could she want him back after learning this? But when had she been happy, wasn't it with Max and Kris? Wasn't that the only time in her whole life that she'd really enjoyed things? And what they could create together, it would take moviegoers' breath away.

She would stay here, she decided. She would put up with Nicole, who would soon tire of the cold and leave anyway. Plus, this way she could keep an eye on her, talk to her, learn more about why and how her father died. Nicole was devious, but then, so was she. Time together might be just what they needed.

Nicole showed up on location the next day, surprising Max and Kristen as she had Maggie. She was particularly fascinated by an outburst of Bruce Borger's later that morning. After Maggie ran Kristen ragged in a scene the actress was not delivering on, he suddenly stepped in front of the cameras and told Maggie, "Lay off the girl!" Everyone was shocked. Had the prop master gone mad? "Don't you see what you are doing to her?" he shouted at an astonished Maggie.

Never at a loss for words, Maggie snapped, "Whatever I'm *doing to her* is none of your fucking business."

But he felt it was. He put his arm around Kristen, helping her from the ski lift chair where she had been trying to do her lines, shouting to Max, who was going up the lift opposite her. It was an emotional outburst that Kristen didn't seem to have the strength for today. Bruce took Maggie's pressing the actress as some kind of cruelty, and even when Kristen told him it was okay, he kept raving. "This girl has had a terrible day," he bellowed. "She's not had a break, she's not eaten, she's falling apart—and she's pregnant. Cut her a little slack."

Maggie glared at him. "Bruce, I would appreciate it if you went back to your props, and quickly."

"I'm not going to have you—"

"You were not hired to be the company shrink," she reminded him. "You're stepping over a line that could be disastrous for you."

Finally, he backed down. Max had been on his way up the mountain in his chair, so he missed the entire encounter. But everyone within earshot had heard it. And for the first time Kristen's pregnancy was made public.

That night, Nicole went into the Campo de Fiori, an Italian restaurant and nightspot where the movie crew usually got sloshed. She ordered a Campari and soda from a waitress. Bruce was already three sheets to the wind as she came over and sat in his lap. "Do we know each other?" he jokingly asked.

"Not really, but we should. We have something in common."

He smiled and sucked on his beer bottle, while she balanced on his thigh. "What would that be?"

"We both want what we can't have."

He blinked. "Don't say."

"A certain guy, for me, and a certain girl, for you."

His good humor died. He moved her to her own chair. "You were there, I recall. I saw you."

"You know who I am?" she purred.

"Heard."

"Maggie thinks I'm here because I'm in love with Max."

He became more alert. Annoyed, he said, "What's everyone see in this guy?"

"Same thing you see in Kristen. Magic." Nicole fished a folded newspaper out of her bag and showed him. The Oscar nominations had been announced. Maggie, Max, and Kristen had all been nominated for *Scandals*.

Bruce looked stricken as he stared at a photograph of the girl he loved. "Yeah," he whispered.

Nicole hadn't expected him to reveal his feelings so openly. She knew his outburst earlier in the day had embarrassed him, and when she'd seen him apologize to Maggie later, she suspected that he had felt too protective of Kristen to keep his feelings in. But the rawness on his face now intrigued her. This was a man head over heels in love. "Tell me something, Mr. Borger."

"Bruce."

"Tell me, Bruce. What would you do to have her?"

"Anything," he said. Then he modified that. "I mean, within reason. I mean, I'm not gonna go try to kill Max." A waitress was setting down another beer in front of him and arched her eyebrows when she heard that. "Movie talk," he explained.

Nicole took a sip of her drink. "Their upcoming offspring has changed everything, for everyone. Kristen thinks Max is going to marry her. She believes he's now being faithful to her."

He nodded. "Yeah?"

"If she learned that wasn't true, I don't think wedding bells would ring for them anytime soon."

"Max is an asshole," Bruce said. "I don't doubt that he's still fucking Maggie."

"Of course he is."

"I hate the bastard," he continued. "He's a self-centered prick. All he cares about is his stardom. And he needs Maggie for that."

Nicole leaned closer to him. "Bruce, I like you. I'd like to see you happy."

He stared at her as if she was nuts. "You don't even know me."

"Having Kristen would make you happy, wouldn't it?"

"What are you getting at?"

"You having Kristen would leave Max open for me."

His eyes lit up. He saw what she wanted. "I see." He stretched his legs out, put his hands behind his head, and said, "So, how the hell do I accomplish that?"

She reached into her purse and handed him an envelope. "With this."

"Kris?" Bruce said as he stuck his head in Kristen's dressing trailer.

Kristen turned toward him, newspapers in her hands. "How could you?"

Bruce stepped in and closed the door. "How could I what?"

"Look." She showed him the headline. ON-SET RIFT REVEALS CAULFIELD PREGANCY. And another one: OSCAR NOMINEE PG.

"Kris," he pleaded, "they were going to find out anyhow. You're going to start showing."

"I wanted to keep it private till then, Bruce. Till Max and I were married. The scrutiny, the prying, it's going to be hell—as if the problems with Maggie and Max aren't enough." She threw the newspapers to the floor. "Damn it, I should never have come back to finish this film."

"You would have lost Max."

She sniffed, "You'd like that, wouldn't you?"

He took a deep breath. "I'm sorry. I'm upsetting you, and that's the opposite of what I want to accomplish here."

"Just what do you hope to accomplish?" she asked in a biting tone.

"Are you going to Los Angeles with him?"

"For the Oscars? Of course. We're both nominated. How could you think Max and I wouldn't go?" She started to get into her parka for the upcoming scene. "Remind me to do something set in Hawaii next."

"Kris, you're too trusting."

"How?"

"Of Max."

Kristen looked surprised. "Why would you say something like that?"

"Be careful."

"Bruce," she said, shaking her head, "I just don't get it. What do you want from me? This jealousy is going to put a wall between us. Either you accept what I've chosen or you don't." She opened the door. "Just be my friend, Bruce, okay? Nothing more." And she left.

That Sunday morning, as Nicole was filing out of St. Mary's Catholic Church, she was surprised to see Kristen kneeling at the back. *"Bonjour."*

Kristen smiled, nodded, blessed herself and got up.

"You attend mass regularly?"

Kristen shrugged. "Lately."

"You should bring Max with you." Both of them stopped in the vestibule as the crush of parishioners greeted the priest who'd said the mass, and bundled up before leaving the building. "He needs to plant his feet on the ground, now that he's going to be a father."

Kristen didn't quite understand. "You think religion would help?"

"Of course. It gave Charles a peace inside him that he'd never known before."

Kristen dismissed the idea. "I think it might cause more guilt, and Max has enough of that already."

"He has never seemed conscience-stricken to me," Nicole said. "Even when we had our affair, he never seemed—" Nicole stopped when she saw Kristen's shocked face. "You mean, he never told you?"

Kristen shook her head. "When was this?"

"Back before you came into the picture. When he

was so in love with Maggie. It didn't seem to bother him at all."

Kristen was clearly unnerved. "Did it bother you?"

"Oh, I couldn't live with myself. I cut it off, stopped it dead. I went home and told Charles. My honesty saved me. He forgave me."

They were getting closer to the priest, who was shaking everyone's hand. Kristen quickly asked, "Did Maggie never find out?"

Nicole snorted. "She just did."

"You told her? Not Max?"

Nicole gave a Gallic shrug. "Ask him." She took the priest's hand, "Ah, Father, what an inspiring sermon . . ."

"Did you sleep with Nicole?"

Max whirled around, almost cutting his neck with his shaver. "What?"

"Did you have an affair with Nicole?" Kristen stood with her arms folded, leaning against the door frame. "Answer me, Max."

He grabbed a towel and wiped the rest of the shaving foam from his chin. "Yes. To the first version. I *slept* with Nicole, once, when I was drunk. I didn't have an affair with her."

"Why didn't you tell Maggie?"

He wasn't sure why she was angry. He could understand if she had asked why he didn't tell *her*. But Maggie? "Because I felt like such a heel," he admitted.

"And you were afraid she'd walk out on you and deep-six your career."

"Something like that. I'm not proud of it." He walked past her, into the bedroom, undid the towel around his waist and slid on a pair of boxer shorts. "How did you find out?"

"Nicole told me."

He stopped short. "How? Why?"

"She was suggesting that I drag you to church."

He laughed uncomfortably. "Save my soul? Kris, don't be naive here. She's got an evil streak that few people see. Maggie even thinks she murdered Charles."

This time it was Kristen that froze. "That's ridiculous," she said.

"Perhaps. But she has always wanted me, from the first day I showed up at the villa. She couldn't care less that Charles was upstairs sleeping. She would have made love to me right there under his nose. She is immoral, but she likes to justify it as 'being French.' "

Kristen didn't know what to believe. "She said *she* broke it off."

"*I* did," he said vehemently. "I'd been very drunk one night in Paris, hurting because Maggie had abandoned me, and she reeled me in. I've been remorseful ever since."

"She made it sound completely opposite."

"She's a liar."

"Why would she do that?" she said skeptically.

"Because she wants to destroy our trust. She wanted to get me away from Maggie, and now that I'm not with Maggie anymore, she wants to do the same to you."

"Why?"

"To have me for herself."

The day before Max, Kristen, and Maggie were to fly to California for the Oscars, they wrapped up the outdoor shooting, with the exception of the hang gliding scene still to be shot on location in Telluride. An air of excitement pervaded the entire cast and crew because all three of them stood a good chance of winning the prize.

At the Aspen Club Lodge, at the Colorado wrap party, Max and Kristen gave an interview to several reporters about the baby, and Maggie chimed in, saying how she hoped to be "godmother, at least." Bruce Borger watched from the sidelines, seething. Nicole seemed amused. Maggie couldn't stand having her around and was glad to be leaving her behind. Max was happier than Maggie about the prospect. He had not spoken a word to Nicole since Kristen told him what she'd said.

About midnight, when the party really got rocking, everyone turned around when someone shouted above the band, "Fuck you!" It was Max, in Bruce's face. Couple by couple, people stopped dancing.

"You don't know shit about me," Max yelled. "I've had enough of your puppy-dog eyes undressing Kristen. Go find some other girl, man."

Bruce grabbed him by his sweater and shook him. "You lying, cheating prick!"

Max became enraged, for it was obvious that Nicole had also told Bruce. Kristen started to rush toward them, but Maggie held her back. "You can't risk getting involved in this," Maggie said. Even so, Kristen called out for them to stop, but they did not hear her.

As the song ended, a young man dressed in a caterer's uniform approached them. "Listen, guys, cool off."

"Screw you," Bruce said, startled that a mere kid was telling him what to do.

"I'm moonlighting tonight," the boy said, reaching under the apron into his back pocket, producing his badge. "Officer Brad Stonecipher, Aspen Police. Now, chill or you're going to get into trouble here."

The music started up again, and everyone had started dancing when Bruce suddenly shoved Max backward into the guitar player. He was on top of Max in a second, landing a hard punch to his mouth. "Fucking asshole, I should kill you!"

Max decked him, sending blood spattering all over the fallen sheet music. The young cop dropped the tray he was carrying and rushed to them, along with several other men. When they pulled Bruce off Max, Bruce muttered, "I'll get you, you fucker!"

Several of the crew dragged Bruce outside. Kristen was appalled. Maggie dashed to put a wet towel on Max's bleeding lip. "He's nuts," Max kept saying. "He's sick. That guy is dangerous."

The cop asked if Max was okay, and he nodded. Did he want to press charges? Maggie gave Max a stern look. He shook his head.

"Ma'am," the young officer offered to Maggie, "if

you have any more trouble tonight, you just call for help, hear?''

Maggie assured him there would be no more trouble.

Back at the Jerome, Kristen and Maggie tended to Max's wounds. Maggie was worried that they wouldn't be able to shoot the interior scenes in L.A. until he healed, but the damage seemed to be superficial. Kristen put him to bed with one of the knock-out sleeping pills Maggie always carried ''just in case.''

In the living room of the suite, Maggie looked at Kristen and said, ''You want me to fire him?''

''Bruce? No. He was drunk. But I do expect him to apologize to X.''

''You're too good.''

Maggie got her bag and put on her coat. Kristen was saying good night to her when she felt a wave of nausea overpower her. Maggie caught her, helped her to a chair. ''You okay, honey?''

Kris tried to shake it off. She put her hands on her stomach. She closed her eyes.

''Hey, what is it?''

Kris thought it was just the emotional upset. ''I hate fighting.''

''You want me to call the doctor?''

''No.'' Kris brightened up. ''I''m fine, just tired. I should get to bed. We have to fly tomorrow.''

Maggie bent forward, and for the first time since Kristen had told them that she was pregnant, she held her shoulders and kissed her forehead. ''Sleep well.'' And she left.

Kristen watched her get into the elevator. She was about to shut the door to the suite when she saw Bruce step out from the other elevator. "Oh, no," Kristen murmured, trying to close the door before he saw her.

But he had. "Kris, wait!"

She slammed it in his face. "Go away, please, Bruce." She leaned against the door, feeling faint and hot again. "Just leave me alone, please. I just saved your job. And I want you to apologize to Max. Do you hear me?"

She heard nothing from the hall. "Bruce?" Still no response. But then, as she opened her eyes, she saw something sliding underneath the door. It was an envelope.

Figuring Bruce had written an apology, she bent down. While still on one knee, she opened it. Looked at the contents. And felt her breath giving out.

Christopher Daniel was reviewing his interviews with his different suspects when Maggie Nash burst into his office. "Forgive the intrusion," she said, looking as though she didn't mean it. "I have something you may be interested in."

He put the interviews into their case file. "Yes?"

She tossed a small plastic bag on his desk. Inside it was a Catholic rosary.

"I don't understand."

"Those beads belonged to my father. Agnes, his devoted maid back in Avignon, sent them to me."

He lifted the bag. "Rosary beads? What are they made from?"

"Beans from Peru." She paced the room, explaining. "My father turned to religion when the slut came into his life."

"Nicole, you mean?"

"Yes." Her mouth quirked with dislike. "The sparrow was always dragging him to church. They said the rosary together every night before bed." She laughed out loud. "Christ! My father, it's hard to imagine. Anyway, Agnes got suspicious when he kept getting sick, then recovering, then getting sick again. When he died, she told me everything she suspected. And we both are sure Nicole killed him. With those."

He was finding this very implausible. "How do you kill someone with a rosary?"

"You do when the beads are made from beans that are poisonous."

He dropped the package.

"It's okay. I think they have to be wet to be dangerous. That's what Agnes thinks. She used to see Nicole lift them to Daddy's lips for him to kiss. We kept trying to figure out what had changed once he married her. The rosary thing started happening after they returned from South America, and that's precisely when he started getting sick."

"You think Nicole poisoned him with rosary beads? By making him kiss them?" He gave her a dismissive look. "Now I've heard them all."

"I was skeptical, too, when I first heard it from Agnes. But feast your eyes on this." She withdrew a thick novel from her bag and set it on his desk. "Turn to page three-ten. It's dog-eared."

He did so. "They found early symptoms of *abrus precatories* poisoning. Jaquirity beans. The rosary beans from South America," he read aloud.

"Nicole bought these when she and Papa went to South America after the Oscars last year."

Daniel looked at the cover of the novel. *Anthem.* "Whose book is this?"

"Look inside the front cover."

Daniel did. There was an inscription from Jerry K. Loeb, the author, to Charles Nash and "beautiful Nicole Richaud."

"It's the sparrow's. Of course, she's so slow that she's been reading it for more than a year. I suppose she didn't think it would give her away."

Daniel rubbed his chin. "I'll have these tested. But I have to explain something to you. There's nothing I can do about this. Charles Nash didn't die in Aspen, or even in America. This is a matter for the French authorities. I am powerless here."

"Yes," Maggie said, "I know that. And I'm going to make sure she gets prosecuted in France. They'll put the murdering little bitch away forever. But the reason I brought them to you is this: Don't you think that if Nicole could kill my father, she was capable of killing Max too?"

Twenty-five

Max was beside himself in the morning when he awoke to find Kristen gone. The lipsticked scrawl on the suite's ornate foyer mirror said, GO TO HELL, MAX! Kristen's things had vanished, so he called Maggie. She was as astonished as he was, for the evening had ended almost sweetly. "What in God's name did you do now?" she asked him.

"How the hell do I know?"

They could not locate her anywhere. They tried Bruce's room at the Aspen Club Lodge, but he'd checked out. All three of them had noon tickets to LAX. Tomorrow was the Academy Awards. No one knew what to do. Maggie tried to keep a level head. "She's gone to L.A. before us. Something happened— probably Bruce Borger—and she went back with him. I think we should go as planned and figure it out once we're there."

And so they flew to Los Angeles. When they got to the Beverly Hills Hotel, they tried Kristen's apartment in Santa Monica. No answer. Maggie called

Bruce's home in Studio City. No answer. Max called Kristen's parents. They had not heard from her, and they became alarmed. Max was anguished. Could she have been kidnapped? She couldn't have just disappeared.

On the afternoon of the Oscars, having slept two hours the night before, Max turned on the television set. On some kind of pre-Oscar show was a guy talking about "Best Actress nominee Kristen Caulfield, who was seen this morning having breakfast at Art's Deli on Ventura Boulevard." There was a shot of Kristen, looking awful, Max thought, on Bruce Borger's arm. He called Bruce's number again. This time he answered.

Yes, Bruce admitted, Kristen was there with him. Yes, she would be going to the Oscars, but not with Max. No, she would not speak to either Max or Maggie, for the rest of her life. Dial tone.

Max stood there frozen, with the phone in his hand. She wouldn't talk to him for the *rest of her life*? What in the hell had happened?

When he told Maggie, she advised him to give her time, that whatever it was would come to the surface sooner or later. She reminded him again and again that Kristen was pregnant, and hadn't looked well lately, and the best thing he could do for her, if he really loved her, was to leave her alone right now.

And so Max Jaxon, in anguish, dolled himself up in his Armani tuxedo and stepped out of the limo with Maggie Nash in front of the Kodak Theater on Hollywood Boulevard, painting a grin on his face for the throng of adoring fans screaming, "We want Kristen! We want Kristen!"

"I do too," he said softly to Maggie as they entered the vast auditorium.

Max kept waiting for Kristen to show up. When she had not arrived by the time the ceremony started, and a seat sitter in a gown temporarily took Kristen's place to the right of him, he had a sick feeling that she was not coming at all. Maggie told him to focus on their film and send energy toward the stage. *Scandals* won the award for editing, and as Maggie's "scissors lady," Ellie Storey, bent over and kissed Maggie on her way up to the podium, she whispered, "Where in the hell is Kristen?"

Scandals won Best Cinematography and then Best Original Score. Kristen had still not shown up by the time Maggie won the Best Original Screenplay honors. She hugged Max before she went to the podium to accept the statue from Sean Connery and made her speech short and heartfelt, with nothing but thanks and praise for "the brilliant costars who brought my words to life and etched them in our minds forever, Max Jaxon and our dear Kristen Caulfield." The audience cheered. Max choked back a cry of pain that got caught in his rib cage. He had never missed Kristen so much as at this moment. If only she had come.

Max did not win for his performance in *Scandals*, which did not surprise anyone, least of all Max, for the money had been—rightly so—on Antonio Banderas, who had "frightened the Academy members into voting for him" (so joked Constance Heller), by playing an unforgettable psychotic killer. *Scandals* was not named Best Picture, and Maggie did not win for directing it. But the Best Actress award went to the odds-on favorite, the one who many felt should have won last time around for *Snow Angel*, Kristen Caulfield—who wasn't there.

Max accepted the award for her, with gratitude, and with love. He tried a little humor, reflecting a famous speech the newly elected John Kennedy once made when he said, "And now we're going to prepare for a new administration . . . and, uh, a new baby." Max delighted the audience by saying, "And now we are going to prepare for a new movie . . . and, uh, a new baby." Only Maggie understood the pain behind his toothy smile.

Late that night, Max slipped out of the *Vanity Fair* party to the alley and smashed his fist against the wall. He felt completely let down, hurt, betrayed by her inexplicable no-show and all that happened in Aspen. An hour later, after several drinks to bolster his confidence, he dialed Bruce's number, got his machine, and left a simple, heartfelt message: "That's my girl, Krissy. I'll never stop loving you. I only wish you could have been there to feel the adoration. You are so special. I don't know what happened, what caused this, and I won't press you. I don't want to detract from your triumph tonight. Let's talk tomorrow. I miss you more than I can say. Ciao."

After pulling in at four in the morning, Max and Maggie slept till midafternoon the next day. Then, while Maggie read the newspapers, all of which featured pictures of Kristen from *Scandals* along with other live shots from the Oscars, Max turned on the TV. The newscasters were now reporting what the morning headlines had been too early too know: that when Max Jaxon stood on stage at the Kodak Theater last night accepting the Oscar for Kristen Caulfield in *Scandals*, she was in St. Joseph's Hospital. Just after midnight, she had lost her baby.

Twenty-six

Maggie was furious. "What did you do to her? What did you say to her? Jesus Christ, I can't replace her now. We're down to the Telluride scene. That's all that's left. Shit!" She slammed her fist on the table. "I've got one star recovering from a miscarriage and the other one acting like he had one."

"It was *my* baby!"

"You'll make another one," she yelled. "I've never had such problems with talent, not in all the years—"

"Oh, go fuck yourself," he said. "Get over your self-absorption for a minute. Kristen thinks I did or said something that made her so emotionally upset that she lost the baby and turned back to that idiot prop man for protection. All you care about is your movie."

"She's been out of the hospital for almost three days. And she won't speak to either of us."

"Ask fucking Borger what's going on in her head!" he shouted, as frustrated as he had ever been.

She stood up and faced him, strong and fiery. "*You* did this. *You* chased her away."

He was incredulous. "Me? How?"

"It wasn't *my* dick that got her pregnant!" Maggie hissed, as if putting a curse on him.

He gasped, stunned at her animosity, completely at a loss for words. "This didn't happen because she was pregnant."

"Like hell." She grabbed her Visor and looked for a phone number.

"Who are you calling?"

"Your agent, Bill Barber, who, I want to remind you, is also *her* agent. She has to return to work."

"Maggie, have a heart."

"Goddamn it, Max, be professional." Her eyes glared at him, enunciating the order. "She has to finish it, Max." She glanced down at Kristen being wheeled from the hospital on the front page of the *Los Angeles Times*. "There's no other option."

She stalked off, leaving him speechless.

While Maggie buried herself in the editing room, Max flew alone to Colorado the next day. She had given him the keys to the chalet, since no one else was there. Another winter snowstorm had buried the town in white. Telluride was going to give Maggie Nash what she wanted: a scene that fit snugly into the rest of the movie. Max would get a good night's rest and then spend three days practicing the hang gliding scene that was to be the movie's spectacular opening sequence.

He was glad he was alone. He needed the concentration, the time for himself, despite his anger and frustration at being blamed for something he hadn't done. He had found integrity in himself, but it bit him in the ass. What good was the truth if people didn't believe it?

In the middle of the night, he felt another body close to his. He drowsily remembered the Agnelli yacht, that night that Maggie had slid into the bed against his naked body, and thought he might be having a recollective dream. Or had Maggie shown up? Was that why she'd given him the keys to the place? But it was not Maggie who was in bed with him. It was Nicole.

He was startled. Both he and Maggie had assumed she'd gone back to France. Before he could speak, she pressed her lips to his, kissing him passionately, searching his mouth with her tongue, running her hands over his side, down under his buttocks, between his legs. He tried to pull away, but she seemed glued to his mouth. When he finally managed to say her name, and tried to sit up, she slid down under the duvet, under the sheets, to take him in her mouth. It felt so good, these lips on his cock, that he almost said, *To hell with integrity, let her blow me. If I'm going to be blamed anyway, why not enjoy it?*

But he did stop her. He knew that Nicole was in love with him, and he was not going to be the reward for someone's obsession. "I can't," he said.

He got up, quickly pulling on sweats, and said, "I like you, Nicole. I honestly do, I feel close to you.

But we just can't do this. I don't love you, and so there's no return here, you know?"

Nicole's eagerness diminished in front of his eyes. "You have lost Kristen, you have given up Maggie, but I am here, Max. I still want you."

"But," he said, in the only words that could explain the situation, "I don't want you." And he left the room.

Just before she grabbed the lamp and flung it at the door.

The storm was raging, so he didn't even try to leave the chalet. He collapsed on the living room sofa, where he and Kristen had made love so many months ago. He had lost everyone now. He was empty. First he'd felt he was nothing without Maggie, but Kristen had given him a sense of worth he'd never had before. And now that was gone. He knew he could crawl back to Maggie, but he also knew that if he let those fears rule him, he would cling to her the rest of his life. Nicole was wrong, however; Maggie had not abandoned him, he had abandoned her. In choosing Kristen, he had emotionally left Maggie forever. And now Kristen hated him. Nicole hated him. Maggie hated him. Christ, was he that bad a person?

He added another person to the list of Max haters: himself. He thought *he* was feeling pain right now. But how about Kris? She had loved two people: him and the baby she was carrying. She had lost both because of him. He had killed his own child by running off to Southern France and playing in the Mediterranean with Maggie while Kristen's trust diminished. He put a pillow over his head, knowing it would not smother him but wishing it would, for he felt he really wanted to die.

Then Maggie walked in. She announced that she had gotten the last flight tonight and had somehow braved the snow to get to the chalet. "What are you doing on the sofa?"

"Nicole's still in residence."

She saw that he was crying, and it startled her. She had never seen him cry, except for fake tears on film.

Max pulled his knees up and hugged them. "I don't believe either of us will ever see her again after the gliding sequence, Maggie. And that hurts me more than I can say."

Maggie pulled a tissue from her pocket and walked to the windows. Standing by the French panes reminded her of the villa. She pictured herself there now, peering down the slope, past the old olive tree where her father was buried. She remembered watching Max out there on their first visit, lit by the glow of the house. Then she thought of the first time she'd seen Kristen in person, in London, waiting for her there at the Ritz, nervous and fidgety and vulnerable. What a mess they had made of everything.

She brought the tissue up to her own eyes and dabbed them, for, to her astonishment, she found herself crying as well. It was as if some virus had swept into her body, a virulent strain of unfulfilled longing that threatened to choke her. That was replaced by a wave of bitterness, a contempt rooting inside her.

She saw Max get up and stoke the fire. "I'm filled with those bad feelings again, Maggie," he said softly.

She did not answer. For all she could feel was revulsion for this man, the boy she had once loved.

Kristen returned to Aspen the next week, after her agent convinced her that Maggie would sue her. The first day she spoke not a word to Max, other than the lines she needed to do, and little more to Maggie. When Maggie tried to break through, following her to her dressing room to tell her how sorry she was, how upset she had been, Kristen wouldn't hear it. "You hate Max, that's obvious," Maggie said. "But you hate me now too?"

Kristen gave her a look that, had it been carried out, would have left spit on her face.

As Kristen entered her dressing room, Max was waiting. "I don't want to talk to you, X," she curtly fired off. "You know that, and I want you to respect it."

"No more."

"What?"

"You heard me." He boldly approached her. "I deserve to know what the hell it is that I did."

"You know damn well what you did." She started throwing things into a big leather bag on the sofa. "I trusted you, but I expected too much. When you expect nothing, everything you get is a pleasure. That's what I've learned. Not to have expectations anymore."

"What are you talking about?"

"I hate you," she said, stopping to look at him.

He could barely breathe. "Why?"

"You lied to me! You promised me! It cost me our baby!" She closed the bag and emptied a drawer into another one. "Liar."

"Liar? About what?" He tried to ascertain what she meant. "Maggie? Is it Maggie you're talking about?" The lightbulb lit up in his head. "Sure, that's why you've ostracized us both. You think we've been together, don't you?"

She let out a shrill, mocking laugh.

He grabbed her, turned her toward him. She had a hairbrush in her hand and gripped it tightly, almost freezing at his touch. "You don't believe I told Maggie it's over, do you? You don't believe I told her I want to marry you. You think I'm still sleeping with her."

"*You* believe I'm some kind of fool."

"Kris, I'm not sleeping with Maggie."

"You're staying with her again!"

"I haven't touched Maggie sexually since I promised you I wouldn't, back when the three of us first split up."

She turned her head and closed her eyes. Then, quietly and measuredly, she said, "Nothing destroys trust like lying, X. Please don't make it even worse, okay? It's over, done, finished. I'll do my lines up on that mountaintop, and then I hope to never lay eyes on you again." She burst into tears, grabbed her things and ran from the dressing room.

He caught up with her. "Kris, you've got to believe me!"

She whirled around as several stagehands stared at them. "Don't you come near me, you hear? If I could hurt you the way you did me, I would jump at the chance."

"Kris . . ."

"Don't tempt me, Max." And with that, she fled.

Twenty-seven

Maggie was kneeling next to the hang glider he was going to fly the next morning when Max came in. He was surprised to find her there. "What are you doing?"

She smiled more warmly than she had in months. "Contemplating the color of the silk."

"Nylon," he corrected her.

"Yeah, right. I don't know much about these things." She seemed unsure of something. "I wonder if red would photograph better."

"The yellow is spectacular against the sky. Gonna be a beautiful day tomorrow. Snow on the ground, clear sky. The fitting ending."

She laughed. "Gloom might be more appropriate. After all we've been through." She patted the glider, then stood up. They faced each other.

"I was walking by, saw the light."

She shrugged, then eyed him with a look of reconciliation. "I've behaved badly."

"You hate me too?"

"I apologize."

He laughed. Then he looked suddenly frightened.

"Max? Still having those bad feelings? We can find a stunt double to do tomorrow's—"

"No," he said emphatically. "The bad feelings have nothing to do with the scene."

"Ah."

He pulled himself together, put his hands on her shoulders, and peered into her eyes in a way he hadn't been able to do in months. This was as good a time as any for courage. "I think after we are done today, I'm going to go off on my own for a while."

She eyed him with steely silence. Only a slight nod told him she had even heard him.

He continued bravely. "I lost you both, you see. That's why I was crying night before last. I have never felt more alone, worse than I did as a kid bounced from relative to relative." He threw his arms around her and clung to her. "Maggie, I'm scared," he admitted, talking into her hair. "I was terrified, frightened. I didn't want to lose you, too."

"You haven't lost me," she assured him. "And I understand your need to walk on your own two feet. Do a movie for someone else. Experiment. You are still young, famous now, with lots of money. The world is at your feet."

"You're not angry?"

She smiled. "I told you to trust me." She kissed him. "I'm the wise one, remember?"

He clung to her again. "I'll always love you."

"We had," she said softly, "a good run." Then she

pulled away. She was the filmmaker again. "Okay, one more thing. Are you *sure* you don't want a stunt double?"

"Sure."

"Positive?"

"Yes." He exuded confidence.

"I thought the insurance people were going to force me to use one, but your experience apparently persuaded them, and Marty Stern agreed."

"I know these mountains."

"Actually, I should be less concerned with your flying and concentrate on the fact that we don't have costumes yet."

"Huh?"

"For the extras. They didn't show."

"Let them wear their own stuff."

"Tell that to the hysterical broad who designed them."

He laughed. "Hey, it's all going to work out. You'll see. I'm gonna soar! It's gonna be awesome!"

She walked to the door and hit the light switch. "I'm counting on it."

"I'm not going to disappoint anyone," he promised, walking out before her, "not ever again."

When Maggie left the prop trailer, she heard raised voices coming from around the corner. She stopped after she had locked the padlock and listened. It was Nicole's voice. And Bruce Borger's. "And when the movie is finished?" Bruce was saying.

"I'm taking him on a cruise."

Bruce laughed. "Does he know this?"

"Not yet. But he'll go. Kristen has dumped him, and he's determined to free himself from Maggie. It's the natural progression. And you'll have Kristen."

They must have moved away, for Maggie could no longer hear them. She risked them seeing her by following them. They stopped in the trees near the movie equipment. "Putting Max on a ship somewhere isn't going to remove him from Kris's heart," Borger was saying. "It's going to take time. I'm not so obsessed with her not to know that she still loves him."

Nicole laughed. "I will see to it that his mind is wiped free of any memories. He'll be so overwhelmed by the birthday gift—sailing on my yacht, which he already loves, to South America—that Kristen will become a faded memory."

"You'd do anything to have him, wouldn't you?"

"I knew from the moment Maggie brought him to the villa that we were destined to be together. I get what I want."

"I got news for you, honey," Borger said. "It's not going to work. No way. Max will do another film for Maggie—he's too weak to go off on his own—and she hates you enough to prevent him from ever getting into a rowboat with you, much less your fancy yacht. No, you're never going to have him. Max is powerless to leave the life Maggie has created for him. Even Kris knows that."

Nicole was silent. Maggie watched her as fire brimmed in her eyes and her fists clenched. Then she

faced Borger again and said, "He will be with me."
It was a statement of fact, not a hope. Then she
added, "Or he will be with no one."

When Nicole stomped away, she ran right into
Maggie. "When my father first plucked whatever
nest you came from, I told him not to trust you. I
accused him of attempting to stay young by telling
himself you actually loved him, but he wouldn't listen. I knew you were evil from the start."

"Charles is dead," Nicole reminded her.

"You should know. You caused it."

Nicole's eyes widened. "How dare you?"

"Say the rosary lately?" Maggie said with venom
in her voice.

"I don't know what you are talking about."

"It's only a matter of time before you do."

Nicole turned the tables on her. "What are you
doing spying on us?"

Maggie glanced back toward Borger, who was
watching the confrontation. "It won't work, Nicole.
Bruce is right. You'll never have Max."

"Oh, Maggie, come on, *laisse tomber*. He's already
left you."

"Go to hell." Maggie turned to leave.

"I've invited him to the villa already," Nicole
shouted. "Told him I'm throwing him the biggest
birthday party ever next month."

"I hope they arrest you the minute you set foot on
French soil."

Nicole ignored her. "He'll be longing to go out on
the boat. He'll forget about you and Kristen in hours.
Especially when I'm fucking him. Again!"

Maggie returned and slapped her across the face.

Nicole reeled, holding her jaw. She muttered something in unintelligible French and then spat on the ground in front of her. "You won't win. I'd rather see Max dead than with you." She disappeared into the trees.

Borger looked at Maggie.

All Maggie could say was, "That woman is dangerous."

Max showed up at Kristen's hotel room. When he asked her to see him, promising he'd only stay a minute, she let him in. He thought she had never looked so beautiful, but he did not say that. "I came to say good-bye. I know you'll leave right after we finish tomorrow, probably before I get out of my harness."

She nodded.

"I think, all things considered, we did good work."

She laughed in derision. "If this movie manages to come together, it'll be despite us. My God, it's a wonder anything creative ever comes out of situations like this."

Max wanted to say he'd done nothing to cause it, but instead he went on quietly, "I've had a tough week, Kris. The bad feelings are haunting me."

"I know, X."

"I love you, Kris. It won't ever change. I can hold my head high saying that because I know that I never betrayed you or your trust. Believe what you like, I know what is true." He shoved his hands into his pockets. "I only wish it had ended differently."

She looked like she wanted to say a lot of things, but it was clear she felt there was no point. She only said, "Me too, X. Me too."

He felt an urge to throw himself at her feet and beg for a new start, another chance. But he merely said, "So. See you on the mountaintop bright and early, huh?"

She nodded.

"Hey, do me a favor?" he said with a twinkle in his eye.

"What?"

"Don't use real bullets, okay?"

The sun arrived after the cameras and the crew, and it promised to be a glorious day. Crisp, billowy clouds dotted the sky, as if Maggie had written them in herself. Max had managed to get a decent night's sleep and was now filled with energy. The marvelous sequence was so much a part of the character he was playing. It was the opening of the film, before the titles. He was going to be wild and reckless, until a gunshot frightened him, a gunshot that would just miss him, but would bring him together with the girl of his dreams.

Max and the property master set the hang glider in place. While he and Borger had not made up, they behaved like professionals. Max was happy about one thing. After today he would never have to see this jerk again.

Max started to go over the glider, as he always did before a flight, checking the assembly, for safety reasons, even though he knew no one had been near it since he and Maggie had left the property trailer the night before. But he was suddenly ordered into hair and makeup.

When he returned, he saw that Kristen had arrived, never looking better. His heart tugged. He almost could not bear it when she smiled at him. He turned away and held his emotions inside. The beauticians took charge of her, readying her for the shot, and then she was whisked away in a van to the other bluff, the cabin location. In the back of the van was Kathy Tam, Bruce's assistant, and all the props they would need, including a 30.06 rifle.

Then Maggie distracted Max from his checklist with a bunch of questions from the cameramen, and he did not finish his inspection. But he was not worried. The glider had been locked up all night. He was brimming with confidence, even when he spied Nicole getting out of a car. He wondered if they would ever be rid of her. He didn't let her get to him, even when she came over and wished him a good flight. He thought she really was hoping he would crash. He'd be damned if he would give her that satisfaction.

The costume people were rushing around, steaming the just-unboxed outfits that had finally arrived for the gathered extras. He saw Nicole slipping one on. So she had wormed her way into being an extra today. Well, why not? She had been as much a part of this emotional roller coaster as any of them. Hell, he thought, Borger himself should be in the final se-

quence. It would only be fitting to have all the misbe-
gotten lovers gathered for the last shot.

They were about ready to roll. The extras, all lo-
cals, those gathered on top of the cliff and those
down in the valley, were ready for their fifteen minutes of fame. The great winged contraption was
going to float in the heavens, and the sequence was
going to be magical.

"Places," Maggie called, very much in control.
"Max, darling, ready?"

"No," he said suddenly. "Maggie, I need gloves. I
usually hold on to the control bar with my bare
hands, but it's too cold."

"Get him gloves," Maggie shouted to Borger.

"In my trailer," Borger called to Max, since he was
stuck helping dress the extras. "In the bag on the
chair."

Max ran over to the prop trailer. He saw a black
leather bag on the table and quickly opened it,
searching for gloves. He didn't see any. This was
Borger's own backpack, he realized, packed with ap-
pointment book, plastic pill bottles, high-protein bars,
and a photograph that was sticking out of a well-
worn white envelope. The photograph sent shivers
of shock—but also of understanding—through him.
It showed him and Maggie lying together on the Agnelli yacht.

He marveled for a moment at the snapshot's very
existence, and then the mysteries of the past few
weeks all came clear to him. This was why Kristen
had believed he was a liar. Bruce had shown her this.

It was that simple. And that is why she had lost their baby.

"Max? Find them?" a voice called from outside.

He crumpled the photograph viciously in his fist and dropped it back into Borger's backpack. Then he saw the black leather bag on the chair, the one he was supposed to be looking into. Inside was a large selection of gloves. He found a pair that fit, bicycle gloves. As he put them on, he thought he'd like to strangle Borger with them. When he rushed back into the sunlight, everyone was waiting for him. He was holding up the shot.

But they would have to wait a few minutes longer, for there was had something he had to do first. He went straight to Bruce Borger and slugged him so hard that he knocked the man off his feet. Bruce landed unconscious in the frozen dirt.

Everyone watched in shock, stunned. The doctor and paramedics—who were stationed there in case Max got into trouble—ran to Bruce's aid. Max went to the glider and took his position, assuring Maggie on the mike that he was fine.

"What was that about?" she asked.

"A good-bye present," he said, "and when you hear the whole story, you'll know he deserved it." He took a deep breath. "Okay, I'm ready."

Maggie put her sunglasses on and took a seat in her high director's chair. "Okay, everybody, places, marker. Let's go. Let's finish this cursed movie before anyone else gets hurt."

* * *

Kristen stood on the other bluff, watching him take off. Boy, he was good. Even though she had flown with him, he never ceased to take her breath away when he lifted his feet from the earth and started to soar. Just like that first time in California, she gaped in awe and felt shivers down her spine. She brought her hand up and brushed her hair back. That was a mistake, for two makeup girls rushed to her and sprayed the strands back into place. She'd almost forgotten she was going to be in the next shot.

She stood there, near the cabin from which she would emerge on-screen, watching him cling expertly to the control bar, circling over Trout Lake and then back to where he'd lifted off. "Maggie's gonna have him buzz them," the second unit director said to her, listening to his earphones. "We've got time yet."

She watched as he did just that. But the second unit director had a puzzled expression on his face. "They're arguing about something, it seems." He uncovered his mouthpiece with his hand and listened some more. "Max said tell Kris it's not over yet." Kristen blinked. What? What had made him talk about her when he was supposed to be concentrating on flying for the cameras? It's not over yet?

He sailed through the sky for what seemed like half an hour, and garnered applause from the gathered extras and the crew for a somersault flip he pulled off expertly. Kristen knew how dangerous a maneuver it was, and she breathed a sigh of relief once it was over.

"Places, Kristen," the unit director ordered, and

Kristen went inside the cabin. The sight of the rifle resting against the wall of the cabin unnerved her. She hated what she was going to have to do: grab it, point it at Max, and pull the trigger. But she was a pro. She calmed herself. Outside the cabin, Kathy Tam assured the unit director that Kristen was ready for her cue. He relayed it to Maggie, and she told Max to go for it.

When Max neared the bluff, the unit director said, "Now," repeating Maggie's cue to him. Kristen ran from the cabin, looking up to the sky, as the cameras caught her every move. She looked terrified. She looked around, as if thinking what to do, then hurried back into the cabin, grabbed the gun, and rushed back outside just as the glider was swinging over the cabin for a second time. She lifted the gun. He was very close to her. She planted her feet squarely on the ground, her heels apart as Bruce had taught her, aimed the rifle, and fired twice, in rapid succession.

She was supposed to pull the trigger again for a third shot, but her finger froze as she saw what was happening above her. Without even realizing it, as if in slow motion, she set the butt of the gun down on the ground, her eyes captivated by the blood. The underside of Max's bright nylon yellow pod was turning red, dark red, blood red, and his right arm, which should have been rigid on the control bar, dangled at his side. Kristen realized people were standing at the edge of the bluff now, holding their hands to their mouths. She heard the unit manager say, "He's bleeding!" So it *was* true. It was blood.

Kathy Tam yelled, "What?"

Kristen ran to the group at the edge. Someone handed her binoculars. She gasped as she saw the blood on the pod, the huge spot that was getting bigger and bigger. From that moment on, it seemed like a blur of time and anguish. She watched with the others as Max desperately tried to bring the disintegrating glider back for a landing. Over and over her mind replayed the gunshots, shots she had fired, wounding him. How could she have shot real bullets? Who had done this? Bruce?

Her heart soared when it looked like Max was going to make it. He was going to land! He would hit the ground, and they would help him, get him to a hospital, save him. As she watched the metal frame holding ragged yellow nylon near the clearing where Maggie and all the others stood, she prayed for him. But then everyone started screaming as the glider fell short of the top of the mountain and smacked hard into the wall of rock below.

She could not stand to look any longer. Her legs gave way and she fell into someone's arms. All she kept thinking was, *This didn't happen, it did not happen.*

But she knew it had.

Twenty-eight

When Maggie finally got to the Telluride Trauma Center after the chaos that surrounded the accident, she learned the news. Max hadn't died. "Not yet," a nurse informed her.

They allowed her to go down the corridor to the trauma room, where she found Kristen already standing guard over the battered, unconscious young man. Maggie rushed to pull Kristen into her arms, and while Kristen did let Maggie hold her, she was unresponsive, numb. "He's not going to die," Kristen said, looking down at the love of her life, alive only because the machine was breathing for him.

When the doctors motioned for the women to get out of the way, Kristen and Maggie went into the hall to wait.

Nicole showed up, distraught, filled with the same questions that Maggie and Kristen had. Would he live? If so, would he be all right? How did this happen? How did real bullets get into the gun? A Telluride police officer came in and conducted interviews with each of them individually, and then a doctor told them they were taking Max to Aspen by helicopter. "Why not Denver?" Maggie snapped. "He deserves the best care."

The doctor in charge explained that Neil Sandberg, one of the world's foremost neurosurgeons, was vacationing in Aspen and had agreed to take a look at Max. It wasn't the bullet wound that was endangering his life, it was his head injury. Dr. Sandberg was also a big fan. He would be meeting them at Aspen Valley Hospital on Castle Creek Road as soon as the helicopter landed. Kristen said, "I want to go with him."

"I'm sorry," the doctor explained, "but he needs medical attention on the flight. You can all see him there when you arrive."

Kristen hurried out without even a good-bye to Maggie or Nicole.

Maggie studied Nicole when she finished giving her statement. "What picture?"

Nicole had no idea what she was talking about. "What?"

"Max said to me—to himself—while he was flying, 'It was *her*. *Nicole! She took the picture!*'"

Nicole looked blank. "I don't know what that means."

Maggie pressed. "He added something about you being on the boat that night."

"What boat? What night?" Nicole acted like she hadn't a clue.

Maggie pushed her to the wall. "Listen, you little

cunt. He shouted that he loved Kristen no matter what the picture suggested. Now what the hell was he talking about?"

"Get away from me!" Nicole squeezed out of Maggie's grasp. "Leave me alone."

"If you don't want to tell me, maybe the police can answer my question."

Max Jaxon, suffering from a collapsed lung and an enormous loss of blood, had the bullet lodged in his shoulder removed in surgery in Aspen, but remained in a coma. Dr. Sandberg, a dark, handsome man in his late thirties, described Max's condition to Maggie and Kristen in medical terms, then put it into English: "His lung will heal—thank God the shot hit him on his right side instead of his left—but I don't know if he'll ever regain consciousness." They both gasped. He had hopes for a new drug called eflorinthine, which had been developed for fever victims in Africa and had turned out to aid the recovery of comatose patients. But he would not get their hopes up. "It's a wonder he survived at all with a head injury like this."

So they had no choice but to keep vigil, through that day and all of the next. Flowers poured in, get-well cards and messages from all over the world, a teddy bear from Nicky Dee. The columns were running what seemed like obituaries, but Kristen's faith never wavered. "I believe he can hear us," she assured Maggie and anyone else who came to the room. "I believe he knows we are here now."

After hours of sitting by Max's bedside, Maggie finally took Kristen to a favorite hangout, Pinions restaurant, on the evening of the second day. They had only just sat down before Kristen demanded, "How did this happen?" She was barely able to keep control of her voice. "I want you to tell me how this happened."

Maggie explained how she'd viewed the accident. It had rendered her speechless, frozen in place. "Everyone ran toward the cliff, but I was completely paralyzed. I just stood there, disbelieving." She looked distraught. "I keep kicking myself. I had a terrible feeling about this. But he was determined. I couldn't talk him into letting a stunt double do it."

"But how did it *happen*?" Kristen repeated. "Who put real bullets into the gun?" She screamed, "I shot him, Maggie! I'm the one who almost killed him!"

Maggie soothed her. "You didn't know. Honey, stop beating yourself up."

"I yelled at Bruce, why real bullets? He didn't know either."

Maggie shook her head. "Kris, I know you're very close to Bruce. And we all know what Bruce feels for you. Is there any chance, given the animosity between Max and Bruce—I mean, Max knocked him out cold just before he took off—that Bruce might have loaded real ammo on purpose?"

Kristen looked horrified. "No," she said quickly. "I don't know what Bruce was capable of doing to X, but he would never have done that to me."

Maggie dropped the thought. "The Telluride police

have turned it over to a detective here in Aspen. They'll find out the truth."

Kristen shook her head. "One of the bullets ripped the wing. He lost control."

Maggie reached across the table and took Kristen's hand. "Yes."

"I did that!"

"Kris, you didn't do it on purpose."

Kristen gripped her hand. "What did he say, Maggie? What did Max say?"

"He said, 'Why did she do this to me?' I don't know who he meant."

Kristen was beside herself. "He meant *me*." Tears welled in her eyes. "Oh, my God."

"Kristen, don't destroy yourself."

"Did you tell the police that?" Kris asked suddenly.

"Of course, and I'm sure they heard it themselves on the tape."

Kristen could not get over it. "Someone purposely did this to him, put real ammunition in that gun. If it wasn't Bruce, who was it? Nicole?"

Maggie bristled. "I wouldn't put it past the little bitch. If she could murder Daddy, she's capable of trying to kill Max."

Kristen started crying. "You know I didn't need to pull the trigger. We shot the insert already. We had the gunshot on film just in case. I just wanted to make it more realistic, thought it would be—"

"Kristen, stop doing this to yourself!" Maggie gripped the girl's shoulder for a long moment, and then, as she saw the tears beginning to fall down her soft, golden cheeks, she whispered, "Oh, Kris, darling, we'll find out. We'll do everything we can to learn who wanted to harm Max." She put her other hand on Kristen's cheek. "Kris, I've missed you."

Kristen turned her head away. "Please, don't . . ."

"No, honey, you have to hear me out. I never wanted it to end. I loved Max, I loved you, I loved us. You two made your choice, and I hated it, but I knew I would have to live with it."

Kristen pulled her arm out of Maggie's grasp and jumped to her feet. "Is that why you were still sleeping with him? Is that how you 'lived with it'?" Kristen didn't give Maggie a chance to speak. "Max may have the body of an athlete, but he's filled with all the fears of a child. He was too insecure about his career. I was right. He would never have been able to resist you sexually."

"You're wrong," Maggie protested, standing up as well. "I'm not going to be blamed for something I didn't do. I never slept with Max after he told me he had chosen you."

"I saw the photograph, Maggie!"

Maggie blinked. The picture—a photograph. Sure, he said Nicole had taken it. That would make the "picture" a photo. But she was clueless. "What photo? Kristen, you've got to tell me. You're blaming me like you blamed Max, and we aren't guilty."

"Ask Bruce to show it to you!" Kristen snapped, and stormed out of the restaurant, leaving Maggie standing there with everyone in the room gaping at her.

* * *

The pretty, dark-haired waitress at Campo de Fiori set a drink down in front of Bruce Borger. "I think this is Absolut number fifteen."

"Twelve," Borger snapped. "You exaggerate."

"Last one."

"Easy for you to say."

"You trying to kill yourself?"

"What's your name?" Bruce looked at her with glassy eyes. "I'm Bruce."

"Tanya."

"You're a nosy bitch, Tanya."

"You're a nasty drunk, Bruce."

He giggled. Then looked thoroughly defeated. "I'm also fucked."

"How?"

"I'm gonna take the fall." He swirled the little piece of lemon rind with his index finger, then drank all the vodka in one gulp. "I shoulda told him about the picture. I could have cleared myself. But I was scared, you know?"

She shrugged. Another drunk babbling. She heard it nightly. But she was more curious about this one because she'd seen him several times with the movie company. The restaurant and bar was their hangout when they were filming. She'd overheard him talking with that Frenchwoman one night, the one who ordered Campari. Tanya had figured she was either mistress to one of the Saudi princes or Eurotrash doing the slopes. Now, with the photos in the paper, and the case the talk of the town, she knew who the Frenchwoman was. And who this guy was. So she egged him on. "What are you scared about?"

"Taking the blame. No way out. Oh, she manufactured it like that. Aimed them at me while making me think we would keep each other's secret."

Normally, Tanya would have cut off the drinks long ago. Instead, she refilled his glass without him even asking for it. "That's on me." Her curiosity was piqued. She bent forward over the table and asked, "Who are you talking about?"

With a conspiratorial tone, he whispered dramatically, "*Her*. You know. And I coulda stopped her, I coulda changed all that happened." He sipped the drink this time. "It's my fault."

"What is?"

"All of it. This whole fucking mess." He slugged down the rest of the Absolut and shuddered. Tears welled up in his eyes. "I coulda prevented the whole thing."

Did he mean the accident? "How?"

"Or I coulda told what I knew. But she said I'd go down too. Now I'm gonna go down while she stands there laughing . . ."

"Bruce, I don't know what you're saying."

He almost shouted, "I told her, 'I saw you do it— I can bring you down!' "

She played along. "What did she say back?"

He wiped his mouth on his sleeve. " 'We have a deal.' "

"An understanding?" She leaned forward, smiling, trying to make him think he could trust her, urging him to open up.

"That's right." Bruce ran his hand nervously over his beard. "You sound like you understand, Donna."

"Tanya."

"I'm drunk."

She risked it again. She brought him another. There was no fear he would drive drunk tonight; it would amaze her if he could even walk out of this place. "Bruce, you sound like you need a friend."

"I need a fucking lawyer." He laughed. "I didn't do it. But I did, you know? Letting it happen is the same thing. Not stopping it. Conspiracy. Collusion. Murder charges apply to the whole group, to all who knew, who covered up. But she's making it look like I was the only one."

"Who's *she*?" Tanya figured he was talking about the Frenchwoman.

"I lied about the photo. Dumb move. I told Kris to lie. Stupid. I should have admitted what I saw."

Tanya put her hand on his shoulder. "Man, you're troubled."

Bruce shook like a snake was crawling under his skin. He stood up. "I think I'm gonna be sick."

"Bathroom's down—"

Bruce grabbed her hand. "Maybe it's not too late?"

"You need to talk to my dad. He could help you."

He blinked. Then burped, looked almost green, but recovered. "Who the hell is your dad and why would I wanna talk to him?"

"I'm Tanya Schierling. My father is Hans Schierling, the chief of—"

Before she finished the sentence, Bruce fled, making a perfect beeline for the door that belied how drunk he was.

Tanya went to the bar, picked up the phone, and dialed a number. "Mom? Dad there? Put him on. I gotta talk to him."

Kristen returned to the hospital early the next morning and sat there for the rest of the day, watching Max, sometimes talking to him, singing to him, hoping that somehow he was aware of her presence and that he would wake up. Maggie showed up late, after she'd been editing. Kristen told her that Max's condition had not changed. Then Nicole walked in. Maggie was outraged. "Get the hell out of here!"

But Christopher Daniel followed on Nicole's heels. "I'm glad you are all here," he said.

"Yeah," Maggie tried to joke, "Macbeth's witches."

Daniel added, "It's time to put our heads together rather than speaking with each of you separately, as I've been doing. Now, about this 'picture' that Max spoke of."

"Yes," Maggie said, "will someone finally tell me what was in this photograph?"

"You and Max making love," Kristen blurted.

Maggie was shocked. "In a photograph? No one ever took photos of us making love. I think I'd know about that."

Kristen said, "The date stamped on it coincided with the week after your father's funeral. I guessed it was on the Agnelli yacht."

Maggie protested. "I never made love to Max on any yacht, including my father's." Then her eyes narrowed as she remembered something. "Wait. That last night I went to Max's stateroom. He held me . . ." She took a step toward Nicole. "You little monster."

Nicole took a step back, as if Maggie were going to strike her. "You were fucking him just like before!" she spat.

Maggie was seething. "*You* photographed us."

"I didn't say that."

"You don't have to," Daniel said. While they'd been arguing, he had reached into his pocket and withdrawn a photo that was lined with creases where Max had crumpled it in his fist. "Bruce threw this away, but thanks to a curious hotel employee, it managed to find its way to the police station."

Maggie snatched it from him and gasped. "But how?"

Nicole angrily said, "Look at the angle. Through the stateroom window, how do you think? Max didn't pull the drapes."

Maggie lunged for her. "*You're* the one who should have hit the side of the mountain!"

Daniel stepped between them, holding Maggie back. He looked at Nicole. "What prompted you to do this?"

Nicole said defensively, "I knew Kristen was waiting for Max to return to her, to marry her. And there he was, naked with *her* again."

Kristen objected. "Don't act like you did it for me."

"You've never cared about anyone but yourself," Maggie accusingly said to Nicole. "Your motivation has always been selfish. Like with Papa."

"You don't know me at all."

"I know you killed my father!" Maggie shouted.

"Stop it," Daniel ordered Maggie. He snapped his head back to face Nicole. "Why did you really take that photo?"

Nicole looked away.

"Mrs. Nash, if you refuse to answer me, I'll start asking you about rosary beads."

That startled her. She suddenly looked fearful.

"I swear," Daniel warned her, "if you don't start cooperating with me, I'll start investigating Charles Nash's death as well. All I learn will be turned over to the French authorities."

Nicole glanced at Maggie, who hadn't stopped glaring at her. She finally said, "That would serve no purpose, Detective. But I do want to see justice done here. I took the photo because Max turned me down. I was hurt."

"Papa wasn't even cold, and you went after Max? You're disgusting."

Kristen added, "Turned you down. Jesus."

Nicole said, defying them, "Max felt something for me since that night in Paris."

Maggie's eyes flashed. "Spare me the violins."

"Perhaps," Nicole said, "I should have photographed him then too."

Daniel tried to rein the conversation in. "You gave that photograph to Borger, right?"

Nicole nodded. "I did."

"Why?" Maggie demanded.

"Because it would win him Kristen. And Max would be free for me."

Maggie lunged for Nicole again. This time she managed to grab her shoulders before Daniel pulled her back. "Max and I did not make love on the boat. He held me, that was all. Yes, I wanted sex, but we did not do it." She faced Kristen, begging her to believe her. "He wouldn't do it, Kris."

Kristen wanted to believe her. Then other pieces fell in place for her. "Max must have seen the picture in the prop trailer when he went back in to get the gloves. That's why he hit Bruce."

"Bruce has a terrible temper," Nicole said. "He's dangerous."

"You should talk," Maggie snapped.

"You hate me because Charles loved me more than he did you!" Nicole shouted at her.

Daniel pressed himself between the two of them. "Stop it."

"No," Maggie retorted, "I hate you because you're lying garbage. I saw through you the minute Daddy dragged you out from whatever rock he lifted up to find you!"

Nicole tried to strike her, but Daniel deflected her arm. "All right," he ordered. "That's enough—"

Nicole suddenly grabbed her bag and fled, muttering something in French.

Daniel looked at Maggie and Kristen. Maggie seemed to be coming apart. "She killed my father! She caused Max's accident! Can't somebody stop her?"

"If Borger did load the gun and slit the nylon, yes, she may be guilty of conspiracy. But do you both feel that Bruce could have been so wildly jealous of Max that he would have tried to kill him?"

Kristen shivered, but admitted, "I think Bruce might have done anything to have me." She felt relieved now that she'd voiced her deepest fear. "It scares me to say this, but he wouldn't have trusted anything short of Max's being out of my life for good." She turned and sat next to the bed, taking Max's limp hand.

Daniel slid the photo into his jacket. "Don't leave town, either of you."

Kristen looked appalled. "How can you think I could leave him?"

Maggie was more practical. "I have a film to finish editing in Los Angeles."

"Do it here," Daniel suggested. "And don't tell Borger what we just discussed."

They shared discomforted glances. Then he left.

Maggie looked at Kristen. "I mean it, honey. I swear. Max held me that night. And that was all." And with that, she walked out, leaving Kristen and Max alone.

The phone in Borger's room rang late that evening. "So," the familiar woman's voice began, "Aspen's Columbo wants us to stay in town."

Bruce said, "Guess we're stuck here."

"How about having a drink with me?"

"Why?"

"So we can talk. You know we need to."

He thought about it. It made sense. Suspicion was an oddly disconcerting thing to live with, especially when you were a suspect. "Yes. When?"

"Now."

"It's late."

She laughed. "Never stopped you before."

He yawned. "How about going skiing with me in the morning instead?"

"Make you a deal. One drink tonight, slopes in the morning. It's important, Bruce."

"Okay. Where?"

"The base of run 1-A."

"That's kinda remote this time of night."

"You want the Prada store on Galena Street?"

He laughed. "I guess we should be circumspect."

"It's private. Ski bum country. It will be fairly deserted."

"There a place to drink there?"

"Nearby."

"Ten minutes."

"I'm leaving now."

When he arrived at the base of 1-A, she was already standing in the parking lot. "What's up?"

"I'm wrong. Thought there was a bar down here, an après-ski place."

He looked around. It was deserted and dark. "This is pretty shabby."

"It's the oldest run. Let's take a walk, so we can talk."

He followed her around the back of the dark building, where they faced the slopes. He looked up. "Look at the moon."

She did not look at the sky but continued walking farther from the building. "So," she said soberly, "no more games. Christopher Cop is getting close. We have to come up with a strategy."

He stopped walking, smiling at her. "It seems that there's not much you can do about it at this point. It's more my call."

She nodded. "I agree. You've got the power."

He kicked some snow, his hands shoved in his parka pockets. "Well, I'm not an unreasonable man. I hated him too, as you well know. Kristen is free now, and I'm going to give her some time. She'll come around once Max has stopped breathing."

"What makes you think he will?"

"Come on," he said, almost laughing. "With those kind of injuries . . ." He stooped down, cupped some snow into his hands and formed a ball. He threw it at a nearby tree. And missed.

"So what's our deal going to be?"

He remained crouched down, making another snowball. "I'll have to think about it."

"I'm afraid you won't be able to."

He lined up the tree with his eye once again. "What do you mean?"

"With a bullet through your brain, it won't be possible."

He froze, holding the snowball in his hand, as he felt the icy cold steel of the pistol pressing against his temple. Held his breath. He dropped the snowball. "You don't need to do this. You can trust me. I have no reason to want to harm you."

"But I have very good reason to want to kill you."

He kept looking straight ahead, blinking. "Why?"

"You're the only person who can give me up."

He felt his knees shaking. "Why would I do that?"

He didn't hear the answer. Because she shot him through the head.

Twenty-nine

Twenty-nine

Christopher Daniel stood near the body. Young Officer Stonecipher told him that he'd been the first to arrive when the call came in at seven in the morning. As ski lift 1-A was about to open, a caretaker had found Bruce Borger's frozen, crumpled corpse behind the building, his brains spattered over the blood-soaked snow, a perfectly formed snowball right next to his head. "Nobody touched a thing," the deputy assured Daniel. In Bruce's hand was the .38 revolver, finger frozen to the trigger. "Sure looks like he did himself in."

"Could be." Daniel studied the scene, the body. "It seems strange that he'd make a snowball but decide not to throw it when he was going to shoot himself."

"We found something else," the deputy offered. "Sir, over there." He pointed to another cop, who was waving toward them, holding something in his hand.

Daniel hurried over to the man. He was holding a woman's leather glove, a very small size, so small that one might describe it as birdlike.

*　　*　　*

Christopher Daniel handed Chief Hans Schierling a Ziploc bag containing the gun, and another with the camel-colored leather glove. "The gun is a .38 that came from the prop trailer they used on *Never Forget*. The glove was manufactured in Paris, and we found the match when we searched the car Nicole has been renting."

Hans sat down. "That the only evidence?"

"The light snow that fell through the night covered the tire tracks and footprints, but one of the officers kicked this up as he searched the area. See the dark spot on the little finger?"

Hans noticed the blood for the first time. "Borger's?"

Daniel nodded.

"What did Nicole say?"

"She was framed."

Hans shook his head. "Goddamned movie people. So what do we have here, Daniel? Where are we exactly?"

"Bruce knew something. When I questioned the ladies at the hospital yesterday, someone obviously got spooked and decided to silence Bruce before he could do her in."

"You got a preference?" Hans asked.

"Nicole."

"Why?"

Daniel handed over a page that had been faxed to him a few minutes before the chief entered his office. It was a report from the head of homicide in Avignon. At Daniel's urging, citing the evidence of the rosary beads, Charles Nash's body had been exhumed from its resting place under his olive tree. Testing for residual poison came back positive. A warrant had been issued in France for the arrest of Nicole Richaud Nash. "Bring her in," Chief Schierling said. "Might be a doubleheader."

After Nicole was arrested on suspicion of murder and brought to the Aspen jail to be held, the reporters found Kristen at the hospital and bombarded her with questions. She did her best to answer them, but halfway through, the emotional distress caught up with her and she asked the nurse to throw them out. She felt better when she was alone with Max. The nurse asked if she wanted some tea, or could she turn on the TV for her? The last thing Kristen needed was to see a replay of the bloody snow where Bruce's body had been found, or Nicole looking defiant in handcuffs, being hustled into the Aspen police station. "X, come back," Kristen pleaded. "Please, before somebody else gets hurt." She stared at his unmoving face. "I know you can hear me. I know you're listening. Maggie was right. They think Nicole murdered Charles. It looks like she shot Bruce because he knew that she did this to you." Tears flooded her cheeks.

Neil Sandberg entered. As Kristen tried to compose herself, he offered a clean tissue from the box near the bed. "You holding up?"

She nodded, reeling her emotions in. "How is he, Doctor?"

The physician looked Max over. "I'd hoped to see some change by now because of the eflorinthine, but we won't give up."

She took a deep breath. "No, we won't."

After the doctor left, Kristen sat on the bed with Max. How could love and desire have gotten so tainted? How could Nicole have become so obsessed with Max? And she had killed Maggie's father. Thinking of that, Kristen realized she had not spoken to Maggie since she'd learned Charles was murdered. She should go over, console Maggie for her loss. Now that the truth behind the photo had been revealed, she knew that comforting Maggie was the right thing to do.

When Kristen got to the chalet, the press was camped there as well. They attacked as they saw her driving up the steep driveway, causing her to nearly run them over. When she got out, she pushed through the field of mikes being held toward her face, shouting, "I have nothing to say!" Maggie opened the door and pulled her inside.

"It's been like that since they took Nicole away." She pulled the drapes tight in all the windows. "Fucking leeches."

Kristen flopped into an easy chair. "It's funny, you know? We love the press when we need them, when we're looking for more fame. But we hate them when we really have something for them to chew on."

"Let them gag on it," Maggie said, kicking off her shoes, curling her feet up under her on the sofa. She was wearing an oversized sweater and wool slacks. "There's another storm coming."

"Perfect," Kristen muttered. Then she asked, "Did Nicole give up easily?"

"She didn't hole up and shoot at them, if that's what you mean. She marched off in handcuffs, screaming that they had the wrong person, they should have been arresting me. Can you imagine?" She put her head back on the leather. "I think it's finally over. I hope they put her in prison for life for murdering my father."

"That's why I came over, to say how sorry I am for your loss."

They talked for a while, and then Kristen shut her eyes. They said nothing more for a long time. Maggie realized that Kristen had fallen asleep. After her three-day vigil, she must be exhausted. She got up, careful not to disturb Kristen, and covered her gently with a throw. She went to the window, and saw that it was snowing again. The sky was heavy with storm clouds, and the wind was blowing.

Maggie poured herself a strong cocktail, and, though it was something she seldom did, she cooked dinner. Kristen awakened to the smell of frying onions, feeling better after her sleep. She came over to help put a salad together. Maggie uncorked some French wine, dumped some into the skillet holding the chicken breasts and onions, and then poured the rest into oversized glasses for the two of them. Kristen took the bread from the oven, and they sat down to a quiet, tasty meal.

And another bottle of wine after the food was gone.

"I think Christopher Daniel is a hunk," Maggie said, a little tipsy.

"What? Where'd that come from?"

"Sultry eyes. I bet he's got a great body under those winter clothes."

Kristen said she had never thought about it. "Nicole should have set her sights on *him*. None of this would have happened."

"I have a surprise," Maggie said over the rim of her wineglass. "Been working on a new script every night for the past year. It's the best part you'll ever play."

Kristen was apprehensive. "I don't think we can make a movie together again, Maggie."

Maggie looked wounded. "Why?"

Kristen shrugged. "Let's forget it."

Maggie wasn't about to. "Shit happens, Kristen. It happened to us, to you in spades, and worse, the very worst, to Max. God, I almost wish he'd died rather than to lie there like a vegetable, a breathing corpse."

Kristen shouted, "He isn't brain-dead! He could still come out of it!"

"I'm a realist," Maggie said, "and I don't live in denial. We have to face facts."

"The fact is, *you* controlled him so strongly that he never had a chance to be himself."

Maggie said, "Blaming me won't help your healing. Do something constructive. You can't squander your talent, Kris. To work again is what Max would want. It's what you owe the world."

"I don't owe anybody anything!" Kristen's anger exploded. "I'm trying to decide if acting is worth it. There was a purity that I found in my work, and I'm not that naive to think it would have lasted forever, but I have no interest in being a star."

"You're brilliant."

"But look at all that's happened to me. Do you see why I might want to go home to Wisconsin and marry a nice plumber?"

"You're lying to yourself. You don't believe that." Maggie was stern, knowing. "I'm not going to let you get away with cloaking yourself in middle-class values that you long ago left behind. You loved what we had. You were a willing participant, you were hungry for it, voracious, and you just can't admit that—it's easier—and safer—to be the victim of Max's cock. Oh, what a monster he was! Oh, sorry, I have it wrong, *I* was the monster and he was the sap. So I'm the villain to your perpetual victim, and Max will always be your hero now that he's conveniently on ice."

Kristen's mouth opened in shock. "How can you speak about him that way?"

Maggie took a sip of her wine. "Max is as good as dead, Kris. Face it."

Kristen was stunned by her coldness. "Where's your heart?"

Maggie rushed to the desk across the room to pull pages of a script out of a leather briefcase. She tapped it with her fingers. "My heart's right here. Where yours should be as well."

Kristen closed her eyes. "I don't have the confidence."

Maggie put her hands on Kristen's shoulders. "I can restore that for you. Trust me, Kris. The spark will return, we'll create a masterpiece together, the two of us." Maggie peered deep into her eyes. "You still love me," she whispered confidently. "I feel it. I know it. Now trust me as well."

Kristen tried to make sense of what she was hearing. Love her? Yes, some part of her would always love this woman who had had such an impact on her life, but what was this about? Kristen sensed a switching of gears that she could not have predicted. Maggie was begging Kristen to come back to her films, her talent, her aura, perhaps even her arms. A thought hit Kristen like a meteor suddenly—who needed Max?

Maggie pulled her toward her, clinging to her, her face buried in Kristen's hair, one hand at the back of her head, whispering to her, "Give us a chance. Please don't leave me again . . ."

As Maggie held her, cried over her shoulder, Kristen said, "I have to go, Maggie."

Maggie protested. "Stay, please stay. Stay the night. Oh, darling. Neither of us should be alone now."

But Kristen, confused and upset, needed to get out.

Where she felt safe.

Where she could process the terrible scenario that was now emerging full-blown in her thoughts.

Thirty

At ten minutes to five o'clock the next afternoon, Maggie Nash rushed into Aspen Valley Hospital, hurrying down the hall to the nurse's station near Max's room. "Someone called," she told the familiar woman at the desk. "They said something happened."

The nurse impassively pointed down the hall.

Maggie ran to Max's room. Inside, she saw the bed had been stripped of the sheets and was being disinfected by a man dressed in a blue outfit, rubber gloves on his hands. "No!" she cried, bringing her hands to her mouth.

The nurse came in right behind her. "I'm sorry, Miss Nash."

"He . . . he's gone?"

The nurse nodded. "It happened late this morning. Miss Caulfield was with him when he died. They did everything they could."

"It happened this morning, and you waited till now to tell me?"

"No one could find you," the woman politely explained.

"I was editing my—" Maggie let out her breath. "Max is dead." Then she turned to the woman again. "How is Kristen? How did she take it?"

The woman shrugged. "I don't know. I just came on at three. I was told they gave her Max's things from the room, the cards and flowers."

Maggie felt her head spinning. "Poor Kris! Oh, God, she must be beside herself. I've got to find her."

She called the Jerome, and then anyone she thought might know where Kristen was. She dialed the Caulfields in Wisconsin, who said they had just heard on the news that Max had died. They didn't seem too upset about that, but they were greatly concerned about their daughter. They begged Maggie to have her call them. She tried the chalet, on a slight hope that Kristen had gone there to tell her. But that was senseless. She was about to hang up after the third ring when someone, surprisingly, answered. "Yes?" a soft voice, obviously in pain, asked.

"Kristen?"

"Maggie?"

"You're there!"

"I didn't . . . I didn't know where else to go." She sounded lost and empty.

"Oh, my darling, I'm so sorry."

"He looked like he was still breathing, just lying there like he had been all along, but his chest wasn't moving."

Maggie felt tears welling in her eyes at the sound of the heartbroken voice. "Kris, are you alone?"

"I don't know what I'm going to do without Max."

"I'm coming, darling. I'm on my way. The roads are terrible, but I'll be there as soon as I can. I'll take care of you, we'll talk. It will be all right, I promise."

"Maggie . . ." Kristen started to cry.

"I'm almost there, sweetheart." She hung up and turned to see an orderly facing her. He had cared for Max each afternoon of the three days he had clung to life, and she said, "Thank you for caring."

He nodded. "I'm so sorry. We all are. We all loved him."

"So did I," she said, turning to start down the stairs. "Once."

The windshield wipers sagged under the weight of the heavy, wet snow. The Mercedes growled as its four powerful wheels churned in the mush, slowly climbing. Maggie had only about ten kilometers to go, and then she would feel safe. The drive would have gotten her down except for the fact that she knew she had won. She heard confirmation of it on the only station she could get on the radio in this storm, the local easy-listening channel. "The motion picture star Max Jaxon died in Aspen Valley Hospital today after spending several days in a coma."

She turned onto the road that led to Snow Canyon Road, but had to stop the vehicle after a few kilometers to brush the snow off the hood. The snow was falling so rapidly that it had no time to melt, despite the fact that the metal was warm from the heat of the engine. It was piling up so fast, she could not see the terrain in front of her. Or where the roadway was. She was simply pointing herself down the middle of the open space between pine trees. She'd never seen a storm like this.

As she moved around to the passenger side of the vehicle, she allowed herself to drink in the beauty, if only for a moment. Despite the tragedy of the day, and the anguish she knew had paralyzed Kristen, she felt a kind of freedom, even a joy, that she had not experienced in a long while. The branches of the trees were weighted down so that they touched the mounds of white on the ground. The enormous dark brown trunks were plastered with ivory spray. In a matter of moments, as she stood outside the car, her hair went from auburn to white as well.

Once inside the warm, cozy compartment, Maggie shook her head like a dog, splattering snow everywhere, which turned immediately to water. She took a sip from the Evian bottle in the cup holder, put the vehicle into gear again, and began to move—after sliding right and left slightly. The radio went to static and died. She suddenly realized it was getting dark.

It took her forty minutes to go a distance that should have taken only ten, and she found herself facing a huge snowplow and two Aspen police vehicles with their lights flashing. They were both GMC all-wheel-drive vehicles, one of which seemed to have spun into the ditch. She came to a stop, grabbed a scarf to put over her head, and got out just as a cop emerged from the big truck. "Miss Nash, we've closed Snow Canyon," he called. "Car went off the ridge about a mile up a few hours ago. Can't risk another situation like that."

"I've got to get to the chalet."

"Sorry."

Another cop got out of the hulking vehicle, an older man. "I'm Officer Raines, Miss Nash. You want to get to your place?"

"I do. I'm sure I can make it. In this." She gestured to the Mercedes.

The young cop said, "I'm not even sure you'd make it in *that*," pointing to the huge machine with the plow affixed to it.

"You have chains?" Raines asked.

Maggie shrugged. "It's four-wheel-drive."

Raines laughed. "So is that." He pointed to the GMC truck in the ditch. "Brilliant here was driving it without chains."

The younger cop looked embarrassed.

Raines said to Maggie, "Surprised you made it this far."

Maggie thought so too, but she wasn't about to tell them that. "It's only ten kilometers up the hill."

"There are chains under the seats down there in the ditch," Raines reminded his partner.

The young man gave a reluctant nod. "You want my opinion, too dangerous even with them."

Maggie batted her eyelashes. "Guys, gimme a break. Please. There's someone waiting at the house who needs me very badly."

The older one nodded. "Heard about Max. I'm truly sorry."

They put the chains on for her and led the way in the huge vehicle. It churned up the snow like it was confetti and plowed a path right to her driveway. She told them good night, and they said they hoped she had enough firewood and food for a long siege. "This is gonna get worse before it gets better."

When they drove off, Maggie put the Mercedes into first gear and gripped the wheel with all her might. The chains, combined with the snow tires, didn't fail her. She made it all the way to the garage. She didn't want to have to dig it out when this was finished. Already she could see the snow had begun to obliterate Kristen's white Outback in the driveway. She rushed into the house.

Inside the chalet, Maggie found burning pine scenting the air. Kristen was curled on the sofa near the fireplace. Maggie took her coat off. "Darling," she said, hugging her tightly. "The storm is getting worse out there. Are you okay?"

"I've been thinking about what you said."

"I wondered where you'd gone."

"And I came to the conclusion that you are right. We have to go on."

Maggie instantly relaxed. Getting comfortable, she took off her coat, shoes, and poured herself a drink. They toasted Max, the memories, and the future. Kristen's hand trembled so badly that some of the wine spilled. Maggie grabbed her arm, steadying her. "Honey?"

Kristen cried in her arms. Maggie held her gently, letting her sorrow pour out. She caressed her, running her hands through the girl's silken hair, until Kristen's tears dried and she settled into Maggie's arms. When Kristen finally sat up, Maggie asked, "You all right?"

Kristen nodded. "I'm okay. I guess I just didn't believe I'd lose him."

"You must be hungry. Let me make some dinner."

Kristen shook off her melancholy. "No, you cooked for me yesterday, so it's my turn. Why don't you go up and have a bath while I make us something?"

"Just reheat anything you have."

Kristen nodded. "I'll give you a call when it's ready."

Maggie hesitated. "Are you sure you want to cook?"

Kristen looked anguished. "I can't just sit around thinking about it, you know?"

Maggie nodded, kissed her on the cheek, and went upstairs.

When the bubbles cascaded over the rim of the tub up in the master bedroom, and Maggie turned off the water and slipped into the water, Kristen walked into the bathroom with Maggie's drink and a lit candle. She doused the overhead light, transforming the room into a romantic, peaceful reverie. She had turned on soft jazz downstairs, and Maggie could hear it now. She knelt by the tub, stroked Maggie's hair, kissed her forehead, and told her a casserole was reheating in the microwave, to relax while she put a salad together. Maggie grabbed the hem of her skirt. "Why don't you join me? Like we used to do."

Kristen looked tempted. "I don't know."

Maggie was careful not to press her, push her too far. "I'm not going to force you."

Kristen nodded and hurried back downstairs.

After dinner, and drinking a whole bottle of wine together, they again sat near the fireplace, on the floor this time. Kristen let Maggie stroke her hair. Maggie admitted how much she had missed her when she left them, admitting how empty she had felt. "I knew you had to feel the same." She caressed Kristen's forehead, rubbing it gently.

"You almost sounded last night like you blamed Max for everything."

Maggie blinked. "I blamed him for getting you pregnant." She began to stroke her arms. "Collette said women bond in a place no man can ever enter. I felt it with you that first time we were together. Max was very much a part of it, but he was always an outsider, as far as my heart was concerned."

"Oh, Maggie," Kristen said. "Hold me, just hold me."

Maggie set her drink down. She put her arms around Kristen as she stretched out next to her on the pile of pillows on the floor. "My darling, I'm going to hold you for the rest of time." And with that promise, she kissed her, full, passionately, on the mouth. Kristen did not resist. She gave herself wholly, willingly, moving her hands behind Maggie's head and holding her there. Then they slowly undressed one another and lay naked in front of the dancing fire. "The flames reflect in your eyes," Maggie said, kissing the girl again.

"What do my eyes tell you?"

"That you still love me," Maggie sighed, and brought her lips to Kristen's left breast, which made Maggie shudder with desire. "Oh, God, I denied my feelings for you for so long, so very long . . ."

"Wait," Kristen said, sitting up.

"What?"

"Wait." Kristen backed up, to the side of the fireplace, propping herself against the pillows, her legs outstretched in front of her, looking sensual and passionate, but with an impish grin on her face that Maggie remembered from so many of their three-way sessions. It turned Maggie on. "How much do you want me?" Kristen whispered.

"More than I can express," Maggie answered, kneeling just feet from her outstretched legs.

"How much? Tell me."

Maggie swallowed. She liked this. She liked talking, domination. "I need you. It's like my lifeblood."

"You want this?" Kristen asked, looking down to her right breast, which she cupped in her hand.

"Yes."

"You want this too?" She caressed the left one.

"I love your body. I want your tits, I want to make love to them." Maggie leaned forward, as if ready to lap them like a dog. "Let me have them, please, darling."

"You want this too?" Kristen brought both hands down. "Is this what you have been waiting for?"

Kristen could tell Maggie's heart was racing. She was feeling caught in a haze of desire she had never known. "Yes. Yes, please."

"Would you grovel on the floor for me?"

"Yes." Maggie said with a cockeyed grin, enjoying this game. She leaned farther forward, putting her chin on the floor, her breasts resting on the old faded carpet.

Kristen stood up before Maggie could touch her feet. "Would you crawl on your hands and knees for me?"

Maggie crawled toward her. Kristen moved away quickly. Maggie continued. "I want you. I need you. Anything, say it and I'll do it."

"Will you buy me anything my heart desires?"

"Yes."

"Will you bathe me?"

"Yes, yes." Maggie was overcome with desire. "I'll bathe you, clean you, powder you, perfume you, fuck you . . ."

"Do you want me all for yourself?" Kristen was teasing Maggie with her nipples, bringing her breasts only inches from her face. But when Maggie reached up, Kristen pulled away. "What will you do to guys who want me?"

Maggie shouted, "I'll stop them." She grabbed Kristen by the leg and pulled herself to her flesh, pressing her cheek against Kristen's thigh.

Kristen said, "What will you do to them if they try to take me away?"

"I won't let them have you! You're mine!" Maggie pressed her face into the V of the girl's crotch, drinking in the odor, the scent, the dampness of the girl she loved. Her body was wracked with sobs of desire. "I'd do *anything* for you."

Kristen froze.

Maggie pulled away. Her passion had suddenly been quelled, as if by ice water. "I didn't mean . . ."

Kristen said, "I know. In the heat of passion, we all say things we don't mean. Things that should never be mentioned in the light of day."

"I think I've had too much to drink."

Kristen, seemingly as embarrassed, said, "Or maybe not enough." With a smile, she poured herself another glass of wine.

"You're drunker than I am!"

"Not!" Kristen giggled.

"Yes, you are."

"Then," Kristen said, grabbing the wine bottle, "you have to catch up." She poured Maggie another glass. They clicked them together. Then Kristen closed her eyes. "I'm suddenly feeling very tired."

Maggie nodded. "Listen, I'll put the things away in the kitchen and see you upstairs, all right?"

"I'll be waiting."

After putting the dishes in the dishwasher, Maggie stood nursing the last of the wine, looking out at the snow. The storm was all a kind of gray-black, whirling, powerfully static. Then, without warning, the electricity went out. She found the candles kept in the kitchen for just such an emergency, lit one and carried it to the foyer, where she lit the three kerosene lamps that sat decoratively on a corner table. She left one to illuminate the steps and carried the other two upstairs, setting one in the hallway, and taking the other to the master bedroom. When she set the lamp on the dresser, she saw immediately Kristen's prone form buried under the blankets in bed.

She sat down on the near side of the bed and kicked off her slippers. The clock said it was only two o'clock, but it felt like four. She set her glass of wine at the side of the bed. "You're not already asleep, are you?"

She climbed under the covers and let her head fall to the down pillow. She lay on her back, waiting for Kristen to roll over. Instead she felt fingers wrap around her hand, gently at first, and then gripping firmly. Only it didn't seem like Kristen's fingers. They felt like Max's from long ago, when he would take her hand every night in bed, just as he had done when they took their walks anywhere and everywhere they had been in the world.

She blinked. It felt like Max's hand, but of course it wasn't. It was . . . ? Whose? Kristen's? No, this was a man's hand.

"Good night, Maggie."

His voice sounded like gentle music. "Good night, Max, my darling," she whispered in return.

And then she opened her eyes.

And she sat up with a start. And let out a scream. For this was no dream. He was really there.

Max Jaxon sat up in bed, staring at Maggie, who had jumped up and pressed herself to the wall behind her so hard it seemed she was trying to force herself through it. "You're afraid of me?" Max asked softly.

"I'm dreaming," she gasped. The beard that had covered his chin in the hospital was gone now. He looked like he used to look. It proved she was hallucinating.

"What are you talking about? Come back to bed."

She clenched her hands into fists and brought one to her face and bit her thumb. She shuddered. "My God, I've lost my mind!"

"Maggie, come on," Max said, sounding slightly annoyed, "we're going skiing in the morning. We need a good night's sleep." He slid down in the bed and pulled the duvet to his neck.

Maggie cupped her palm over her mouth. She trembled, shook all over, as she took a step toward the bed, reached forward and felt for him, tapped his shoulder—his eyes opened, and he smiled—and then recoiled in fear again. She tried to get a grip. She knew she wasn't dreaming, this wasn't the past coming alive again, they were not going skiing. This was today, this was some horrible trick that he was playing. Her head filled with a dizzying array of questions: *Why isn't he dead? Didn't the radio report he was dead?*

"Come on, Maggie, you need some rest too." He patted the sheet where she had been lying with his left hand. "Even though my right arm's in a sling, I think we could make love, if you want . . ."

She shuddered. His beard had been shaved, but his arm was still in the sling from the accident. This couldn't be happening. "Stop it! Stop fucking with my head!" She started flinging everything within reach at him. "You're not real! You're not here!" Everything on the bedstand, the lamp and framed photo of her mother and father, the clock, crashed to the floor.

He held the duvet up to shield himself and then said, with a giggle, as if it didn't faze him, "Hey, I never did anything to hurt you. Why would I start now?"

She kept her distance, eyeing him like a bullfighter in the ring, apprehensive, yet trying not to show it. "You bastard! You never died! It's all a setup, you tricked me. This is *her* doing, her game! That performance in the living room earlier, it was all a sham." Maggie was drunk, and she knew it, but she also knew that what she was saying was true. "Kristen!" she shouted through the wall.

"Maggie, Maggie," Max said, as if placating her, "you're being ridiculous." He turned to face the window, pulled the duvet over his head, and moaned, "Just come to sleep."

The intensity of her humiliation overcame her. She turned and dashed out of the room. She flew down the stairs, almost stumbling in the darkness. The kerosene lamp flickered in the foyer. She went to a breakfront across the living room, pulled a drawer open and withdrew a gun. "Kristen!" She bolted upright, looking around. "You tricked me! You ungrateful bitch!"

There was no reply.

She rushed back up the stairs. As she lurched into the master bedroom, she pointed the gun at the outline of Max's body still snug under the feather comforter. "Kristen!" she screamed, knowing the girl was somewhere where she could hear her. "Your trick didn't work. Now he *will* die." She pulled the trigger over and over again.

The shots, in rapid succession, tore up the duvet. Feathers flew. Max let out a cry that sounded like pain and fury. The last bullet struck the window, and the glass shattered. And the room started filling with billowing snow. Maggie, her finger still glued to the trigger, took a step forward. There was no blood on the bed, no gore coming from the duvet, no sign of a body where she had emptied the bullets. She reached out and grasped the edge of the comforter with one hand, then lifted it. Only pillows were underneath. There was no sign of Max.

"Drop the gun," the voice behind her said. "And put your hands into the air. Slowly."

She knew the voice well. So it had all been a trap, a device to catch her. For a moment she thought it was brilliant, the kind of thing she'd write into one of her own films. Then she turned and saw not only the figure of the detective standing there holding a gun on her in the dancing light of the kerosene lamp, but Kristen next to him as well.

"Drop the gun," Christopher Daniel repeated.

Maggie brought her right hand down slowly, though the gun remained gripped in her fingers. She took a step toward Kristen. Daniel forced Kristen back behind him, afraid Maggie was going to try to shoot her. But Maggie suddenly looked as if she were sleepwalking, her face filled with anguish. "How could you do this to me?" she asked Kristen.

"Give me the gun, Maggie," Daniel ordered again. He reached out for it.

She let him take it.

Then Max walked out of the closet.

"You," Maggie growled at him, seething. "One of the great disappointments of my life was when you didn't die on that damn glider."

Max said, "I feel sorry for you."

"Shove your pity," Maggie snapped back. "And rot in hell."

A terrible gust of wind filled the room. The kerosene lamp flickered. Daniel pulled handcuffs from his jacket pocket.

Maggie took a step backward, looking at Kristen again. "You!" She sounded possessed. "I did it for you! This was all because of *you*."

Daniel grabbed Maggie and pulled her to one side, while Max leaped onto the bed, crossed over it, and protectively put his arms around Kristen. Pain filled his shoulder, but he didn't show it.

Daniel told Maggie to turn around. She did no such thing. Her eyes were still intent on Kristen. "I gotta hand it to you, your deception was clever. How did you pull this off?"

"Max came out of the coma early this morning," Kristen said. "The eflorinthine worked, but last night I realized you did it. And that you did it because you wanted only me. You drew me into your relationship to hold on to Max, but you fell obsessively in love with me. You came to hate him for chasing me away." She waited for a reaction but there was none.

"Bruce knew, didn't he?" Daniel asked.

Maggie spit out her words in bitter defiance. "He caught me in the prop trailer the night before."

"That's when you cut the nylon on the wings?"

"No," Max said, certain of it. "I would have seen it in the morning."

Daniel asked, "You loaded the gun that night?"

"I didn't do anything that night but think," Maggie corrected him. "I loaded the gun before Little Mary Sunshine got there with her baked goods at sunrise."

"But when—how—did you cut the nylon?" Max asked.

She shook her head and laughed, almost proudly. "Right there, under everyone's nose, when we were opening the boxes."

Max remembered. "The costume boxes."

Maggie sounded smug. "I mean, even *you* were standing there." She glared at Max as if asking how he could have been so stupid not to see her. "It was a last-minute decision, kind of an insurance policy."

"And Bruce saw you do it," Kristen said. All the pieces were now fitting into place. "Catching you in the prop trailer wasn't proof of anything. He witnessed you actually cutting the sails."

"Was Borger blackmailing you?" Daniel asked.

She laughed. "He wasn't smart enough for that. He was willing to forget about it as long as he thought he'd get Kristen." She glanced at the girl. "But he wasn't willing to go to jail for it."

"My God," Kristen gasped, shivering as snow howled through the jagged glass.

Max said, "That's why you set Nicole up."

"She *is* a murderer!" Maggie answered.

"So are you," Max said.

"And the price is pretty much the same." Daniel leaned toward her, lifting the handcuffs.

Maggie shrugged, looked at Kristen, and seemed suddenly lost in a lovesick haze. "I'll never forget the first time we were together, my darling," she whispered. With a furious glance at Max, she said, "He made you pregnant, he drove you away, he took you from me—"

Daniel put a hand on Maggie's shoulder to turn her around to cuff her. But she whirled around faster than he anticipated, and in doing so deliberately knocked the kerosene lamp off the table and onto Daniel. Flames followed the splash of kerosene up the side of his body.

Max thought fast. He shoved Daniel to the bed and pulled the ripped duvet over the flames. Pressing his own body on the duvet, he smothered the flames in seconds. But the room was on fire as well. Kristen was trapped in the corner, flames leaping in front of her. Max jumped up, reached through the fire to grab Kristen, yanking her toward the bed. "You okay?"

"Yes. Daniel?"

Daniel gasped. The fire had burned the side of his neck, blistered his ear, and singed his hair, but he was all right thanks to Max's quick move. "I'm okay. But we have to get out of here. Now."

"Maggie!" Kristen said, realizing she was gone.

"Fuck Maggie," Max said, "come on!" Assessing whether or not they could run through the flames to get downstairs, he knew immediately that it was impossible.

"The window," Daniel said.

Kristen pushed a chair in front of it. It was feeding the flames oxygen, but it was also their only means of escape. Max jumped up on the chair, kicked out the remaining pieces of jagged glass, and looked out. "The snow will cushion the jump."

"You sure?" Kristen asked.

"Do we have a choice?" Max answered, helping her up.

"Careful," Kristen warned. "Maggie probably picked up the gun."

"Raines is downstairs," Daniel assured them. "Stonecipher too. I'm sure they've got her by now."

Kristen leaped from the burning building. The deep mound of snow directly underneath indeed cushioned her fall. She looked up to see Max helping Daniel onto the windowsill. Max jumped while still holding on to Daniel, as the drapes behind them suddenly ignited with crimson flames.

In the snow, Daniel said, "I'm okay, I'm okay."

The three of them moved as fast as they could around to the front of the burning building. The younger deputy was on his knees just inside the front door, tending to the fallen Officer Raines. "She shot him, sir," Stonecipher explained to Daniel. He was pressing on Raines's shoulder, where he was bleeding.

"I'll be fine," Raines assured them through his pain. "Daniel, your face—"

"Where is she?" Daniel shouted.

Raines whispered, "She stopped on the stairs. I told her to freeze. She shot me."

"I came in the door," the younger cop explained, "as she was running back up."

"Back up?" Max said.

They looked up at the smoke and fire as Stonecipher told them, "She ran back upstairs."

"My God," Max said.

Kristen closed her eyes for a moment.

"Can't let her burn to death," Daniel said. He rushed up the stairs.

Max followed.

"No!" Stonecipher called to him, "I can't let you—"

"Call for an ambulance," Kristen shouted at him, and then, without thinking twice, ran up the stairs herself.

The master bedroom door frame was a wall of flame and smoke filled the hallway, but the fire had not yet spread out there. Kristen dashed past the burning room and felt Max grab her.

He panicked on seeing her. "Get back, go back down!" His eyes were stinging from the smoke. He coughed.

"No! I won't leave you," Kristen said, grabbing his arm.

Together they moved toward the open door of the guest room. "Daniel?" Max called. No answer. "Daniel?"

Then they heard Daniel's voice shout, "No!"

And they heard the shot. A single shot, and then silence.

They raced into the room to find Christopher Daniel, who stood with his gun still in his hand—but it was not the gun that had gone off. Across the room, lying facedown on the bed where she had fallen when she had pulled the trigger, when she knew she was trapped and that there was no way out, was the body of Maggie Nash.

With a bullet through her head.

ONYX

PAUL EDDY
FLINT

**"The creepiest denouement since
Thomas Harris's *Hannibal*."
—*The Wall Street Journal***

**"Not since Modesty Blaise has spy literature seen a
heroine as determined or spunky as Flint."
—*Time***

Undercover cop Grace Flint barely escaped with
her life after a blown sting operation. She still
bears the scars of her attacker. She will find him.
She will make him pay. Revenge has a new name.

0-451-40995-7

ONYX

A KISS GONE BAD

Jeff Abbott

"A BREAKTHROUGH NOVEL."
—*New York Times* bestselling author Sharyn McCrumb

"Rocks big time...pure, white-knuckled suspense. I read it in one sitting."
—*New York Times* bestselling author Harlan Coben

A death rocks the Gulf Coast town of Port Leo, Texas. Was it suicide, fueled by a family tragedy? Or did an obsessed killer use the dead man as a pawn in a twisted game? Beach-bum-turned judge Whit Mosley must risk everything to find out.

"Exciting, shrewd and beautifully crafted...A book worth including on any year's best list."

—*Chicago Tribune*

0-451-41010-6

To order call: 1-800-788-6262

S425/Abbott